DATE DUE			
GAYLORD			PRINTED IN U.S.A.

THE OXFORD BOOK OF AGING

THE OXFORD BOOK OF
AGING

Edited by
Thomas R. Cole and Mary G. Winkler

Oxford   New York
OXFORD UNIVERSITY PRESS
1994

Oxford University Press

Oxford   New York   Toronto
Delhi   Bombay   Calcutta   Madras   Karachi
Kuala Lumpur   Singapore   Hong Kong   Tokyo
Nairobi   Dar es Salaam   Cape Town
Melbourne   Auckland   Madrid

and associated companies in
Berlin   Ibadan

Copyright © 1994 by Thomas R. Cole and Mary G. Winkler

Published by Oxford University Press, Inc.,
198 Madison Avenue, New York, New York 10016

Oxford is a registered trademark of Oxford University Press

Library of Congress Cataloging-in-Publication Data
The Oxford book of aging
/ edited by Thomas R. Cole and Mary G. Winkler.
p.   cm.
Includes index.
ISBN 0–19–507369–X
1. Old age in literature.   2. Aging in literature.
I. Cole, Thomas R., 1949–   .   II. Winkler, Mary G.
PN56.0409   1994
305.26—dc20   94–19848

2 4 6 8 9 7 5 3

Printed in the United States of America
on acid free paper

CONTENTS

III. GENERATIONS
100

IV. SOLITUDE / LONELINESS
149

V. WORKS
183

IX.   REMEMBRANCE
359

CREDITS
405

REFERENCES
415

AUTHOR INDEX
417

ACKNOWLEDGMENTS

The editors are grateful for the assistance of many people who helped bring this volume to fruition. While the project was still only a proposal, Wayne Booth, David Troyansky, Judith de Luce, Bertram Cohler, and Ronald Manheimer provided valuable advice. Bob Atchley, Kate Farrell, Anne Wyatt-Brown, Rick Moody, Bob Kastenbaum, Carter Williams, and Kathleen Woodward all generously commented on a draft of the manuscript. Their ideas and suggested readings substantially improved the book. Kate Farrell, in particular, sent a large number of photocopied suggestions, many of which we included. Shreela Ray, Leah Buturain Schneider, and Rod Olsen also alerted us to valuable material. Kathleen Woodward, Marc Kaminsky, and Ron Carson provided invaluable suggestions for the introduction. Kathleen Modd helped with correspondence and bibliographic citations, always with good humor.

At Oxford, our editors Linda Halvorson Morse and Liza Ewell gave special time and attention to shaping the volume over a period of more than three years. Vida Petronis and Susan Hannan patiently wrestled with an inordinate number of details during copy editing and production. Margaret Gorenstein performed the difficult and vital job of securing reprint permissions.

The Interlibrary Loan staff—Laura Donaldson, John Young, Marisela Sifuentes, Lashanda Long, Enrique Puentes, Jr., Trish Douglas—of the Moody Medical Library at the University of Texas Medical Branch were unstinting in filling endless requests for loan materials. Alex Bienkowski helped track down answers to innumerable reference questions. Larry Wygant, Ph.D., Associate Director of the Library, often guided us to appropriate sources of information or personnel.

We are also grateful to the scholars and editors whose recent anthologies and guides to literature on aging have been essential resources in our own foraging for material. In particular, we are indebted to *Perceptions of Aging in Literature: A Cross-Cultural Study,* edited by Prisca von Dorotka Bagnell and Patricia Spencer Soper (Greenwood Press, 1989); *Aging in Literature: A Reader's Guide,* by Robert E. Yahnke and Richard M. Eastman (American

Library Association, 1990); *Songs of Experience: An Anthology of Literature on Growing Old*, edited by Margaret Fowler and Priscilla McCutcheon (Ballantine Books, 1991); *The Ageless Spirit*, edited by Phillip Berman and Connie Goldman (Ballantine Books, 1992); *Vital Signs: International Stories on Aging*, edited by Dorothy Sennett with Anne Czarniecki (Graywolf Press, 1991); *Full Measure: Modern Short Stories on Aging*, edited by Dorothy Sennett (Graywolf Press, 1988); *The Art of Growing Older: Writers on Living and Aging*, edited by Wayne Booth (Poseidon Press, 1992); and *Literature and Aging: An Anthology*, edited by Martin Kohn, Carol Donley, and Delese Wear (Kent State University Press, 1992).

This volume was supported in part by a National Endowment for the Humanities Challenge Grant and the Jesse Jones Memorial Research Fund at the Institute for the Medical Humanities at the University of Texas Medical Branch.

Finally, we wish to acknowledge the indispensable work of our editorial associates, Mary Terrell White and Eleanor Porter, who have participated in the development of this project since its inception. The selections in the *Oxford Book of Aging* represent only about twenty percent of the materials that were gathered and read over the course of three years. Mary White did most of the library digging for these materials, participated in reading and evaluating all of them, and helped provide background research. Eleanor Porter organized the materials, made them available for evaluation, and participated in the selection process. While tracking a mass of biographical and bibliographical details, Eleanor was responsible for day-to-day editorial and production work in our offices.

Galveston, Texas　　　　　　　　　　　　　　　　　　　　T. R. C.
February 1994　　　　　　　　　　　　　　　　　　　　 M. G. W.

THE OXFORD BOOK OF AGING

INTRODUCTION

The Oxford Book of Aging is guided by the understanding that later life in the West today is a season in search of its purposes. For the first time in human history, most people can expect to live into their seventies in reasonably good health; those over age eighty-five are the fastest-growing age group in the population. Yet the words of Ecclesiastes—"To every thing there is a season, and a time to every purpose under heaven"—carry little conviction when applied to the second half of life.

Between the sixteenth century and the third quarter of the twentieth century, Western ideas about aging underwent a fundamental transformation, spurred by the development of modern society. Ancient and medieval understandings of aging as a mysterious part of the eternal order of things gradually gave way to the secular, scientific, and individualist tendencies of modernity. Old age was removed from its place as a way station along life's spiritual journey and redefined as a problem to be solved by science and medicine. By the mid-twentieth century, older people were moved to society's margins and defined primarily as patients or pensioners.

Because long lives have become the rule rather than the exception, and because collective meaning systems have lost their power to infuse aging with widely shared significance, we have become deeply uncertain about what it means to grow old. Ancient myths and modern stereotypes alike fail to articulate the challenges or capture the uncertainty of generations moving into the still-lengthening later years. The modernization of aging has generated a host of unanswered questions: Does aging have an intrinsic purpose? Is there anything really important to be done after children are raised, jobs left, careers completed? Is old age the culmination of life? Does it contain potential for self-completion? What are the avenues of spiritual growth in later life? What are the roles, rights, and responsibilities of older people? What are the particular strengths and virtues of old age? Is there such a thing as a "good" old age?

In 1979, the English writer Ronald Blythe wrote in *The View in Winter* that "the ordinariness of living to be old" was too new to appreciate. "The old have . . . been sentenced to life and turned into a matter for public concern," he wrote. "They are the first generations of full-timers and thus the first generations of old people for whom the state, experimentally, grudgingly and uncertainly, is having to make special supportive conditions." Blythe suggested that it would soon be necessary for people to learn to grow old as they once learned to grow up.

These perceptive remarks already have the feel of a bygone era. In the late twentieth century Western world, the long-rising tide of modernity has begun to turn; beneath the much-heralded population "age wave," uncharted cultural currents are breaking up conventional images, norms, and expectations about aging and old age. The large percentage of public economic and medical resources devoted to older people has spawned a fierce debate over intergenerational equity in shrinking welfare states. Meanwhile, writers, filmmakers, advocates, and elders are defying negative stereotypes and images of old age.

The recent growth, for example, of fiction featuring older people as complex and exciting protagonists has overturned the harsh generalization made by the French writer Simone de Beauvoir in 1970. In *The Coming of Age,* Beauvoir asserted that literature had no interest in the inner life of the old, who were considered "finished, set, with no hope, no development to be looked for." On the contrary, many contemporary writers of mid-life and late-life fiction (some of which is included here) are not preoccupied with loss and decline. Rather, they are giving expression to growing cultural impulses to explore the experiences of aging, to move *toward* something as one grows older—a unity of understanding; loving relations with others; the return of wonder; acceptance of mortality; God. In *The Fountain of Age* (1993), for example, Betty Friedan's affirmation of her own experience of aging offers a model that combines both freedom and care for others. New roles for older people in the media, the development of new forms of education, productivity and self-help among retired people, the growth of theological and pastoral concern about aging—these are only some of the signs that our aging society is drawing what the American historian Peter Laslett calls *A Fresh Map of Life* (1989).

Thus our era offers new opportunities for reclaiming the moral and spiritual dimensions of later life, for bridging the gap between existential mystery and scientific mastery, for reconciling the modern value of individual development with the ancient virtues of accepting natural limits and social responsibilities. Nevertheless, formidable obstacles remain. Many of our most troubling dilemmas are linked to the fact that Western culture offers few convincing ways to make sense of physical decline and the inevitability of death. For the most part, physical decay and death are still culturally construed as personal or medical failures, devoid of social or cosmic meaning.

When faced with loss, frailty, disease, imminent mortality, or dependency, we come up against many barriers to living *with* the passage of time: anxiety about growing old; exaggerated stereotypes (both negative and positive) about old age; denial of death, punctuated by nightmares of medically protracted dying; dreams of physical rejuvenation; feelings of shame or inferiority associated with loss of independence. These barriers tend to block the experience of time as flowing; they create a sense of stagnation, of being stuck or frozen. In Western culture, people in mid-life and beyond often appear (to themselves as well as to others) as strangers, liminal figures. Nevertheless, the gradual erosion of modern culture's strong temporal prejudices—that progress renders the past obsolete, that the new is better than the old, that youth is better than age—has begun to allay our society's traumatic fear and denial of aging. More and more people are coming face to face with an interesting truth: we have met the aged, and they are us.

While scientific research and medical technology will continue to alter the biological possibilities of human life, they cannot free us from the necessity of living within limits. Time—invisible, intangible, yet inexorable—is perhaps the most mysterious limit of all. Aging is about living in time. Born into the world at a certain historical moment, destined to pass out of it at a later, uncertain moment, we are creatures who change significantly over a lifetime. For groups as well as individuals, time brings changes of form and condition. "And there are always new thresholds to cross," writes the Dutch anthropologist Arnold van Gennep in *Rites of Passage* (1908), "the thresholds of summer and winter, of a season and a year . . . the thresholds of birth, adolescence, maturity, and old age; the thresholds of death and that of afterlife—for those who believe in it."

While aging poses universal questions about life and death, these do not admit of universal or univocal answers. "If by the time we're sixty we haven't learnt what a knot of paradox and contradiction life is, and how exquisitely the good and the bad are mingled in every action we take, and what a compromising hostess Our Lady of Truth is, we haven't grown old to much purpose," argues the English writer John Cowper Powys in *The Art of Growing Old* (1944). Moral and spiritual truths about aging are both possible and necessary, but they do not come in one-size-fits-all garments.

To become personally inhabited, such truths must be cut from the historical cloth of particular cultures, measured by the yardstick of individual experience, and stitched together during an evolution of the spirit that "pilgrims" of every tradition have experienced along life's way. "We who are old know that age is more than a disability," writes Florida Scott-Maxwell in

The Measure of My Days (1968), then in her early eighties. "It is an intense and varied experience, almost beyond our capacity at times, but something to be carried high. If it is a long defeat, it is also a victory, meaningful for the initiates of time, if not for those who have come less far." Put in more stoic language, *growing* old is not a matter of accumulating years. "Age is not decisive," writes the German sociologist of modernity, Max Weber, in *Politics as a Vocation* (1919). What is decisive is the "trained relentlessness in viewing the realities of life and the ability to face such realities and to measure up to them inwardly." Inwardly. Selections in the *Oxford Book of Aging* were chosen with an eye toward enlarging readers' capacities for viewing, facing, and measuring up to the challenges and opportunities of later life.

Perhaps the most interesting finding of recent humanistic and social gerontology is that creativity remains a powerful source of growth, regardless of age. While usually associated with a visible product (a painting, poem, book, or piece of furniture, for example), creativity often results in less tangible outcomes: the altered self-image of an individual or group; a change in how one lives; the deepening of a long-term relationship; a more acutely felt intuition of one's place in a family, in a religious group, or in nature.

Creativity, as the American scholar and writer Robert Kastenbaum suggests in *Generations* (Spring 1991), "may be the aging individual's most profound response to the limits and uncertainties of existence. . . . Indeed, the sheer joy and being-aliveness in creative activity has its own way of triumphing over the inroads of debilitation and the unrelenting movement of time. . . . And if *every* moment of life is a passage, both a becoming and a perishing, then is the creative integration of experience not also demanded of all who would treasure what has gone before and embrace that which is yet to come?" Applied to the work of growing old, creativity—which involves affirming life and taking risks—demands continual wrestling with limits amidst changing inner and outer circumstances.

The Oxford Book of Aging encourages just such personal wrestling with angels. Its nine chapters are organized around themes that symbolize and illuminate the pleasures, mysteries, agonies, and ideals of human beings striving to know themselves and live out their days in the fullness of time. The selections within each chapter are loosely sequenced in groups that are explained in that chapter's headnote, but are not explicitly marked in the text itself. Each chapter's headnote, in other words, provides the editors' rationale for the movement of ideas, images, and feelings contained in the following sequence of readings; but the selections stand on their own, preserving the reader's freedom of reaction and interpretation.

In constructing the organizing themes for each chapter, we have avoided fixed categories that reinforce the notion of growing old as the pursuit of static abstractions such as wisdom, health, spirituality, or retirement. We have also avoided categories based on binary opposites: gain versus loss; health versus disease; work versus retirement; age versus youth; life versus death.

A good deal of Western (and especially American) cultural illiteracy about aging derives from middle-class stereotypes that drive out nuanced thinking in favor of moralistic dualism (for example, good things happen to good people; bad things happen to bad people). Many people have trouble reading their own experience outside culturally dominant expectations of youthfulness, health, or success. Conventional wisdom fails to convince. Stereotypes blunt the imagination. They fail to offer symbolic avenues of self-renewal and inhibit appreciation for the simple realities of daily life—what Thoreau called "the bloom of the present moment." By juxtaposing ideas and images that are often considered opposites, we have constructed categories that allow surprise, tension, paradox, ambiguity, and contradiction.

We have brought together different or opposing points of view—even within individual works—to encourage personal engagement with various ideas and moods. We have included several passages from Ecclesiastes, for example, because it is a rich literary dialogue in which both skepticism and piety have their day. As the American classicist T. A. Perry argues in *Dialogues with Kohelet* (1993), the notion that human efforts are ultimately futile is offered not as a foregone conclusion, but as a debatable position. The idea that time sweeps aside all pleasure and accomplishment is to be weighed against the notion that God has made everything beautiful in its own time.

The Oxford Book of Aging presents a multiplicity of experiences and aspirations rather than singular truths about aging and the human spirit. "I wonder if old people want truth more than anything else, and they cannot find it," writes Florida Scott-Maxwell. "Perhaps truth is diversity so each seeks his own." In this book, readers will find expressions of despair, foolishness, greed, and unfulfilled longing, as well as images of accomplishment, joy, peacefulness, and wisdom. The selections are offered in a spirit of creative dialogue to encourage personal and cultural conversations about what it means to grow old.

Although many selections reflect Jewish and Christian traditions as well as our grounding in American and European cultural history, we have also abundantly sampled writing from various other cultures, religious traditions, and ethnic backgrounds. Readers will find many old chestnuts, including Shakespeare's seventy-third sonnet, Robert Browning's "Rabbi Ben Ezra," and Cicero's "De Senectute." They will also find unexpected African folktales, Islamic poetry, ancient Hebrew epigrams, historical medical writings, fragments from personal journals, and selections from contemporary Buddhist thought.

Along with poetry, fiction, and drama, we have included sacred writings from the world's religions, philosophical speculations, journalistic interviews, letters, diaries, essays, satire, and scientific and medical writing. The works extend from the canonical art of Sappho, Dante, or Yeats to the untutored, deeply felt autobiographical narratives of the former American slave Gus Alexander or the contemporary Appalachian woman Rena Cornett.

In addition to ranging widely across cultures and genres, we have also ranged widely across history. It is often assumed that before the nineteenth century almost nothing was written on the subjects of aging and old age. This is only partially true. As a separate topic of scientific inquiry, medical practice, philosophic speculation, personal meditation, or literary and artistic representation, aging is largely a creation of the last 150 years. But as an aspect of human temporality embedded in larger views of society, nature, and the cosmos, the subject of aging appears in virtually all historical periods and human cultures. In fact, the meaning of aging has been linked historically to the way that cultures symbolize life as a whole. Our first and most traditional chapter, therefore, is organized around two ancient and universal metaphors that situate aging within the life cycle: the stages and journey of life.

The power of these images derives from their capacity to map human lifetime as if it consisted of movement through space. Metaphorically, stages are resting places or milestones along the temporal journey of life. Often analogized to seasons of the year or times of the day, the motif of stages conveys a pattern of fixed periods throughout life. The motif of the journey, which is also represented as a voyage, sacred pilgrimage, or mystical inner way, highlights movement from stage to stage—the spiritual drama of the traveler's search. "Life's racecourse is fixed," writes Cicero in *De Senectute.* "Nature has only a single path and that path is run but once, and to each stage of existence has been allotted its appropriate quality." In many cultures, these organizing metaphors appear not as mere cognitive abstractions, but as ritualized elements of individual and social life.

Because of their traditional associations, the metaphors of the stages and journey of life may strike some readers as remnants of obsolete worldviews. For others, they may have historical or nostalgic value, but may fail to communicate the complexity of personal experience. For still others, they may offer a renewed way of envisioning a meaningful pattern of time, one in which the later years are woven into the earlier years and into the lives of others.

While Chapter One, Stages/Journey, offers traditional metaphors that attempt to make meaning of life as a whole, Chapter Two, Change/Metamorphosis highlights the inevitability of change over time—the disruption and recovery of personal and cultural meanings. "I ask myself often: 'Why is it that everything changes?' And only one answer comes back to me," writes the contemporary Buddhist master Sogyal Rinpoche, "'That is how life is.'" The selections in this chapter articulate different kinds of change and various attitudes toward change itself. Excerpts from the Oglala Sioux holy man's *Black Elk Speaks* reveal devastating historical forces that may influence personal development. Selections from the work of Christine Downing and Ursula K. Le Guin—contemporary women who are reclaiming menopause from its connotations of shame and disease—demonstrate the power of ideas to shape the personal experience of biological change.

How do we understand the direction of change in the second half of life? As movement toward ultimate dissolution? Toward fulfillment? Entropy? Reincarnation? Salvation? As the theologians Henri J. M. Nouwen and Walter J. Gaffney write in *Aging: The Fulfillment of Life* (1974), "Everyone will age and die, but this knowledge has no inherent direction. It can be destructive as well as creative, oppressive as well as liberating." Why is it that so many people view aging with dread? In the 1930s, the Swiss psychiatrist Carl Jung argued that modern Western culture's denial of death and preoccupation with youth inhibited spiritual and psychological growth in the later years. Many of his older patients suffered from vague anxiety and feelings of meaninglessness. "They look back and cling to the past with a secret fear of death in their hearts," writes Jung in "The Soul and Death" (1934). "They withdraw from the life process, at least psychologically, and consequently remain fixed like nostalgic pillars of salt, with vivid recollections of youth but no living relation to the present. From the middle of life onward, only he remains alive who is ready to *die with life.*"

Remaining alive and vital in the second half of life requires finding or knowing one's place in the chain of generations or in a larger community. Chapter Three, Generations, therefore, emphasizes the importance of relationships between the young and the old—a subject rendered increasingly complex in our era of four-generational families and terribly expensive care for frail, disabled, or ill older people. We have not tried to present solutions to contemporary problems of eldercare or intergenerational equity. Rather, we have selected writings that illuminate a wide spectrum of issues, such as the obligations of the young toward the old; ideals of honor or behavior in old age; the unexpected loss of children; fear of abandonment; ageism; and the special connection between children and grandparents. One of the fruits of growing older may be a deeper sense that one's individual, separate self consists paradoxically of its relationships with others, past and present.

In Chapter Four, Solitude/Loneliness, the voices range from the ancient Psalmist to the modern nursing-home resident. Many seem to support John Cowper Powys's bold generalization: "the older we get the lonelier we get."

The selections give expression to the positive, reflective, and meditative dimensions of solitude, as well as to the melancholy, sometimes tragic, sometimes pathetic aspects of loneliness. In this chapter and others, moving testimony from personal journals suggests that the very act of writing a journal can be a means of sustaining a sense of self. In a diary, as the gerontologist Harry Berman shows in "From the Pages of My Life" (1991), writers (and not only professionals) may find clarity of purpose and confidence to withstand necessary losses, to maintain intense attachments to what they truly value. As the American psychoanalyst Martin Grotjahn wrote in "The Day I Got Old" (1981):

> I don't work anymore. I don't walk anymore. Peculiarly enough, I feel well about it. . . . I sit in the sun watching the falling leaves slowly sail across the waters of the swimming pool. I think, I dream, I draw, I sit—I feel free of worry—almost free of this world of reality.
>
> If anyone had told me that I would be quietly happy just sitting here, reading a little, writing a little, and enjoying life in a quiet and modest way, I, of course, would not have believed. That a walk across the street to the corner of the park satisfies me when I always thought a four-hour walk was just not good enough: that surprises me.

Chapter Five, Works, brings together several different kinds of activity that are generally considered separately: artistic production; work as paid employment; the work of retirement; spiritual work; and preparation for death. The work of relating to others, for example, remains important even when one longs for death. In a letter to her children, the seventy-seven-year-old German artist Kaethe Kollwitz announced her desire to die: "Do not be frightened and do not try to talk me out of it," she wrote in 1944. "I bless my life, which has given me such an infinitude of good along with its hardships. Nor have I wasted it; I have used what strength I had to the best of my ability. All I ask of you now is to let me go—my time is up. . . . I thank you with all my heart." Some readings cast doubt on the traditional expectation that hard work and good habits are rewarded with health or wealth. Others draw attention to the economic conditions that affect the experience of old age.

Chapter Six, Eros/Thanatos, is inspired by the German poet Rainer Maria Rilke's insight that "love and death are the great gifts given to us that mostly are passed on unopened." Linking love with death suggests both their inextricable physical connection and the hope that some form of life-giving love may continue growing until the moment of death. The selections explore traditional quandaries: the persistence (and taboo) of sexuality in old age; the longing for physical expressions of love and beauty; the pain of feeling young and desirous, but being perceived as unattractive, perhaps even repulsive.

Death appears in many guises: as friend, enemy, erotic experience, mutual suicide, and divine kiss. The Dalai Lama discusses the importance of the moment of death from the Buddhist point of view.

Chapter Seven, Celebration/Lament, also brings together apparently contradictory ideas. Celebration of life may include—even require—lament for aspects of life that are irrevocably lost. According to a Hasidic saying: "There are three aspects of mourning: with tears, that is the lowest; with silence, that is higher; and with a song, that is the highest." The importance of celebration in old age is beautifully captured in the famous stanza from Yeats's "Sailing to Byzantium":

> An aged man is but a paltry thing,
> A tattered coat upon a stick, unless
> Soul clap its hands and sing, and louder still,
> for every tatter in its mortal dress.

The selections in this chapter range from examples of traditional Christian virtues and optimistic odes to painful lament, bitter satire, and fearless rejection of illusory ideals.

Chapter Eight, Body/Spirit, challenges the most basic dichotomy in Western thought, implying that both are part of a larger unity that eludes easy conceptualization. Several sources celebrate the physical self and glory in the beauty of aging flesh. Others struggle to express the paradox of an embodied, limited, yet somehow timeless self. At age eighty-two, the American writer M. F. K. Fisher speaks bluntly and with great wit about dignity and her aged body. Medical, religious, literary, and autobiographical writings explore longevity, wisdom, and suffering.

Chapter Nine, Remembrance, highlights the importance of personal and collective memory. Memory is not simply a matter of retrieving information aimed at empirical truths; it is an act of imagination, a creative process of crafting meaning from the remnants of time. As such, it is a crucial source of hope for the future—for individuals and for groups. "Memory implies a certain act of redemption," writes the English critic John Berger in "The Uses of Photography" (1980). "What is remembered has been saved from nothingness. What is forgotten has been abandoned. . . . Such a presentiment, extracted from man's long, painful experience of time, is to be found . . . in almost every culture and religion."

Forms of remembrance—stories, memoirs, epitaphs, poetry, history, reminiscence—help preserve and transmit lives, meanings, and values from generation to generation. As the American poet and scholar Marc Kaminsky puts it in "The Story of the Shoe Box" (1992), these arts of memory are powerful oars for rowing across the wide waters of forgetfulness toward the shores of meaning.

The Oxford Book of Aging, then, approaches aging as a physical, moral, and spiritual frontier whose terrain can be explored but never fully tamed. Our basic stance is one of hope girded by realism. Affirming the incalculable goodness of the gift of life, we do not flinch from the intractable realities of pain and suffering, loss, and evil.

We believe that the joys, fears, sufferings, and mysteries of aging can be successfully explored with humility and self-knowledge, with love and compassion, with a sense of the sacred, and with acceptance of physical decline and mortality. This exploration requires a delicate reciprocity between individuals and society. Individuals must be willing to persist in their growth toward self-knowledge, which means acknowledging their fated place within the cycle of generations. At the same time, society must value the aged of diverse class, racial, and ethnic backgrounds; to care for and about old people who are poor or sick; to accept the elderly "stranger" raging against fate or injustice; to encourage more people to become responsible elders in their own families and communities.

This volume, then, is meant to be a contribution to the imagination of our aging society. It aims to enhance the reader's personal search for, and the growing public dialogue about the meanings and purposes of later life. We encourage people to read poignant, striking, or troubling passages out loud— to themselves and to others—as a means of enacting and engaging the views of different authors. By encountering many voices across the boundaries of time, race, culture, ethnicity, and gender, readers may find new ways to make sense of their own experience and to appreciate the experience of others.

T. R. C.

CHAPTER ONE
STAGES/JOURNEY

This chapter is organized around two primal metaphors that all cultures use to craft meaning and order from the chaotic events of human lifetime: the stages of life and the journey of life. Unlike other chapters in *The Oxford Book of Aging*, which are filled with differences and discontinuities, this chapter emphasizes the remarkable historical continuity of these two overarching metaphors. Readers will find these metaphors echoed and reformulated in every other chapter. Stages/Journey is roughly organized into five sections: traditional Western images of life's journey; cross-cultural material on the stages of life; medical ideas about life's stages; philosophical/religious reflections on old age and the progression through life; and personal, poetic meditations on being old.

We begin with the journey motif. Using Christian imagery dating from the fourteenth century, the first section moves from the middle to the end of life. The opening lines of Dante's medieval *Divine Comedy* depict strikingly resonant experiences of mid-life: fear of the unknown and search for illumination. In Petrarch's letter, the Renaissance Italian humanist argues that fear of old age is unnecessary: a well-lived Christian life leads not to shipwreck in later life, but to a harbor. African-American poet Sterling A. Brown uses a Negro spiritual idiom to depict the heavenly passage on "de las' train." The American theologian Richard R. Niebuhr offers an insight for and about contemporary "pilgrims."

The next grouping offers various views on the stages of life. Every human culture divides the life cycle into a number of stages and provides appropriate images, explanations, and behavioral prescriptions for each period. The selections here range from the Native American folktale "The Four Hills of Life" to Shakespeare's famous rendition of the seven ages of man in *As You Like It*. Ancient Greek thought about the three ages of life is exemplified by Aesop's fable and by Aristotle's extended description of the moral and emotional qualities of youth, manhood, and old age. Confucius and Rabbi Judah ben Tema offer pithy, ancient Chinese and Hebrew descriptions and prescriptions for the various stages of life. Isidore of Seville, the encyclopedic scholar known for transmitting knowledge of a dying Roman culture to the Germanic Middle Ages, describes six ages of life. Finally, Jaques's cynical speech from *As You Like It* reminds us, with biting humor, of the limits of all idealized images of life's stages.

The Yellow Emperor's Classic of Internal Medicine introduces a short series of medical writings about the stages of life. Huang Ti, who is thought to have lived almost forty-seven hundred years ago, illustrates the interweaving of medical and religious thought. The ancient Roman physician Celsus, who introduced Hippocrates' writings to Roman society, observes variations in health and disease brought on by changes in the seasons of the year and the ages of life. Eliza W. Farnham, a nineteenth-century American reformer who promulgated the superiority of woman, is our lone female voice in a tradition of medical men. More than a century before contemporary feminists began writing about menopause, Farnham applied the idea of progress to the female life course, envisioning the "post-maternal" period as one of great power and generativity.

The next series contains several reflections on living according to one's stage of life or, in contemporary parlance, "acting your age." In the late twentieth century, Western culture is increasingly disinclined to apply this idea to old age, both because the old rules seem outmoded or demeaning, and because many people reject the idea of *any* age-appropriate rules for behavior in later life. Sir Thomas Browne, the English physician and moralist, provides a seventeenth-century Christian version of this doctrine of "tempestivitas," or acting according to one's season of life. The late-nineteenth-century German philosopher Arthur Schopenhauer presents a bracingly pessimistic view, echoing the tone found commonly in ancient wisdom literature. Modern developmental psychology, ancient Hindu prescription, and ancient Roman Stoicism find expression in the selections from Erik Erikson, the Manu Smriti, and Cicero's *De Senectute*.

Cicero's decidedly masculine, patrician perspective contrasts interestingly with the nineteenth-century Protestant optimism of Abigail House, whose letter opens the chapter's final grouping of personal meditations in old age. This series moves from House to the contemporary American Ruth Jacobs, who defiantly rejects the cult of youth. Early in the twentieth century the American psychologist G. Stanley Hall anticipated modern gerontology's view of later life as greatly misunderstood and underutilized. The chapter ends with the poetry of Ralph Waldo Emerson, Kathleen Raine, and Walt Whitman, who convey feelings of movement, spaciousness, and gratitude— as well as the need of courage to face the fleeting beauty and toil at the journey's end.

DANTE ALIGHIERI *(Italian, 1265–1321)*

In the middle of the journey of our life
    I found myself astray in a dark wood
    where the straight road had been lost sight of.
How hard it is to say what it was like
    in the thick of thickets, in a wood so dense and gnarled
    the very thought of it renews my panic.
It is bitter almost as death itself is bitter.
    But to rehearse the good it also brought me
    I will speak about the other things I saw there.
How I got into it I cannot clearly say
    for I was moving like a sleepwalker
    the moment I stepped out of the right way,
But when I came to the bottom of a hill
    standing off at the far end of that valley
    where a great terror had disheartened me
I looked up, and saw how its shoulders glowed
    already in the rays of the planet
    which leads and keeps men straight on every road.
Then I sensed a quiet influence settling
    into those depths in me that had been rocked
    and pitifully troubled all night long . . . .

From "Canto I—Inferno," in *The Divine Comedy*, 1310

EMILY DICKINSON *(American, 1830–1886)*

Down Time's quaint stream
Without an oar
We are enforced to sail
Our Port a secret
Our Perchance a Gale
What Skipper would
Incur the Risk
What Buccaneer would ride
Without a surety from the Wind
Or schedule of the Tide—

"Down Time's quaint stream," c. 1862–1866

15

FRANÇOIS MAURIAC *(French, 1885–1970)*

Strive as I will, I cannot keep my ship from drifting either toward God or toward death. I would like to find again the current of life, forget my age, but it is impossible: the estuary is too wide and already has some of the characteristics of the ocean. I can see the shores only through a veil of mist. What I still have in common with other men are the seasons, the transition from one to the other, to which I have always so keenly responded. It is the familiar current that I must find again by opening the books I have loved, and thus, in regard to them, pursue a meditation that is peaceful and down to earth.

The forward spring weather invites melancholy. For me, these mild days in February are coins too precious; in Auteuil, they are not legal tender. They merely help me to recompose indefinitely in my mind the Guyenne landscape that I have a tendency to embellish, for surely it is not as luminous as I imagine. The painter or poet sees in his mind's eye the human portion of a landscape, his eternity. Utrillo's painting of the white wall in Montmartre, which he made the 4th of August, 1914, is infinitely more beautiful than the actual wall, if it still exists today.

When, each year, the time comes for me to take the road toward the southwest, the treasure of the summer days will have been squandered in advance. The real springtime, when it appears, will have nothing more to give us. No matter! I can enjoy even a return in winter, even in the icy rain; I will welcome those days with closed eyes and will find in them my delight. No matter how cold the hand on our forehead, it is enough that it be a loved hand. Even a dull and rainy month of March knows some moments of remission: one minute of light glorifies chilled nature.

What I called mild weather and which I so highly prized in former times I can now easily do without, having reached the age of contemplation. The picture framed by the open window in the Malagar drawing-room enchants me even if the rain is streaming on the still leafless linden-trees and on the ancient roof-tiles—a rose-pink that is unique in the world for me, a color that has never been rendered except in words, that supernatural color needed for a roof-tile. And perhaps toward the end of the rainy afternoon, the rainbow, like the one painted by Millet, in the Louvre, will spring from the hornbeam hedgerows and straddle the terrace.

Fine weather is a prejudice of youth. For an old man, the weather can be neither fine nor bad; it is the very texture of the weather that seems priceless, whether brightened by shafts of sunlight or clouded with darkness. Each thread of the tapestry woven by time is precious, since all the faces that have disappeared from the earth are projected on it by our memory. But even without any face projected there, and without any of my dead reappearing there, it still keeps in my eyes the splendor of being a season of time, mankind's time, the time in which our destiny will have been experienced and inscribed, among millions of others.

From "Man and Nature, and Art, and What It Should Be" in
The Inner Presence: Recollections of My Spiritual Life, 1968

PETRARCH (*Italian, 1304–1374*)

I have grown old. I can no longer hide the fact if I would, and I would not if I could. I bid you who are my coevals rejoice if you can resist better than I the advance of age, or if you are more ingenious in hiding its effects, or if you are readier than I to trust in a vain hope based on fallacious and fleeting promises. I can no longer believe in the enticements of an age that is silently slipping away. Take your pleasure, you young men who want to gain the public eye! It is time for me to yield my place; I shall leave an empty seat for you. Sit firm in your chair, and write as your age may dictate.

I admit that I am an old man. I read my years in my mirror, others read them on my brow. My familiar expression has changed; the bright look of my eyes is veiled, but I feel the clouding with no distress. My falling hair, my roughened skin, my snowy crown, testify that my winter has come. But I render my thanks to him who watches and guides us at dawning and at evening, from childhood to decrepitude. In this state I feel my mental powers undiminished, and I notice no dwindling in my bodily vigor, in my application to familiar studies, in my capacity for honest activities. For other activities I am incompetent, and thereat I rejoice. I strive to become the more incompetent, aiding the work of time with fasting, toil, and night vigils. By such means, if I am tempted to imagine foul deeds that I cannot commit, I banish them, and think myself stronger than Milo or Hercules. I feel that I have triumphed over my body, that old enemy which waged many a cruel war on me, and I seem to be driving a laureled chariot up the sacred way to the Capitol of my soul, dragging at chariot-tail my conquered passions, the insidious foes of virtue firmly bound, and pleasure in chains.

Some of you will perhaps be surprised—though not those who best understand that nothing is surprising in the human spirit—when I say that life never seemed so beautiful as it does now, when to many others it begins to be a burden. May God, who has brought me to this age, transport me from this vain mortal life to the true eternal life, as now I prize higher one day of this ripeness than do most young men prize a year of their bloom. . . .

I have grown old, and I give my thanks to nature therefor, whether or not she may will that I complete the journey. I know that after old age nothing remains but death, the final state of senescence. The end of life may better appear the end of one's labors. Wherever the traveler stops is the end of his journey; his last effort has been made. What boots it how much farther he could have gone, since he went no farther? I leave the judgment in this matter, and all my concern, to him who, as it is written, guides aright all the steps of men, in whom every man's term is fixed, the number of his months and days, in whose sight a thousand years are but a passing day. He will call me and I shall answer, hoping that my faith in him will bring me to bliss. So I advance the more happily from day to day. And I say to any who may follow me with reluctant steps: "Come with assurance; fear not; do not listen to those dismal old men who weep that they have been released from the toils of evil lusts, while they should have wept when they were bound. Do not believe them because of their years, which make them venerable without but repulsive within. Age, toward which you draw amid the storms of life, is nothing so dreadful. Those who call it so have found all stages of life unwelcome, thanks to their mishandling of life, not to a particular age. The latter years of a learned, modest man are sheltered and serene. He has appeased the storms within his breast, he has left behind the reefs of strife and labor, he is protected as by a ring of sunny hills from the outer storms. So go securely, do not delay; a harbor opens where you feared a shipwreck."

From a letter to his friends, from Pavia, 29 November 1366 or 1367

STERLING A. BROWN (*African American, 1901–1989*)

> Honey
> When de man
> Calls out de las' train
> You're gonna ride,
> Tell him howdy.
>
> Gather up yo' basket
> An' yo' knittin' an' yo' things,
> An' go on up an' visit
> Wid frien' Jesus fo' a spell.
>
> Show Marfa
> How to make yo' greengrape jellies,
> An' give po' Lazarus
> A passel of them Golden Biscuits.
>
> Scald some meal
> Fo' some righdown good spoonbread
> Fo' li'l box-plunkin' David.
>
> An' sit aroun'
> An' tell them Hebrew Chillen
> All yo' stories. . . .

Honey
Don't be feared of them pearly gates,
Don't go 'round to de back,
No mo' dataway
Not evah no mo'.

Let Michael tote yo' burden
An' yo' pocketbook an' evahthing
'Cept yo' Bible,
While Gabriel blows somp'n
Solemn but loudsome
On dat horn of his'n.

Honey
Go straight on to de Big House,
An' speak to yo' God
Widout no fear an' tremblin'.

Then sit down
An' pass de time of day awhile.

Give a good talkin' to
To yo' favorite 'postle Peter,
An' rub the po' head
Of mixed-up Judas,
An' joke awhile wid Jonah.

Then, when you gits de chance,
Always rememberin' yo' raisin',
Let 'em know youse tired
Jest a mite tired.

Jesus will find yo' bed fo' you
Won't no servant evah bother wid yo' room.
Jesus will lead you
To a room wid windows
Openin' on cherry trees an' plum trees
Bloomin' everlastin'.

An' dat will be yours
Fo' keeps.
Den take yo' time. . . .
Honey, take yo' bressed time.

"Sister Lou," 1980

RICHARD R. NIEBUHR *(American, b. 1926)*

> Pilgrims are persons in motion—passing
> through territories not their own—seeking
> something we might call completion, or per-
> haps the word clarity will do as well, a goal to
> which only the spirit's compass points the way.

"Pilgrims and Pioneers," 1984

TRADITIONAL OJIBWAY STORY *(Native American)*

Weegwauss (Birch) awoke sweating and trembling from the midst of a dream which so disturbed him that he could not go back to sleep. He had to understand his dream. For the remainder of the night he pondered, but at dawn Weegwauss was no closer to a satisfactory interpretation. He got up, put on his clothes, and went out of his lodge to look for Chejauk (Crane), the wise man.

When he arrived at Chejauk's lodge, Weegwauss called out, "Chejauk! I must see you. I need your guidance."

"Come in," said Chejauk, yawning and stretching.

Weegwauss walked into the lodge and sat down.

"Why do you disturb my rest, Weegwauss?" said Chejauk. "What can be so important that you arise at dawn before the birds?"

"I have had a very strange dream. It disturbs me a great deal so much that I cannot go back to sleep. I must know what it means," said Weegwauss in agitation.

Chejauk indicated that Weegwauss should sit and then stirred up the fire. He filled his pipe and lit it before inviting, "Tell me your dream."

Weegwauss began: "I was standing on a high hill overlooking a deep, wide, and enchanting valley. It was quite unlike any valley I had ever seen and I gazed upon it, captivated. After a long time I turned my gaze from the valley to the other side. Across this vast expanse I saw four great hills. The first was steep and jagged; the second and third were less steep and rugged; the fourth was craggy and almost perpendicular, the top enshrouded by a thick white mist. And even though the hills were distant, I saw them clearly and everything upon them.

"On the slope of the first hill were countless infants crawling from bottom to the crown. At the base, only the smallest, youngest, and frailest were to be seen. As the infants proceeded toward the crest they got older and stronger. Near the top were the oldest infants. Of the vast number who began the ascent, only half, it seems, reached the top. Some scarcely began the journey before they slumped to the ground and lay still. Others continued a little further before they collapsed to move no more; still others, stronger and sturdier struggled on, but they too were stricken and breathed no more. Happily, some survived, attained the crest and descended the other side of the hill. I was among that crowd of infants. I saw myself survive the hardships of that first hill.

"I next looked upon the second hill. How different; yet, how similar. Here those who had been infants on the first hill were now young boys and girls, bigger, stronger, and sturdier; some appeared to be quite well on in years. Others were hardly seven or eight.

"Unlike the quiet nature of those on the first hill, the boys and girls on the second hill were full of energy. They could do many things. They had greater scope, greater powers; they played games of racing, wrestling, swimming, shooting; they worked, carrying wood, picking berries, hunting, and fishing. Laughter filled the hillside. But just as often as the youths were happy, they were grave. In moods and abilities and scope those on the second hill had greater range than those on the first.

"In other respects the scene was very much like that which took place on the first hill. There was the same compelling irresistible motion toward the top of the hill. There were the same calamities on that vast wide road. Boys and girls perished along the way; some in their play; some in their work; others in sleep. They drowned in streams and lakes; a few had violent choking; some were slain by human shadows. There was life; there was motion; there was death; there was no stopping.

"Seldom did the survivors stop to help the stricken. When they did pause, it was to remain only for a few moments and hurry on again. None turned back. They seemed unconcerned about the sick and the dying and the injured; it was as if they cared only for themselves. Something, a force, an object, a purpose drew them ever forward toward the summit of the hill. When they reached the crest they hurried down the fatal slope. I, too, hurried with them. Ahead was the third hill.

"There seemed to be little difference between the third and second hills. Some of the faces that I have seen on the first and second hills appeared among the crowd of climbers. There was the same unflagging, constant and forward pace. There was the same loss of life and unremitting reduction in numbers. There was the same indifference to the dying by the living.

"But how different all else; how changed. There were, on the third hill, no infants or youths to be seen, few games to be witnessed, little laughter to be heard. Men and women began to travel in pairs, although there were

21

solitary travellers, both men and women. All, paired or alone, were bent upon reaching the top. Little else mattered; pleasures were few and short-lived.

"Men worked at various tasks, hunting, fishing, making and repairing tools and instruments; women laboured by a fireplace cooking; or in a lodge making and mending clothing; blending medicines.

"In between the tasks and the infrequent joys, there were shouts of anger and hatred. There were battles between peoples over matters of little importance. Too frequently quarrels ended in pain, injury, and death.

"On and on the masses marched with unperturbed pace. Two by two, one by one the marchers stumbled and slumped to the ground to rise no more. But no calamity, no impediment, no pleasure halted that surge of human beings. There was no pause, no rest, no turning or looking back. There was only one motion, forward.

"At the peak, the marchers and I among them, who had survived, shouted in triumph. The goal so difficult was attained. The descent looked easy but was fraught with dangers and perils. Men and women fell, got up, stumbled, gasped, and lay still forever; women sat down to rest and sleep, never to wake again. The way down was as treacherous as was the way up.

"Above the wayfarers towered the fourth hill. How few we were; how old; how creased and wrinkled; how white of hair; how frail. It seemed impossible that these feeble and broken bodies could scale or even attempt to crawl the jagged rocks of the heights.

"Still we went on. Had we not overcome the first and second hills? Had we not conquered the third mountain? Why not the fourth hill? With faltering steps, halting strengths, gasping breaths the decrepit struggled on. Some inner strength of spirit urged us on; some outer force pushed or enticed us onward, forward, upward.

"But neither inner strength nor external force was enough to carry us all to our distant goals. Old men and ancient women crumbled to the ground and were engulfed into the mountain soil to become one with it. Those living on looked back, shouted encouragement to the fallen, to the faint. They shouted even to those on the third hill.

"On we went, undaunted by the loss of companions or life partners, undismayed by the ordeal, anxious to reach the misted crest. Most succumbed on the incline. Few reached the summit. But I was one of those who did not collapse. I lived on. I struggled on. Those of us who continued to live slowly vanished into the shroud that hid the crest.

"At this point I woke up. I do not know whether the dream is good or evil. I come to you for guidance." Weegwauss waited for Chejauk to answer.

The medicine man spoke calmly without looking up. "It was a good dream, Weegwauss. You saw life from beginning to end. You saw man's life in its entirety, in all its stages, in all its moods, and in all its forms. Kitche Manitou, the Great Spirit, has been generous to you. He has allowed you to see all of life in dream. He grants this privilege to only a few. As you saw life, whole, continuous, and uninterrupted, so will you live out your own life to its very end. You will see your grandchildren and your great-grandchildren. You will suffer sickness and enjoy good health; you will endure adversity and know prosperity; you will encounter both good and evil. You will survive, while others will never reach the fourth and final hill. You need not fear that death will cut off your life before you have lived it out in its entirety and before you have served your brothers."

From "The Four Hills of Life," in *Ojibway Heritage,* 1976

AESOP *(Greek, c. 620–560 B.C.E.)*

A Horse, an Ox, and a Dog, driven to great straits by the cold, sought shelter and protection from Man. He received them kindly, lighted a fire, and warmed them. He made the Horse free of his oats, gave the Ox abundance of hay, and fed the Dog with meat from his own table. Grateful for these favors, they determined to repay him to the best of their ability. They divided for this purpose the term of his life between them, and each endowed one portion of it with the qualities which chiefly characterized himself. The Horse chose his earliest years, and endowed them with his own attributes: hence every man is in his youth impetuous, headstrong, and obstinate in maintaining his own opinion. The Ox took under his patronage the next term of life, and therefore man in his middle age is fond of work, devoted to labor, and resolute to amass wealth, and to husband his resources. The end of life was reserved to the Dog, wherefore an old man is often snappish, irritable, hard to please, and selfish, tolerant only of his own household, but averse to strangers, and to all who do not administer to his comfort or to his necessities.

"The Man, The Horse, The Ox, and The Dog," in *Aesop's Fables,* 1949

ARISTOTLE *(Greek, c. 384–322 B.C.E.)*

Let us now consider the various types of human character, in relation to the emotions and moral qualities, showing how they correspond to our various ages and fortunes. By emotions I mean anger, desire, and the like; these we have discussed already. By moral qualities I mean virtues and vices; these also have been discussed already, as well as the various things that various types of men tend to will and to do. By ages I mean youth, the prime of life, and old age. By fortune I mean birth, wealth, power, and their opposites—in fact, good fortune and ill fortune.

To begin with the Youthful type of character. Young men have strong passions, and tend to gratify them indiscriminately. Of the bodily desires, it is the sexual by which they are most swayed and in which they show absence of self-control. They are changeable and fickle in their desires, which are violent while they last, but quickly over: their impulses are keen but not deep-rooted, and are like sick people's attacks of hunger and thirst. They are hot-tempered and quick-tempered, and apt to give way to their anger; bad temper often gets the better of them, for owing to their love of honour they cannot bear being slighted, and are indignant if they imagine themselves unfairly treated. While they love honour, they love victory still more; for youth is eager for superiority over others, and victory is one form of this. They love both more than they love money, which indeed they love very little, not having yet learnt what it means to be without it—this is the point of Pittacus' remark about Amphiaraus. They look at the good side rather than the bad, not having yet witnessed many instances of wickedness. They trust others readily, because they have not yet often been cheated. They are sanguine; nature warms their blood as though with excess of wine; and besides that, they have as yet met with few disappointments. Their lives are mainly spent not in memory but in expectation; for expectation refers to the future, memory to the past, and youth has a long future before it and a short past behind it: on the first day of one's life one has nothing at all to remember, and can only look forward. They are easily cheated, owing to the sanguine disposition just mentioned. Their hot tempers and hopeful dispositions make them more courageous than older men are; the hot temper prevents fear, and the hopeful disposition creates confidence; we cannot feel fear so long as we are feeling angry, and any expectation of good makes us confident. They are shy, accepting the rules of society in which they have been trained, and not yet believing in any other standard of honour. They have exalted notions, because they have not yet been humbled by life or learnt its necessary limitations; moreover, their hopeful disposition makes them think themselves equal to great things—and that means having exalted notions. They would always rather do noble deeds than useful ones: their lives are regulated more by moral feeling than by reasoning; and whereas reasoning leads us to choose what is useful, moral goodness leads us to choose what is noble. They are fonder of their friends, intimates, and companions than older men are, because they like spending their days in the company of others, and have not yet come to value either their friends or anything else by their usefulness to themselves. All their mistakes are in the direction of doing things excessively and vehemently. They disobey Chilon's precept by overdoing everything; they love too much and hate too much, and the same with everything else. They think they know everything, and are always quite sure about it; this, in fact, is why they overdo everything. If they do wrong to others, it is because they mean to insult them, not to do them actual harm. They are ready to pity others, because they think every one an honest man, or anyhow better than he is: they judge their neighbour by their own harmless natures, and so cannot think he deserves to be treated in that way. They are fond of fun and therefore witty, wit being well-bred insolence.

Such, then, is the character of the Young. The character of Elderly Men— men who are past their prime—may be said to be formed for the most part of elements that are the contrary of all these. They have lived many years; they have often been taken in, and often made mistakes; and life on the whole is a bad business. The result is that they are sure about nothing and *under-do* everything. They 'think', but they never 'know'; and because of their hesita- tion they always add a 'possibly' or a 'perhaps', putting everything this way and nothing positively. They are cynical; that is, they tend to put the worse construction on everything. Further, their experience makes them distrustful and therefore suspicious of evil. Consequently they neither love warmly nor hate bitterly, but following the hint of Bias they love as though they will some day hate and hate as though they will some day love. They are small- minded, because they have been humbled by life: their desires are set upon nothing more exalted or unusual than what will help them to keep alive. They are not generous, because money is one of the things they must have, and at the same time their experience has taught them how hard it is to get and how easy to lose. They are cowardly, and are always anticipating dan- ger; unlike that of the young, who are warm-blooded, their temperament is chilly; old age has paved the way for cowardice; fear is, in fact, a form of chill. They love life; and all the more when their last day has come, because the object of all desire is something we have not got, and also because we desire most strongly that which we need most urgently. They are too fond of themselves; this is one form that small-mindedness takes. Because of this, they guide their lives too much by considerations of what is useful and too little by what is noble—for the useful is what is good for oneself, and the noble what is good absolutely. They are not shy, but shameless rather; caring less for what is noble than for what is useful, they feel contempt for what people may think of them. They lack confidence in the future; partly through experience—for most things go wrong, or anyhow turn out worse than one expects; and partly because of their cowardice. They live by mem- ory rather than by hope; for what is left to them of life is but little as compared with the long past; and hope is of the future, memory of the past. This, again, is the cause of their loquacity; they are continually talking of the past, because they enjoy remembering it. Their fits of anger are sudden but feeble. Their sensual passions have either altogether gone or have lost their vigour; consequently they do not feel their passions much, and their actions are inspired less by what they do feel than by the love of gain. Hence men at this time of life are often supposed to have a self-controlled character; the fact is that their passions have slackened, and they are slaves to the love of gain. They guide their lives by reasoning more than by moral feeling; reasoning being directed to utility and moral feeling to moral goodness. If they wrong others, they mean to injure them, not to insult them. Old men may feel pity, as well as young men, but not for the same reason. Young men feel it out of kindness; old men out of weakness, imagining that anything that befalls any one else might easily happen to them, which, as we saw, is a thought that excites pity. Hence they are querulous, and not disposed to jesting or laughter—the love of laughter being the very opposite of querulousness.

Such are the characters of Young Men and Elderly Men. People always think well of speeches adapted to, and reflecting, their own character; and we can now see how to compose our speeches so as to adapt both them and ourselves to our audiences.

As for Men in their Prime, clearly we shall find that they have a character between that of the young and that of the old, free from the extremes of either. They have neither that excess of confidence which amounts to rashness, not too much timidity, but the right amount of each. They neither trust everybody nor distrust everybody, but judge people correctly. Their lives will be guided not by the sole consideration either of what is noble or of what is useful, but by both; neither by parsimony nor by prodigality, but by what is fit and proper. So, too, in regard to anger and desire; they will be brave as well as temperate, and temperate as well as brave; these virtues are divided between the young and the old; the young are brave but intemperate, the old temperate but cowardly. To put it generally, all the valuable qualities that youth and age divide between them are united in the prime of life, while all their excesses or defects are replaced by moderation and fitness. The body is in its prime from thirty to five-and-thirty; the mind about forty-nine.

Rhetoric, book 2, chapters 12–14, last half of the fourth century B.C.E.

CONFUCIUS (*Chinese, c. 551–479 B.C.E.*)

> At fifteen I set my heart upon learning.
> At thirty I established myself [in accordance with ritual].
> At forty I no longer had perplexities.
> At fifty I knew the Mandate of Heaven.

At sixty I was at ease with whatever I heard.
At seventy I could follow my heart's desire without
transgressing the boundaries of right.

From *Analects*

PTOLEMY (*Born in Greece, second century* c.e.)

In the matter of the age divisions of mankind in general there is one and the
same approach, which for likeness and comparison depends upon the order
of the seven planets: it begins with the first age of man and with the first
sphere from us, that is, the moon's, and ends with the last of the ages and the
outermost of the planetary spheres, which is called that of Saturn. And in
truth the accidental qualities of each of the ages are those which are naturally proper to the planet compared with it, and these it will be needful to
observe, in order that by this means we may investigate the general questions of the temporal divisions, while we determine particular differences
from the special qualities which are discovered in the nativities.

For up to about the fourth year, following the number which belongs to
the quadrennium, the moon takes over the age of infancy and produces the
suppleness and lack of fixity in its body, its quick growth and the moist
nature, as a rule, of its food, the changeability of its condition, and the
imperfection and inarticulate state of its soul, suitably to her own active
qualities.

In the following period of ten years, Mercury, to whom falls the second
place and the second age, that of childhood, for the period which is half of
the space of twenty years, begins to articulate and fashion the intelligent and
logical part of the soul, to implant certain seeds and rudiments of learning,
and to bring to light individual peculiarities of character and faculties, awak-
ing the soul at this stage by instruction, tutelage, and the first gymnastic
exercises.

Venus, taking in charge the third age, that of youth, for the next eight
years, corresponding in number to her own period, begins, as is natural, to
inspire, at their maturity, an activity of the seminal passages and to implant
an impulse toward the embrace of love. At this time particularly a kind of
frenzy enters the soul, incontinence, desire for any chance sexual gratification, burning passion, guile, and the blindness of the impetuous lover.

The lord of the middle sphere, the sun, takes over the fourth age, which
is the middle one in order, young manhood, for the period of nineteen years,
wherein he implants in the soul at length the mastery and direction of its
actions, desire for substance, glory, and position, and a change from playful,
ingenuous error to seriousness, decorum, and ambition.

27

After the sun, Mars, fifth in order, assumes command of manhood for the space of fifteen years, equal to his own period. He introduces severity and misery into life, and implants cares and troubles in the soul and in the body, giving it, as it were, some sense and notion of passing its prime and urging it, before it approaches its end, by labour to accomplish something among its undertakings that is worthy of note.

Sixth, Jupiter, taking as his lot the elderly age, again for the space of his own period, twelve years, brings about the renunciation of manual labour, toil, turmoil, and dangerous activity, and in their place brings decorum, foresight, retirement, together with all-embracing deliberation, admonition, and consolation; now especially he brings men to set store by honour, praise, and independence, accompanied by modesty and dignity.

Finally to Saturn falls as his lot old age, the latest period, which lasts for the rest of life. Now the movements both of body and of soul are cooled and impeded in their impulses, enjoyments, desires, and speed; for the natural decline supervenes upon life, which has become worn down with age, dispirited, weak, easily offended, and hard to please in all situations, in keeping with the sluggishness of his movements.

From Tetrabiblos, book 4, chapter 10

OVID *(Roman, 43 B.C.E.–17 or 18 C.E.)*

Then again, do you not see the year assuming four aspects, in imitation of our own lifetime? For in early spring it is tender and full of fresh life, just like a little child; at that time the herbage is bright, swelling with life, but as yet without strength and solidity, and fills the farmers with joyful expectation. Then all things are in bloom and the fertile fields run riot with their bright-coloured flowers; but as yet there is no strength in the green foliage. After spring has passed, the year, grown more sturdy, passes into summer and becomes like a strong young man. For there is no hardier time than this, none more abounding in rich, warm life. Then autumn comes, with its first flush of youth gone, but ripe and mellow, midway in time between youth and age, with sprinkled grey showing on the temples. And then comes aged winter, with faltering step and shivering, its locks all gone or hoary.

'Our own bodies also go through a ceaseless round of change, nor what we have been or are to-day shall we be to-morrow. There was a time when we lay in our first mother's womb, mere seeds and hopes of men. Then Nature wrought with her cunning hands, willed not that our bodies should lie cramped in our strained mother's body, and from our home sent us forth into the free air. Thus brought forth into the light, the infant lay without strength; but soon it lifted itself up on all fours after the manner of the beasts; then gradually in a wabbling, weak-kneed fashion it stood erect, supported by some convenient prop. Thereafter, strong and fleet, it passed over the span of youth; and when the years of middle life also have been spent, it glides along the downhill path of declining age. This undermines and pulls down the strength of former years; and Milon, grown old, weeps when he looks at those arms, which once had been like the arms of Hercules with their firm mass of muscles, and sees them now hanging weak and flabby. Helen also weeps when she sees her aged wrinkles in the looking-glass, and tearfully asks herself why she should twice have been a lover's prey. O Time, thou great devourer, and thou, envious Age, together you destroy all things; and, slowly gnawing with your teeth, you finally consume all things in lingering death!'

From *Metamorphoses*, book 15, chapter 2, 1–8, c. 5 C.E.

RABBI JUDAH BEN TEMA (*Hebrew, c. middle of the second century C.E.*)

At five years of age the study of Scripture;
At ten, the study of Mishnah;
At thirteen, subject to the commandments;
At fifteen, the study of Talmud;
At eighteen, marriage;
At twenty, the pursuit [of a livelihood];
At thirty, the peak of strength;
At forty, wisdom;
At fifty, able to give counsel;
At sixty, old age creeping on;
At seventy, fullness of years;
At eighty, the age of "strength";
At ninety, body bent;
At a hundred, as good as dead and gone completely out
    of the world.

From *Ethics of the Fathers*, second century C.E.

ISIDORE OF SEVILLE (*Roman/lived in Spain, c. 560–636*)

Of the Ages of Man. The stages of life are six: infancy, boyhood, adolescence, youth, maturity, and old age. The first age, infancy, belongs to the child entering life and extends for seven years. The second age is boyhood, an age of purity not yet able to produce offspring, which lasts until the fourteenth year. The third is adolescence, an age mature enough for reproduction, which extends up to twenty-eight years. The fourth is youth, the strongest of all the ages, ending in the fiftieth year. The fifth is the age of the elder, or maturity, which is a period of decline from youth towards old age. It is not yet old age, but neither is it any longer youth: it is that age of the elder which the Greeks call πρεσβύτην (an old man being called by the Greeks not 'presbyter' but γέρων). This age begins in the fiftieth year and ends in the seventieth. Sixth comes old age, which is limited to no particular number of years, for whatever remains of life after the previous five ages is assigned to it. Decrepitude is the last part of old age, to be understood as the conclusion of the sixth age. Thus it is that the authorities have divided human life into these six stages, through which it suffers change, and hurries by, and arrives at its conclusion in death.

From *Etymologiae*, book 11, chapter 2, seventh century C.E.

WILLIAM SHAKESPEARE (*English, 1564–1616*)

> All the world's a stage,
> And all the men and women merely players:
> They have their exits and their entrances;
> And one man in his time plays many parts,
> His acts being seven ages. As, first the infant,
> Mewling and puking in the nurse's arms.
> And then the whining schoolboy, with his satchel
> And shining morning face, creeping like snail
> Unwillingly to school. And then the lover,
> Sighing like furnace, with a woeful ballad
> Made to his mistress' eyebrow. Then the soldier,
> Full of strange oaths, and bearded like the pard,
> Jealous in honour, sudden and quick in quarrel,
> Seeking the bubble reputation
> Even in the cannon's mouth. And then the justice,
> In fair round belly with good capon lined,
> With eyes severe and beard of formal cut,
> Full of wise saws and modern instances;
> And so he plays his part. The sixth age shifts
> Into the lean and slipper'd pantaloon,
> With spectacles on nose and pouch on side;
> His youthful hose, well saved, a world too wide
> For his shrunk shank; and his big manly voice,
> Turning again toward childish treble, pipes
> And whistles in his sound. Last scene of all,
> That ends this strange eventful history,

Is second childishness and mere oblivion,
Sans teeth, sans eyes, sans taste, sans everything.

From *As You Like It*, act 2, scene 7, 1600

HUANG TI (*Chinese, possibly legendary, attributed dates of reign are c. 2697–2597 B.C.E.*)

[*The teacher, Ch'i Po, answered Huang Ti, the Yellow Emperor:*]

"In the most ancient times the teachings of the sages were followed by those beneath them; they said that weakness and noxious influences and injurious winds should be avoided at specific times. They [the sages] were tranquilly content in nothingness and the true vital force accompanied them always; their vital (original) spirit was preserved within; thus, how could illness come to them?

"They exercised restraint of their wills and reduced their desires; their hearts were at peace and without any fear; their bodies toiled and yet did not become weary.

"Their spirit followed in harmony and obedience; everything was satisfactory to their wishes and they could achieve whatever they wished. Any kind of food was beautiful (to them); and any kind of clothing was satisfactory. They felt happy under any condition. To them it did not matter whether a man held a high or a low position in life. These men can be called pure at heart. No kind of desire can tempt the eyes of those pure people and their mind cannot be misled by excessiveness and evil.

"(In such a society) no matter whether men are wise or foolish, virtuous or bad, they are without fear of anything; they are in harmony with Tao, the Right Way. Thus they could live more than one hundred years and remain active without becoming decrepit, because their virtue was perfect and never imperiled."

The Emperor asked: "When people grow old then they cannot give birth to children. Is it because they have exhausted their strength in depravity or is it because of natural fate?"

Ch'i Po answered: "When a girl is seven years of age, the emanations of the kidneys become abundant, she begins to change her teeth and her hair grows longer. When she reaches her fourteenth year she begins to menstruate and is able to become pregnant and the circulation in the great thoroughfare pulse is strong. Menstruation comes at regular times, thus the girl is able to give birth to a child.

"When the girl reaches the age of twenty-one years the emanations of the kidneys are regular, the last tooth has come out, and she is fully grown.

31

When the woman reaches the age of twenty-eight, her muscles and bones are strong, her hair has reached its full length and her body is flourishing and fertile.

"When the woman reaches the age of thirty-five, the pulse indicating [the region of] the 'Sunlight' deteriorates, her face begins to wrinkle and her hair begins to fall. When she reaches the age of forty-two, the pulse of the three [regions of] Yang deteriorates in the upper part (of the body), her entire face is wrinkled and her hair begins to turn white.

"When she reaches the age of forty-nine she can no longer become pregnant and the circulation of the great thoroughfare pulse is decreased. Her menstruation is exhausted, and the gates of menstruation are no longer open; her body deteriorates and she is no longer able to bear children.

"When a boy is eight years old the emanations of his testes (kidneys) are fully developed; his hair grows longer and he begins to change his teeth. When he is sixteen years of age the emanations of his testicles become abundant and he begins to secrete semen. He has an abundance of semen which he seeks to dispel; and if at this point the male and female element unite in harmony, a child can be conceived.

"At the age of twenty-four the emanations of his testicles are regular; his muscles and bones are firm and strong, the last tooth has grown, and he has reached his full height. At thirty-two his muscles and bones are flourishing, his flesh is healthy and he is able-bodied and fertile.

"At the age of forty the emanations of his testicles become smaller, he begins to lose his hair and his teeth begin to decay. At forty-eight his masculine vigor is reduced or exhausted; wrinkles appear on his face and the hair on his temples turns white. At fifty-six the force of his liver deteriorates, his muscles can no longer function properly, his secretion of semen is exhausted, his vitality diminishes, his testicles (kidneys) deteriorate, and his physical strength reaches its end. At sixty-four he loses his teeth and his hair.

"Man's kidneys rule over the water which receives and stores the secretion of the five 'viscera' and of the six 'bowels.' When the five viscera are filled abundantly, they are able to dispel secretion; but when, at this stage, the five viscera are dry, the muscles and bones decay, the generative secretions are exhausted and therefore his hair at the temples turns white, his body grows heavy, his posture is no longer straight and he is unable to produce offspring."

The Emperor asked: "But there are men who, though already old in years, produce offspring. How is this possible?"

Ch'i Po answered: "Those are men whose natural limit of age is higher. The vigor of their pulse remains active and there is a surplus of secretion of their testicles (kidneys). Yet if they have children, their sons will not exceed their sixty-fourth year and their daughters will not exceed their forty-ninth year, because at that time the essence of Heaven and Earth will be exhausted."

The Emperor asked: "Those who follow Tao, the Right Way, and thus reach the age of about a hundred years, can they beget children?"

Ch'i Po answered: "Those who follow Tao, the Right Way, can escape old age and keep their body in perfect condition. Although they are old in years they are still able to produce offspring."

Huang Ti said: "I have heard that in ancient times there were the so-called Spiritual Men; they mastered the Universe and controlled Yin and Yang [the two principles in nature]. They breathed the essence of life, they were independent in preserving their spirit, and their muscles and flesh remained unchanged. Therefore they could enjoy a long life, just as there is no end for Heaven and Earth. All this was the result of their life in accordance with Tao, the Right Way."

From *The Yellow Emperor's Classic of Internal Medicine*, 2697–2597 B.C.E.

CELSUS (*Roman, 25 B.C.E.–50 C.E.*)

The middle period of life is the safest, for it is not disturbed by the heat of youth, nor by the chill of age. Old age is more exposed to chronic diseases, youth to acute ones. The square-built frame, neither thin nor fat, is the fittest; for tallness, as it is graceful in youth, shrinks in the fulness of age; a thin frame is weak, a fat one sluggish.

*   *   *

As regards the various times of life, children and adolescents enjoy the best health in spring, and are safest in early summer; old people are at their best during summer and the beginning of autumn; young and middle-aged adults in winter. Winter is worst for the aged, summer for young adults. At these periods should any indisposition arise, it is very probable that infants and children still of tender age should suffer from the creeping ulcerations of the mouth which the Greeks call aphthas, vomiting, insomnia, discharges from the ear, and inflammations about the navel. Especially in those teething there arise ulcerations of the gums, slight fevers, sometimes spasms, diarrhoea; and they suffer as the canine teeth in particular are growing up; the most well-nourished children, and those constipated, are especially in danger. In those somewhat older there occur affections of the tonsils, various spinal curvatures, swelling in the neck, the painful kind of warts which the Greeks call acrochordones, and a number of other swellings. At the commencement of puberty, in addition to many of the above troubles, there occur chronic fevers and also nose-bleedings. Throughout childhood there are special dangers, first about the fortieth day, then in the seventh month, next in the seventh year, and after that about puberty. The sorts of affections which occur in infancy, when not ended by the time of puberty, or of the first coitions, or of the first menstruations in the females, generally become chronic; more often, however, puerile affections, after persisting for a rather long while, come to an end. Adolescence is liable to acute diseases, such as fits, especially to consumption; those who spit blood are generally youths. After that age come on pain in the side and lung, lethargy, cholera, madness, and outpourings of blood from certain mouths of veins which the Greeks call haemorrhoids. In old age there occur breathing and urinary difficulties, choked nostrils, joint and renal pains, paralysis, the bad habit of body which the Greeks call cachexia, insomnias, the more chronic maladies of the ears, eyes, also of the nostrils, and especially looseness of the bowels with its sequences, dysentery, intestinal lubricity, and the other ills due to bowel looseness. In addition thin people are fatigued by consumption, diarrhoea, running from the nose, pain in the lung and side. The obese, many of them, are throttled by acute diseases and difficult breathing; they die often suddenly, which rarely happens in a thinner person.

From *De Medicina*, book 2, Augustan Age

SIR FRANCIS BACON *(English, 1561–1626)*

The scale or ladder of man's life hath these steps: conception, quickening in the womb, birth, sucking, weaning, feeding on pap, and spoon-meat in infancy, breeding of teeth at two years old, secret hair at twelve or fourteen, ability for generation, flowers, hair on the knees, and under the armholes, a budding beard, full growth, full strength and agility, grayness, baldness, ceasing of flowers, and of generative ability, inclining to dryness, a creature with three feet, Death. . . .

The differences of youth and age are these following: In youth the skin is moist and smooth, in age dry, and wrinkled, especially about the forehead, and eyes: the flesh in youth is tender, and soft, in age hard; youth is strong, and nimble, age weak, and unwieldy; in youth good digestion, in age weak: the bowels in youth are soft, and moist, in age salt and dry; in youth the body is straight, in age bowed, and crooked, the sinews in youth are steady, in age weak, and trembling, choleric humors in youth, and hot blood, in age phlegmatic, melancholy humors, and cold blood, youth prone to venery, age slow in performance: the moisture of the body in youth oily, in age raw, and watery, in youth many swelling spirits, in age few, and weak; in youth spirits thick, and lively; in age sharp, and thin; in youth sharp and sound senses, in age dull, and decaying; in youth strong sound teeth, in age weak, worn, and falling out; in youth colored hair, in age the former color turns grey, hair in youth, in age baldness, quick, and strong pulse in youth, in age weak and slow; in youth sharp curable sicknesses and diseases, in age tedious and incurable: wounds heal soon in youth, in age slowly, in youth flesh-colored cheeks, in age pale, or of a deep sanguine red: youth not much trouble with rheums, age rhematic, the body grows fatter only in age than youth. Perspiration and digestion in age being bad, and fatness being the abundance of nourishment over and above that which is perfectly assimilated and converted into the substance of the body. And the appetite is sometimes in age increased, by sharp humors, digestion being then weaker: this and the rest being by physicians ascribed to the decay of natural heat, and radical moisture, but dryness in the course of age doth precede coldness, and the lusty heat of flourishing youth declines to dryness, then to coldness.

The affections also of youth and age differ: I remember in my youth I was familiarly acquainted at Poitiers in France with an ingenious young gentleman, after an eminent man, who inveighing against the conditions of age, would usually say, "that old men's minds being visible, would appear as deformed as their bodies," wittily afterward comparing the mind's vices in age to the body's defects, saying "They were dry skinned and impudent, hard boweled, and unmerciful; bleary eyed, and envious; downlooking, and stooping, and atheists; earth, not heaven, being their constant object: trembling limbs, wavering, and unconstant, crooked fingered, greedy and covetous, knees trembling, and fearful, wrinkled, and crafty." But to make a more serious comparison, youth is shamefaced, and modest, age is hardened; youth is liberal and merciful, age is hard; youth emulates, age envies, youth is religious, and fervently zealous, being unexperienced in the miseries of this world, age cold in piety and charity, through much experience, and incredulity; youth is forward in desire, age moderate; youth light and inconstant, age grave, and constant; youth is liberal, bountiful, and loving, age covetous, and wisely provident; youth confident, and presumptuous, age distrustful and suspicious; youth gentle, and tractable, age forward, and disdainful; youth sincere, and simple, age cautious, and close; youth haughty in desires, age careful for necessaries; youth a time-pleaser, age a time-rememberer; youth an adorer of superiors, age a censurer. And by many other characters impertinent to the present matter, the different conditions of youth and age may be described: But the body growing fat in age, so the judgement, not the fancy grows stronger, preferring safe sure courses before shows and appearances: and lastly, age loves to prattle and brag, and being desirous to do less, is desirous to talk most. Poets therefore feigned, that old Tithonius was changed into a chirping grasshopper.

From "The Differences of Youth and Age," in *The History of Life and Death*, 1638

ELIZA W. FARNHAM (*American, 1815–1864*)

Procreation is the highest *function* of life, in whatever form, vegetable or animal. It is the End to which all attainable perfection is Means, the one office for which innumerable inferior types are brought forward to their ultimate stage of development.

*　　*　　*

Again, the suspension of this function in Woman marks her life by a physical change—an experience peculiar to herself. The masculine life is divisible, physiologically, into two periods, youth and maturity—ante-paternal and paternal; the feminine into three, Ante-Maternal, Maternal, and Post-Maternal—and the transition from the second to the third is a physiological experience exclusive to Woman, which is balanced by nothing in the functional experience of man.

Now what is the language of natural physiological change? It is advancement—never degradation. It is the unequivocal testimony, in any life which it marks, of a degree of differentiation beyond that of another life, into which it cannot come. And unless we reject advancement as the Aim, and progress from condition to condition as the Method of Nature, we must acknowledge that it marks a stage of growth in the ultimate, if not in the present powers of the life, at whatever time it takes place and with, whatever manifest diminution of existing capacities. I speak not here of the change to old age, which comes upon all living (though of that also it is equally to be affirmed that it is advancement toward the ultimate), but of those changes which mark functional stages in the life.

Now of this great change in Woman, from the Maternal to the Post-Maternal period, nothing could be more natural than that, in the material ages which are past, it should, happening to Woman alone of all living, have been read as a sign of her descent from a full to a limited life—from capacity to incapacity: an absolute, uncompensated loss of power; because no material compensation appeared, to take its place in the circuit of her corporeal capacities.

*　　*　　*

This phenomenon of the human feminine is significantly called by names which indicate a dim perception of its true character. The "turn of life," into new channels—the "change of life," from old forms of expression to new, but never is it, in popular language, named diminution of life or loss of it. . . .

In vain will man send forth his Imagination, with pinion all unloosed, to picture this era of Woman's life. There are no dyes in which her brush may be dipped, that will lay in the colors of that matchless mosaic. Look back over the long road she has traveled, since incipient Maternity, in her tiny body, kissed and caressed its first doll—childhood and its natural, graceful, refined, artistic joys; Motherhood and its timid, shy, palpitating hopes, yearnings, fears, trusts, loves; Womanhood and its deep, grand, awful experiences—all leading up to this mysterious gateway, by which she is to pass to a still unknown, separated, Beyond. What valleys of early hope lie cool and dewy, pure and fragrant, in that far distance which she re-members—what wide, monotonous plains spread all about her, as she ad-vanced—what shining heights, bathed in the auroral airs of love, promised for their fullness of joy, their perfect peace—what hills of difficulty presently arose—what black, forbidding steeps of impossibility—what vast continents, over which the winds of experience blew in alternate zephyr and tornado—what deserts, where death withered every bud and leaf that made life sweet; where sorrow turned fairest flowers to ashes, and sweetest savors to bitter-ness; where suffering dried every fountain and parched all the little, gurgling springs, and sucked up the tiny streams, whose flow would have adorned and made vocal the landscape. . . .

. . . What marvel that, in her desperation, arrived at this great transit, only darkness, mystery and loss of power before—only swiftly perishing capacity behind—around her only skepticism as to the most profound real-ities of her daily life, happy if it be but skepticism, in gentle, patient form, instead of jeering sarcasm, or harshness—nowhere a ray of intelligent sympathy—books dumb, persons blind to her emotions of joy and suffering; looking cold or forbearingly askance if she chance to utter so much as a word of some unfamiliar thought or feeling that possesses her—younger women pitying or half despising her—elder women, who give their sympathy, hav-ing no real light to give—the husband making the same demands upon her, respecting only corporeal disability—even affectionate children, loving daughters, and tender, manly sons, plainly showing that it is pity rather than reverence that controls their treatment of her; all her relations, in short, shaping themselves to the theory of a diminished instead of an expanded self-hood—what marvel, I repeat, that thousands of women, as good as the best, as true as the truest, have given way, in these fearful years, and drifted into the dreary wilderness of insanity, or rushed to the swift escape of self-destruction!

*　　*　　*

She stands at this portal, now, which separates her past and present from a future that is unknown to her, and that is made forbidding by the theory she has received of it. No wonder that she looks upon these gates, as the condemned upon the door which is next to open the way to his scaffold—that she counts sadly every step which brings her nearer to them—that she would fain convince herself and the world that she is yet far off; thirty-five instead of forty-five; fresh with youth instead of cosmetics; gay from happiness instead of simulation. For that awful future! Wherein it is not mysterious it is worse; insulting, neglectful, chilling. And, whatever its aspect to her, the near approaches to it are through trials of soul and sense that call for the most delicate consideration, the deepest tenderness, the finest sympathy of the spirit. It is the winding up of a set of functions, the most august of her gifts—of a circuit of nerve-activities, and the transfer of the finer powers, capacities, and sensibilities involved in them, from the corporeal to the psychical level. All this does not take place without perturbations of heart, and nerve, and brain, hard to bear at the best—appalling at times, in the darkness wherein she has to grope her lonely way.

From *Woman and Her Era*, 1864

SIR THOMAS BROWNE (*English, 1605–1682*)

Confound not the distinctions of thy Life which Nature hath divided: that is, Youth, Adolescence, Manhood, and old Age, nor in these divided Periods, wherein thou art in a manner Four, conceive thyself but One. Let every division be happy in its proper Virtues, nor one Vice run through all. Let each distinction have its salutary transition, and critically deliver thee from the imperfections of the former, so ordering the whole, that Prudence and Virtue may have the largest Section. Do as a Child but when thou art a Child, and ride not on a Reed at twenty. He who hath not taken leave of the follies of his Youth, and in his maturer state scarce got out of that division, disproportionately divideth his Days, crowds up the latter part of his Life, and leaves too narrow a corner for the Age of Wisdom, and so hath room to be a Man scarce longer than he hath been a Youth. Rather than to make this confusion, anticipate the Virtues of Age, and live long without the infirmities of it.

From *Christian Morals*, part 3, section 8, 1643

JOHANN WOLFGANG von GOETHE (*German, 1749–1832*)

People always fancy that we must become old to become wise; but, in truth, as years advance, it is hard to keep ourselves as wise as we were. Man becomes, indeed, in the different stages of life, a different being; but cannot say that he is a better one, and in certain matters he is as likely to be right in his twentieth as in his sixtieth year.

We see the world one way from a plain, another way from the heights of a promontory, another from the glacier fields of the primary mountains. We see, from one of these points, a larger piece of world than from the others; but that is all, and we cannot say that we see more truly from any one than from the rest. When a writer leaves monuments on the different steps of his life, it is chiefly important that he should have an innate foundation and good will; that he should, at each step, have seen and felt clearly, and that, without any secondary aims, he should have said distinctly and truly what has passed in his mind. Then will his writings, if they were right at the step where they originated, remain always right, however the writer may develop or alter himself in after times.

From *Conversations of Goethe with Eckermann and Soret,* 17 February 1831

LIN YUTANG *(Chinese, 1895–1976)*

I think that, from a biological standpoint, human life almost reads like a poem. It has its own rhythm and beat, its internal cycles of growth and decay. It begins with innocent childhood, followed by awkward adolescence trying awkwardly to adapt itself to mature society, with its young passions and follies, its ideals and ambitions; then it reaches a manhood of intense activities, profiting from experience and learning more about society and human nature; at middle age, there is a slight easing of tension, a mellowing of character like the ripening of fruit or the mellowing of good wine, and the gradual acquiring of a more tolerant, more cynical and at the same time a kindlier view of life; then in the sunset of our life, the endocrine glands decrease their activity, and if we have a true philosophy of old age and have ordered our life pattern according to it, it is for us the age of peace and security and leisure and contentment; finally, life flickers out and one goes into eternal sleep, never to wake up again. One should be able to sense the beauty of this rhythm of life, to appreciate, as we do in grand symphonies, its main theme, its strains of conflict and the final resolution. The movements of these cycles are very much the same in a normal life, but the music must be provided by the individual himself. In some souls, the discordant note becomes harsher and harsher and finally overwhelms or submerges the main melody. Sometimes the discordant note gains so much power that the music can no longer go on, and the individual shoots himself with a pistol or jumps into a river. But that is because his original *leit-motif* has been hopelessly over-shadowed through the lack of a good self-education. Otherwise the normal human life runs to its normal end in a kind of dignified movement and procession. There are sometimes in many of us too many *staccatos* or *impetuosos,* and because the tempo is wrong, the music is not pleasing to the ear; we might have more of the grand rhythm and majestic tempo of the Ganges, flowing slowly and eternally into the sea.

No one can say that a life with childhood, manhood and old age is not a beautiful arrangement; the day has its morning, noon and sunset, and the year has its seasons, and it is good that it is so. There is no good or bad in life, except what is good according to its own season. And if we take this biological view of life and try to live according to the seasons, no one but a conceited fool or an impossible idealist can deny that human life can be lived like a poem.

From "Human Life a Poem," in *The Importance of Living,* 1937

ARTHUR SCHOPENHAUER *(German, 1788–1860)*

There is a very fine saying of Voltaire's to the effect that every age of life has its own peculiar mental character, and that a man will feel completely unhappy if his mind is not in accordance with his years

> Qui n'a pas l'esprit de son âge,
> De son âge atout-le malheur. . . .

*   *   *

I have elsewhere stated that in childhood we are more given to using our intellect than our will; and I have explained why this is so. It is just for this reason that the first quarter of life is so happy: as we look back upon it in after years, it seems a sort of lost paradise. In childhood our relations with others are limited, our wants are few—in a word, there is little stimulus for the will; and so our chief concern is the extension of our knowledge.

*   *   *

In this way the earliest years of a man's life lay the foundation of his view of the world, whether it be shallow or deep; and although this view may be extended and perfected later on, it is not materially altered.

*   *   *

It is the depth and intensity of this early intuitive knowledge of the external world that explain why the experiences of childhood take such a firm hold on the memory. When we were young, we were completely absorbed in our immediate surroundings; there was nothing to distract our attention from them; we looked upon the objects about us as though they were the only ones of their kind, as though, indeed, nothing else existed at all. Later on, when we come to find out how many things there are in the world, this primitive state of mind vanishes, and with it our patience. . . .

Accordingly, we find that, in the years of childhood, the world is much better known to us on its outer or objective side, namely, as the presentation of will, than on the side of its inner nature, namely, as the will itself. . . . So the world lies before [the youth] like another Eden; and this is the Arcadia in which we are all born.

A little later, this state of mind gives birth to a thirst for real life—the impulse to do and suffer—which drives a man forth into the hurly-burly of the world. There he learns the other side of existence—the inner side, the will, which is thwarted at every step. Then comes the great period of disillusion, a period of very gradual growth; but once it has fairly begun, a man will tell you that he has got over all his false notions—*l'âge des illusions est passé;* and yet the process is only beginning, and it goes on extending its sway and applying more and more to the whole of life. . . .

The period of youth, which forms the remainder of this earlier half of our existence (and how many advantages it has over the later half!) is troubled and made miserable by the pursuit of happiness, as though there were no doubt that it can be met with somewhere in life, a hope that always ends in failure and leads to discontent.

*   *   *

In the bright dawn of our youthful days, the poetry of life spreads out a gorgeous vision before us, and we torture ourselves by longing to see it realized. We might as well wish to grasp the rainbow! . . .

If the chief feature of the earlier half of life is a never satisfied longing after happiness, the later half is characterized by the dread of misfortune. For, as we advance in years, it becomes in a greater or less degree clear that all happiness is chimerical in its nature, and that pain alone is real.

*   *   *

The consequence of this is that, as compared with the earlier, the later half of life, like the second part of a musical period, has less of passionate longing and more restfulness about it. And why is this the case? Simply because, in youth, a man fancies that there is a prodigious amount of happiness and pleasure to be had in the world, only that it is difficult to come by it; whereas, when he becomes old, he knows that there is nothing of the kind; he makes his mind completely at ease on the matter, enjoys the present hour as well as he can, and even takes a pleasure in trifles.

The chief result gained by experience of life is clearness of view. This is what distinguishes the man of mature age, and makes the world wear such a different aspect from that which it presented in his youth or boyhood. It is only then that he sees things quite plain, and takes them for that which they really are: while in earlier years he saw a phantom world, put together out of the whims and crotchets of his own mind, inherited prejudice and strange delusion: the real world was hidden from him, or the vision of it distorted. The first thing that experience finds to do is to free us from the

41

phantoms of the brain—those false notions that have been put into us in youth.

*   *   *

From the point of view we have been taking up until now, life may be compared to a piece of embroidery, of which, during the first half of his time, a man gets a sight of the right side, and during the second half, of the wrong. The wrong side is not so pretty as the right, but it is more instructive; it shows the way in which the threads have been worked together.

Intellectual superiority, even if it is of the highest kind, will not secure for a man a preponderating place in conversation until after he is forty years of age. . . .

And on passing his fortieth year, any man of the slightest power of mind—any man, that is, who has more than the sorry share of intellect with which Nature has endowed five-sixths of mankind—will hardly fail to show some trace of misanthropy.

*   *   *

From the standpoint of youth, life seems to stretch away into an endless future; from the standpoint of old age, to go back but a little way into the past; so that, at the beginning, life presents us with a picture in which the objects appear a great way off, as though we had reversed our telescope; while in the end everything seems so close. To see how short life is, a man must have grown old, that is to say, he must have lived long.

On the other hand, as the years increase, things look smaller, one and all; and Life, which had so firm and stable a base in the days of our youth, now seems nothing but a rapid flight of moments, every one of them illusory: we have come to see that the whole world is vanity!

*   *   *

I have said that almost every man's character seems to be specially suited to some one period of life, so that on reaching it the man is at his best. Some people are charming so long as they are young, and afterwards there is nothing attractive about them; others are vigorous and active in manhood, and then lose all the value they possess as they advance in years; many appear to best advantage in old age, when their character assumes a gentler tone, as becomes men who have seen the world and take life easily. . . .

This peculiarity must be due to the fact that the man's character has something in it akin to the qualities of youth or manhood or old age— something which accords with one or another of these periods of life, or perhaps acts as a corrective to its special failings. . . .

There is thus a sense in which it may be said that it is only in youth that a man lives with a full degree of consciousness, and that he is only half alive when he is old. As the years advance, his consciousness of what goes on about him dwindles, and the things of life hurry by without making any impression upon him, just as none is made by a work of art seen for the thousandth time. A man does what his hand finds to do, and afterwards he does not know whether he has done it or not.

As life becomes more and more unconscious, the nearer it approaches the point at which all consciousness ceases, the course of time itself seems to increase in rapidity.

*   *   *

A complete and adequate notion of life can never be attained by anyone who does not reach old age; for it is only the old man who sees life whole and knows its natural course; it is only he who is acquainted—and this is most important—not only with its entrance, like the rest of mankind, but with its exit too; so that he alone has a full sense of its utter vanity; whilst the others never cease to labor under the false notion that everything will come right in the end.

*   *   *

The same truth may be more broadly expressed by saying that the first forty years of life furnish the text, while the remaining thirty supply the commentary; and that without the commentary we are unable to understand aright the true sense and coherence of the text, together with the moral it contains and all the subtle application of which it admits. . . .

But the most curious fact is that it is also only towards the close of life when a man really recognizes and understands his own true self—the aims and objects he has followed in life, more especially the kind of relation in which he has stood to other people and to the world. It will often happen that as a result of this knowledge, a man will have to assign himself a lower place than he formerly thought was his due. But there are exceptions to this rule; and it will occasionally be the case that he will take a higher position than he had before. This will be owing to the fact that he had no adequate notion of the *baseness* of the world, and that he set up a higher aim for himself than was followed by the rest of mankind.

The progress of life shows a man the stuff of which he is made.

*   *   *

Disillusion is the chief characteristic of old age; for by that time the fictions are gone which gave life its charm and spurred on the mind to activity; the splendors of the world have been proved null and vain; its pomp, grandeur, and magnificence are faded. A man has then found out that behind most of the things he wants, and most of the pleasures he longs for, there is very little after all; and so he comes by degrees to see that our existence is all empty and void. . . .

From *Counsels and Maxims*, 1892

ERIK H. ERIKSON (*American, 1902–1994*)

As we come to the last stage, we become aware of the fact that our civilization really does not harbor a concept of the whole of life, as do the civilizations of the East: "In office a Confucian, in retirement a Taoist." In fact, it is astonishing to behold, how (until quite recently and with a few notable exceptions) Western psychology has avoided looking at the range of the whole cycle. As our world-image is a one-way street to never ending progress interrupted only by small and big catastrophes, our lives are to be one-way streets to success—and sudden oblivion. Yet, if we speak of a cycle of life we really mean two cycles in one: the cycle of one generation concluding itself in the next, and the cycle of individual life coming to a conclusion. If the cycle, in many ways, turns back on its own beginnings, so that the very old become again like children, the question is whether the return is to a childlikeness seasoned with wisdom—or to a finite childishness. This is not only important within the cycle of individual life, but also within that of generations, for it can only weaken the vital fiber of the younger generation if the evidence of daily living verifies man's prolonged last phase as a sanctioned period of childishness. Any span of the cycle lived without vigorous meaning, at the beginning, in the middle, or at the end, endangers the sense of life and the meaning of death in all whose life stages are intertwined.

Individuality here finds its ultimate test, namely, man's existence at the entrance to that valley which he must cross alone. I am not ready to discuss the psychology of "ultimate concern." But . . . I cannot help feeling that the order depicted suggests an existential complementarity of the great Nothingness and the actuality of the cycle of generations. For if there is any responsibility in the cycle of life it must be that one generation owes to the next that strength by which it can come to face ultimate concerns in its own way—unmarred by debilitating poverty or by the neurotic concerns caused by emotional exploitation.

For each generation must find the wisdom of the ages in the form of its own wisdom. Strength in the old, therefore, takes the form of wisdom in all of its connotations from ripened "wits" to accumulated knowledge and matured judgment. It is the essence of knowledge freed from temporal relativity.

Wisdom, then, is detached concern with life itself, in the face of death itself. It maintains and conveys the integrity of experience, in spite of the decline of bodily and mental functions. It responds to the need of the on-coming generation for an integrated heritage and yet remains aware of the relativity of all knowledge.

Potency, performance, and adaptability decline; but if vigor of mind combines with the gift of responsible renunciation, some old people can envisage human problems in their entirety (which is what "integrity" means) and can represent to the coming generation a living example of the "closure" of a style of life. Only such integrity can balance the despair of the knowledge that a limited life is coming to a conscious conclusion, only such wholeness can transcend the petty disgust of feeling finished and passed by, and the despair of facing the period of relative helplessness which marks the end as it marked the beginning.

There are the leaders, of course, and the thinkers, who round out long productive lives in positions in which wisdom is of the essence and is of service. There are those who feel verified in a numerous and vigorous progeny. But they, too, eventually join the over-aged who are reduced to a narrowing space-time, in which only a few things, in their self-contained form, offer a last but firm whisper of confirmation.

From *Insight and Responsibility*, 1964

MANU SMRITI (*The laws of Manu; sacred Hindu treatise, probably composed sometime around the beginning of the common era.*)

A twice-born Snâtaka, who has thus lived according to the law in the order of householders, may, taking a firm resolution and keeping his organs in subjection, dwell in the forest, duly observing the rules given below.

When a householder sees his skin wrinkled, and his hair white, and the sons of his sons, then he may resort to the forest.

Abandoning all food raised by cultivation, and all his belongings, he may depart into the forest, either committing his wife to his sons, or accompanied by her.

Taking with him the sacred fire and the implements required for domestic sacrifices, he may go forth from the village into the forest and reside there, duly controlling his senses.

Let him offer those five great sacrifices according to the rule, with various kinds of pure food fit for ascetics, or with herbs, roots, and fruit.

Let him wear a skin or a tattered garment; let him bathe in the evening or in the morning; and let him always wear his hair in braids, the hair on his body, his beard, and his nails being unclipped.

*   *   *

Let him eat vegetables that grow on dry land or in water, flowers, roots, and fruits, the productions of pure trees, and oils extracted from forest-fruits.

Let him avoid honey, flesh, and mushrooms growing on the ground or elsewhere, the vegetables called Bhûstri*n*a, and *S*igruka, and the *S*leshmân-taka fruit.

*   *   *

45

He may eat either what has been cooked with fire, or what has been ripened by time; he either may use a stone for grinding, or his teeth may be his mortar.

He may either at once after his daily meal cleanse his vessel for collecting food, or lay up a store sufficient for a month, or gather what suffices for six months or for a year.

Having collected food according to his ability, he may either eat at night only, or in the daytime only, or at every fourth mealtime, or at every eighth.

*   *   *

Or he may constantly subsist on flowers, roots, and fruit alone, which have been ripened by time and have fallen spontaneously, following the rule of the Institutes of Vikhanas.

*   *   *

But having thus passed the third part of a man's natural term of life in the forest, he may live as an ascetic during the fourth part of his existence, after abandoning all attachment to worldly objects.

He who after passing from order to order, after offering sacrifices and subduing his senses, becomes tired with giving alms and offerings of food, an ascetic, gains bliss after death.

When he has paid the three debts, let him apply his mind to the attainment of final liberation; he who seeks it without having paid his debts sinks downwards.

Having studied the Vedas in accordance with the rule, having begat sons according to the sacred law, and having offered sacrifices according to his ability, he may direct his mind to the attainment of final liberation.

*   *   *

Worlds, radiant in brilliancy, become the portion of him who recites the texts regarding Brahman and departs from his house as an ascetic, after giving a promise of safety to all created beings.

For that twice-born man, by whom not the smallest danger even is caused to created beings, there will be no danger from any quarter, after he is freed from his body.

Departing from his house fully provided with the means of purification Pavitra, let him wander about absolutely silent, and caring nothing for enjoyments that may be offered to him.

Let him always wander alone, without any companion, in order to attain final liberation, fully understanding that the solitary man, who neither forsakes nor is forsaken, gains his end.

He shall neither possess a fire, nor a dwelling, he may go to a village for his food, he shall be indifferent to everything, firm of purpose, meditating, and concentrating his mind on Brahman.

46

A potsherd instead of an alms-bowl, the roots of trees for a dwelling, coarse worn-out garments, life in solitude and indifference towards everything, are the marks of one who has attained liberation.

Let him not desire to die, let him not desire to live; let him wait for his appointed time, as a servant waits for the payment of his wages.

Let him put down his foot purified by his sight, let him drink water purified by straining with a cloth, let him utter speech purified by truth, let him keep his heart pure.

Let him patiently bear hard words, let him not insult anybody, and let him not become anybody's enemy for the sake of this perishable body.

*   *   *

Let him not be sorry when he obtains nothing, nor rejoice when he obtains something, let him accept so much only as will sustain life, let him not care about the quality of his utensils.

Let him disdain all food obtained in consequence of humble salutations, for even an ascetic who has attained final liberation, is bound with the fetters of the Samsâra by accepting food given in consequence of humble salutations.

By eating little, and by standing and sitting in solitude, let him restrain his senses, if they are attracted by sensual objects.

By the restraint of his senses, by the destruction of love and hatred, and by the abstention from injuring the creatures, he becomes fit for immortality.

Let him reflect on the transmigration of men, caused by their sinful deeds, on their falling into hell, and on the torments in the world of Yama.

*   *   *

By not injuring any creatures, by detaching the senses from objects of enjoyment, by the rites prescribed in the Veda, and by rigorously practicing austerities, men gain that state even in this world.

Let him quit this dwelling, composed of the five elements, where the bones are the beams, which is held together by tendons instead of cords, where the flesh and the blood are the mortar, which is thatched with the skin, which is foul-smelling, filled with urine and ordure, infested by old age and sorrow, the seat of disease, harassed by pain, gloomy with passion, and perishable.

*   *   *

Contentment, forgiveness, self-control, abstention from unrighteously appropriating anything, obedience to the rules of purification, coercion of the organs, wisdom, knowledge of the supreme Soul, truthfulness, and abstention from anger, form the tenfold law.

Those Brâhmaɳas who thoroughly study the tenfold law, and after studying obey it, enter the highest state.

A twice-born man who, with collected mind, follows the tenfold law and has paid his three debts, may, after learning the Vedânta according to the prescribed rule, become an ascetic.

Having given up the performance of all rites, throwing off the guilt of his sinful acts, subduing his organs and having studied the Veda, he may live at his ease under the protection of his son.

He who has thus given up the performance of all rites, who is solely intent on his own particular object, and free from desires, destroys his guilt by his renunciation and obtains the highest state.

Thus the fourfold holy law of Brâhma*n*as, which after death yields imperishable rewards, has been declared to you.

CICERO *(Roman, 106–43 B.C.E.)*

And, indeed, when I reflect on this subject I find four reasons why old age appears to be unhappy: first, that it withdraws us from active pursuits; second, that it makes the body weaker; third, that it deprives us of almost all physical pleasures; and, fourth, that it is not far removed from death. Let us, if you please, examine each of these reasons separately and see how much truth they contain.

"Old age withdraws us from active pursuits." From what pursuits? Is it not from those which are followed because of youth and vigour? Are there, then, no intellectual employments in which aged men may engage, even though their bodies are infirm.

*   *   *

Those . . . who allege that old age is devoid of useful activity adduce nothing to the purpose, and are like those who would say that the pilot does nothing in the sailing of the ship, because, while others are climbing the masts, or running about the gangways, or working at the pumps, he sits quietly in the stern and simply holds the tiller. He may not be doing what younger members of the crew are doing, but what he does is better and much more important. It is not by muscle, speed, or physical dexterity that great things are achieved, but by reflection, force of character, and judgement; in these qualities old age is usually not only not poorer, but is even richer.

*   *   *

True enough, for rashness is the product of the budding-time of youth, prudence of the harvest-time of age.

But, it is alleged, the memory is impaired. Of course, if you do not exercise it, or also if you are by nature somewhat dull. . . . I, for instance, know not only the people who are living, but I recall their fathers and grandfathers, too; and as I read their epitaphs I am not afraid of the super-stititon that, in so doing, I shall lose my memory; for by reading them I refresh my recollection of the dead. I certainly never heard of any old man forgetting where he had hidden his money! The aged remember everything that interests them, their appointments to appear in court, and who are their creditors and who their debtors.

And how is it with aged lawyers, pontiffs, augurs, and philosophers? What a multitude of things they remember! Old men retain their mental faculties, provided their interest and application continue; and this is true, not only of men in exalted public station, but likewise of those in the quiet of private life. Sophocles composed tragedies to extreme old age; and when, because of his absorption in literary work, he was thought to be neglecting his business affairs, his sons haled him into court in order to secure a verdict removing him from the control of his property on the ground of imbecility, under a law similar to ours, whereby it is customary to restrain heads of families from wasting their estates. Thereupon, it is said, the old man read to the jury his play, *Oedipus at Colonus,* which he had just written and was revising, and inquired: "Does that poem seem to you to be the work of an imbecile?" When he had finished he was acquitted by the verdict of the jury.

*   *   *

And . . . Caecilius, in writing of the old man making provision for a future generation, spoke to better purpose than he did in the following lines:

> In truth, Old Age, if you did bring no bane
> But this alone, 'twould me suffice: that one,
> By living long, sees much he hates to see.

Possibly, also, many things he likes; and as for things one does not wish to see, even youth often encounters them. However, this other sentiment from the same Caecilius is worse:

> But saddest bane of age, I think, is this:
> That old men feel their years a bore to youth.

A pleasure, rather than a bore, say I. For just as wise men, when they are old, take delight in the society of youths endowed with sprightly wit, and the burdens of age are rendered lighter to those who are courted and highly esteemed by the young, so young men find pleasure in their elders, by whose precepts they are led into virtue's paths; nor indeed do I feel that I am any less of a pleasure to you than you are to me. But you see how old age, so far from being feeble and inactive, is even busy and is always doing and effecting something—that is to say, something of the same nature in each case as were the pursuits of earlier years. And what of those who even go on adding to their store of knowledge? Such was the case with Solon, whom we see boasting in his verses that he grows old learning something every day. And I have done the same, for in my old age I have learned Greek, which I seized upon as eagerly as if I had been desirous of satisfying a long-continued thirst, with the result that I have acquired first-hand the information which you see me using in this discussion by way of illustration. And when I read what Socrates had done in the case of the lyre, an instrument much cultivated by the ancients, I should have liked to do that too, if I could; but in literature I have certainly laboured hard.

I do not now feel the need of the strength of youth—for that was the second head under the faults of old age—any more than when a young man I felt the need of the strength of the bull or of the elephant.

*   *   *

And yet, even that very loss of strength is more often chargeable to the dissipations of youth than to any fault of old age; for an intemperate and indulgent youth delivers to old age a body all worn out.

*   *   *

But I return to myself. I am in my eighty-fourth year and . . . can say this much: that while I am not now, indeed, possessed of that physical strength which I had as a private soldier in the Punic War, or as a quaestor in the same war, or as commander-in-chief in Spain, or when as military tribune four years later I fought the war out at Thermopylae under the command of Manius Acilius Glabrio; yet, as you see, old age has not quite unnerved or shattered me. The senate and the popular assembly never find my vigour wanting, nor do my friends, my dependents, or my guests; for I have never assented to that ancient and much-quoted proverb, which advises: "Become old early if you would be old long." For my part I would rather not be old so long than be old before my time. Accordingly, I have so far never refused an audience to anyone who wished to consult me. . . .

Only let every man make a proper use of his strength and strive to his utmost, then assuredly he will have no regret for his want of strength.

*   *   *

But, grant that old age is devoid of strength; none is even expected of it. Hence both by law and by custom men of my age are exempt from those public services which cannot be rendered without strength of body. Therefore, we are not only not required to do what we cannot perform, but we are not required to do even as much as we can. Yet, it may be urged, many old men are so feeble that they can perform no function that duty or indeed any position in life demands. True, but that is not peculiar to old age; generally it is a characteristic of ill-health. . . .

But it is our duty, my young friends, to resist old age; to compensate for its defects by a watchful care; to fight against it as we would fight against

50

disease; to adopt a regimen of health; to practise moderate exercise; and to take just enough of food and drink to restore our strength and not to over-burden it. Nor, indeed, are we to give our attention solely to the body; much greater care is due to the mind and soul; for they, too, like lamps, grow dim with time, unless we keep them supplied with oil. Moreover, exercise causes the body to become heavy with fatigue, but intellectual activity gives buoy-ancy to the mind.

* * *

We come now to the third ground for abusing old age, and that is, that it is devoid of sensual pleasures. O glorious boon of age, if it does indeed free us from youth's most vicious fault! Now listen, most noble young men, to what that remarkably great and distinguished man, Archytas of Tarentum, said in an ancient speech repeated to me when I was a young man serving with Quintus Maximus at Tarentum: "No more deadly curse," said he, "has been given by nature to man than carnal pleasure, through eagerness for which the passions are driven recklessly and uncontrollably to its gratifica-tion. From it come treason and the overthrow of states; and from it spring secret and corrupt conferences with public foes. In short, there is no criminal purpose and no evil deed which the lust for pleasure will not drive men to undertake. Indeed, rape, adultery, and every like offence are set in motion by the enticements of pleasure and by nothing else; and since nature—or some god, perhaps—has given to man nothing more excellent than his intellect, therefore this divine gift has no deadlier foe than pleasure; for where lust holds despotic sway self-control has no place, and in pleasure's realm there is not a single spot where virtue can put her foot."

* * *

Why then, do I dwell at such length on pleasure. Because the fact that old age feels little longing for sensual pleasures not only is no cause for reproach, but rather is ground for the highest praise. Old age lacks the heavy banquet, the loaded table, and the oft-filled cup; therefore it also lacks drunkenness, indigestion, and loss of sleep. But if some concession must be made to pleasure, since her allurements are difficult to resist, and she is, as Plato happily says, "the bait of sin,"—evidently because men are caught therewith like fish—then I admit that old age, though it lacks immoderate banquets, may find delight in temperate repasts.

* * *

. . . Nothing is more enjoyable than a leisured old age. Scipio, I used to see your father's intimate friend, Gaius Gallus, engaged in the task of mea-suring, almost bit by bit, the heavens and the earth. How often the morning sun has surprised him working on some chart which he had begun at night! and how often night has surprised him at a task begun at the break of day! How much joy he took in telling us, long in advance, of eclipses of the sun

51

and moon! And what of those men occupied in studies which, though not so exacting, yet demand keenness of intellect?

*   *   *

It remains to consider now the fourth reason—one that seems especially calculated to render my time of life anxious and full of care—the nearness of death; for death, in truth, cannot be far away. O wretched indeed is that old man who has not learned in the course of his long life that death should be held of no account! For clearly death is negligible, if it utterly annihilates the soul, or even desirable, if it conducts the soul to some place where it is to live for ever. Surely no other alternative can be found. What, then, shall I fear, if after death I am destined to be either not unhappy or happy? And yet is there anyone so foolish, even though he is young, as to feel absolutely sure that he will be alive when evening comes? Nay, even youth, much more than old age, is subject to the accident of death; the young fall sick more easily, their sufferings are more intense, and they are cured with greater difficulty. Therefore few arrive at old age, and, but for this, life would be lived in better and wiser fashion. For it is in old men that reason and good judgement are found, and had it not been for old men no state would have existed at all.

*   *   *

Now the fruit of old age, as I have often said, is the memory of abundant blessings previously acquired. Moreover, whatever befalls in accordance with Nature should be accounted good; and indeed, what is more consonant with Nature than for the old to die? But the same fate befalls the young, though Nature in their case struggles and rebels. Therefore, when the young die I am reminded of a strong flame extinguished by a torrent; but when old men die it is as if a fire had gone out without the use of force and of its own accord, after the fuel had been consumed; and, just as apples when they are green are with difficulty plucked from the tree, but when ripe and mellow fall of themselves, so, with the young, death comes as a result of force, while with the old it is the result of ripeness. To me, indeed, the thought of this "ripeness" for death is so pleasant, that the nearer I approach death the more I feel like one who is in sight of land at last and is about to anchor in his home port after a long voyage.

But old age has no certain term, and there is good cause for an old man living so long as he can fulfil and support his proper duties and hold death of no account. By this means old age actually becomes more spirited and more courageous than youth. . . .

Hence, it follows that old men ought neither to cling too fondly to their little remnant of life, nor give it up without a cause. Pythagoras bids us stand like faithful sentries and not quit our post until God, our Captain, gives the word. . . .

Now, there may be some sensation in the process of dying, but it is a fleeting one, especially to the old; after death the sensation is either pleasant or there is none at all. But this should be thought on from our youth up, so that we may be indifferent to death, and without this thought no one can be in a tranquil state of mind. For it is certain that we must die, and, for aught we know, this very day. Therefore, since death threatens every hour, how can he who fears it have any steadfastness of soul?

*   *   *

I do not mean to complain of life as many men, and they learned ones, have often done; nor do I regret that I have lived, since I have so lived that I think I was not born in vain, and I quit life as if it were an inn, not a home. For Nature has given us an hostelry in which to sojourn, not to abide.

O glorious day, when I shall set out to join the assembled hosts of souls divine and leave this world of strife and sin! . . .

For these reasons, Scipio, my old age sits light upon me (for you said that this has been a cause of wonder to you and Laelius), and not only is not burdensome, but is even happy. And if I err in my belief that the souls of men are immortal, I gladly err, nor do I wish this error which gives me pleasure to be wrested from me while I live. . . . Again, if we are not going to be immortal, nevertheless, it is desirable for a man to be blotted out at his proper time. For as Nature has marked the bounds of everything else, so she has marked the bounds of life. Moreover, old age is the final scene, as it were, in life's drama, from which we ought to escape when it grows wearisome and, certainly, when we have had our fill.

Such, my friends, are my views on old age. May you both attain it, and thus be able to prove by experience the truth of what you have heard from me.

From *Cato Maior de senectute*, 44 B.C.E.

ABIGAIL HOUSE (*American, 1790–1861*)

My Dear Friend in Old Age:

As the winter is passed and gone, and spring comes with all its beauty, how it reminds me of my fallen nature. Once a child, and helpless from that to youth; gay and cheerful, and perhaps vain. From that to riper years, and more active in life; soon old age comes on, and infirmities and cares increase, and we give way for others. Our knowledge and judgment pass away; intellect and memory fail, and our substance, wealth if we have any, is conveyed into other hands, and nought but the old stump is left. What can there be desirable in old age, or any other age, if it were not for the expectation of a brighter day? There are, it is true, in all stages of human life, some pleasing enjoyments, which attach us to earth—and no time nor state, ex-

53

empts us from trials, and death. But having well grounded hope, we can say: Blessed be old age, as we are nearer ripe for the grave, and glory heaves in view; although our eyes are dim, that we cannot look out of the windows, and the grinders are few, and fears shall be in the way, and the grasshopper shall be a burden and all these things which are incident to the aged. Yet there is something in it which animates and buoys up the spirits of such, because nature has its proper course. The Sun, Moon, and Stars, all move in their order, and the seasons, Spring, Summer, Autumn, and Winter, all have their beauties and luxuries. He that made heaven and earth said there should be seed time and harvest. Summer and winter, cold and heat, and that he would rain upon the just and unjust. I say because all these things are promised us in things of nature. Shall we not also believe the gracious promises? Be thou faithful unto death, and I will give thee a crown of life.

From a letter, in *Memoirs of Abigail House,* 1861

RUTH HARRIET JACOBS (*American, b. 1927*)

Don't call me a young woman.
I was a young woman for years
but that was then and this is now.
I was a mid life woman for a time
and I celebrated that good span.
Now I am somebody magnificent, new,
a seer, wise woman, old proud crone,
an example and mentor to the young
who need to learn old women wisdom.
I look back on jobs well done
and learn to do different tasks now.
I think great thoughts and share them.

Don't call me a young woman.
You reveal your own fears of aging.
Maybe you'd better come learn from
all of us wonderful old women
how to take the sum of your life
with all its experience and knowledge
and show how a fully developed life
can know the joy of a past well done
and the joy of life left to live.

Don't call me a young woman;
it's not a compliment or courtesy

but rather a grating discourtesy.
Being old is a hard won achievement
not something to be brushed aside
treated as infirmity or ugliness
or apologized away by "young woman."
I am an old woman, a long liver.
I'm proud of it. I revel in it.
I wear my grey hair and wrinkles
as badges of triumphant survival
and I intend to grow even older.

"Don't Call Me a Young Woman," 1991

G. STANLEY HALL (American, 1844–1924)

To learn that we are really old is a long, complex, and painful experience. Each decade the circle of the Great Fatigue narrows around us, restricting the intensity and endurance of our activities. In the thirties the athletic power passes its prime, for muscular energy begins to abate. There is also some loss of deftness, subtlety, and power of making fine, complex movements of the accessory motor system, and a loss of facility for acquiring new skills. In the forties grayness and, in men, baldness may begin and eyesight is a little less acute so that we hold our book or paper farther off. We are less fond of "roughing" it or of severe forms of exercise. We may become so discontented with our achievements or our environment that we change our whole plan of life. In the fifties we feel that half a century is a long time to have lived and compare our vitality with that of our forbears and contemporaries of the same age. Memory for names may occasionally slip a cog. We go to the physician for a "once over" to be sure that all our organs are functioning properly. We realize that if we are ever to accomplish anything more in the world we must be up and at it and give up many old hopes and ambitions as vain. Perhaps we indulge ourselves in certain pleasures hitherto denied before it is forever too late. At sixty we realize that there is but one more threshold to cross before we find ourselves in the great hall of discard where most lay their burdens down and that what remains yet to do must be done quickly. Hence this is a decade peculiarly prone to overwork. We refuse to compromise with failing powers but drive ourselves all the more because we are on the home stretch. We anticipate leaving but must leave things right and feel we can rest up afterwards. So we are prone to overdraw our account of energy and brave the danger of collapse if our overdraft is not honored. Thus some cross the conventional deadline of seventy in a state of exhaustion that nature can never entirely make good. Added to all this is the struggle, never so intense for men as in the sixties, to seem younger, to be and remain necessary, and perhaps to circumvent the looming possibilities of displacement by younger men. Thus it is that men often shorten their lives and, what is far more important, impair the quality of their old age, so that we yet see and know but little of what it could, should, or would be if we could order life according to its true nature and intent. Only greater easement between fifty and seventy can bring ripe, healthful, vigorous senectitude, the services of which to the race constitute, as I have elsewhere tried to show, probably the very greatest need of our civilization to-day.

From *Senescence: The Last Half of Life*, chapter 8, 1922

HERMANN HESSE *(German, 1897–1962)*

Old age is a stage in our lives, and like all other stages it has a face of its own, its own atmosphere and temperature, its own joys and miseries. We old white-haired folk, like all our younger human brothers, have a part to play that gives meaning to our lives, and even someone mortally ill and dying, who can hardly be reached in his own bed by a cry from this world, has his task, has something important and necessary to accomplish. Being old is just as beautiful and holy a task as being young, learning to die and dying are just as valuable functions as any other—assuming that they are carried out with reverence toward the meaning and holiness of all life. A man who hates being old and gray, who fears the nearness of death, is no more worthy a representative of his stage of life than a strong young person who hates and tries to escape his profession and his daily tasks.

To put it briefly, to fulfill the meaning of age and to perform its duty one must be reconciled with old age and everything it brings with it. One must say yes to it. Without this yea, without submission to what nature demands of us, the worth and meaning of our days—whether we are old or young—are lost and we betray life.

From "On Old Age," in *My Belief: Essays on Life and Art*, 1952

RALPH WALDO EMERSON *(American, 1805–1882)*

It is time to be old,
To take in sail:—
The god of bounds,
Who sets to seas a shore,
Came to me in his fatal rounds,
And said: "No more!

No farther shoot
Thy broad ambitious branches, and thy root.
Fancy departs: no more invent;
Contract thy firmament
To compass of a tent.
There's not enough for this and that,
Make thy option which of two;
Economize the failing river,
Not the less revere the Giver,
Leave the many and hold the few.
Timely wise accept the terms,
Soften the fall with wary foot;
A little while
Still plan and smile,
And,—fault of novel germs,—
Mature the unfallen fruit.
Curse, if thou wilt, thy sires,

Bad husbands of their fires,
Who, when they gave thee breath,
Failed to bequeath
The needful sinew stark as once,
The Baresark marrow to thy bones,
But left a legacy of ebbing veins,
Inconstant heat and nerveless reins,—
Amid the Muses, left thee deaf and dumb,
Amid the gladiators, halt and numb."

    As the bird trims her to the gale,
I trim myself to the storm of time,
I man the rudder, reef the sail,
Obey the voice at eve obeyed at prime:
"Lowly faithful, banish fear,
Right onward drive unharmed;
The port, well worth the cruise, is near,
And every wave is charmed."

                                  "Terminus," 1867

KATHLEEN RAINE (*English, b. 1908*)

Now I am old and free from time
How spacious life,
Unbeginning unending sky where the wind blows

The ever-moving clouds and clouds of starlings on the wing,
Chaffinch and apple-leaf across my garden lawn,
Winter paradise
With its own birds and daisies
And all the near and far that eye can see,
Each blade of grass signed with the mystery
Across whose face unchanging everchanging pass
Summer and winter, day and night.
Great countenance of the unknown known
You have looked upon me all my days,
More loved than lover's face,
More merciful than the heart, more wise
Than spoken word, unspoken theme
Simple as earth in whom we live and move.

"Winter Paradise," 1977

WALT WHITMAN (*American, 1819–1892*)

Thanks in old age—thanks ere I go,
For health, the midday sun, the impalpable air—for life, mere life,
For precious ever-lingering memories, (of you my mother dear—you,
   father—you, brothers, sisters, friends,)
For all my days—not those of peace alone—the days of war the same,
For gentle words, caresses, gifts from foreign lands,
For shelter, wine and meat—for sweet appreciation,
(You distant, dim unknown—or young or old—countless, unspecified,
   readers belov'd,
We never met, and ne'er shall meet—and yet our souls embrace, long, close
   and long;)
For beings, groups, love, deeds, words, books—for colors, forms,
For all the brave strong men—devoted, hardy men—who've forward sprung
   in freedom's help, all years, all lands,
For braver, stronger, more devoted men—(a special laurel ere I go, to life's
   war's chosen ones,
The cannoneers of song and thought—the great artillerists—the foremost
   leaders, captains of the soul:)
As soldier from an ended war return'd—As traveler out of myriads, to the
   long procession retrospective,
Thanks—joyful thanks!—a soldier's, traveler's thanks.

"Thanks in Old Age," c. 1890

CHAPTER TWO
CHANGE/METAMORPHOSIS

Change/Metamorphosis aims to capture a twofold sense of alteration: barely noticeable movement along a continuum and transformation from one form or condition to another. "In human life as in the rest of nature," wrote the humanistic psychologist William Bridges in *Transitions* (1980), "change accumulates slowly and almost invisibly until it is made manifest in the sudden form of fledging out or thawing or leaf-fall." This chapter is about physical change and human development. As Shakespeare put it in "As You Like It": "From hour to hour we ripe and ripe, from hour to hour we rot and rot, and thereby hangs a tale."

The first several selections remind us that—for better or for worse—time brings changes that overwhelm all human efforts at control. The famous passage from Ecclesiastes—"To every thing there is a season, and a time to every purpose under the heaven"—contains the consolation of God's ultimate power and goodness. Sogyal Rinpoche's Buddhist message of impermanence, on the other hand, leads to an appreciation of "nowness," the possibilities for what T. S. Eliot called a "lifetime burning in every moment." Henry James's question, "How does the look of age come?," invites the reader to the next section on the human experience of physical change.

Eda LeShan tells a story of lobsters and their shells, a metaphor for the human need to move and to dare at mid-life. Menopause is the subject of selections by Christine Downing, Ursula K. Le Guin, and Kathy Kozachenko. But these women writers address more than a physical "change of life." They approach this physical rite of passage as an opportunity for self-knowledge or as a liberation. Feminist writer Ursula K. Le Guin speaks of the potential hidden in the metamorphosis from woman to crone, urging each woman to "become pregnant with herself at last."

Next follow readings based on the metaphor of ripening fruit. D. H. Lawrence's poem "When the Ripe Fruit Falls" offers powerful images of death as fulfillment, in particular the death of fulfilled people. Yet people are not fruit. According to Carl Jung's classic essay "The Soul and Death," human ripening, fulfillment, or soul-ful-ness in the second half of life requires conscious acceptance of mortality and acquiescence in the loss of physical youth.

The next series—from the ancient Taoist classic *Chuang Tzu* to the seventh-century Japanese poem "We are helpless before time"—consists of responses to illness, war, debility, and pain. Writers variously accept their fortune, pray for God's assistance, lament over the body's decay, and struggle against disease.

Is there a real self that endures amidst all the emotional and physical changes of a lifetime and its historical era? The remaining readings explore this question and highlight the struggle for self-re-formation in the face of physical weakness and suffering. Heinz Kohut, the founder of psychoanalytic self-psychology, briefly muses over a shift in his own aging self. In Richard Stern's short story, "Dr. Cahn's Visit," a senile father is brought to the hospital to visit his dying wife. In that brief, sad meeting, the old physician momentarily regains an earlier self, sparked by loving contact with his wife.

Reality comes when one is loved for a long time. That is the message of *The Velveteen Rabbit,* a children's story. By the time you become real, the toy rabbit learns from the old Skin Horse, you have also become shabby and threadbare. But "once you are Real you can't be ugly, except to people who don't understand."

The ancient Greeks used the butterfly as an image for the soul. Meridel Le Sueur uses the sunflower to convey the Native American culture's approach to change and death. She reminds us that things in nature do not age—they ripen. In her poem "Rites of Ancient Ripening," she equates age with light: "I am luminous with light." The sunflower metaphor ties human change to the great, inexorable cycles of the natural world—seed time; ripening; harvest.

From Le Sueur we move to Jalal ad-Din Rumi, the great thirteenth-century Islamic poet, who envisioned life's metamorphoses culminating in a return to the origin of existence. He echoes the Koranic terms: "Truly we belong to God and unto Him we return." The chapter ends with the words of Swiss minister and psychiatrist Paul Tournier. Echoing Noah benShea's story, "Jacob the Baker," Tournier urges middle-aged readers to open themselves up to the broader horizons of life.

ECCLESIASTES 3:1–11, HEBREW SCRIPTURES

To every thing there is a season, and a time to every purpose under the heaven:

> A time to be born, and a time to die;
> A time to plant, and a time to pluck up that which is planted;

A time to kill, and a time to heal;
A time to break down, and a time to build up;

A time to weep, and a time to laugh;
A time to mourn, and a time to dance;

A time to cast away stones, and a time to gather stones together;
A time to embrace, and a time to refrain from embracing;

A time to seek, and a time to lose;
A time to keep, and a time to cast away;

A time to rend, and a time to sew;
A time to keep silence, and a time to speak;

A time to love, and a time to hate;
A time for war, and a time for peace.

What profit hath he that worketh in that he laboureth? I have seen the task which God hath given to the sons of men to be exercised therewith. He hath made every thing beautiful in its time; also He hath set the world in their heart, yet so that man cannot find out the work that God hath done from the beginning even to the end.

SOGYAL RINPOCHE (Tibetan, b. 1950)

I ask myself often: "Why is it that everything changes?" And only one answer comes back to me: *That is how life is.* Nothing, nothing at all, has any lasting character. The Buddha said:

> *This existence of ours is as transient as autumn clouds.*
> *To watch the birth and death of beings is like looking at the*
> *movements of a dance.*
> *A lifetime is like a flash of lightning in the sky,*
> *Rushing by, like a torrent down a steep mountain.*

One of the chief reasons we have so much anguish and difficulty facing death is that we ignore the truth of impermanence. We so desperately want everything to continue as it is that we have to believe that things will always stay the same. But this is only make-believe. And as we so often discover, belief has little or nothing to do with reality. This make-believe, with its misinformation, ideas, and assumptions, is the rickety foundation on which we construct our lives. No matter how much the truth keeps interrupting, we prefer to go on trying, with hopeless bravado, to keep up our pretense.

In our minds changes always equal loss and suffering. And if they come, we try to anesthetize ourselves as far as possible. We assume, stubbornly and unquestioningly, that permanence provides security and impermanence does not. But, in fact, impermanence is like some of the people we meet in life—difficult and disturbing at first, but on deeper acquaintance far friendlier and less unnerving than we could have imagined.

Reflect on this: The realization of impermanence is paradoxically the only thing we can hold onto, perhaps our only lasting possession. It is like the sky, or the earth. No matter how much everything around us may change or collapse, they endure. Say we go through a shattering emotional crisis . . . our whole life seems to be disintegrating . . . our husband or wife suddenly leaves us without warning. The earth is still there; the sky is still there. Of course, even the earth trembles now and again, just to remind us we cannot take anything for granted . . .

Even Buddha died. His death was a teaching, to shock the naive, the indolent, and complacent, to wake us up to the truth that everything is impermanent and death an inescapable fact of life. As he was approaching death, the Buddha said:

> *Of all footprints*
> *That of the elephant is supreme;*
> *Of all mindfulness meditations*
> *That on death is supreme.*

Whenever we lose our perspective, or fall prey to laziness, reflecting on death and impermanence shakes us back into the truth:

> *What is born will die,*
> *What has been gathered will be dispersed,*
> *What has been accumulated will be exhausted,*
> *What has been built up will collapse,*
> *And what has been high will be brought low.*

The whole universe, scientists now tell us, is nothing but change, activity, and process—a totality of flux that is the ground of all things:

Every subatomic interaction consists of the annihilation of the original particles and the creation of new subatomic particles. The subatomic world is a continual dance of creation and annihilation, of mass changing into energy and energy changing to mass. Transient forms sparkle in and out of existence, creating a never-ending, forever newly created reality.

What is our life but this dance of transient forms? Isn't everything always changing: the leaves on the trees in the park, the light in your room as you read this, the seasons, the weather, the time of day, the people passing you in the street? And what about us? Doesn't everything we have done in the past seem like a dream now? The friends we grew up with, the childhood haunts, those views and opinions we once held with such single-minded passion:

We have left them all behind. Now, at this moment, reading this book seems vividly real to you. Even this page will soon be only a memory.

The cells of our body are dying, the neurons in our brain are decaying, even the expression on our face is always changing, depending on our mood. What we call our basic character is only a "mindstream," nothing more. Today we feel good because things are going well; tomorrow we feel the opposite. Where did that good feeling go? New influences took us over as circumstances changed: We are impermanent, the influences are impermanent, and there is nothing solid or lasting anywhere that we can point to.

What could be more unpredictable than our thoughts and emotions: do you have any idea what you are going to think or feel next? Our mind, in fact, is as empty, as impermanent, and as transient as a dream. Look at a thought: It comes, it stays, and it goes. The past is past, the future not yet risen, and even the present thought, as we experience it, becomes the past.

The only thing we really have is nowness, is now.

From *The Tibetan Book of Living and Dying*, 1992

SURA 2:266, THE KORAN

> Would any of you wish to have a garden
> of palms and vines, with rivers flowing
> beneath it, and all manner of fruit there
> for him, then old age smites him, and he has
> seed, but weaklings, then a whirlwind with
> fire smites it, and it is consumed?
> So God makes clear the signs to you; haply
> you will reflect.

BLACK ELK (*Native American/Oglala-Sioux, 1863–1950*)

After the heyoka ceremony, I came to live here where I am now between Wounded Knee Creek and Grass Creek. Others came too, and we made these little gray houses of logs that you see, and they are square. It is a bad way to live, for there can be no power in a square.

You have noticed that everything an Indian does is in a circle, and that is because the Power of the World always works in circles, and everything tries to be round. In the old days when we were a strong and happy people, all our power came to us from the sacred hoop of the nation, and so long as the hoop was unbroken, the people flourished. The flowering tree was the living center of the hoop, and the circle of the four quarters nourished it. The east gave peace and light, the south gave warmth, the west gave rain, and the north with its cold and mighty wind gave strength and endurance. This knowledge came to us from the outer world with our religion. Everything the Power of the World does is done in a circle. The sky is round, and I have heard that the earth is round like a ball, and so are all the stars. The wind, in its greatest power, whirls. Birds make their nests in circles, for theirs is the same religion as ours. The sun comes forth and goes down again in a circle. The moon does the same, and both are round. Even the seasons form a great circle in their changing, and always come back again to where they were. The life of a man is a circle from childhood to childhood, and so it is in everything where power moves. Our tepees were round like the nests of birds, and these were always set in a circle, the nation's hoop, a nest of many nests, where the Great Spirit meant for us to hatch our children.

But the Wasichus have put us in these square boxes. Our power is gone and we are dying, for the power is not in us any more. You can look at our boys and see how it is with us. When we were living by the power of the circle in the way we should, boys were men at twelve or thirteen years of age. But now it takes them very much longer to mature.

Well, it is as it is. We are prisoners of war while we are waiting here. But there is another world.

AUTHOR'S POSTSCRIPT

After the conclusion of the narrative, Black Elk and our party were sitting at the north edge of Cuny Table, looking off across the Badlands ("the beauty and the strangeness of the earth," as the old man expressed it). Pointing at Harney Peak that loomed black above the far skyrim, Black Elk said: "There, when I was young, the spirits took me in my vision to the center of the earth and showed me all the good things in the sacred hoop of the world. I wish I could stand up there in the flesh before I die, for there is something I want to say to the Six Grandfathers."

So the trip to Harney Peak was arranged, and a few days later we were there. On the way up to the summit, Black Elk remarked to his son, Ben: "Something should happen to-day. If I have any power left, the thunder beings of the west should hear me when I send a voice, and there should be at least a little thunder and a little rain." What happened is, of course, related to Wasichu readers as being merely a more or less striking coincidence. It was a bright and cloudless day, and after we had reached the summit the sky was perfectly clear. It was a season of drouth, one of the worst in the memory of the old men. The sky remained clear until about the conclusion of the ceremony.

"Right over there," said Black Elk, indicating a point of rock, "is where I stood in my vision, but the hoop of the world about me was different, for what I saw was in the spirit."

Having dressed and painted himself as he was in his great vision, he faced the west, holding the sacred pipe before him in his right hand. Then he sent forth a voice; and a thin, pathetic voice it seemed in that vast space around us:

"Hey-a-a-hey! Hey-a-a-hey! Hey-a-a-hey! Hey-a-a-hey! Grandfather, Great Spirit, once more behold me on earth and lean to hear my feeble voice. You lived first, and you are older than all need, older than all prayer. All things belong to you—the two-leggeds, the four-leggeds, the wings of the air and all green things that live. You have set the powers of the four quarters to cross each other. The good road and the road of difficulties you have made to cross; and where they cross, the place is holy. Day in and day out, forever, you are the life of things.

"Therefore I am sending a voice, Great Spirit, my Grandfather, forgetting nothing you have made, the stars of the universe and the grasses of the earth.

"You have said to me, when I was still young and could hope, that in difficulty I should send a voice four times, once for each quarter of the earth, and you would hear me.

"To-day I send a voice for a people in despair.

"You have given me a sacred pipe, and through this I should make my offering. You see it now.

"From the west, you have given me the cup of living water and the sacred bow, the power to make live and to destroy. You have given me a sacred wind and the herb from where the white giant lives—the cleansing power and the healing. The daybreak star and the pipe, you have given from the east; and from the south, the nation's sacred hoop and the tree that was to bloom. To the center of the world you have taken me and showed the goodness and the beauty and the strangeness of the greening earth, the only mother—and there the spirit shapes of things, as they should be, you have shown to me and I have seen. At the center of this sacred hoop you have said that I should make the tree to bloom.

"With tears running, O Great Spirit, Great Spirit, my Grandfather—with running tears I must say now that the tree has never bloomed. A pitiful old man, you see me here, and I have fallen away and have done nothing. Here at the center of the world, where you took me when I was young and taught me; here, old, I stand, and the tree is withered, Grandfather, my Grandfather!

"Again, and maybe the last time on this earth, I recall the great vision you sent me. It may be that some little root of the sacred tree still lives. Nourish it then, that it may leaf and bloom and fill with singing birds. Hear me, not for myself, but for my people; I am old. Hear me that they may once more go back into the sacred hoop and find the good red road, the shielding tree!"

We who listened now noted that thin clouds had gathered about us. A scant chill rain began to fall and there was low, muttering thunder without lightning. With tears running down his cheeks, the old man raised his voice to a thin high wail, and chanted: "In sorrow I am sending a feeble voice, O Six Powers of the World. Hear me in my sorrow, for I may never call again. O make my people live!"

For some minutes the old man stood silent, with face uplifted, weeping in the drizzling rain.

In a little while the sky was clear again.

As told to John G. Neihardt in Black Elk Speaks: Being the Life Story of a Holy Man of the Oglala-Sioux, 1932

NOAH BEN SHEA (*American, b. 1945*)

The children arrived after school. They folded their bodies onto the flour sacks.

A warmth reflected between the faces of the children and the child in Jacob.

The proximity to this warmth caused Jacob to reflect, "Vision is often the distance I need to see what is directly in front of me."

A boy found his courage and asked Jacob, "Why do you say, 'A child sees what I only understand'?"

Jacob paused a moment before answering, letting the silence draw the boy's face upward.

When Jacob spoke, his voice had a long-ago quality.

"Imagine a boy, sitting on a hill, looking out through his innocence on the beauty of the world.

"Slowly, the child begins to learn. He does this by collecting small stones of knowledge, placing one on top of the other.

"Over time, his learning becomes a wall, a wall he has built in front of himself.

"Now, when he looks out, he can see his learning, but he has lost his view.

"This makes the man, who was once the boy, both proud and sad.

"The man, looking at his predicament, decides to take down the wall. But, to take down a wall also takes time, and, when he accomplishes this task, he has become an old man.

"The old man rests on the hill and looks out through his experience on the beauty of the world.

"He understands what has happened to him. He understands what he sees. But, he does not see, and will never see the world again, the way he saw it as a child on that first, clear morning."

"Yes . . . but," interjected a little girl unable to contain herself, "the old man can remember what he once saw!"

Jacob's head swiveled toward the child.

"You are right. Experience matures to memory. But memory is the gentlest of truths."

"Are you afraid of growing old, Jacob?" asked a child, giggling while she spoke.

"What grows never grows old," said Jacob.

"Reality Rides the Current," in *Jacob the Baker*, 1989

SENECA (*Roman, 4 B.C.E.–65 C.E.*)

[*Seneca, born in Cordoba, Spain, took his own life at Nero's orders. Here he provides insight into slave labor, an aspect of old age ignored in most literary references.*]

Wherever I turn, I find indications that I am getting old. I was visiting a suburban estate of mine and complaining about the expense of the dilapidated building. My caretaker told me that this was not the fault of neglect on his part—he was doing everything, but the fact was that the building was old. In fact this house was built under my own supervision—what will happen to me, if stones of the same age as myself are in such a crumbling state? I was upset at what he said and took the next suitable opportunity for an outburst of anger. "These plane-trees are obviously not being looked after," I said. "There are no leaves on them; the branches are all knotted and parched, and the bark is flaking off those squalid trunks. That would not happen if someone was digging round them and giving them water." He swore by my own soul that he was doing whatever possible, that there was no respect in which his efforts were falling short—but they were old. Between ourselves, I planted them myself; I saw their first growth of leaves. I went up to the entrance. "Who," I said, "is that decrepit fellow? How suitable that he should have been moved to the door—he is clearly waiting to move on. Where on earth did you get hold of him? What possessed you to steal a corpse from someone else?" But the fellow said to me, "Don't you recognize me? I am Felicio—you used to give me puppets at the Saturnalia. I am the son of your manager Philositus; I was your playmate when I was little." "The man is absolutely mad," I said. "Now he has turned into a little boy and playmate of mine. It could be true, though—he is as toothless as a child."

From *Epistolae morales*, 63–65 C.E.

HENRY JAMES (*American, 1843–1916*)

How does the look of age come? . . .

Does it come of itself, unobserved, unrecorded, unmeasured? Or do you woo it and set baits and traps for it, and watch it like the dawning brownness of a meerschaum pipe, and nail it down when it appears, just where it peeps out, and light a votive taper beneath it and give thanks to it daily? Or do you forbid it and fight it and resist it, and yet feel it settling and deepening about you, as irresistible as fate?

From *A Passionate Pilgrim*, 1871

EDA LeSHAN (*American, b. 1922*)

While working on a book I was writing on middle age I was asked by an oceanographer if I knew anything about lobsters. "Lobsters? I'm sorry, but it really has never been very high on my list of priorities to wonder about that." And he said, "Well, I'm going to explain it to you. Did you know that lobsters know when they have to deshell? They get real crowded inside this three-pound shell—they're terribly uncomfortable—and it's not possible for them to go on living if they stay in that shell. So what they do is go out to the sea unprotected, which is very dangerous—they might get hit by a reef, they might be eaten by another lobster or a fish—but they must deshell. That whole, hard shell comes off and the pink membrane that's inside grows and becomes a harder shell, but a bigger one."

At first it didn't hit me, but soon I became preoccupied with lobsters. I kept coming back to the idea and I thought, That's the most interesting thing. I dreamed about it. Finally, I mentioned it to my therapist and she said, "Eda, that's what you're writing this book on middle age about. Going to the reef, even if it's dangerous." And that really has been my philosophy of life, at any age, and it certainly is now. You know, if you stay stifled where you are, you're dead before you're dead.

From an interview, in *The Ageless Spirit*, 1992

CHRISTINE DOWNING (*American, b. 1931*)

On my fiftieth birthday I realized: if I live to be as old as my mother already is, I am now just beginning the second half of my adult life. I knew myself to be at the point of transition from early to late adulthood. I knew that because I am a woman this turning would be definitively marked by the physiological phenomenon of menopause. I suspected that the social, psychological, and spiritual dimensions of my experiencing this life-change were all likely to be so affected by the biological event as to make what had been written about mid-life crisis by men (for whom aging is a continuous process) seem mostly beside the point. Yet I knew almost nothing of the distinctively female ways of navigating this passage and felt myself to be confronting a transition for which my culture had somehow conspired to keep me unprepared. I felt alone, uninformed, somewhat afraid—and yet also curious and expectant. I was at the brink of a centrally important life-change and had no knowledge of the myths or rituals that had helped women throughout history live this transition with hope, dignity, and depth.

I knew that from the day of birth to that of death individuals in traditional cultures submit to ceremonies which make possible the passage from one social category or life phase to another. Sometimes individuals have to undergo the transition alone; sometimes they are led through it in the company of other members of a particular group within the society. As Arnold Van Gennep noted in his classical study, *Les rites des passage*, published some seventy-five years ago, participation in such ritualized passages was regarded as an ineluctable feature of human life:

> For groups, as well as for individuals, life itself means to separate and to be reunited, to change form and condition, to die and be reborn. It is to act and to cease, to wait and rest, and then to begin acting again, but in a different way. And there are always new thresholds to cross: the thresholds of summer and winter, of a season or a year, of a month or a night; the thresholds of

birth, adolescence, maturity, and old age; the threshold of death and that of the afterlife—for those who believe in it . . .

The series of human transitions has, among some peoples, been linked to the celestial passages, the revolutions of the planets, and the phases of the moon. It is indeed a cosmic conception that relates the stages of human existence to those of plant and animal life and, by a sort of pre-scientific divination, joins them to the great rhythms of the universe.

Rites of passage serve to reveal the social significance of what might otherwise appear as individual crises (puberty, childbirth, illness, journeys, death); their purpose is to integrate the personal and the transpersonal. Through participation in such rites one discovers that one's suffering and confusion are not unique and isolating. The pain one endures in giving up and leaving behind a familiar and cherished life form is simply the pain of being human, what Freud calls "common unhappiness." Because the ritual was communal, participation in it provides validation that, having passed through the initiatory experience, one is truly a new person. One is not only different to oneself, one is met by others as being different. Participation in a sequence of such rites which have always the same form—separation, initiation, reincorporation—leads one toward an appreciation of the rhythms of life and gives meaning to the transition time as going somewhere, as not a cul-de-sac or dead end. The rites are often supplemented by myths which recount how a prototypical goddess or god, heroine or hero, was the first to undergo the same trial and to discover its hidden significance. The rituals and myths serve to alleviate the potentially harmful effects of significant life transitions on the affected individuals and their communities.

Although in modern societies there are few such explicit transitional rituals, the initiatory pattern may still continue to function, albeit unconsciously, in our imaginative and dream life and in certain real challenges we undergo. Mircea Eliade believes the pattern to be visible "in the spiritual crises, the solitude and despair through which every human being must pass in order to attain to a responsible, genuine and creative life":

Even if the initiatory character of these ordeals is not apprehended, as such, nevertheless it remains true that humans become themselves only after having solved a series of desperately difficult and even dangerous situations; that is, after having undergone "tortures" and "death," followed by an awakening to another life, qualitatively different because regenerated. If we look closely, we see that every human life is made up of a series of ordeals, of "deaths," and of "resurrections." . . . Initiation lies at the core of any genuine human life.

It makes me sad to know that if someone speaks of the myths of menstruation or menopause, they mean the untruths, the fallacies, the misogynist distortions. I cannot believe that I am alone in my hunger for a more symbolic connection to these mysteries of feminine life. Our relation to these profoundly life-transforming transitions (and thus to ourselves and to our sisters) seems so obviously diminished when we live them as though they don't really matter very much, when we experience them as degrading, as isolating and isolated events, as taboo.

From "Female Rites of Passage," in *Journey through Menopause*, 1987

URSULA K. LE GUIN (*American, b. 1929*)

The menopause is probably the least glamorous topic imaginable; and this is interesting, because it is one of the very few topics to which cling some shreds and remnants of taboo. A serious mention of menopause is usually met with uneasy silence; a sneering reference to it is usually met with relieved sniggers. Both the silence and the sniggering are pretty sure indications of taboo.

Most people would consider the old phrase "change of life" a euphemism for the medical term "menopause," but I, who am now going through the change, begin to wonder if it isn't the other way round. "Change of life" is too blunt a phrase, too factual. "Menopause," with its chime-suggestion of a mere pause after which things go on as before, is reassuringly trivial.

But the change is not trivial, and I wonder how many women are brave enough to carry it out wholeheartedly. They give up their reproductive capacity with more or less of a struggle, and when it's gone they think that's all there is to it. Well, at least I don't get the Curse any more, they say, and the only reason I felt so depressed sometimes was hormones. Now I'm myself again. But this is to evade the real challenge, and to lose, not only the capacity to ovulate, but the opportunity to become a Crone.

In the old days women who survived long enough to attain the menopause more often accepted the challenge. They had, after all, had practice. They had already changed their life radically once before, when they ceased to be virgins and became mature women/wives/matrons/mothers/mistresses/whores/etc. This change involved not only the physiological alterations of puberty—the shift from barren childhood to fruitful maturity—but a socially recognized alteration of being: a change of condition from the sacred to the profane.

With the secularization of virginity now complete, so that the once awesome term "virgin" is now a sneer or at best a slightly dated word for a person who hasn't copulated yet, the opportunity of gaining or regaining the dangerous/sacred condition of being at the Second Change has ceased to be apparent.

Virginity is now a mere preamble or waiting room to be got out of as soon as possible; it is without significance. Old age is similarly a waiting room, where you go after life's over and wait for cancer or a stroke. The years before and after the menstrual years are vestigial: the only meaningful condition left to women is that of fruitfulness. Curiously, this restriction of significance coincided with the development of chemicals and instruments that make fertility itself a meaningless or at least secondary characteristic of female maturity. The significance of maturity now is not the capacity to conceive but the mere ability to have sex. As this ability is shared by pubescents and by postclimacterics, the blurring of distinctions and elimination of opportunities is almost complete. There are no rites of passage because there is no significant change. The Triple Goddess has only one face: Marilyn Monroe's, maybe. The entire life of a woman from ten or twelve through seventy or eighty has become secular, uniform, changeless. As there is no longer any virtue in virginity, so there is no longer any meaning in menopause. It requires fanatical determination now to become a Crone.

Women have thus, by imitating the life condition of men, surrendered a very strong position of their own. Men are afraid of virgins, but they have a cure for their own fear and the virgin's virginity: fucking. Men are afraid of crones, so afraid of them that their cure for virginity fails them; they know it won't work. Faced with the fulfilled Crone, all but the bravest men wilt and retreat, crestfallen and cockadroop.

Menopause Manor is not merely a defensive stronghold, however. It is a house or household, fully furnished with the necessities of life. In abandoning it, women have narrowed their domain and impoverished their souls. There are things the Old Woman can do, say, and think that the Woman cannot do, say, or think. The Woman has to give up more than her menstrual periods before she can do, say, or think them. She has got to change her life.

The nature of that change is now clearer than it used to be. Old age is not virginity but a third and new condition; the virgin must be celibate, but the crone need not. There was a confusion there, which the separation of female sexuality from reproductive capacity, via modern contraceptives, has cleared up. Loss of fertility does not mean loss of desire and fulfillment. But it does entail a change, a change involving matters even more important—if I may venture a heresy—than sex.

The woman who is willing to make that change must become pregnant with herself, at last. She must bear herself, her third self, her old age, with travail and alone. Not many will help her with that birth. Certainly no male obstetrician will time her contractions, inject her with sedatives, stand ready with forceps, and neatly stitch up the torn membranes. It's hard even to find an old-fashioned midwife, these days. That pregnancy is long, that labor is hard. Only one is harder, and that's the final one, the one that men also must suffer and perform.

It may well be easier to die if you have already given birth to others or yourself, at least once before. This would be an argument for going through all the discomfort and embarrassment of becoming a Crone. Anyhow it seems a pity to have a built-in rite of passage and to dodge it, evade it, and pretend nothing has changed. That is to dodge and evade one's woman-hood, to pretend one's like a man. Men, once initiated, never get the second chance. They never change again. That's their loss, not ours. Why borrow poverty?

Certainly the effort to remain unchanged, young, when the body gives so impressive a signal of change as the menopause, is gallant; but it is a stupid, self-sacrificial gallantry, better befitting a boy of twenty than a woman of forty-five or fifty. Let the athletes die young and laurel-crowned. Let the soldiers earn the Purple Hearts. Let women die old, white-crowned, with human hearts.

If a space ship came by from the friendly natives of the fourth planet of Altair, and the polite captain of the space ship said, "We have room for one passenger; will you spare us a single human being, so that we may converse at leisure during the long trip back to Altair and learn from an exemplary person the nature of the race?"—I suppose what most people would want to do is provide them with a fine, bright, brave young man, highly educated and in peak physical condition. A Russian cosmonaut would be ideal (American astronauts are mostly too old). There would surely be hundreds, thousands of volunteers, just such young men, all worthy. But I would not pick any of them. Nor would I pick any of the young women who would volunteer, some out of magnanimity and intellectual courage, others out of a profound conviction that Altair couldn't possibly be any worse for a woman than Earth is.

What I would do is go down to the local Woolworth's, or the local village marketplace, and pick an old woman, over sixty, from behind the costume jewelry counter or the betel-nut booth. Her hair would not be red or blonde or lustrous dark, her skin would not be dewy fresh, she would not have the secret of eternal youth. She might, however, show you a small snapshot of her grandson, who is working in Nairobi. She is a bit vague about where Nairobi is, but extremely proud of the grandson. She has worked hard at small, unimportant jobs all her life, jobs like cooking, cleaning, bringing up kids, selling little objects of adornment or pleasure to other people. She was a virgin once, a long time ago, and then a sexually potent fertile female, and then went through menopause. She has given birth several times and faced death several times—the same times. She is facing the final birth/death a little more nearly and clearly every day now. Sometimes her feet hurt something terrible. She never was educated to anything like her capacity, and that is a shameful waste and a crime against humanity, but so common a crime should not and cannot be hidden from Altair. And anyhow she's not dumb. She has a stock of sense, wit, patience, and experiential shrewdness, which the Altaireans might, or might not, perceive as wisdom. If they are wiser than we, then of course we don't know how they'd perceive it. But if they are wiser than we, they may know how to perceive that inmost mind and heart which we, working on mere guess and hope, proclaim to be humane. In any case, since they are curious and kindly, let's give them the best we have to give.

The trouble is, she will be very reluctant to volunteer. "What would an old woman like me do on Altair?" she'll say. "You ought to send one of those scientist men, they can talk to those funny-looking green people. Maybe Dr. Kissinger should go. What about sending the Shaman?" It will be very hard to explain to her that we want her to go because only a person who has experienced, accepted, and acted the entire human condition—the essential quality of which is Change—can fairly represent humanity. "Me?" she'll say, just a trifle slyly. "But I never did anything."

But it won't wash. She knows, though she won't admit it, that Dr. Kissinger has not gone and will never go where she has gone, that the scientists and the shamans have not done what she has done. Into the space ship, Granny.

"The Space Crone," 1976

KATHY KOZACHENKO (*American, contemporary*)

She stored up the anger
for twenty-five years,
then she laid it on the table
like a casserole for dinner.

"I have stolen back
my life," she said.
"I have taken possession
of the rain and the sun
and the grasses," she said.

"You are talking
like a madwoman,"
he said.

"My hands are rocks,
my teeth are bullets,"
she said.

"You are
my wife,"
he said.

"My throat is an eagle,
my breasts
are two white hurricanes," she said.

"Stop!" he said.
"Stop or I shall call
a doctor."

"My hair
is a hornet's nest,
my lips
are thin snakes
waiting for their victim."

He cooked his own dinners,
after that.

The doctors diagnosed it
common change-of-life.

She, too, diagnosed
it change of life.
And on leaving the hospital
she said to her woman-friend
"My cheeks
are the wings
of a young
virgin dove.
Kiss them."

"Mid-Point," 1978

JEFFREY STEINGARTEN (*American, b. 1942*)

Isn't ripening a chaotic, degenerative breakdown of the flesh and skin of a fruit as it plunges toward the death and decay that await us all? Where did you get that idea? Ripening is a tightly structured, programmed series of changes a fruit undergoes as it prepares to seduce every gastronomically aware animal in the neighborhood. Nearly every change makes the fruit more alluring, often just when its seeds are ready to germinate.

 Isn't this a teleological explanation bordering on the religious? So?

 When does ripening begin? Ripening can begin only when a fruit has fully matured and reached its ultimate size and intended shape. Fruit picked immature can never ripen. And even fruit picked at a mature stage will undergo only some of the changes that we mean by ripening.

How many changes are there? Twelve, but I'll mention only a few. Most fruits synthesize an enzyme called polygalacturonase that attacks the pectin cement holding their own cells rigidly in place. The cells slide around, which makes the fruit soft, and the cells spill out their contents, which makes it juicy. Apples lack polygalacturonase, which is why they remain crisp until they degenerate and decay. Most fruits also manufacture a natural wax to protect their surface and slow the loss of water when they are later cut off from fresh supplies.

Fruits become much sweeter as they ripen. Some of them have already stored up lots of starch or insipid sugars like glucose; they synthesize enzymes to convert these into intensely sweet sugars like sucrose and fructose. Other fruits simply fill up with sweet sap but only while attached to the mother plant. And most fruits become less sour as their acids are used up in other ripening processes. It takes the average fruit only a week or two to go from full maturity to perfect ripeness.

From "Ripe Now," 1992

D. H. LAWRENCE (*English, 1885–1930*)

When the ripe fruit falls
its sweetness distils and trickles away into the veins of the earth.

When fulfilled people die
the essential oil of their experience enters
the veins of living space, and adds a glisten
to the atom, to the body of immortal chaos.

For space is alive
and it stirs like a swan
whose feathers glisten
silky with oil of distilled experience.

"When the Ripe Fruit Falls," 1929

CARL G. JUNG (*Swiss, 1875–1961*)

How different does the meaning of life seem to us when we see a young person striving for distant goals and shaping the future, and compare this with an incurable invalid, or with an old man who is sinking reluctantly and without strength to resist into the grave! Youth—we should like to think—has purpose, future, meaning, and value, whereas the coming to an end is only a meaningless cessation. If a young man is afraid of the world, of life and the future, then everyone finds it regrettable, senseless, neurotic; he is considered a cowardly shirker. But when an aging person secretly shudders and is even mortally afraid at the thought that his reasonable expectation of life now amounts to only so many years, then we are painfully reminded of certain feelings within our own breast; we look away and turn the conversation to some other topic. The optimism with which we judge the young man fails us here. Naturally we have on hand for every eventuality one or two suitable banalities about life which we occasionally hand out to the other fellow, such as "everyone must die sometime," "one doesn't live forever," etc. But when one is alone and it is night and so dark and still that one hears nothing and sees nothing but the thoughts which add and subtract the years, and the long row of disagreeable facts which remorselessly indicate how far the hand of the clock has moved forward, and the slow, irresistible approach of the wall of darkness which will eventually engulf everything you love, possess, wish, strive, and hope for—then all our profundities about life slink off to some undiscoverable hiding place, and fear envelops the sleepless one like a smothering blanket.

Many young people have at bottom a panic-fear of life (though at the same time they intensely desire it), and an even greater number of the aging have the same fear of death. Yes, I have known those people who most feared life when they were young to suffer later just as much from the fear of death. When they are young, one says they have infantile resistances against the normal demands of life; one should really say the same thing when they are old, for they are likewise afraid of one of life's normal demands. We are so convinced that death is simply the end of a process that it does not ordinarily occur to us to conceive of death as a goal and a fulfillment, as we do without hesitation the aims and purposes of youthful life in its ascendance.

Life is an energy process. Like every energy process, it is in principle irreversible and is therefore unequivocally directed towards a goal. That goal is a state of rest. In the long run everything that happens is, as it were, nothing more than the initial disturbance of a perpetual state of rest which forever attempts to reestablish itself. Life is teleology par excellence; it is the intrinsic striving towards a goal, and the living organism is a system of directed aims which seek to fulfill themselves. The end of every process is its goal. All energy flow is like a runner who strives with the greatest effort and the utmost expenditure of strength to reach his goal. Youthful longing for the world and for life, for the attainment of high hopes and distant goals, is life's obvious teleological urge which at once changes into fear of life, neurotic resistances, depressions and phobias if at some point it remains caught in the past, or shrinks from risks without which the unseen goal cannot be achieved. With the attainment of maturity and at the zenith of biological existence, life's drive towards a goal in no wise halts. With the same intensity and irresistibility with which it strove upward before middle age, life now descends; for the goal no longer lies on the summit, but in the valley where the ascent began. The curve of life is like the parabola of a projectile which, disturbed from its initial state of rest, rises and then returns to a state of repose.

The psychological curve of life, however, refuses to conform to this law of nature. Sometimes the lack of accord begins early in the ascent. The projectile ascends biologically, but psychologically it lags behind. We straggle behind our years, hugging our childhood as if we could not tear ourselves away. We stop the hands of the clock and imagine that time will stand still. When after some delay we finally reach the summit, there again, psychologically, we settle down to rest, and although we can see ourselves sliding down the other side, we cling, if only with longing backward glances, to the peak once attained. Just as, earlier, fear was a deterrent to life, so now it stands in the way of death. We may even admit that fear of life held us back on the upward slope, but just because of this delay we claim all the more right to hold fast to the summit we have now reached. Though it may be obvious that in spite of all our resistances (now so deeply regretted) life has reasserted itself, yet we pay no attention and keep on trying to make it stand still. Our psychology then loses its natural basis. Consciousness stays up in the air, while the curve of the parabola sinks downward with ever increasing speed.

Natural life is the nourishing soil of the soul. Anyone who fails to go along with life remains suspended, stiff and rigid in mid-air. That is why so many people get wooden in old age; they look back and cling to the past with a secret fear of death in their hearts. They withdraw from the life process, at least psychologically, and consequently remain fixed like nostalgic pillars of salt, with vivid recollections of youth but no living relation to the present. From the middle of life onward, only he remains vitally alive who is ready to *die with life*. For in the secret hour of life's midday the parabola is reversed, death is born. The second half of life does not signify ascent, unfolding, increase, exuberance, but death, since the end is its goal. The negation of life's fulfillment is synonymous with the refusal to accept its ending. Both mean not wanting to live; not wanting to live is identical with not wanting to die. Waxing and waning make one curve.

Whenever possible our consciousness refuses to accommodate itself to this undeniable truth. Ordinarily we cling to our past and remain stuck in the illusion of youthfulness. Being old is highly unpopular. Nobody seems to

78

consider that not being able to grow old is precisely as absurd as not being able to outgrow child-sized shoes. A still infantile man of thirty is surely to be deplored, but a youthful septuagenarian—isn't that delightful? And yet both are perverse, lacking in style, psychological monstrosities. A young man who does not fight and conquer has missed the best part of his youth, and an old man who does not know how to listen to the secrets of the brooks as they tumble down from the peaks to the valleys makes no sense; he is a spiritual mummy who is nothing but a rigid relic of the past. He stands apart from life, mechanically repeating himself to the last triviality.

Our relative longevity, substantiated by present-day statistics, is a product of civilization. It is quite exceptional for primitive people to reach old age. For instance, when I visited the primitive tribes of East Africa I saw very few men with white hair who might have been over sixty. But they were really old, they seemed to have always been old, so fully had they assimilated their age. They were exactly what they were in every respect. We are forever only more or less than we actually are. It is as if our consciousness had somehow slipped from its natural foundations and no longer quite knew how to get along on nature's timing. It seems as though we are suffering from a *hubris* of consciousness which fools us into believing that one's time of life is a mere illusion which can be altered according to one's desire. (One asks oneself where our consciousness gets its ability to be so contrary to nature and what such arbitrariness might signify.)

Like a projectile flying to its goal, life ends in death. Even its ascent and its zenith are only steps and means to this goal. This paradoxical formula is no more than a logical deduction from the fact that life strives towards a goal and is determined by an aim. I do not believe that I am guilty here of playing with syllogisms. We grant goal and purpose to the ascent of life, why not to the descent? The birth of a human being is pregnant with meaning, why not death? For twenty years and more the growing man is being prepared for the complete unfolding of his individual nature, why should not the older man prepare himself twenty years and more for his death? Of course, with the zenith one has obviously reached something, one is it and has it. But what is attained with death?

At this point, just when it might be expected, I do not want suddenly to pull a belief out of my pocket and invite my reader to do what nobody can do, that is, believe something. I must confess that I myself could never do it either. Therefore I shall certainly not assert now that one must believe death to be a second birth leading to a survival beyond the grave. But I can at least mention that the *consensus gentium* has decided views about death, unmistakably expressed in all the great religions of the world. One might even say that the majority of these religions are complicated systems of preparation for death, so much so that life, in agreement with my paradoxical formula, actually has no significance except as a preparation for the ultimate goal of death. In both the greatest living religions, Christianity and Buddhism, the meaning of existence is consummated in its end.

"The Soul and Death," 1934

ATTRIBUTED TO CHUANG TZU (*Chinese, late fourth to early third century* B.C.E.)

When Chuang Tzu was going to Ch'u he saw by the roadside a skull, clean and bare, but with every bone in its place. Touching it gently with his chariot-whip he bent over it and asked, "Sir, was it some insatiable ambition that drove you to transgress the law and brought you to this? Was it the fall of a kingdom, the blow of the executioner's axe that brought you to this? Or had you done some shameful deed and could not face the reproaches of father and mother, of wife and child, and so were brought to this? Was it hunger and cold that brought you to this, or was it that the springs and autumns of your span had in their due course carried you to this?"

Having thus addressed the skull, he put it under his head as a pillow and went to sleep. At midnight the skull appeared to him in a dream and said to him, "All that you said to me—your glib, commonplace chatter—is just what I should expect from a live man, showing as it does in every phase a mind hampered by trammels from which we dead are entirely free. Would you like to hear a word or two about the dead?"

"I certainly should," said Chuang Tzu.

"Among the dead," said the skull, "none is king, none is subject. There is no division of the seasons: for us the whole world is spring, the whole world is autumn. No monarch on his throne has joy greater than ours."

Chuang Tzu did not believe this. "Suppose," he said, "I could get the Clerk of Destinies to make your frame anew, to clothe your bones once more with flesh and skin, send you back to father and mother, wife and child, friends and home, I do not think you would refuse."

A deep frown furrowed the skeleton's brow. "How can you imagine," it asked, "that I would cast away joy greater than that of a king upon his throne, only to go back to the toils of the living world?"

Master Ssu, Master Yü, Master Li and Master Lai were all four talking together. "Who can look upon inaction as his head, upon life as his back, upon death as his rump?" they asked. "Who knows that life and death, existence and annihilation, are all parts of a single body? I will be his friend!"

The four men looked at each other and smiled. There was no disagreement in their hearts and so the four of them became friends.

All at once Master Yü fell ill, and Master Ssu went to ask how he was. "Amazing!" exclaimed Master Yü. "Look, the Creator is making me all crookedy! My back sticks up like a hunchback's so that my vital organs are on top of me. My chin is hidden down around my navel, my shoulders are up above my head, and my pigtail points at the sky. It must be due to some dislocation of the forces of the yin and the yang."

Yet he seemed quite calm at heart and unconcerned. Dragging himself faltingly to the edge of a well, he looked at his reflection and cried, "My, my! Look, the Creator is making me all crookedy!"

"Do you resent it?" asked Master Ssu.

"Why no," replied Master Yü. "What is there to resent? If the process continues, perhaps in time he'll transform my left arm into a rooster: in that case I'll herald the dawn with my crowing. Or in time he may transform my right arm into a crossbow pellet and I'll shoot down an owl for roasting. Or perhaps he will even turn my buttocks into cartwheels: then with my spirit for a horse, I'll climb up and go for a ride, and never again have need for a carriage.

"I received life because the time had come; I will lose it because the order of things passes on. If only a man will be content with this time and dwell in this order neither sorrow nor joy can touch him. In ancient times this was called 'the freeing of the bound.' Yet there are those who cannot free themselves, because they are bound by mere things. Creatures such as I can never win against Heaven. That is the way it has always been: what is there to resent?"

Then suddenly Master Lai also fell ill. Gasping for breath he lay at the point of death. His wife and children gathered round in a circle and wept. Master Li, who had come to find out how he was, said to them, "Shoo! Get back! Don't disturb the process of change!"

And he leaned against the doorway and chatted with Master Lai. "How marvelous the Creator is!" he exclaimed. "What is he going to make out of you next? Where is he going to send you? Will he make you into a rat's liver? Will he make you into a bug's arm?"

"A child obeys his father and mother and goes wherever he is told, east or west, south or north," said Master Lai. "And the yin and the yang—how much more are they to a man than father or mother! Now that they have brought me to the verge of death, how perverse it would be of me to refuse to obey them. What fault is it of theirs? The Great Clod burdens me with form, labors me with life, eases me in old age and rests me in death. So if I think well of my life, by the same token I must think well of my death. When a

81

skilled smith is casting metal, if the metal should leap up and cry, 'I insist upon being made into a famous sword like the sword Mu-yeh of old!'—he would surely regard it as very inauspicious metal indeed. In the same way, if I who have once had the audacity to take on human form should now cry, 'I don't want to be anything but a man! Nothing but a man!'—the Creator would surely consider me a most inauspicious sort of person. So now I think of heaven and earth as a great furnace and the Creator as a skilled smith. What place could he send me that would not be all right? I will go off peacefully to sleep, and then with a start I will wake up.''

Dialogues from *Chuang Tzu*

MARGARET BOURKE-WHITE (*American, 1904–1971*)

My mysterious malady began so quietly I could hardly believe there was anything wrong. Nothing to see or feel except a slight dull ache in my left leg, which I noticed when I walked upstairs. This was not strong enough to dignify by the name of pain. Just strong enough to make me aware that my left leg was not properly sharing the duty of carrying around one photographer on shank's mare. I had the uneasy feeling that this was different from any ache I had ever had. Little did I dream this was the stealthy beginning of a lifetime siege during which I would have to add a new word to my vocabulary—"incurable."

For half a year there were no further developments except that the dull ache moved about in a will-o'-the-wisp fashion to other parts of my leg and even to my arm. But it confined its wanderings to my left side. Then something small but very peculiar crept into my life. I discovered that after sitting for perhaps an hour, as at lunch, on rising from the table my first three steps were grotesque staggers. On the fourth step my ability to walk returned. I first noticed these difficulties at the luncheon table in the Tokyo Press Club. I had already been in and out of Korea several times.

I was highly embarrassed by these staggers and thought up little concealing devices such as dropping my gloves and retrieving them; with the smallest delaying action I could walk. I consulted with doctors I ran across, but my wisp of a symptom meant as little to them as it did to me.

When it refused to disappear after I got back to the States, I started the weary, time-consuming round of specialists. I learned the long list of diseases I did not have. I did not have cancer, heart trouble, infantile paralysis or arthritis. I was amazed that I could have contracted anything when I thought of the near misses of two wars. I had always been arrogantly proud of my health and durability. Strong men might fall by the wayside, but I was "Maggie the Indestructible."

*   *   *

And then a few weeks later something happened that frightened me out of all that nonsense. I found I was losing my ability to write on the typewriter, even my own electric typewriter with its featherlight touch. My fingers were becoming far too stiff to reach the keys properly. The letter "C," for instance, seemed to have removed itself by miles from any position that I could reach. I was working on this book. Dictating is no good to me. When it comes to writing, my flow of thoughts always comes best on the typewriter. Maybe I won't even be able to finish my book, I thought with alarm. . . .

From then on everything became an exercise. A *Life* assignment to the Colorado Dust Bowl, which included airplane photographs, meant that instead of setting the clock for 4:00 A.M. so as to meet the pilot on the airstrip just before sunrise, I set the alarm for 3:30 A.M. so that I would have time to crumple newspapers. When I left the tourist room or the motel where I had spent the night, the floor would be nearly hidden in the rising piles of crumpled newspapers squeezed into popcorn-ball size. If I traveled by myself on an airplane, train or bus, when I disembarked, the space under the seat overflowed with popcorn balls. Any well-appointed hotel bathroom was a clear invitation from the management to wring out all the beautiful turkish towels under the warm-water tap. The bath mat was last. When my camera cases were all packed and my hastily assembled suitcases were bulging, I called for the bellhop, squeezed out the mat, plopped it into the bathtub, and out I went.

*   *   *

Of greatest help to my strength of spirit was the fact that I could continue to work to some extent. Work to me is a sacred thing, and while writing the book was important to me, photography is my profession. My great dread in connection with my illness was that people would try to spare me too much. My editors were wonderfully understanding of this. When I told them I was under doctor's orders to walk four miles a day, they shuddered at the thought but gave me assignments where I could walk, run, climb, fly.

*   *   *

Not knowing the name of my ailment, I dramatized it, told myself I had something very rare. My doctors need not have been so cautious about naming it. When I did learn that I had Parkinson's disease, the name could not frighten me because I did not know what in the world it was. Then, slowly, an old memory came back: of a dinner meeting of photographers perhaps eight or ten years earlier. Captain Steichen spoke with tears on his cheeks of the illness of the "dean of photographers," the great Edward Weston, who had Parkinson's disease. I can still hear the break in Steichen's voice. "A terrible disease . . . you can't work because you can't hold things . . . you grow stiffer and stiffer each year until you are a walking prison . . . no known cure. . . ."

But the discovery that astonished me most was to learn that, far from being a rare malady, it could hardly be less exclusive. We don't know how many people have it, but they are in the hundreds of thousands. Its existence has been known for more than four thousand years (Parkinsonism is the shaking palsy of the Bible), and it has been named and documented for more than a century.

The disease's odd name comes from Dr. James Parkinson, a paleontologist as well as a practicing physician. In 1817, he published his observations of six victims of the disease, noting each weird and ugly symptom. This chronicle has become a medical classic, and yet in the 128 years from Dr. Parkinson's death to the onset of my own siege, little more had been learned.

Parkinsonism does not affect the thinking part of the brain but the brain's motor centers which coordinate voluntary movements. It is Hydra-headed. Push it down in one spot and it rears up in another. It is easy to list its two main symptoms: rigidity and tremor. But to know what Parkinsonism is you must know the surprise of finding yourself standing in a sloping position as though you were trying to impersonate the leaning tower of Pisa. You must know the bewilderment of finding yourself prisoner in your own clothes closet, unable to back out of it. You must experience the awkwardness of trying to turn around in your own kitchen—eleven cautious little steps when one swift pivot used to do the job. You must live with the near panic which you face when you have to walk into a roomful of people, and the uneasiness of the questions you ask yourself: Do I just imagine that I can't seem to turn over in bed any more? How will I get my feet moving when they want to stay glued to the floor? How will I disengage myself from a group of people and step away if they're all around me? How will I keep from knocking them down? What can I do with my hands when I'm only standing still? How will I get my meat cut up? What a waste of good steak! You feel so clumsy if you cut it yourself and so conspicuous if you have someone do it for you. How did I look this time? Did I get through it all right? Did people notice anything wrong?

*   *   *

If I could give only one message after sifting down this experience, it would be to urge others to banish the secrecy. I see now how futile are the obsessive efforts to keep the illness hidden. In most cases it isn't secret anyway, and it is the most harmful possible course to follow, because it robs you of the release of talking it over. I found that many of my friends knew all about it—in some cases they knew more than I. They were distressed most by not knowing how to help me. I was surrounded by a wall of loving silence which no one dared to break through.

Parkinsonism is a strange malady. It works its way into all paths of life, into all that is graceful and human and outgiving in our lives, and poisons it all.

I often thought with thankfulness that if I had to be saddled with some kind of ailment, I was fortunate that it was something where my own efforts could help. I was amazed to see what the human body will do for you if you insist. Having to plug away at some exercise and finding I could make small advances gave me the feeling I was still captain of my ship—an attitude which is very important to me.

*   *   *

Well-meaning people frequently advise that you must learn to accept your illness. My conviction was just the opposite. Try to take a realistic approach, yes. But accept an illness, never. Laying down my weapons in the middle of the fight was unthinkable. And there was, too, another reason, which went much deeper. Somehow I had the unshakable faith that if I could just manage to hang on and keep myself in good shape, somewhere a door would open.

And that door did indeed open.

From *Portrait of Myself,* 1963

TU FU (*Chinese, 713–770 c.e.*)

In the eighth moon of autumn, the wind howling viciously,
Three layers of thatch were whirled away from my roof.
The thatch flying over the river sprinkled the embankment
And some of it was entangled in the treetops,
And some whirled away and sank in the marshlands.
A swarm of small boys from South Village laughing at me because I am old
    and feeble.
They know they can rob me even in my face.
What effrontery! Stealing my thatch, taking it to the bamboo grove.
With parched lips and tongue I screamed at them—it was no use—
And so I came back sighing to my old place.
Then the wind fell and the clouds were inky black,
The autumn sky a web of darkness, stretching toward the dusk,
And my old cotton quilt was as cold as iron,
And my darling son tossed in his sleep, bare feet tearing through the blanket,
And the rain dripped through the roof, and there was no dry place on the
    bed.
Like strings of wax the rain fell, unending.
After all these disasters of war, I have had little sleep or rest.

When will this long night of drizzle come to an end?
Now I dream of an immense mansion, tens of thousands of rooms,
Where all the cold creatures can take shelter, their faces alight;
Not moved by the wind or the rain, a mansion as solid as a mountain—
Alas, when shall I see such a majestic house?
If I could see this, even though my poor house were torn down,
Even though I were frozen to death I would be content.

"The Roof Whirled Away by Winds," T'ang Dynasty, 618–954 C.E.

PSALM 102:1–13, HEBREW SCRIPTURES

A prayer of the lowly man when he is faint and pours forth his plea before
the LORD.

O LORD, hear my prayer;
let my cry come before You.
Do not hide Your face from me
in my time of trouble;
turn Your ear to me;
when I cry, answer me speedily.

For my days have vanished like smoke
and my bones are charred like a hearth.
My body is stricken and withered like grass;
too wasted to eat my food;
on account of my vehement groaning
my bones show through my skin.
I am like a great owl in the wilderness,
an owl among the ruins.
I lie awake; I am like
a lone bird upon a roof.
All day long my enemies revile me;
my deriders use my name to curse.
For I have eaten ashes like bread
and mixed my drink with tears,
because of Your wrath and Your fury:
for You have cast me far away.
My days are like a lengthening shadow;
I wither like grass.

But You, O LORD, are enthroned forever;
Your fame endures throughout the ages.

YAMANOUE OKURA *(Japanese, 660–733 C.E.)*

We are helpless before time
Which ever speeds away.
And pains of a hundred kinds
Pursue us one after another.
Maidens joy in girlish pleasures,
With ship-borne gems on their wrists,
And hand in hand with their friends;
But the bloom of maidenhood,
As it cannot be stopped,
Too swiftly steals away.
When do their ample tresses
Black as a mud-snail's bowels
Turn white with the frost of age?
Whence come those wrinkles
Which furrow their rosy cheeks?
The lusty young men, warrior-like,
Bearing their sword blades at their waists,
In their hands the hunting bows,
And mounting their bay horses,
With saddles dressed with twill,
Ride about in triumph;
But can their prime of youth
Favor them for ever?
Few are the nights they keep,
When, sliding back the plank doors,
They reach their beloved ones
And sleep, arms intertwined,
Before, with staffs at their waists,
They totter along the road,
Laughed at here, and hated there.
This is the way of the world;
And, cling as I may to life,
I know no help!

ENVOY

Although I wish I were thus;
Like the rocks that stay for ever,
In this world of humanity
I cannot keep old age away.

"We are helpless before time," in *Man'yōshū*, Ancient Period, to 794 C.E.

HEINZ KOHUT *(Austrian American, 1913–1981)*

The influence of aging (and with it the inescapable necessity of facing the reality of the final dissolution of individual existence) is producing a shift. There is less enthusiasm in me now (and less Pollyanna) and more concern for the continuity (i.e., for the survival) of the values for which I have lived.

Be that as it may, the point I wish to make is that even the *nuclear* self changes and that, under the impact of new internal and external factors, the task of reforming the self is repeatedly imposed on us, and may evoke in us, temporarily, old fragmentation fears until a new self is again firmly established.

From "Discussion of 'On the Adolescent Process as a Transformation of the Self,' by Ernest S. Wolf, John E. Gedo, and David M. Terman," 1972

MAY SARTON *(American, b. 1912)*

Now I become myself. It's taken
Time, many years and places;
I have been dissolved and shaken,
Worn other people's faces,
Run madly, as if Time were there,
Terribly old, crying a warning,
"Hurry, you will be dead before—"
(What? Before you reach the morning?
Or the end of the poem is clear?
Or love safe in the walled city?)
Now to stand still, to be here,
Feel my own weight and density!
The black shadow on the paper
Is my hand; the shadow of a word
As thought shapes the shaper
Falls heavy on the page, is heard.
All fuses now, falls into place
From wish to action, word to silence,
My work, my love, my time, my face
Gathered into one intense
Gesture of growing like a plant.
As slowly as the ripening fruit
Fertile, detached, and always spent,
Falls but does not exhaust the root,
So all the poem is, can give,

Grows in me to become the song;
Made so and rooted so by love.
Now there is time and Time is young.
O, in this single hour I live
All of myself and do not move.
I, the pursued, who madly ran,
Stand still, stand still, and stop the sun!

"Now I Become Myself," c. 1952

W. B. YEATS *(Irish, 1865–1939)*

The trees are in their autumn beauty,
The woodland paths are dry,
Under the October twilight the water
Mirrors a still sky;
Upon the brimming water among the stones
Are nine-and-fifty swans.

The nineteenth autumn has come upon me
Since I first made my count;
I saw, before I had well finished,
All suddenly mount
And scatter wheeling in great broken rings
Upon their clamorous wings.

I have looked upon those brilliant creatures,
And now my heart is sore.
All's changed since I, hearing at twilight,
The first time on this shore,
The bell-beat of their wings above my head,
Trod with a lighter tread.

Unwearied still, lover by lover,
They paddle in the cold
Companionable streams or climb the air;
Their hearts have not grown old;
Passion or conquest, wander where they will,
Attend upon them still.

But now they drift on the still water,
Mysterious, beautiful;
Among what rushes will they build,

By what lake's edge or pool
Delight men's eyes when I awake some day
To find they have flown away?

"The Wild Swans at Coole," 1917

HENRI J. M. NOUWEN *(Dutch, b. 1932)*
WALTER J. GAFFNEY *(American, b. 1938)*

Is aging a way to the darkness or a way to the light? It is not given to anyone to make a final judgment, since the answer can only be brought forth from the center of our being. No one can decide for anyone else how his or her aging shall or should be. It belongs to the greatness of men and women that the meaning of their existence escapes the power of calculations and predictions. Ultimately, it can only be discovered and affirmed in the freedom of the heart. There we are able to decide between segregation and unity, between desolation and hope, between loss of self and a new, recreating vision. Everyone will age and die, but this knowledge has no inherent direction. It can be destructive as well as creative, oppressive as well as liberating.

What seems the most frightening period of life, marked by excommunication and rejection, might turn into the most joyful opportunity to tell our community top from bottom.

From *Aging*, 1974

RICHARD STERN *(American, b. 1928)*

"How far is it now, George?"

The old man was riding next to his son, Will. George was his brother, dead the day after Franklin Roosevelt.

"Almost there, Dad."

"What does 'almost' mean?"

"It's Eighty-sixth and Park. The hospital's at Ninety-ninth and Fifth. Mother's in the Klingenstein Pavilion."

"Mother's not well?"

"No, she's not well. Liss and I took her to the hospital a couple of weeks ago."

"It must have slipped my mind." The green eyes darkened with sympathy. "I'm sure you did the right thing. Is it a good hospital?"

"Very good. You were on staff there half a century."

"Of course I was. For many years, I believe."

"Fifty."

"Many as that?"

"A little slower, pal. These jolts are hard on the old man."

The cabbie was no chicken himself. "It's your ride."

"Are we nearly there, George?"

"Two minutes more."

"The day isn't friendly," said Dr. Cahn. "I don't remember such—such—"

"Heat."

"Heat in New York." He took off his gray fedora and scratched at the hairless, liver-spotted skin. Circulatory difficulty left it dry, itchy. Scratching had shredded and inflamed its soft center.

"It's damned hot. In the nineties. Like you."

"What's that?"

"It's as hot as you are old. Ninety-one."

"Ninety-one. That's not good."

"It's a grand age."

"That's your view."

"And Mother's eighty. You've lived good, long lives."

"Mother's not well, son?"

"Not too well. That's why Liss and I thought you ought to see her. Mother's looking forward to seeing you."

"Of course. I should be with her. Is this the first time I've come to visit?"

"Yes."

"I should be with her."

The last weeks had been difficult. Dr. Cahn had been the center of the household. Suddenly, his wife was. The nurses looked after her. And when he talked, she didn't answer. He grew angry, sullen. When her ulcerous mouth improved, her voice was rough and her thought harsh. "I wish you'd stop smoking for five minutes. Look at the ashes on your coat. Please stop smoking."

"Of course, dear. I didn't know I was annoying you." The ash tumbled like a suicide from thirty stories, the butt was crushed into its dead brothers. "I'll smoke inside." And he was off, but, in two minutes, back. Lighting up. Sometimes he lit two cigarettes at once. Or lit the filtered end. The odor was foul, and sometimes his wife was too weak to register her disgust.

They sat and lay within silent yards of each other. Dr. Cahn was in his favorite armchair, the *Times* bridge column inches from his cigarette. He read it all day long. The vocabulary of the game deformed his speech. "I need some clubs" might mean "I'm hungry." "My spades are tired" meant he was. Or his eyes were. Praise of someone might come out "He laid his hand out clearly." In the bedridden weeks, such mistakes intensified his wife's exasperation. "He's become such a penny-pincher," she said to Liss when

Dr. Cahn refused to pay her for the carton of cigarettes she brought, saying, "They can't charge so much. You've been cheated."

"Liss has paid. Give her the money."

"Are you telling me what's trump? I've played this game all my life."

"You certainly have. And I can't bear it."

In sixty marital years, there had never been such anger. When Will came from Chicago to persuade his mother into the hospital, the bitterness dismayed him.

It was, therefore, not so clear that Dr. Cahn should visit his wife. Why disturb her last days? Besides, Dr. Cahn seldom went out anywhere. He wouldn't walk with the black nurses (women whom he loved, teased, and was teased by). It wasn't done. "I'll go out later. My feet aren't friendly today." Or, lowering the paper, "My legs can't trump."

Liss opposed his visit. "Mother's afraid he'll make a scene."

"It doesn't matter," said Will. "He has to have some sense of what's happening. They've been the center of each other's lives. It wouldn't be right."

The hope had been that Dr. Cahn would die first. He was ten years older, his mind had slipped its moorings years ago. Mrs. Cahn was clearheaded, and, except near the end, energetic. She loved to travel, wanted especially to visit Will in Chicago—she had not seen his new apartment—but she wouldn't leave her husband even for a day. "Suppose something happened." "Bring him along." "He can't travel. He'd make an awful scene."

Only old friends tolerated him, played bridge with him, forgiving his lapses and muddled critiques of their play. "If you don't understand a two bid now, you never will." Dr. Cahn was the most gentlemanly of men, but his tongue roughened with his memory. It was as if a lifetime of restraint were only the rind of a wicked impatience.

"He's so spoiled," said Mrs. Cahn, the spoiler.

"Here we are, Dad."

They parked under the blue awning. Dr. Cahn got out his wallet—he always paid for taxis, meals, shows—looked at the few bills, then handed it to his son. Will took a dollar, added two of his own, and thanked his father.

"This is a weak elevator," he said of one of the monsters made to drift the ill from floor to floor. A nurse wheeled in a stretcher and Dr. Cahn removed his fedora.

"Mother's on eight."

"Minnie is here?"

"Yes. She's ill. Step out now."

"I don't need your hand."

Each day, his mother filled less of the bed. Her face, unsupported by dentures, seemed shot away. Asleep, it looked to Will as if the universe leaned on the crumpled cheeks. When he kissed them, he feared they'd turn to dust, so astonishingly delicate was the flesh. The only vanity left was love of attention, and that was part of the only thing that counted, the thought of those who cared for her. How she appreciated the good nurses, and her children. They—who'd never seen before their mother's naked body—would change her nightgown if the nurse was gone. They brought her the bedpan and, though she usually suggested they leave the room, sat beside her while, under the sheets, her weak body emptied its small waste.

For the first time in his adult life, Will found her beautiful. Her flesh was mottled like a Pollock canvas, the facial skin trenched with the awful last ditches of self-defense, but her look melted him. It was human beauty.

Day by day, manners that seemed as much a part of her as her eyes—fussiness, bossiness, nagging inquisitiveness—dropped away. She was down to what she was.

Not since childhood had she held him so closely, kissed his cheek with such force. "This is mine. This is what lasts," said the force.

What was she to him? Sometimes, little more than the old organic scenery of his life. Sometimes she was the meaning of it. "Hello, darling," she'd say. "I'm so glad to see you." The voice, never melodious, was rusty, avian. Beautiful. No actress could match it. "How are you? What's happening?"

"Very little. How are you today?"

She told her news. "Dr. Vacarian was in, he wanted to give me another treatment. I told him, 'No more.' And no more medicine." Each day, she renounced more therapy. An unspoken decision had been made afer a five-hour barium treatment which usurped the last of her strength. (Will thought that might have been its point.) It had given her her last moments of eloquence, a frightening jeremiad about life dark beyond belief, nothing left, nothing right. It was the last complaint of an old champion of complaint, and after it, she had made up her mind to go. There was no more talk of going home.

"Hello, darling. How are you today?"

Will bent over, was kissed and held against her cheek. "Mother, Dad's here."

To his delight, she showed hers. "Where is he?" Dr. Cahn had waited at the door. Now he came in, looked at the bed, realized where he was and who was there.

"Dolph, dear. How are you, my darling? I'm so happy you came to see me."

The old man stooped over and took her face in his hands. For seconds, there was silence. "My dearest," he said; then, "I didn't know. I had no idea. I've been so worried about you. But don't worry now. You look wonderful. A little thin, perhaps. We'll fix that. We'll have you out in no time."

The old man's pounding heart must have driven blood through the clogged vessels. There was no talk of trumps.

"You can kiss me, dear." Dr. Cahn put his lips on hers.

He sat next to the bed and held his wife's hand through the low rail. Over and over he told her she'd be well. She asked about home and the nurses. He answered well for a while. Then they both saw him grow vague and tired. To Will he said, "I don't like the way she's looking. Are you sure she has a good doctor?"

Of course Mrs. Cahn heard. Her happiness watered a bit, not at the facts, but at his inattention. Still, she held on. She knew he could not sit so long in a strange room. "I'm so glad you came, darling."

Dr. Cahn heard his cue and rose. "We mustn't tire you Minnie, dear. We'll come back soon."

She held out her small arms, he managed to lean over, and they kissed again.

In the taxi, he was very tired. "Are we home?"

"Almost, Dad. You're happy you saw Mother, aren't you?"

"Of course I'm happy. But it's not a good day. It's a very poor day. Not a good bid at all."

"Dr. Cahn's Visit," 1980

MARGERY WILLIAMS (*English, 1880–1944*)

The Skin Horse had lived longer in the nursery than any of the others. He was so old that his brown coat was bald in patches and showed the seams underneath, and most of the hairs in his tail had been pulled out to string bead necklaces. He was wise, for he had seen a long succession of mechanical toys arrive to boast and swagger, and by-and-by break their mainsprings and pass away, and he knew that they were only toys, and would never turn into anything else. For nursery magic is very strange and wonderful, and only those playthings that are old and wise and experienced like the Skin Horse understand all about it.

"What is REAL?" asked the Rabbit one day, when they were lying side by side near the nursery fender, before Nana came to tidy the room. "Does it mean having things buzz inside you and a stick-out handle?"

"Real isn't how you are made," said the Skin Horse. "It's a thing that happens to you. When a child loves you for a long, long time, not just to play with, but REALLY loves you, then you become Real."

"Does it hurt?" asked the Rabbit.

"Sometimes," said the Skin Horse, for he was always truthful. "When you are Real you don't mind being hurt."

"Does it happen all at once, like being wound up," he asked, "or bit by bit?"

"It doesn't happen all at once," said the Skin Horse. "You become. It takes a long time. That's why it doesn't often happen to people who break easily, or have sharp edges, or who have to be carefully kept. Generally, by the time you are Real, most of your hair has been loved off, and your eyes drop out and you get loose in the joints and very shabby. But these things don't matter at all, because once you are Real you can't be ugly, except to people who don't understand."

From *The Velveteen Rabbit, or How Toys Became Real,* 1922

MERIDEL LE SUEUR (*American, b. 1900*)

I would like to read my litany to age and death. The title of this comes of the fact that I'm doing away with the word "age." Aging? You've heard of that? Aging or age or death? Aging? You never hear of anything in nature aging, or a sunflower saying, "Well, I'm growing old," and leaning over and vomiting. You know, it *ripens*, it drops its seed and the cycle goes on. So I'm ripening. For "Age" you can say "ripening."

It's a terrible thing in women's culture that you're supposed to be dead after menopause in our culture. You're not beautiful any more, nothing. Since I was 60 I've written more and had better energy and more energy than I ever had in my life. I went to a doctor when I was about 70 and he said, "Oh, just take these tranquilizers." I said, "Are you kidding?" I said, "I'm going to do my best work before I'm 70, between 70 and 80." "Oh," he said, "that's riduculous!" And he gave me the most brilliant description of decay you ever heard. He described sclerosis, and cutting off your wind, and total decay, stroke, and on. "Just take these tranquilizers." I said, "No, I'm not going to do that. I'm really going to do my best writing before I'm 80." In three years *he* was dead!"

That's really a terrible thing. In American Indian culture after you give your children to the world, serve socially your nation, and contribute, *then* you can become a shaman, women too, or a medicine man, or a holy person. And you're considered an asset to the nation as an elder, because of your history.

I was broke in New York, and they had an agency. You could rent yourself out as a grandmother, at minimum wage an hour, $3.40 or something. The children never saw an old person! They wanted to touch you, take out your teeth. They really wanted to know what age was. They never saw older people! I must say the younger persons weren't so great to look at.

So this is the title, "Rites of Ancient Ripening."

I am luminous with age
In my lap I hold the valley.
I see on the horizon what has been taken
What is gone lies prone fleshless.
In my breast I hold the middle valley
The corn kernels cry to me in the fields
     Take us home.
Like corn I cry in the last sunset
Gleam like plums.

     My bones shine in fever
Smoked with the fires of age.
Herbal, I contain the final juice,
Shadow, I crouch in the ash
     never breaking to fire.
Winter iron bough
     unseen my buds,
Hanging close I live in the beloved bone
Speaking in the marrow
     alive in green memory.

The light was brighter then.
Now spiders creep at my eyes' edge.
I peek between my fingers
     at my fathers' dust.
The old stones have been taken away
     there is no path.
The fathering fields are gone.
The wind is stronger than it used to be.
My stone feet far below me grip the dust.
I run and crouch in corners with thin dogs.
I tie myself to the children like a kite.
I fall and burst beneath the sacred human tree.
Release my seed and let me fall.
Toward the shadow of the great earth
     let me fall.
Without child or man
     I turn I fall.
Into shadows,
     the dancers are gone.
My salted pelt stirs at the final warmth
Pound me death
     stretch and tan me death

Hang me up, ancestral shield
    against the dark.
Burn and bright and take me quick.
Pod and light me into dark.

Are those flies or bats or mother eagles?
I shrink I cringe
Trees tilt upon me like young men.
The bowl I made I cannot lift.
All is running past me.
The earth tilts and turns over me.
I am shrinking
 and lean against the warm walls of old summers.
With knees and chin I grip the dark
Swim out the shores of night in old meadows.
Remember buffalo hunts
Great hunters returning
Councils of the fathers to be fed
Round sacred fires.
The faces of profound deer who
      gave themselves for food.
We faced the east the golden pollened
    sacrifice of brothers.
The little seeds of my children
    with faces of mothers and fathers
Fold in my flesh
    in future summers.
My body a canoe turning to stone
Moves among the bursting flowers of memory
Through the meadows of flowers and food,
I float and wave to my grandchildren in the
Tipis of many fires
    In the winter of the many slain
I hear the moaning.
I ground my corn daily
In my pestle many children
Summer grasses in my daughters
Strength and fathers in my sons
All was ground in the bodies bowl
  corn died to bread
   woman to child
    deer to the hunters.

Sires of our people
Wombs of mothering night
Guardian mothers of the corn
Hill borne torrents of the plains
Sing all grinding songs
    of healing herbs
Many tasselled summers
                    Flower in my old bones
                Now.
Ceremonials of water and fire
Lodge me in the deep earth
    grind my harvested seed.

The rites of ancient ripening
Make my flesh plume
And summer winds stir in my smoked bowl.
Do no look for me till I return
                    rot of greater summers
Struck from fires and dark,
Mother struck to future child.
Unbud me now
Unfurl me now
Flesh and fire
            burn
                requicken
                    Death.

"Rites of Ancient Ripening," 1986

JALAL AD-DIN RŪMĪ (*Persian, 1207–1273*)

I died as mineral and became a plant
I died as plant and rose to animal,
I died as animal and I was Man.
Why should I fear? When was I less by dying?
Yet once more I shall die as Man, to soar
With angels blest; but even from angelhood
I must pass on; **all except God doth perish.**
When I have sacrificed my angel-soul,
I shall become what no mind e'er conceived.
Oh, let me not exist! for Non-existence
Proclaims in organ tones, "To Him we shall return."

From the *Masnavi,* thirteenth century

PAUL TOURNIER *(Swiss, 1898–1986)*

You, my forty- and fifty-year-old readers, you have had to specialize narrowly in order to build up the fruitful life you lead today. You have had to give up many things which might have interested you. You have worked hard. You have used your time off only for pleasure and relaxation, and you have been disciplined enough not to spend too much time on such things. You have had to direct your energies and to train for success, but in rather too narrow a field. And success has even further enslaved you to your career. It is not enough for you to complain that you no longer have time for anything else. Consider, therefore, what is at stake: it is to make sure that your life will be able to expand once more. It is already time for you to begin a movement in a reverse direction, away from specialization, and to reopen your mind to a wider horizon.

From "Work and Leisure," in *Learning to Grow Old*, 1971

CHAPTER THREE
GENERATIONS

Growing old is a fundamental dynamic in all cycles of social and biological reproduction. Each aging individual forms a precious, necessary, yet fragile link in a chain of parents, children, and grandchildren, ancestors and descendants. Each individual—even the most solitary—has a life that is both personal and social, one that is physically and culturally linked to past and future. This chapter about generational relations includes both the personal and the social. It focuses on tensions, breakdowns, frictions, and strengths that connect the individual to his or her own family—and to the human family. The chapter's readings explore not only familial but also religious, social, and personal relations between people of different generations. Loosely grouped sections address filial piety; conflict, ambiguity, and uncertainty in age relations; personal perceptions of changing relationships; the death of adult children; and leave-takings.

The first group of selections—from the fifth commandment of the Hebrew decalogue to Lin Yutang's passage on the traditional Chinese family system—exemplifies filial piety in various cultures. For traditional Christians, the story of Ruth and her daughter-in-law is about genealogy: Ruth and Boaz (Naomi's kinsman) founded a lineage that led to David, Solomon, Mary, and Jesus. But the story is also a model of mutual help and friendship between generations. Ruth's support and loyalty meet Naomi's wisdom so that they can secure a common future. In his essay "On Growing Old Gracefully," the twentieth-century Chinese writer Lin Yutang argues that intergenerational respect and love are the wellsprings of a harmonious life and a good society.

The next series of readings articulates humor, conflict, suffering, and anxiety in generational relations. It opens with Lewis Carroll's hilarious satire of Robert Southey's "The Old Man's Comforts and How He Gained Them." Problems such as abuse, abandonment, or measuring up to the ideal of filial piety are explored in poetry, folklore, and political writing. The difficulties of intergenerational living are epitomized in Shakespeare's famous words: "Crabbed age and youth cannot live together."

A third group articulates the commonalities of young and old, the wonderful discoveries—sometimes achieved after decades of estrangement—of what different generations share. Bernard Cooper writes of a father and son who acknowledge each other's need for sexual love and companionship. In "Loving Mother, at Last," Linda Bird Francke finds a giddy young girl still alive in her previously precise and impeccable mother. In the giving and receiving that weaves the fabric of our lives, writes Carter Catlett Williams, "we find ourselves in each other and in all ages." The ninth-century (B.C.E.) Chinese writer Po Chü-i speaks of his love for grandchildren with emotion that crosses cultures and spans centuries.

The fourth section, one of the most poignant in the chapter, is about parents who suffer the death of a child. These selections, beginning with the aged David's piteous lament for his son Absalom, are arranged as a unit. The well-known and tragic story of the Brontë family follows. Patrick Brontë (1777–1861) survived his wife and all six of his children (an alcoholic son and five daughters, three of whom were famous novelists). The unit ends with a verse from the Gospel According to Matthew, bewailing Herod's massacre of Bethlehem's firstborns. The selections speak to the grief of all mothers and fathers who outlive their children, and of all who live into a bereft and lonely old age.

Next are two selections about children facing the death of parents. The eighteenth-century composer Wolfgang Amadeus Mozart writes to comfort and encourage his dying father. While the thirty-one-year-old Mozart believes death to be "the true goal of our existence," he hopes that his father will recover. If not, he wants to "come to [his] arms" as quickly as possible. In the humorous excerpt from John Nichols's *The Milagro Beanfield War*, the patriarch Amarante is always on the verge of death, always bidding a ritual farewell. Farewells between parents and children can sometimes take a long time.

The chapter begins with the commandment that most great religious traditions hold sacred: the commandment that the young honor the old, the parents. It ends with Rena Cornett's Appalachian autobiographical narrative as told to Wendy Ewald, which pleads for elders to pass traditions on to the next generation, for oral history that carries the ancestors forward to the descendants. Cornett centers the aged in the succession of generations. Let parents and grandparents teach the young about the past, she implores, for great-grandparents are "the roots of our souls."

DEUTERONOMY 5:16, HEBREW SCRIPTURES

Honor thy father and thy mother, as the Lord thy God commanded thee; that thy days may be long and that it may go well with thee, upon the land which the Lord thy God giveth thee.

SURA 17:23, THE KORAN

Thy Lord has decreed
you shall not serve
any but Him,
and to be good to parents,
whether one or both of them
attains old age with thee;
say not to them 'Fie'
neither chide them, but
speak unto them words
respectful,
and lower to them the
wing of humbleness
out of mercy and say,
'My Lord,
have mercy upon them,
as they raised me up
when I was little.'

FROM THE BOOK OF RUTH, HEBREW SCRIPTURES

And it came to pass in the days when the judges judged, that there was a famine in the land. And a certain man of Beth-lehem in Judah went to sojourn in the field of Moab, he, and his wife, and his two sons. And the name of the man was Elimelech, and the name of his wife Naomi, and the name of his two sons Mahlon and Chilion, Ephrathites of Beth-lehem in Judah. And they came into the field of Moab, and continued there. And Elimelech Naomi's husband died; and she was left, and her two sons. And they took them wives of the women of Moab; the name of the one was Orpah, and the name of the other Ruth; and they dwelt there about ten years. And Mahlon and Chilion died both of them; and the woman was left of her two children and of her husband. Then she arose with her daughters-in-law, that she might return from the field of Moab; for she had heard in the field of Moab how that the LORD had remembered His people in giving them bread. And she went forth out of the place where she was, and her two daughters-in-law with her; and they went on the way to return unto the land of Judah. And Naomi said unto her two daughters-in-law: 'Go, return each of you to her mother's house; the LORD deal kindly with you, as ye have dealt with the dead, and with me. The LORD grant you that ye may find rest, each of you in the house of her husband.' Then she kissed them; and they lifted up their voice, and wept. And they said unto her: 'Nay, but we will return with thee unto thy people.'

And Naomi said: 'Turn back, my daughters; why will ye go with me? have I yet sons in my womb, that they may be your husbands? Turn back, my daughters, go your way; for I am too old to have a husband. If I should say: I have hope, should I even have a husband to-night, and also bear sons; would ye tarry for them till they were grown? would ye shut yourselves off for them and have no husbands? nay, my daughters; for it grieveth me much for your sakes, for the hand of the LORD is gone forth against me.' And they lifted up their voice, and wept again and Orpah kissed her mother-in-law; but Ruth cleaved unto her.

And she said: 'Behold, thy sister-in-law is gone back unto her people, and unto her god; return thou after thy sister-in-law.' And Ruth said: 'Entreat me not to leave thee, and to return from following after thee; for whither thou goest, I will go; and where thou lodgest, I will lodge; thy people shall be my people, and thy God my God; where thou diest, will I die, and there will I be buried; the LORD do so to me, and more also, if aught but death part thee and me.' And when she saw that she was stedfastly minded to go with her, she left off speaking unto her. So they two went until they came to Beth-lehem. And it came to pass, when they were come to Beth-lehem, that all the city was astir concerning them, and the women said: 'Is this Naomi?' And she said unto them: 'Call me not Naomi, call me Marah; for the Almighty hath dealt very bitterly with me. I went out full, and the LORD hath brought me back home empty; why call ye me Naomi, seeing the LORD hath testified against me, and the Almighty hath afflicted me?' So Naomi returned, and Ruth the Moabitess, her daughter-in-law, with her, who returned out of the field of Moab—and they came to Beth-lehem in the beginning of barley harvest.

CHAPTER II

And Naomi had a kinsman of her husband's, a mighty man of valour, of the family of Elimelech, and his name was Boaz. And Ruth the Moabitess said unto Naomi: 'Let me now go to the field, and glean among the ears of corn after him in whose sight I shall find favour.' And she said unto her: 'Go, my daughter.' And she went, and came and gleaned in the field after the reapers; and her hap was to light on the portion of the field belonging unto Boaz, who was of the family of Elimelech. And, behold, Boaz came from Beth-lehem, and said unto the reapers: 'The LORD be with you.' And they answered him: ''The LORD bless thee.' Then said Boaz unto his servant that was set over the reapers: 'Whose damsel is this?' And the servant that was set over the reapers answered and said: 'It is a Moabitish damsel that came back with Naomi out of the field of Moab; and she said: Let me glean, I pray you, and gather after the reapers among the sheaves; so she came, and hath continued even from the morning until now, save that she tarried a little in the house.' Then said Boaz unto Ruth: 'Hearest thou not, my daughter? Go not to glean in another field, neither pass from hence, but abide here fast by my maidens. Let thine eyes be on the field that they do reap, and go thou after them; have I not charged the young men that they shall not touch thee? and when thou art athirst, go unto the vessels, and drink of that which the young men have drawn.' Then she fell on her face and bowed down to the ground, and said unto him: 'Why have I found favour in thy sight, that thou shouldest take cognizance of me, seeing I am a foreigner?' And Boaz answered and said unto her: 'It hath fully been told me, all that thou hast done unto thy mother-in-law since the death of thy husband; and how thou hast left thy father and thy mother, and the land of thy nativity, and art come unto a people that thou knowest not heretofore. The LORD recompense thy work, and be thy reward complete from the LORD, the God of Israel, under whose wings thou art come to take refuge.'

* * *

So she kept fast by the maidens of Boaz to glean unto the end of barley harvest and of wheat harvest; and she dwelt with her mother-in-law.

CHAPTER III

And Naomi her mother-in-law said unto her: 'My daughter, shall I not seek rest for thee, that it may be well with thee? And now is there not Boaz our kinsman, with whose maidens thou wast? Behold, he winnoweth barley to-night in the threshing-floor. Wash thyself therefore, and anoint thee, and put thy raiment upon thee, and get thee down to the threshing-floor; but make not thyself known unto the man, until he shall have done eating and drinking. And it shall be, when he lieth down, that thou shalt mark the place where he shall lie, and thou shalt go in, and uncover his feet, and lay thee down; and he will tell thee what thou shalt do.' And she said unto her: 'All that thou sayest unto me I will do.' And she went down unto the threshing-floor, and did according to all that her mother-in-law bade her. And when Boaz had eaten and drunk, and his heart was merry, he went to lie down at the end of the heap of corn; and she came softly, and uncovered his feet, and laid her down. And it came to pass at midnight, that the man was startled, and turned himself; and, behold, a woman lay at his feet. And he said: 'Who art thou?' And she answered: 'I am Ruth thy handmaid; spread therefore thy skirt over thy handmaid; for thou art a near kinsman.' And he said: 'Blessed be thou of the LORD, my daughter; thou hast shown more kindness in the end than at the beginning, inasmuch as thou didst not follow the young men, whether poor or rich. And now, my daughter, fear not; I will do to thee all that thou sayest; for all the men in the gate of my people do know that thou art a virtuous woman. And now it is true that I am a near kinsman; howbeit there is a kinsman nearer than I. Tarry this night, and it shall be in the morning, that if he will perform unto thee the part of a kinsman, well; let him do the kinsman's part; but if he be not willing to do the part of a kinsman to thee, then will I do the part of a kinsman to thee, as the LORD liveth; lie down until the morning.' And she lay at his feet until the morning; and she rose up before one could discern another. For he said: 'Let it not be known that the woman came to the threshing-floor.' And he said: 'Bring the mantle that is upon thee, and hold it'; and she held it; and he measured six measures of barley, and laid it on her; and he went into the city. And when she came to her mother-in-law, she said: 'Who art thou, my daughter?' And she told her all that the man had done to her. And she said: 'These six measures of barley gave he me; for he said to me: Go not empty unto thy mother-in-law.' Then said she: 'Sit still, my daughter, until thou know how the matter will fall; for the man will not rest, until he have finished the thing this day.'

CHAPTER IV

Now Boaz went up to the gate, and sat him down there; and, behold, the near kinsman of whom Boaz spoke came by; unto whom he said: 'Ho, such a one! turn aside, sit down here.' And he turned aside, and sat down. And he took ten men of the elders of the city, and said: 'Sit ye down here.' And they sat down. And he said unto the near kinsman: 'Naomi, that is come back out of the field of Moab, selleth the parcel of land, which was our brother Elimelech's; and I thought to disclose it unto thee, saying: Buy it before them that sit here, and before the elders of my people. If thou wilt redeem it, redeem it; but if it will not be redeemed, then tell me, that I may know; for there is none to redeem it beside thee; and I am after thee.' And he said: 'I will redeem it.' Then said Boaz: 'What day thou buyest the field of the band of Naomi—hast thou also bought of Ruth the Moabitess, the wife of the dead, to raise up the name of the dead upon his inheritance?'

*   *   *

And Boaz said unto the elders, and unto all the people: 'Ye are witnesses this day, that I have bought all that was Elimelech's, and all that was Chilion's and Mahlon's, of the hand of Naomi. Moreover Ruth the Moabitess, the wife of Mahlon, have I acquired to be my wife, to raise up the name of the dead upon his inheritance, that the name of the dead be not cut off from among his brethren, and from the gate of his place; ye are witnesses this day.' . . . So Boaz took Ruth, and she became his wife; and he went in unto her, and the LORD gave her conception, and she bore a son. And the women said unto Naomi: 'Blessed be the LORD, who hath not left thee this day without a near kinsman, and let his name be famous in Israel. And he shall be unto thee a restorer of life, and a nourisher of thine old age; for thy daughter-in-law, who loveth thee, who is better to thee than seven sons, hath borne him.' And Naomi took the child, and laid it in her bosom, and became nurse unto it. And the women her neighbours gave it a name, saying: 'There is a son born to Naomi'; and they called his name Obed; he is the father of Jesse, the father of David.

ANONYMOUS (*Chinese, c. 551–479 B.C.E.*)

CHAPTER I: THE GENERAL THEME

Chung-ni [Confucius], was at leisure, and Tseng Tzu attended him. The Master said: "The early kings possessed the supreme virtue and the basic Tao for the regulation of the world. On account of this, the people lived in peace and harmony; neither superiors nor inferiors had any complaints. Do you know this?"

Tseng Tzu rose from his seat and said: "How can Sheng [Tseng Tzu], dull of intelligence, know this?"

The Master said: "Filial piety is the basis of virtue and the source of culture. Sit down again, and I will explain it to you. The body and the limbs, the hair and the skin, are given to one by one's parents, and to them no injury should come; this is where filial piety begins. To establish oneself and practice the Tao is to immortalize one's name and thereby to glorify one's parents; this is where filial piety ends. Thus filial piety commences with service to parents; it proceeds with service to the sovereign; it is completed by the establishment of one's own personality.

"In the Shih [Book of Odes] it is said:

> May you think of your ancestors,
> And so cultivate their virtues!"

CHAPTER VI: THE COMMON PEOPLE

In order to support their parents, they follow the Tao of Heaven; they utilize the earth in accordance with the quality of its soil, and they are prudent and frugal in their expenditure. This is the filial piety of the common people.

Therefore, from the Son of Heaven down to the common people, there has never been one on whom, if filial piety was not pursued from the beginning to end, disasters did not befall.

CHAPTER IX: GOVERNMENT BY THE SAGE

Tseng Tzu said: "I venture to ask whether in the virtue of the sage there is anything that surpasses filial piety."

The Master said: "It is the nature of Heaven and earth that man is the most honorable of all beings. Of all human conduct none is greater than filial piety. In filial piety nothing is greater than to revere one's father. In revering one's father, nothing is greater than making him a peer in Heaven. The Duke of Chou did this. Formerly the Duke of Chou sacrificed to Hou Chi in the suburbs as the peer of Heaven. He sacrificed to King Wen [his father] at the Ming T'ang [Bright Temple] as the peer of Shang Ti [Supreme Being]. Therefore, all the feudal princes within the four seas came, each with his tribute, to join in the sacrifices. How can there be anything in the virtue of the sage that surpasses filial piety?

"Affection is fostered by parents during childhood, and from there springs the child's reverence, which grows daily, while sustaining his parents. The sage was to follow this innate development by teaching reverence and to follow this innate feeling of affection by teaching love. Thus, the teachings of the sage, though not stringent, were followed, and his government, though not rigorous, was well ordered. All this was brought about because of this innate disposition.

"The Tao of father and son is rooted in the Heaven-endowed nature, and develops into the equity between sovereign and ministers. Parents give one life; no bond is stronger. They bring up and care for their child; no kindness is greater. Therefore, one who does not love one's parents, but others, acts to the detriment of virtue. One who does not revere one's parents, but others, acts to the detriment of li. Should the rules of conduct be modeled on such perversity the people would have no true norm by which to abide. Therein is found no goodness but only evil. Although such a person may gain a high position, the chün tzu will not esteem him.

"The chün-tzu is not like this. His speech is consistent with the Tao, his action with what is good. His virtuous equity is respected: his administration is commendable; his demeanor is pleasing; his movements are proper. In this way he governs the people, and therefore they look upon him with awe and love—make him their model and follow him. Thus he is able to realize his virtuous teachings and to carry out his edicts and orders.

"In the Shih it is said:

The chün-tzu our princely lord—
His fine demeanor is without fault."

CHAPTER X: THE PRACTICE OF FILIAL PIETY

The Master said: "In serving his parents, a filial son reveres them in daily life; he makes them happy while he nourishes them; he takes anxious care of them in sickness; he shows great sorrow over their death; and he sacrifices to them with solemnity. When he has performed these five duties, he has truly served his parents.

"He who really serves his parents will not be proud in a high position; he will not be rebellious in an inferior position; among the multitude he will not be contentious. To be proud in a high position is to be ruined; to be rebellious in an inferior position is to insure punishment; to be contentious among the multitude is to bring about violence. As long as these three evils are not discarded, a son cannot be called filial, even though he treats his parents daily with the three kinds of meat."

CHAPTER XVIII: MOURNING FOR PARENTS

The Master said: "In mourning for his parents, a filial son weeps without wailing, he observes funeral rites without heeding his personal appearance, he speaks without regard for eloquence, he finds no comfort in fine clothing, he feels no joy on hearing music, he has no appetite for good food; all this is the innate expression of grief and sorrow. After three days, he breaks his fast, so as to teach the people that the dead should not hurt the living and that disfigurement should not destroy life; this is the rules of the sages. Mourning only extends to the period of three years, so as to show the people that sorrow comes to an end.

"The body, dressed in fine robes, is placed in the encased coffin. The sacrificial vessels are set out with grief and sorrow. Beating the breasts and stamping the feet, weeping and wailing, the mourners escort the coffin to the resting-place selected by divination. A shrine is built, and there offerings are made to the spirits. Spring and autumn sacrificial rites are performed, for the purpose of thinking about them at the proper season.

"When parents are alive, they are served with love and reverence; when they are dead, they are mourned with grief and sorrow. This is the performance of man's supreme duty, fulfillment of the mutual affection between the living and the dead, and the accomplishment of the filial son's service to his parents."

From *The Book of Filial Piety*, Confucian Era

MUHAMMAD (*Arabian/Islamic, c. 570–632 C.E.*)

To every young person who honoureth the old, on account of their age, may God appoint those who shall honour him in his years.

Verily, to honour an old man is showing respect to God.

From *The Sayings of Muhammad*, 1941

LIN YUTANG (*Chinese, 1895–1976*)

The Chinese family system, as I conceive it, is largely an arrangement of particular provision for the young and the old, for since childhood and youth and old age occupy half of our life, it is important that the young and the old live a satisfactory life. It is true that the young are more helpless and can take less care of themselves, but on the other hand, they can get along better without material comforts than the old people. A child is often scarcely aware of material hardships, with the result that a poor child is often as happy as, if not happier than, a rich child. He may go barefooted, but that is a comfort, rather than a hardship to him, whereas going barefooted is often an intolerable hardship for old people. This comes from the child's greater vitality, the bounce of youth. He may have his temporary sorrows, but how easily he forgets them. He has no idea of money and no millionaire complex, as the old man has. At the worst, he collects only cigar coupons for buying a pop-gun, whereas the dowager collects Liberty Bonds. Between the fun of these two kinds of collection there is no comparison. The reason is the child is not yet intimidated by life as all grown-ups are. His personal habits are as yet unformed and he is not a slave to a particular brand of coffee, and he takes whatever comes along. He has very little racial prejudice and absolutely no religious prejudice. His thoughts and ideas have not fallen into certain ruts. Therefore, strange as it may seem, old people are even more dependent than the young because their fears are more definite and their desires are more delimited.

Something of this tenderness toward old age existed already in the primeval consciousness of the Chinese people, a feeling that I can compare only to the Western chivalry and feeling of tenderness toward women. If the early Chinese people had any chivalry, it was manifested not toward women and children, but toward the old people. That feeling of chivalry found clear expression in Mencius in some such saying as, "The people with grey hair should not be seen carrying burdens on the street," which was expressed as the final goal of a good government. Mencius also described the four classes of the world's most helpless people as: "The widows, widowers, orphans and old people without children." Of these four classes the first two were to be taken care of by a political economy which should be so arranged that there would be no unmarried men and women. What was to be done about the orphans Mencius did not say, so far as we know, although orphanages have always existed throughout the ages, as well as pensions for old people. Every one realizes, however, that orphanages and old age pensions are poor substitutes for the home. The feeling is that the home alone can provide anything resembling a satisfactory arrangement for the old and the young. But for the young, it is to be taken for granted that not much need be said, since there is natural paternal affection. "Water flows downwards and not upwards," the Chinese always say, and therefore the affection for parents and grandparents is something that stands more in need of being taught by culture. A natural man loves his children, but a cultured man loves his parents. In the end, the teaching of love and respect for old people became a generally accepted principle, and if we are to believe some of the writers, the desire to have the privilege of serving their parents in their old age actually became a consuming passion. The greatest regret a Chinese gentleman could have was the eternally lost opportunity of servng his old parents with medicine and soup on their deathbed, or not to be present when they died. For a high official in his fifties or sixties not to be able to invite his parents to come from their native village and stay with his family at the capital, "seeing them to bed every night and greeting them every morning," was to commit a moral sin of which he should be ashamed and for which he had constantly to offer excuses and explanations to his friends and colleagues. This regret was expressed in two lines by a man who returned too late to his home when his parents had already died:

> The tree desires repose, but the wind will not stop;
> The son desires to serve, but his parents are already gone.

It is to be assumed that if man were to live this life like a poem, he would be able to look upon the sunset of his life as his happiest period, and instead of trying to postpone the much feared old age, be able actually to look forward to it, and gradually build up to it as the best and happiest period of his existence. In my efforts to compare and contrast Eastern and Western life, I have found no differences that are absolute except in this matter of the attitude towards age, which is sharp and clearcut and permits of no intermediate positions. The differences in our attitude towards sex, toward women, and toward work, play and achievement are all relative. The relationship between husband and wife in China is not essentially different from that in the West, nor even the relationship between parent and child. Not even the ideas of individual liberty and democracy and the relationship between the people and their ruler are, after all, so very different. But in the matter of our attitude toward age, the difference is absolute, and the East and the West take exactly opposite points of view. This is clearest in the matter of asking about a person's age or telling one's own. In China, the first question a person asks the other on an official call, after asking about his name and surname is, "What is your glorious age?" If the person replies apologetically that he is twenty-three or twenty-eight, the other party generally comforts him by saying that he has still a glorious future, and that one day he may become old. But if the person replies that he is thirty-five or thirty-eight, the other party immediately exclaims with deep respect, "Good luck!"; enthusiasm grows in proportion as the gentleman is able to report a higher and higher age, and if the person is anywhere over fifty, the inquirer immediately drops his voice in humility and respect. That is why all old people, if they can, should go and live in China, where even a beggar with a white beard is treated with extra kindness. People in middle age actually look forward to the time when they can celebrate their fifty-first birthday, and in the case of successful merchants or officials, they would celebrate even their forty-first birthday with great pomp and glory. But the fifty-first birthday, or the half-century mark, is an occasion of rejoicing for people of all classes. The sixty-first is a happier and grander occasion than the fifty-first and the seventy-first is still happier and grander, while a man able to celebrate his eighty-first birthday is actually looked upon as one specially favored by heaven. The wearing of a beard becomes a special prerogative of those who have become grandparents, and a man doing so without the necessary qualifications, either of being a grandfather or being on the other side of fifty, stands in danger of being sneered at behind his back. The result is that young men try to pass themselves off as older than they are by imitating the pose and dignity and point of view of the old people, and I have known young Chinese writers graduated from the middle schools, anywhere between twenty-one and twenty-five, writing articles in the magazines to advise what "the young men ought and ought not to read," and discussing the pitfalls of youth with a fatherly condescension.

This desire to grow old and in any case to appear old is understandable when one understands the premium generally placed upon old age in China. In the first place, it is a privilege of the old people to talk, while the young must listen and hold their tongue. "A young man is supposed to have ears and no mouth," as a Chinese saying goes. Men of twenty are supposed to listen when people of thirty are talking, and these in turn are supposed to listen when men of forty are talking. As the desire to talk and to be listened to is almost universal, it is evident that the further along one gets in years, the better chance he has to talk and to be listened to when he goes about in society. It is a game of life in which no one is favored, for everyone has a chance of becoming old in his time. Thus a father lecturing his son is obliged to stop suddenly and change his demeanor the moment the grandmother opens her mouth. Of course he wishes to be in the grandmother's place. And it is quite fair, for what right have the young to open their mouth when the old men can say, "I have crossed more bridges than you have crossed streets!" What right have the young got to talk?

"On Growing Old Gracefully," in *The Importance of Living*, 1937

ROBERT SOUTHEY (*English, 1774–1843*)

"You are old, father William," the
young man cried,
"The few locks which are left you
are grey;
You are hale, father William, a
hearty old man;
Now tell me the reason, I pray."

"In the days of my youth," father
William replied,
"I remember'd that youth would
fly fast,
And abus'd not my health and my
vigour at first,
That I never might need them at
last."

"You are old, father William," the
young man cried,
"And pleasures with youth pass
away.
And yet you lament not the days that
are gone;
Now tell me the reason, I pray."

"In the days of my youth," father
William replied,
"I remember'd that youth could
not last;
I thought of the future, whatever I
did,
That I never might grieve for the
past."

"You are old, father William," the
young man cried,

"And life must be hast'ning away;
You are cheerful and love to converse
upon death;
Now tell me the reason, I pray."

"I am cheerful, young man," father
William replied,
"Let the cause thy attention
engage;
In the days of my youth I
remember'd my God!
And He hath not forgotten my
age."

"The Old Man's Comforts and How He Gained Them," 1799

LEWIS CARROLL (*English, 1832–1898*)

"You are old, Father William," the young man said,
"And your hair has become very white;
And yet you incessantly stand on your head—
Do you think, at your age, it is right?"

"In my youth," Father William replied to his son,
"I feared it might injure the brain;
But now that I'm perfectly sure I have none,
Why, I do it again and again."

"You are old," said the youth, "as I mentioned before,
And have grown most uncommonly fat;
Yet you turned a back somersault in at the door—
Pray, what is the reason of that?"

"In my youth," said the sage, as he shook his grey locks,
"I kept all my limbs very supple
By the use of this ointment—one shilling the box—
Allow me to sell you a couple."

"You are old," said the youth, "and your jaws are too weak
For anything tougher than suet;
Yet you finished the goose, with the bones and the beak—
Pray, how did you manage to do it?"

"In my youth," said his father, "I took to the law,
And argued each case with my wife;

113

And the muscular strength, which it gave to my jaw,
  Has lasted the rest of my life."

"You are old," said the youth; "one would hardly suppose
  That your eye was as steady as ever;
Yet you balanced an eel on the end of your nose—
  What made you so awfully clever?"

"I have answered three questions, and that is enough,"
  Said his father; "don't give yourself airs!
Do you think I can listen all day to such stuff?
  Be off, or I'll kick you down stairs!"

"You are old, Father William," 1865

THE BROTHERS GRIMM (*German; Jacob, 1785–1863, Wilhelm, 1786–1859*)

There was once a very old man whose eyes had grown dim, his ears deaf, and whose knees shook. When he sat at the table hardly able to hold his spoon he'd spill soup on the tablecloth, and a little would even run out of his mouth. This disgusted his son and his daughter-in-law, and so finally the old grandfather had to sit in a corner behind the stove. They gave him his food in an earthenware bowl and not even enough at that. He used to look sadly toward the table, and tears would come to his eyes. One day his trembling hands couldn't even hold the bowl, and it fell to the floor and broke to pieces. The young woman scolded, but he said nothing and merely sighed. For a few farthings she then bought him a wooden bowl, and he had to eat out of that. As they were sitting thus, his little four-year-old grandson was fitting some little boards together on the floor. "What are you doing there?" asked his father. "I'm making a trough for father and mother to eat out of when I'm grown up," answered the child.

The husband and wife looked at one another for a while, finally began to weep, and at once brought the old grandfather to the table. From then they always let him eat with them, and they didn't say anything even when he did spill a little.

"The Old Grandfather and the Grandson," first half of the nineteenth century

LI MI (*Chinese, Tsin Dynasty, 265–316 C.E.*)

Your subject Mi pleads:
  It was fated that I would have various disasters and ills in life. When I was only six months old, my kind father died. When I was just four years

old, my maternal uncle coerced my mother into a second marriage. My grandmother, Liu, grieved at my helpless orphanage, brought me up with maternal care. And in my early years, I was so entangled with a diversity of sicknesses that even at the age of nine I could not walk. In such solitude and misery did I grow up.

I am not only devoid of uncles, but also devoid of brothers; my family has been poor, and I have not been blessed with any children until late in my age. Abroad I have no distant relatives upon whom I can rely, while at home there is no boy servant, five feet in stature, to answer the door. Thus being solitary and desolate, my body and shadow grieve sympathetically with each other. Moreover, my grandmother has long been sick and confined to bed all the time. In the matter of medicine and diet, I have to attend to her with constancy.

Since the beginning of the present dynasty, I have been benefited by its virtuous rule. At one time, through the recommendation of Prefect Kuei, I was accorded the degree of *Hsiao-lin,* and at another, through that of Governor Yung, the degree of *Hsiu-tsai* was conferred on me. However, because no one would take care of my grandmother, I had to decline these honors. Then an imperial decree was issued appointing me secretary to the court and was soon followed by another decree transferring me to the post of an attendant to the Crown Prince. It was indeed too great an honor for me, as a man of humble birth, to serve His Highness. Hence I would wear my body smooth for the sake of repaying Your Majesty's kindness. However, I have to submit a memorial declining, as before, the assumption of office.

Now the imperial decree in a rather severe tone has reprimanded me as being evasive and tardy. The district officials keep urging me to take to the road, while those of the prefect beset my door in fiery impatience. Shall I accept the decree to hasten away? There is my grandmother whose sickness becomes worse day by day. Shall I persist in my personal wish? All my requests have been rejected. Such being the case, I am now in a stalemate, knowing not what to do.

In my humble opinions, the present enlightened dynasty makes filial piety the governing principle of the empire. So the aged and the infirm are afforded consolation and support. How much more deserving of these am I, who have been more desolate and wretched? Again, in my youth, I served the previous dynasty and held a ministerial post. I wish I could pursue official distinctions, without regard to the fame of pure conduct. At present, I am but a worthless captive of the conquered dynasty, being mean and insignificant. However, Your Majesty confers promotions and honors on me. How should I dare to be hesitant and expect greater honors? But my grandmother is now in the sunset of her days, and, with faint breath, she seems likely to come to the end of her life at every moment. Without my grandmother, I would not have been able to live today, and without me, my grandmother would have no one to comfort her old age. In fact, we, grandmother and grandson, have been depending upon each other for life. This is my humble reason why I cannot leave her behind.

I am now forty-four years old, and my grandmother is reaching her ninety-sixth year. Thus I have more days to serve Your Majesty with loyalty than to repay my grandmother with filiality. As a little crow seeks to show its gratitude to the mother bird, I beg to be allowed to serve my grandmother to the end of her life. As to the misfortunes of my life, not only are the inhabitants of the district and the county magistrates thereof my witnesses, but the Supreme Heaven and August Earth take cognizance of them as well.

Wherefore, I wish that Your Majesty may take pity on my puerile sincerity and grant my humble request, so that my grandmother can fortunately complete her span of life. Then I shall hold my life at your disposal while living, and afford your protection by "tying grass" [to entangle enemy's feet in battle]. With my mind kept in fear and trembling, I respectfully submit this memorial to Your Majesty for consideration.

"A Pleading Memorial," third century c.e.

JAPANESE FOLK LEGEND (*eleventh century*)

In ancient times there prevailed a custom of abandoning old people when they reached the age of sixty. Once an old man was going to be abandoned on a mountain. He was carried there in a sedan chair by his two sons. On the way the old man broke the branches of the trees. "Why do you do such a thing? Do you break the branches in order to recognize the way to come back after we leave you on the mountain?" asked the sons. The old father just recited a poem!

> "To break branches in the mountain
> Is for the dear children
> For whom I am ready to sacrifice myself."

The brothers did not think much about their father's poem, and took him up the mountain and abandoned him. "We shall go another way to return home," they said, and started on the way back.

The sun set in the west, but they could not find the way home. Meanwhile the moon came up and shone on the mountain. The two sons had no recourse but to return to their father. "What have you been doing until now?" he asked. "We tried to go back by a different way, but we could not get home. Please kindly tell us the way." So they carried the father again and went down the mountain, following their father's instructions, according to where he had broken the branches. When the brothers returned home, they hid their father under the floor. They gave him food every day and showed their gratitude for his love.

Some time afterward the lord issued a notice to the people to make a rope with ashes and present it to him. The people tried to make a rope by mixing ashes and water but no one could do it. Then the two brothers talked about this to the old father. The father said: "Moisten straw with salty water and make a rope of the straw; then after it is dried, burn it and present the ashes to the lord in the shape of a rope."

The brothers did just as he told them and presented the ash-rope to the lord. The lord was much pleased and said: "I feel very secure in having such wise men in my country. How is it that you possess such wisdom?" The two brothers explained in detail about their father. The lord heard them out, and then gave notice to all the country that none should abandon old people thereafter. The two brothers returned home with many rewards, which delighted the old father.

The place where the old father was abandoned is said to be Obasute-yama, the Mountain of Abandoned Old People.

"The Mountain of Abandoned Old People"

VALENTE MALANGATANA (*Mozambican, b. 1936*)

Into your arms I came
when you bore me, very anxious
you, who were so alarmed
at that monstrous moment
fearing that God might take me.
Everyone watched in silence
to see if the birth was going well
everyone washed their hands
to be able to receive the one who came from Heaven
and all the women were still and afraid.
But when I emerged
from the place where you sheltered me so long
at once I drew my first breath
at once you cried out with joy
the first kiss was my grandmother's.
And she took me at once to the place
where they kept me, hidden away

everyone was forbidden to enter my room
because everyone smelt bad
and I all fresh, fresh
breathed gently, wrapped in my napkins.
But grandmother, who seemed like a madwoman,
always looking and looking again
because the flies came at me
and the mosquitoes harried me
God who also watched over me
was my old granny's friend.

"To the Anxious Mother," c. 1960

BARBARA MacDONALD (*American, b. 1912*)

From the beginning of this wave of the women's movement, from the beginning of Women's Studies, the message has gone out to those of us over 60 that your "Sisterhood" does not include us, that those of you who are younger see us as men see us—that is, as women who used to be women but aren't any more. You do not see us in our present lives, you do not identify with our issues, you exploit us, you patronize us, you stereotype us. Mainly you ignore us.

Has it never occurred to younger women activists as you organized around "women's" issues, that old women are raped, that old women are battered, that old women are poor, that old women perform unpaid work in the home and out of the home, that old women are exploited by male medical practitioners, that old women are in jail, are political prisoners, that old women have to deal with racism, classism, homophobia, anti-semitism? I open your feminist publications and not once have I read of any group of younger women enraged or marching or organizing legal support because of anything that happened to an old woman. I have to read the *L.A. Times* or *Ageing International* to find out what's happening to the women of my generation, and the news is not good. I have to read these papers to find out that worldwide old women are the largest adult poverty group, or that 44 percent of old Black women are poor, or about the battering of old women, about the conditions in public housing for the elderly in which almost all of the residents are women, or that old women in nursing homes are serving as guinea pigs for experimental drugs—a practice forbidden years ago for prison inmates.

But activists are not alone in their ageism. Has it never occurred to those of you in Women's Studies as you ignore the meaning and the politics of the lives of women beyond our reproductive years, that this is male thinking? Has it never occurred to you as you build feminist theory that ageism is a central feminist issue?

*   *   *

Meanwhile, as the numbers of old women rapidly increase, the young women you taught five years ago are now in the helping professions as geriatricians and social workers because the jobs are there. They still call themselves feminists but, lacking any kind of feminist analysis of women's aging from your classrooms, they are defining old women as needy, simple-minded, and helpless—definitions that correlate conveniently with the services and salaries they have in mind . . .

But it is worse than that. For you yourselves—activists and academicians—do not hesitate to exploit us. We take in the fact that you come to us for "oral histories"—for your own agendas, to learn *your* feminist or lesbian or working-class or ethnic histories—with not the slightest interest in our present struggles as old women. You come to fill in some much-needed data for a thesis, or to justify a grant for some "service" for old women that imitates the mainstream and which you plan to direct, or you come to get material for a biography of our friends and lovers. But you come not as equals, not with any knowledge of who we are, what our issues may be. You come to old women who have been serving young women for a lifetime and ask to be served one more time, and then you cover up your embarrassment as you depart by saying that you felt as though we were your grandmother or your mother or your aunt. And no one in the sisterhood criticizes you for such acts.

But let me say it to you clearly: We are not your mothers, your grandmothers, or your aunts. And we will never build a true women's movement until we can organize together as equals, woman to woman, without the burden of these family roles.

Mother. Grandmother. Aunt. It should come as no surprise to us that ageism has its roots in patriarchal family.

*   *   *

But if we are to understand ageism, we have no choice but to bring family again under the lens of a feminist politic. In the past, we examined the father as oppressor, we examined his oppression of the mother and the daughters, in great detail we examined the mother as oppressor of the daughters, but what has never come under the feminist lens is the daughters' oppression of the mother—that woman who by definition is older than we are.

The source of your ageism, the reason why you see older women as there to serve you, comes from family. It was in patriarchal family that you learned

119

that mother is there to serve you, her child, that serving you is her purpose in life. This is not woman's definition of motherhood. This is man's definition of motherhood, a male myth enforced in family and which you still believe—to your peril and mine. It infantilizes you and it erases me.

From the speech "Outside the Sisterhood: Ageism in Women's Studies," 1985

WILLIAM SHAKESPEARE (*English, 1564–1616*)

Crabbed age and youth cannot live together:
Youth is full of pleasance, age is full of care;
Youth like summer morn, age like winter weather;
Youth like summer brave, age like winter bare.
Youth is full of sport, age's breath is short;
Youth is nimble, age is lame;
Youth is hot and bold, age is weak and cold;
Youth is wild, and age is tame;
Age, I do abhor thee; youth I do adore thee;
O, my love, my love is young!
Age, I do defy thee: O, sweet shepherd, hie thee
For methinks thou stay'st too long.

From *The Passionate Pilgrim*, c. 1590

BERNARD COOPER (*American, b. 1951*)

It has been nearly a year since my father fell while picking plums. The bruises on his leg have healed, and except for a vague absence of pigmentation where the calf had blistered, his recovery is complete. Back in the habit of evening constitutionals, he navigates the neighborhood with his usual stride—"Brisk," he says, "for a man of eighty-five"—dressed in a powder blue jogging suit that bears the telltale stains of jelly doughnuts and Lipton tea, foods which my father, despite doctor's orders, hasn't the will to forsake.

He broke his glasses and his hearing aid in the fall, and when I first stepped into the hospital room for a visit, I was struck by the way my father—head cocked to hear, squinting to see—looked so much older and more remote, a prisoner of his failing senses. "Boychik?" he asked, straining his face in my general direction. He fell back into a stack of pillows, sighed a deep sigh, and without my asking described what had happened:

"There they are, all over the lawn. Purple plums, dozens of them. They look delicious. So what am I supposed to do? Let the birds eat them? Not on your life. It's my tree, right? First I fill a bucket with the ones from the ground. Then I get the ladder out of the garage. I've climbed the thing a hundred times before. I make it to the top, reach out my hand, and . . . who knows what happens. Suddenly I'm an astronaut. Up is down and vice versa. It happened so fast I didn't have time to piss in my pants. I'm flat on my back, not a breath in me. Couldn't have called for help if I tried. And the pain in my leg—you don't want to know."

"Who found you?"

"What?"

I move closer, speak louder.

"Nobody found me," he says, exasperated. "Had to wait till I could get up on my own. It seemed like hours. I'm telling you, I thought it was all over. But eventually I could breathe normal again and—don't ask me how; God only knows—I got in the car and drove here myself." My father shifted his weight and grimaced. The sheet slid off his injured leg, the calf swollen, purple as a plum, what the doctor called "an insult to the tissue."

Throughout my boyhood my father possessed a surplus of energy, or it possessed him. On weekdays he worked hard at the office, and on weekends he gardened in our yard. He was also a man given to unpredicatable episodes of anger. These rages were never precipitated by a crisis—in the face of illness or accident my father remained steady, methodical, even optimistic; when the chips were down he was an incorrigible joker, an inveterate back-slapper, a sentry at the bedside—but something as simple as a drinking glass left out on the table could send him into a frenzy of invective. Spittle shot from his lips. Blood ruddied his face. He'd hurl the glass against the wall.

His temper rarely intimidated my mother. She'd light a Tareyton, stand aside, and watch my father flail and shout until he was purged of the last sharp word. Winded and limp, he'd flee into the living room, where he would draw the shades, sit in his wing chair, and brood for hours.

Even as a boy, I understood how my father's profession had sullied his view of the world, had made him a wary man, prone to explosions. He spent hours taking depositions from jilted wives and cuckolded husbands. He conferred with a miserable clientele: spouses who wept, who spat accusations, who pounded his desk in want of revenge. At the time, California law required that grounds for divorce be proven in court, and toward this end my father carried in his briefcase not only the usual legal tablets and manila files but bills for motel rooms, matchbooks from bars, boxer shorts blooming with lipstick stains.

After one particularly long and vindictive divorce trial, he agreed to a weekend out of town. Mother suggested Palm Springs, rhapsodized about the balmy air, the cacti lit by colored lights, the street named after Bob Hope. When it finally came time to leave, however, my mother kept thinking of things she forgot to pack. No sooner would my father begin to back the car out of the driveway than my mother would shout for him to stop, dash into the house, and retrieve what she needed. A carton of Tareytons. An aerosol can of Solarcaine. A paperback novel to read by the pool. I sat in the back-seat, motionless and mute; with each of her excursions back inside, I felt my father's frustration mount. When my mother insisted she get a package of Saltine crackers in case we got hungry along the way, my father glared at her, bolted from the car, wrenched every piece of luggage from the trunk, and slammed it shut with such a vengeance the car rocked on its springs.

Through the rear window, my mother and I could see him fling two suitcases, a carryall, and a makeup case yards above his balding head. The sky was a huge and cloudless blue; gray chunks of luggage sailed through it, twisting and spinning and falling to earth like the burned-out stages of a booster rocket. When a piece of luggage crashed back to the asphalt, he'd pick it up and hurl it again. With every effort, an involuntary, animal grunt issued from the depths of his chest.

Finally, the largest suitcase came unlatched in mid-flight. Even my father was astonished when articles of his wife's wardrobe began their descent from the summer sky. A yellow scarf dazzled the air like a tangible strand of sunlight. Fuzzy slippers tumbled down. One diaphanous white slip drifted over the driveway and, as if guided by an invisible hand, draped itself across a hedge. With that, my father barreled by us, veins protruding on his temple and neck, and stomped into the house. "I'm getting tired of this," my mother grumbled. Before she stooped to pick up the mess—a vast and random geography of clothes—she flicked her cigarette onto the asphalt and ground the ember out.

One evening, long after I'd moved away from home, I received a phone call from my father telling me that my mother had died the night before. "But I didn't know it happened," he said.

He'd awakened as usual that morning, ruminating over a case while he showered and shaved. My mother appeared to be sound asleep, one arm draped across her face, eyes sheltered beneath the crook of her elbow. When he sat on the bed to pull up his socks, he'd tried not to jar the mattress and wake her. At least he *thought* he'd tried not to wake her, but he couldn't remember, he couldn't be sure. Things looked normal, he kept protesting—the pillow, the blanket, the way she lay there. He decided to grab a doughnut downtown and left in a hurry. But that night my father returned to a house suspiciously unlived-in. The silence caused him to clench his fists, and he called for his wife—"Lillian, Lillian"—as he drifted through quiet, unlit rooms, walking slowly up the stairs.

I once saw a photograph of a woman who had jumped off the Empire

State Building and landed on the roof of a parked car. What is amazing is that she appears merely to have leapt into satin sheets, to be deep in a languid and absolute sleep. Her eyes are closed, lips slightly parted, hair fanned out on a metal pillow. Nowhere is there a trace of blood, her body caught softly in its own impression.

As my father spoke into the telephone, his voice about to break—"I should have realized. I should have known"—that's the state in which I pictured my mother: a long fall of sixty years, an uncanny landing, a miraculous repose.

My father and I had one thing in common after my mother's heart attack: we each maintained a secret life. Secret, at least, from each other.

I'd fallen for a man named Travis Mask. Travis had recently arrived in Los Angeles from Kentucky, and everything I was accustomed to—the billboards lining the Sunset strip, the 7-Elevens open all night—stirred in him a strong allegiance; "I love this town," he'd say every day. Travis's job was to collect change from food vending machines throughout the city. During dinner he would tell me about the office lobbies and college cafeterias he had visited, the trick to opening different machines, the noisy cascade of nickles and dimes. Travis Mask was enthusiastic. Travis Mask was easy to please. In bed I called him by his full name because I found the sound of it exciting.

My father, on the other hand, had fallen for a woman whose identity he meant to keep secret. I knew of her existence only because of a dramatic change in his behavior: he would grow mysterious as quickly and inexplicably as he had once grown angry. Though I resented being barred from this central fact of my father's life, I had no intention of telling him I was gay. It had taken me thirty years to achieve even a modicum of intimacy with the man, and I didn't want to risk a setback. It wasn't as if I was keeping my sexual orientation a secret; I'd told relatives, co-workers, friends. But my father was a man who whistled at waitresses, flirted with bank tellers, his head swiveling like a radar dish toward the nearest pair of breasts and hips. Ever since I was a child my father reminded me of the wolf in cartoons whose ears shoot steam, whose eyes pop out on springs, whose tongue unfurls like a party favor whenever he sees a curvaceous dame. As far as my father was concerned, desire for women fueled the world, compelled every man without exception—his occupation testified to that—was a force as essential as gravity. I didn't want to disappoint him.

Eventually, Travis Mask was transferred to Long Beach. In his absence my nights grew long and ponderous, and I tried to spend more time with my father in the belief that sooner or later an opportunity for disclosure would present itself. We met for dinner once a month in a restaurant whose interior was dim and crimson, our interaction friendly but formal, both of us cautiously skirting the topic of our private lives; we'd become expert at the ambiguous answer, the changed subject, the half-truth. Should my father ask if I was dating, I'd tell him yes, I had been seeing someone. I'd liked them very much, I said, but they were transferred to another city. Them. They. My attempt to neuter the pronouns made it sound as if I were courting people en masse. Just when I thought this subterfuge was becoming obvious, my father began to respond in kind: "Too bad I didn't get a chance to meet them. Where did you say they went?"

Avoidance also worked in reverse: "And how about you, Dad? Are you seeing anybody?"

"Seeing? I don't know if you'd call it *seeing*. What did you order, chicken or fish?"

During one dinner we discovered that we shared a fondness for nature programs on television, and from that night on, when we'd exhausted our comments about the meal or the weather, we'd ask if the other had seen the show about the blind albino fish who live in underwater caves, or the one about the North American moose whose antlers, coated with green moss, provide camouflage in the underbrush. My father and I had adapted like those creatures to the strictures of our shared world.

And then I met her.

I looked up from a rack of stationery at the local Thrify one afternoon and there stood my father with a willowy black woman in her early forties. As she waited for a prescription to be filled, he drew a finger through her hair, nuzzled the nape of her neck, the refracted light of his lenses causing his cheeks to glow. I felt like a child who was witness to something forbidden: his father's helpless, unguarded ardor for an unfamiliar woman. I didn't know whether to run or stay. Had he always been attracted to young black women? Had I ever known him well? Somehow I managed to move myself toward them and mumble hello. They turned around in unison. My father's eyes widened. He reached out and cupped my shoulder, struggled to say my name. Before he could think to introduce us, I shook the woman's hand, startled by its softness. "So you're the son. Where've you been hiding?" She was kind and cordial, though too preoccupied to engage in much conversation, her handsome features furrowed by a hint of melancholy, a sadness which I sensed had little to do with my surprise appearance. Anna excused herself when the pharmacist called her name.

Hours after our encounter, I could still feel the softness of Anna's hand, the softness that stirred my father's yearning. He was seventy-five years old, myopic and hard of hearing, his skin loose and liver-spotted, but one glimpse of his implusive public affection led me to the conclusion that my father possessed, despite his age, a restless sexual energy. The meeting left me elated, expectant. My father and I had something new in common: the pursuit of our unorthodox passions. We were, perhaps, more alike than I'd realized. After years of relative estrangement, I'd been given grounds for a fresh start, a chance to establish a stronger connection.

But none of my expectations mattered. Later that week, they left the country.

The prescription, it turned out, was for a psychotropic drug. Anna had battled bouts of depression since childhood. Her propensity for unhappiness gave my father a vital mission: to make her laugh, to wrest her from despair. Anna worked as an elementary-school substitute teacher and managed a few rental properties in South-Central Los Angeles, but after weeks of functioning normally, she would take to my father's bed for days on end, blank and immobile beneath the quilt she had bought to brighten up the room, unaffected by his jokes, his kisses and cajoling. These spells of depression came without warning and ended just as unexpectedly. Though they both did their best to enjoy each other during the periods of relative calm, they lived, my father later lamented, like people in a thunderstorm, never knowing when lightning would strike. Thinking that a drastic change might help Anna shed a recent depression, they pooled their money and flew to Europe.

They returned with snapshots showing the two of them against innumerable backdrops: the Tower of London, the Vatican, Versailles; monuments, obelisks, statuary. In every pose their faces were unchanged, the faces of people who want to be happy, who try to be happy, and somehow can't.

As if in defiance of all the photographic evidence against them, they were married the following month at the Church of the Holy Trinity. I was one of only two guests at the wedding. The other was an uncle of Anna's. Before the ceremony began, he shot me a glance which attested, I was certain, to an incredulity as great as mine. The vaulted chapel rang with prerecorded organ music, an eerie and pious overture. Light filtered through stained-glass windows, chunks of sweet color that reminded me of Jell-O. My old Jewish father and his Episcopalian lover appeared at opposite ends of the dais, walking step by measured step toward a union in the center. The priest, swimming in white vestments, was somber and almost inaudible. Cryptic gestures, odd props; I watched with a powerful, wordless amazement. Afterward, as if the actual wedding hadn't been surreal enough, my father and Anna formed a kind of receiving line (if two people can constitute a line) in the church parking lot, where the four of us, bathed by hazy sunlight, exchanged pleasantries before the newlyweds returned home for a nap; their honeymoon in Europe, my father joked, had put the cart before the horse.

During the months after the wedding, when I called my father, he answered as though the ringing of the phone had been an affront. When I asked him what the matter was he'd bark, "What makes you think there's something the matter?" I began to suspect that my father's frustration had given rise to those ancient rages. But my father had grown too old and frail to sustain his anger for long. When we saw each other—Anna was always visiting relatives or too busy or tired to join us—he looked worn, embattled, and the pride I had in him for attempting an interracial marriage, for risking condemnation in the eyes of the world, was overwhelmed now by concern. He lost weight. His hands began to shake. I would sit across from him in the dim, red restaurant and marvel that this bewildered man had once hurled glasses against a wall and launched Samsonite into the sky.

Between courses I'd try to distract my father from his problems by pressing him to unearth tidbits of his past, as many as memory would allow. He'd often talk about Atlantic City, where his parents had owned a small grocery. Sometimes my mother turned up in the midst of his sketchy regressions. He would smooth wrinkles from the tablecoth and tell me no one could take her place. He eulogized her loyalty and patience, and I wondered whether he could see her clearly—her auburn hair and freckled hands—wondered whether he wished she were here to sweep up after his current mess. "Remember," he once asked me, without a hint of irony or regret, "what fun we had in Palm Springs?" Then he snapped back into the present and asked what was taking so long with our steaks.

The final rift between my father and Anna must have happened suddenly; she left behind several of her possessions, including the picture of Jesus that sat on the sideboard in the dining room next to my father's brass menorah. And along with Anna's possessions were stacks of leather-bound books, *Law of Torts, California Jurisprudence,* and *Forms of Pleading and Practice,* embossed along their spines. Too weak and distracted to practice law, my father had retired, and the house became a repository for the contents of his former office. I worried about him being alone, wandering through rooms freighted with history, crowded with the evidence of two marriages, fatherhood, and a long and harrowing career; he had nothing to do but pace and sigh and stir up dust. I encouraged him to find a therapist, but as far as my father was concerned, psychiatrists were all conniving witch doctors who fed off the misery of people like Anna.

Brian, the psychotherapist I'd been living with for three years (and live with still), was not at all fazed by my father's aversion to his profession. They'd met only rarely—once we ran into my father at a local supermarket, and twice Brian accompanied us to the restaurant—but when they were together, Brian would draw my father out, compliment him on his plaid pants, ask questions regarding the fine points of law. And when my father spoke, Brian listened intently, embraced him with his cool, blue gaze. My father relished my lover's attention: Brian's cheerfulness and steady disposition must have been refreshing in those troubled, lonely days. "How's that interesting friend of yours?" he sometimes asked. If he was suspicious that Brian and I shared the same house, he never pursued it—until he took his fall from the plum tree.

I drove my father home from the hospital, trying to keep his big unwieldy car, bobbing like a boat, within the lane. I bought him a pair of seersucker shorts because long pants were too painful and constricting. I brought over groceries and my wok, and while I cooked dinner my father sat at the dinette table, leg propped on a vinyl chair, and listened to the hissing oil, happy, abstracted. I helped him up the stairs to his bedroom, where we watched *Wheel of Fortune* and *Jeopardy* on the television and where, for the first time since I was a boy, I sat at his feet and he rubbed my head. It felt so good I'd graze his good leg, contented as a cat. He welcomed my visits with an eagerness bordering on glee and didn't seem to mind being dependent on me for physical assistance; he leaned his bulk on my shoulder wholly, and I felt protective, necessary, inhaling the scents of salve and Old Spice and the base, familiar odor that was all my father's own.

"You know those hostages?" asked my father one evening. He was sitting at the dinette, dressed in the seersucker shorts, his leg propped on the chair. The bruises had faded to lavender, his calf back to its normal size.

I could barely hear him over the broccoli sizzling in the wok. "What about them?" I shouted.

"I heard on the news that some of them are seeing a psychiatrist now that they're back."

"So?"

"Why a psychiatrist?"

I stopped tossing the broccoli. "Dad," I said, "if you'd been held hostage in the Middle East, you might want to see a therapist, too."

The sky dimmed in the kitchen windows. My father's face was a silhouette, his lenses catching the last of the light. "They got their food taken care of, right? And a place to sleep. What's the big deal?"

"You're at gunpoint, for God's sake. A prisoner. I don't think it's like spending a weekend at the Hilton."

"Living alone," he said matter-of-factly, "is like being a prisoner."

I let it stand. I added the pea pods.

"Let me ask you something," said my father. "I get this feeling—I'm not sure how to say it—that something isn't right. That you're keeping something from me. We don't talk much, I grant you that. But maybe now's the time."

127

My heart was pounding. I'd been thoroughly disarmed by his interpretation of world events, his minefield of non sequiturs, and I wasn't prepared for a serious discussion. I switched off the gas. The red jet sputtered. When I turned around, my father was staring at his outstretched leg. "So?" he said.

"You mean Brian?"

"Whatever you want to tell me, tell me."

"You like him, don't you?"

"What's not to like."

"He's been my lover for a long time. He makes me happy. We have a home." Each declaration was a stone in my throat. "I hope you understand. I hope this doesn't come between us."

"Look," said my father without skipping a beat, "you're lucky to have someone. And he's lucky to have you, too. It's no one's business anyway. What the hell else am I going to say?"

But my father thought of something else before I could speak and express my relief. "You know," he said, "when I was a boy of maybe sixteen, my father asked me to hold a ladder while he trimmed the tree in our backyard. So I did, see, when I suddenly remember I have a date with this bee-yoo-tiful girl, and I'm late and I run out of the yard. I don't know what got into me. I'm halfway down the street when I remember my father, and I think, 'Oh, boy. I'm in trouble now.' But when I get back I can hear him laughing way up in the tree. I'd never heard him laugh like that. 'You must like her a lot,' he says when I help him down. Funny thing was, I hadn't told him where I was going."

I pictured my father's father teetering above the earth, a man hugging the trunk of a tree and watching his son run down the street in pursuit of sweet, ineffable pleasure. While my father reminisced, night obscured the branches of the plum tree, the driveway where my mother's clothes once floated down like enormous leaves. When my father finished telling the story, he looked at me, then looked away. A moment of silence lodged between us, an old and obstinate silence. I wondered whether nothing or everything would change. I spooned our food onto separate plates. My father carefully pressed his leg to test the healing flesh.

"Picking Plums: Fathers and Sons and Their Lovers," 1992

LINDA BIRD FRANCKE (*American, b. 1939*)

She had always been an ultimately fastidious person. As a child I wondered at her perfectly manicured fingernails, whose polish never seemed to chip. As if her will were strong enough to dominate anything that touched her person, her stockings never had runs, the seams were always exclamation-point straight, and even the leather heels on her shoes never ran down. Did the wind blow her hair? I search my memory for images of a tousled head just once—but all I can conjure up are perfect curls, sculpted waves or the bouffant style that saw her through to the end.

So the reality of the beginning of my mother's death eight years ago lay quite apart from the doctor's chart, which stated coldly that she had terminal emphysema. She began to look, well, like other people. Her shortness of breath kept her in bed a good part of the time, and her perfect hair began to mat and lie flat in the back. Her chin and upper lip, from which she had meticulously tweezered post-menopausal hairs for years, now were fringed in down and left unplucked.

She began to look like a photo negative that had been washed with yellow. Where once her hair—what is this fixation I have with her hair?— had been blued just enough so that the gray seemed to shimmer, now it went the color of dried egg yolk. Her fingernails, too, with decades of "Fire and Ice" polish removed from them by a no-nonsense nurse, also looked yellow and for once any dirt she had under them showed through. Dirt. Dirty. Those words never had the slightest relevance to my image of my mother. Now her nose showed unmistakable black smudges where the rim of the oxygen mask rested. For the first time in my life, she became vulnerable.

We went through a strange transition. The woman she had been, erect, tailored, spotless, was certainly a woman to be admired, but hardly to love. There had been no room for hugging this perfectly constructed creature for fear that by disarranging even one of her parts, the others might tumble after. Now, as she slouched in a bathrobe which bore dribbles of tea and broth, I could finally get my arms around her. For 35 years, I had longed for physical warmth from this tightly controlled person whom my sister and I incongruously called "Mummy," and finally, ever so gently, I had it. In the vernacular of the day, my mother and I bonded.

I grew possessive of her, this strange new creature whose dependence on me now seemed more than my dependence on her had ever been. To be sure, she had registered nurses around the clock who bustled about, trying to get her to eat and rubbing salve into the raw places on her back where her skin had simply given way. And I watched her struggle to retain the control she always had over her household. Her handwriting grew impossibly spidery on the checks she would write to the nurses, always having to add "R.N." after their names to satisfy her insurance company. But when she began to sign her own name "Janet K. Bird, R.N." I knew I had to take over. And I welcomed it. I would spend two hours a day in her apartment in between my job and my own family eight blocks away, writing checks, making shopping lists, crabbing at the superintendent about the plaster that hung from her living-room ceiling like stalactites. Something inside me began to thaw that last six months. I knew she couldn't hurt me any more. Yet I could hurt her. But I didn't.

Her mind began to wander into fantasy then, seeking refuge from the suffering her body was enduring. The nurses rolled their eyes heavenward and clucked in sorrow during these fantasy forays, but I loved them. It was the first time, after all, that my mother had expressed any whimsy, any sense that order was not all. Her eyesight was going, along with the rest of her body, and she began to see things that were not there. One afternoon she sat in the living room among the plants that friends had sent her, and suddenly announced that "the garden simply did not look right." "How should it look?" I asked her. "This rose bush should be over there," she said, pointing vaguely at a small african violet. I set it down on the rug where she wanted it. "The lillies of the valley belong there," she said. And I put a vase of cut flowers a little farther along on the living-room floor. "Don't be silly, Mrs. Bird," the nurse of the day scolded. "You're not in a garden." "Yes, she is," I hissed at Miss Starch, R.N. And then my mother and I took a little walk around her garden and she smiled. "It's just right now, isn't it?" she said. I agreed, while the nurse clucked and rolled her eyes.

She began to sing, this tiny uptight mother of mine, who had always frowned at any sense of spontaneity. Often now in the afternoons, we would have a chorus or two of "Row, row, row your boat" or "Marezy Doats" and sometimes even the nurse would tentatively enter in. "Oh, it's just terrible," a visitor would say, listening to my mother. "Oh no, indeed, it's wonderful," I would respond. "This must be very hard on you, seeing your mother like this" others would say. Again I would disagree. "I've never seen her so full of life," I said, leaving them, I'm sure, thinking I was madder than my mother. The last time she was ever out of bed she stood in the doorway bracing herself against me and sang the entirety of "Oh, You Beautiful Doll," even belting out the cadence of the last line "oh—oh—oh—oh—oh you BEAU-tiful doll." We applauded. And again she smiled.

She finally, finally died while the nurse was trying to spoon broth into her mouth. I pedaled my bike furiously up Madison Avenue from my job, but I was too late. But it didn't matter really. I sat for a while with my mother/child, child/mother and then called my sister in London to tell her it was finally over. And that was that. My mother was at peace. And so was I.

"Loving Mother, at Last," 1981

CARTER CATLETT WILLIAMS (*American, b. 1923*)

My aunt, Fanny Catlett Montague, is the source of the treasured story I begin with today. She tells in her *Recollections* about being sent one childhood Christmas by my grandfather to their minister, the Rev. Mr. Lee, who lived across the field from their home. Aunt Fanny was to deliver a basket of especially beautiful holly gathered from the fine tree in the Catlett yard as well as some select root vegetables from my grandfather's garden.

Her father had carefully rehearsed what she was to say. She began:

> "Father says, 'What do you see in the basket?'" . . . [Mr. Lee] pried under the holly and answered, "Why, there's salsify and parsnips and onions. It was mighty good of your father to . . . [send these to me]." "But," I said, "Father says there's something else in the basket." The good parson, alarmed at having failed to do full justice to the gift he really thought highly of, hastened to examine its contents once more.
>
> "Father says," I continued, "that the things that are seen are temporal, but the things that are unseen are eternal; the basket is full of love and good wishes."

As my years increase, meaning comes to me in plain things: in the parsnips, onions and salsify of my life, and in some glistening holly moments too.

> Breaking bread together at the close of day hallows
> the routine of preparing our evening meal.
> On a visit to my desperately sick, barely
> conscious aunt I suck orange juice into a
> straw and release it on her parched lips.
> Awe fills the intimacy of the moment, this
> small offering of sustenance.
> Later the same day I spoon warm cereal into my
> infant granddaughter's eager mouth; spirit
> is strengthened, lifted up, as body is
> nourished.
> Standing in the warm September sun in the doorway of my mother's home
> after
> a morning spent helping her enter a nursing home, I am suddenly
> reconnected with my childhood.
> Slashing across red camellias near my mother's casket, the sun sets the
> flowers
> ablaze, claiming life in the midst of death.

As I struggle to understand and absorb these interior responses to the everyday things of my life, the Christian catechism, which I learned by rote so long ago, comes to me again and again: a sacrament is "an outward and visible sign of an inward and spiritual grace."

The holly and the vegetables dug from my grandfather's garden, carefully placed in the basket, and delivered to his dear friend, were the outward and visible signs, the temporal things, of love, the inward and spiritual grace, the unseen and the eternal.

As I advance inexorably in the ranks of the older generation, plain things bring surprising gifts of the spirit. In these moments *things* signify, *routines* transform and are transforming, *relationships* weave patterns of surpassing richness. Plain things become the stuff of wonder, the source of new understanding, the assurance of things unseen, the sacraments of daily living. . . .

One December afternoon in my warm kitchen a sense of comfort enveloped me as I placed filled custard cups in the oven. With eyes squinting as the heat of the oven flooded my face, I poured the not quite boiling water into the pan holding the thick cups with the honey-like glaze. The rich milk and egg mixture, topped with the fragrant sprinkling of nutmeg, rippled as I pushed the pan toward the middle of the oven shelf. Then, without warning or transition, I was my mother in the kitchen of my childhood. I was at one with her who in those innocent pre-cholesterol days, trusted the nourishing, nurturing qualities of eggs and milk and knew how lovely the cool custard could be to the feverish throat.

But in that moment I was my child self too, the child who anticipated the soothing custard that would often be on the supper tray when I was convalescing from one or another of the numerous diseases children succumbed to sixty-five years ago.

The context for this custard making was the overwhelming and frightening illness of my friend of more than sixty years. For days she had been without appetite but responded warmly, "Oh, custard would be *lovely,*" when I suggested it, having shown no interest earlier in fruit yogurt. Fruit yogurt? Totally unknown to us in our rural Virginia childhoods. Clabber was what we knew and loved, not yogurt, but I could not produce clabber with today's store-bought milk.

The warmth of her response had given me the relief of *doing* something for her in my otherwise powerless position. It was good to know, too, that she was anticipating the custard with pleasure.

So with a sense of relief, and satisfaction, I beat the eggs for the custard and saw the milk turn pale gold. I buttered the cups, poured in the rich liquid, placed them tenderly, even lovingly, in the oven in their hot water. There was comfort, not only in the promise of the food, but in the ritual of its preparation, making the moves I had so often seen my mother make: measuring the milk, cracking the eggs, beating, stirring, savoring the scents of vanilla and nutmeg as I closed the oven door.

Then for an indelible moment I was my mother and my child self: in an out-of-time meshing of the joy of giving and receiving, I was at once the receiving child and the giving mother. Somehow I was mother, child, my mother, myself, Giver and Receiver.

This shining moment in my kitchen sends shafts of light across my days, especially new light on what giving and receiving are about, and where I stand in relation to my mother. In that light I see that my friend and I were both givers and receivers—she the giver of a concrete thing that I in my great need could do for her, I the giver of the work of my hands—and surely of my heart—in the time of her mortal sickness. I received in my giving; she gave in her receiving.

In that moment I knew myself to be taking my place in the ranks of women of all the ages, at the heart of the giving and receiving that is at the center of life. Bound up also in this experience of baking custard for my friend was the gift of knowing, despite all the division and points of separation we had suffered, that I rightfully and gladly stood with my mother. This knowing came only after I had lived daughterhood, motherhood, and grandmotherhood, and this knowing is not only powerful but a good and comfortable thing.

Now my daughter is intent on making her father's birthday cake while her daughter makes contented sounds in her bouncing seat nearby. Through all the generations, through all the days and years, the giving and receiving continue to weave the very fabric of our lives, and we find ourselves in each other and in all ages.

From "Salsify and Sacrament," 1993

ROBERT GRAVES (*English, 1895–1985*)

That aged woman with the bass voice
And yellowing white hair: believe her.
Though to your grandfather, her son, she lied
And to your father disingenuously
Told half the tale as the whole,
Yet she was honest with herself,
Knew disclosure was not yet due,
Knows it is due now.

She will conceal nothing of consequence
From you, her great-grandchildren
(So distant the relationship,
So near her term),
Will tell you frankly, she has waited
Only for your sincere indifference
To exorcize that filial regard
Which has estranged her, seventy years,
From the folk of her house.

Confessions of old distaste
For music, sighs and roses—
Their false-innocence assaulting her,
Breaching her hard heart;
Of the pleasures of a full purse,
Of clean brass and clean linen,
Of being alone at last;
Disgust with the ailing poor
To whom she was bountiful;
How the prattle of young children
Vexed more than if they whined;
How she preferred cats.

She will say, yes, she acted well,
Took such pride in the art
That none of them suspected, even,
Her wrathful irony
In doing what they asked
Better than they could ask it. . . .
But, ah, how grudgingly her will returned
After the severance of each navel-cord,
And fled how far again,
When again she was kind!

She has outlasted all man-uses,
As was her first resolve:
Happy and idle like a port
After the sea's recession,
She does not misconceive the nature
Of shipmen or of ships.
Hear her, therefore, as the latest voice;
The intervening generations (drifting
On tides of fancy still), ignore.

"The Great-Grandmother," c. 1930

JOHN CROWE RANSOM (*American, 1888–1974*)

A discreet householder exclaims on the grandsire
In warpaint and feather, with fierce grandsons and axes
Dancing round a backyard fire of boxes:
"Watch grandfather, he'll set the house on fire."

134

But I will unriddle for you the thought of his mind,
An old one you cannot open with conversation.
What animates the thin legs in risky motion?
Mixes the snow on the head with snow on the wind?

"Grandson, grandsire. We are equally boy and boy.
Do not offer your reclining-chair and slippers
With tedious old women talking in wrappers.
This life is not good but in danger and in joy.

"It is you the elder to these and junior to me
Who are penned as slaves by properties and causes
And never walk from your insupportable houses.
Shamefully, when boys shout, you turn and flee.

"May God forgive me, I know your middling ways,
Having taken care and performed ignominies unreckoned
Between the first brief childhood and brief second,
But I will be more honorable in these days."

"The Old Man Playing with Children," 1924

PO CHÜ-I *(Chinese, 772–846 c.e.)*

My nephew, who is six years old, is called
    "Tortoise";
My daughter of three—little "Summer Dress."
One is beginning to learn to joke and talk;
The other can already recite poems and songs.
At morning they play clinging about my feet;
At night they sleep pillowed against my dress.
Why, children, did you reach the world so late,
Coming to me just when my years are spent?
Young things draw our feelings to them;
Old people easily give their hearts.
The sweetest vintage at last turns sour;
The full moon in the end begins to wane.
And so with men the bands of love and affection
Soon may change to a load of sorrow and care.
But all the world is bound by love's ties;
Why did I think that I alone should escape?

"Children," c. 820 c.e.

135

SHEL SILVERSTEIN (*American, b. 1932*)

> Said the little boy, "Sometimes I drop my spoon."
> Said the little old man, "I do that too."
> The little boy whispered, "I wet my pants."
> "I do that too," laughed the little old man.
> Said the little boy, "I often cry."
> The old man nodded, "So do I."
> "But worst of all," said the boy, "it seems
> Grown-ups don't pay attention to me."
> And he felt the warmth of a wrinkled old hand.
> "I know what you mean," said the little old man.

"The Little Boy and the Old Man," 1981

II SAMUEL 18:32–19:1–4, HEBREW SCRIPTURES

The king [David] asked the Cushite, "Is my boy Absalom safe?" And the Cushite replied, "May the enemies of my lord the king and all who rose against you to do you harm fare like that young man!" The king was shaken. He went up to the upper chamber of the gateway and wept, moaning these words as he went, "My son Absalom! O my son, my son Absalom! If only I had died instead of you! O Absalom, my son, my son!"

Joab was told that the king was weeping and mourning over Absalom. And the victory that day was turned into mourning for all the troops, for that day the troops heard that the king was grieving over his son. The troops stole into town that day like troops ashamed after running away in battle. The king covered his face and the king kept crying aloud, "O my son Absalom! O Absalom, my son, my son!"

CHARLOTTE BRONTË (*English, 1816–1855*)

MY DEAR SIR,—We have buried our dead out of our sight. A lull begins to succeed the gloomy tumult of last week. It is not permitted us to grieve for him who is gone as others grieve for those they lose. The removal of our only brother must necessarily be regarded by us rather in the light of a mercy than a chastisement. Branwell was his father's and his sisters' pride and hope in boyhood, but since manhood the case has been otherwise. It has been our lot to see him take a wrong bent; to hope, expect, wait his return to the right path; to know the sickness of hope deferred, the dismay of prayer baffled; to experience despair at last—and now to behold the sudden early obscure close of what might have been a noble career.

I do not weep from a sense of bereavement—there is no prop withdrawn, no consolation torn away, no dear companion lost—but for the wreck of talent, the ruin of promise, the untimely dreary extinction of what might have been a burning and a shining light. My brother was a year my junior. I had aspirations and ambitions for him once, long ago—they have perished mournfully. Nothing remains of him but a memory of errors and sufferings. There is such a bitterness of pity for his life and death, such a yearning for the emptiness of his whole existence as I cannot describe. I trust time will allay these feelings.

My poor father naturally thought more of his *only* son than of his daughters, and, much and long as he had suffered on his account, he cried out for his loss like David for that of Absalom—my son! my son!—and refused at first to be comforted.

From a letter to W. S. Williams, 2 October 1848

E. C. GASKELL (*English, 1810–1865*)

The interior of the church is common-place; it is neither old enough nor modern enough to compel notice. The pews are of black oak, with high divisions; and the names of those to whom they belong are painted in white letters on the doors. There are neither brasses, nor altar-tombs, nor monument, but there is a mural tablet on the right-hand side of the communion-table, bearing the following inscription:—

HERE

LIE THE REMAINS OF

MARIA BRONTË, WIFE

OF THE

REV. P. BRONTË, A.B., MINISTER OF HAWORTH.

HER SOUL

DEPARTED TO THE SAVIOUR, SEPT. 15TH, 1821,

IN THE 39TH YEAR OF HER AGE.

"Be ye also ready: for in such an hour as ye think not the Son of Man cometh."—Matthew xxiv. 44

ALSO HERE LIE THE REMAINS OF

MARIA BRONTË, DAUGHTER OF THE AFORESAID;

SHE DIED ON THE

6TH OF MAY, 1825, IN THE 12TH YEAR OF HER AGE,

AND OF

ELIZABETH BRONTË, HER SISTER,

WHO DIED JUNE 15TH, 1825, IN THE 11TH YEAR OF HER AGE.

"Verily I say unto you, Except ye be converted, and become as little children, ye shall not enter into the kingdom of heaven."—Matthew xviii. 3.

137

HERE ALSO LIE THE REMAINS OF
PATRICK BRANWELL BRONTË,
WHO DIED SEPT. 24TH, 1848, AGED 30 YEARS.

AND OF
EMILY JANE BRONTË,
WHO DIED DEC. 19TH, 1848, AGED 29 YEARS,

SON AND DAUGHTER OF THE

REV. P. BRONTË, INCUMBENT

THIS STONE IS ALSO DEDICATED TO THE
MEMORY OF ANNE BRONTË,
YOUNGEST DAUGHTER OF THE REV. P. BRONTË, A.B.

SHE DIED, AGED 27 YEARS, MAY 28TH, 1849,

AND WAS BURIED AT THE OLD CHURCH, SCARBORO'.

At the upper part of this tablet ample space is allowed between the lines of the inscription; when the first memorials were written down, the survivors, in their fond affection, thought little of the margin and verge they were leaving for those who were still living. But as one dead member of the household follows another fast to the grave, the lines are pressed together, and the letters become small and cramped. After the record of Anne's death, there is room for no other.

But one more of that generation—the last of that nursery of six little motherless children—was yet to follow, before the survivor, the childless and widowed father, found his rest. On another tablet, below the first, the following record has been added to that mournful list:—

ADJOINING LIE THE REMAINS OF
CHARLOTTE, WIFE
OF THE

REV. ARTHUR BELL NICHOLLS, A.B.,

AND DAUGHTER OF THE REV. P. BRONTË, A.B., INCUMBENT.

SHE DIED MARCH 31ST, 1855, IN THE 39TH

YEAR OF HER AGE.

JOHN STORES SMITH (*English, 1815–c. 1892*)

The Reverend Mr. Brontë was the ruin of what had been a striking and singularly handsome man. He was tall, strongly built, and even then perfectly erect. His hair was nearly white, but his eyebrows were still black; his features were large and handsome, but he was quite blind. He was dressed very carelessly, in almost worn-out clothes, had no proper necktie, and was in slippers. He sat beside the fireplace erect in his chair, facing the window, and he seemed to look steadfastly towards the light with his sightless orbs, which were never again to behold it, until the celestial splendour of the New Jerusalem flash upon them, when the sun and moon shall be no more. The blind old dog curled himself on the hearth at his blind old master's feet. He commenced conversation almost immediately upon his daughter. I had read and admired her works? I told him I had, and gave my honest opinion of their fascinating interest and startling originality. And was that the general verdict of the world? I gave him a summary of many criticisms I well remembered, and at every pause he rubbed his knees slowly, and muttered in half soliloquy: 'And I hadn't an idea of it. To think of me never even suspecting it. Strange! Strange!' And then he talked about Emily and the other sister, and told me how he had considered Emily the genius of the family, how he never fancied Charlotte capable of writing anything, and could scarcely realise it, and as he did so, he ever and anon fell into reverie again, and muttered the old refrain: 'And I knew nothing about it, positively nothing. Strange! Strange! Perhaps I might have stopped it if I had. But I knew nothing—nothing.' He seemed to have a threefold feeling—regret that novels should have proceeded from his daughters; paternal pride, evident and sometimes garrulous, demonstrative pride; and a wandering inability altogether to believe it. After a little he turned upon the untimely deaths of his younger children; dwelt much upon both, and then fell into soliloquy once more: 'And she is dead. And Emily dead too! both dead! All dead!'

From "Personal Reminiscences of Charlotte Brontë," in *Free Lance*, 7 March 1868

A. B. NICHOLLS (*English, 1818–1906*)
E. C. GASKELL (*English, 1810–1865*)

Dear Miss Nussey,

Mr. Brontë's letter would prepare you for the sad intelligence I have to communicate. Our dear Charlotte is no more. She died last night of exhaustion. For the last two or three weeks we had become very uneasy about her, but it was not until Sunday evening that it became apparent that her sojourn with us was likely to be short. We intend to bury her on Wednesday morning.—Believe me, sincerely yours,

A. B. NICHOLLS.

Mrs. Gaskell is our only other authority for the last sad days:—

Long days and longer nights went by; still the same relentless nausea and faintness, and still borne on in patient trust. About the third week in March there was a change; a low, wandering delirium came on; and in it she begged constantly for food and even for stimulants. She swallowed eagerly now; but it was too late. Wakening for an instant from this stupor of intelligence she saw her husband's woe-worn face, and caught the sound of some murmured words of prayer that God would spare her. 'Oh!' she whispered forth, 'I am not going to die, am I? He will not separate us, we have been so happy.'

Early on Saturday morning, March 31st, the solemn tolling of Haworth church bell spoke forth the fact of her death to the villagers who had known her from a child, and whose hearts shivered within them as they thought of the two sitting desolate and alone in the old grey house.

Letter to Ellen Nussey, 31 March 1855; and excerpt from *The Life of Charlotte Brontë*,
E. C. Gaskell, 1857

THE GOSPEL ACCORDING TO MATTHEW 2:17–18, THE NEW TESTAMENT

Then was fulfilled that which was spoken by Jeremy the prophet, saying,
In Rama was there a voice heard, lamentation, and weeping, and great mourning, Rachel weeping *for* her children, and would not be comforted, because they are not.

WOLFGANG AMADEUS MOZART (*Austrian, 1756–1791*)

Vienna, 4 April 1787

Mon très cher Père!
. . . . This very moment I have received a piece of news which greatly distresses me, the more so as I gathered from your last letter that, thank God, you were very well indeed. But now I hear that you are really ill. I need hardly tell you how greatly I am longing to receive some reassuring news from yourself. And I still expect it; although I have now made a habit of being prepared in all affairs of life for the worst. As death, when we come to consider it closely, is the true goal of our existence, I have formed during the last few years such close relations with this best and truest friend of mankind, that his image is not only no longer terrifying to me, but is indeed very soothing and consoling! . . . I hope and trust that while I am writing this, you are feeling better. But if, contrary to all expectation, you are not recovering, I implore you by . . . not to hide it from me, but to tell me the whole truth or get someone to write it to me, so that as quickly as is humanly possible I may come to your arms, I entreat you by all that is sacred—to both

of us. Nevertheless I trust that I shall soon have a reassuring letter from you; and cherishing this pleasant hope, I and my wife and our little Karl kiss your hands a thousand times and I am ever

> your most obedient son
> W. A. Mozart
> From a letter to his father, 4 April 1787

JOHN NICHOLS (*American, b. 1940*)

All his life Amarante had lived in the shadow of his own death. When he was two days old he caught pneumonia, they gave him up for dead, somehow he recovered. During his childhood he was always sick, he couldn't work like other boys his age. He had rheumatic fever, chicken pox, pneumonia three or four more times, starting coughing blood when he was six, was anemic, drowsy all the time, constantly sniffling, weak and miserable, and—everybody thought—dying. At eight he had his tonsils out; at ten, his appendix burst. At twelve he was bitten by a rattlesnake, went into a coma, survived. Then a horse kicked him, breaking all the ribs on his left side. He contracted tuberculosis. He hacked and stumbled around, hollow-eyed, gaunt and sniffling, and folks crossed themselves, murmuring Hail Marys whenever he staggered into view. At twenty, when he was already an alcoholic, scarlet fever almost laid him in the grave; at twenty-three, malaria looked like it would do the job. Then came several years of amoebic dysentery. After that he was constipated for seventeen months. At thirty, a lung collapsed; at thirty-four, shortly after he became the first sheriff of Milagro, that old devil pneumonia returned for another whack at it, slowed his pulse to almost nothing, but like a classical and very pretty but fainthearted boxer, couldn't deliver the knockout punch. During the old man's forties a number of contending diseases dropped by Amarante's body for a shot at the title. The clap came and went, had a return bout, was counted out. The measles appeared, as did the mumps, but they did not even last a full round. For old time's sake pneumonia made a token appearance, beat its head against the brick wall that evidently lined Amarante's lungs, then waved a white flag and retreated. Blood poisoning blew all his lymph nodes up to the size of golf balls, stuck around for a month, and lost the battle.

Amarante limped, coughed, wheezed; his chest ached; he spat both blood and gruesome blue-black lungers, drank until his asshole hurt, his flat feet wailed; arthritis took sledgehammers to his knees; his stomach felt like it was bleeding; and all but three of his teeth turned brown and toppled out of his mouth like acorns. In Milagro, waiting for Amarante Córdova to drop dead became like waiting for one of those huge sneezes that just refuses to come. And there was a stretch during Amarante's sixties when people kept running away from him, cutting conversations short and like that, because everybody *knew* he was going to keel over in the very next ten seconds, and nobody likes to be present when somebody drops dead.

In his seventies Amarante's operations began. First they removed a lung. By that time the citizens of Milagro had gotten into the irate, sarcastic, and not a little awed frame of mind which had them saying: "Shit, even if they took out that old bastard's other lung he'd keep on breathing."

A lump in his neck shaped like a miniature cow was removed. After that a piece of his small intestine had to go. There followed, of course, the usual gallbladder, spleen, and kidney operations. People in Milagro chuckled "Here comes the human zipper," whenever Amarante turned a corner into sight. His friends regarded him with a measure of respect and hatred, beseeching him to put in a good word for them with the Angel of Death, or whoever it was with whom he held counsel, even as they capsized over backward into the adobe and caliche darkness of their own graves.

But finally, at seventy-six, there loomed on Amarante's horizon a Waterloo. Doc Gómez in the clinic at Doña Luz sent him to a doctor at the Chamisaville Holy Cross Hospital who did a physical, took X rays, shook his head, and sent the old man to St. Claire's in the capital where a stomach specialist, after doing a number of tests and barium X rays and so forth, came to the conclusion that just about everything below Amarante's neck had to go, and the various family members were notified.

The family had kept in touch in spite of being scattered to the three winds, and those that were still living, including Jorge from Australia, returned to Milagro for a war council, and for a vote on whether or not they could muster the money to go ahead with their father's expensive operation. "If he doesn't have this operation," the Capital City doctor told them, "your father will be dead before six months are out."

Now the various members of the family had heard that tune before, but all the same they took a vote: Nadia, María Ana, Berta, Sally, and Billy voted for the operation; Jorge, Roberto, Nazario, and Ricardo voted against it. And so by a 5–4 margin Amarante went under the knife and had most of his innards removed. He recuperated for several weeks, and then, under Sally's and Ricardo's and Betita's care, went home to Milagro.

But it looked as if this time was really *it*. Slow to get back on his feet, Amarante had jaundice and looked ghastly. He complained he couldn't see anymore, and they discovered he had cataracts in both eyes, so Ricardo and Sally and Betita took him back to St. Claire's and had those removed. Thereafter, he had to wear thick-lensed glasses which made him look more like a poisoned corpse than ever before. His slow, creeping way of progressing forward made snails look like Olympic sprinters. The people of Milagro held their collective breath; and if they had been a different citizenry with a different culture from a different part of the country, they probably would have begun to make book on which day *it* would happen. In fact, the word had spread, so that down in Chamisaville at the Ortega Funeral Home, which handled most of the death from Arroyo Verde to the Colorado border, it became common for Bunny Ortega, Bruce Maés, and Bernardo Medina to wonder, sort of off the cuff during their coffee breaks, when Amarante's body would be coming in. And eventually, although she did not go so far as to have Joe Mondragón or one of the other enterprising kids like him dig a grave out in the camposanto, Sally did drop by Ortega's in order to price coffins and alert the personnel as to what they might expect when the time came.

One gorgeous autumn day when all the mountain aspens looked like a picture postcard from heaven, Amarante had a conversation with Sally. "I guess this old temple of the soul has had it," he began with his usual sly grin. "I think you better write everybody a letter and tell them to come home for Christmas. I want to have all my children gathered around me at Christmastime so I can say good-bye. There won't be no more Navidades for me."

Sally burst into tears, she wasn't quite sure whether of relief or of grief. And, patting her father on the back once she had loudly blown her nose, she said, "Alright, Papa. I know everybody who's left will come."

And *that* was a Christmas to remember! The Celebration of 1956. Jorge came from Australia with his wife and their five children. Nadia journeyed up from the capital with her lover. María Ana took off from the Arthur Murray studios in San Francisco, flying in with her husband and four children. Berta and the lemon grower took a train from the San Jose Valley. Robert, Billy, and Nazario, their wives and fourteen children and some grandchildren, drove in a caravan of disintegrating Oldsmobiles from L.A. And Sally and the remaining two of her brood still in the nest motored up every day from Doña Luz. People stayed at Ricardo's house, at what was left of Amarante's and Betita's adobe, and some commuted from Sally's in Doña Luz.

They had turkeys and pumpkin pie, mince pie and sour cream pie; they had chili and posole, corn and sopaipillas and enchiladas and empanaditas, tequila and mescal, Hamms and Coors and Old Crow, and in the center of it all with the screaming hordes revolving happily about him, chest-deep in satin ribbons and rainbow-colored wrapping paper, so drunk that his lips were flapping like pajamas on a clothesline during the April windy season, sat the old patriarch himself, dying but not quite dead, and loving every minute of it. His children hugged him, whispered sweet nothings in his ear, and waited on his every whim and fancy. They pressed their heads tenderly against his bosom, muttering endearing and melodramatic lovey-doveys, even as they also anxiously listened to see if the old ticker really was on its last legs. They took him by the elbow and held him when he wished to walk somewhere, they gazed at him sorrowfully and shed tears of both joy and sadness, they squeezed his feeble hands and reminisced about the old days and about the ones who were dead, about what all the grandchildren were doing, and about who was pregnant and who had run away, who was making a lot of money and who was broke and a disgrace, who was stationed in Korea and who was stationed in Germany . . . and they joined hands, singing Christmas carols in Spanish, they played guitars and an accordion, they wept and cavorted joyously some more, and finally, tearfully, emotionally, tragically, they all kissed his shrunken cheeks and bid him a fond and loving adios, told their mama Betita to be strong, and scattered to the three winds.

Three years later when Jorge in Australia received a letter from Sally in Doña Luz, he replied:

> What do you mean he wants us all to meet again for Christmas so he can say good-bye? What am I made out of, gold and silver? I said good-bye two winters ago, it cost me a fortune! I can't come back right now!

Nevertheless, when Sally a little hysterically wrote that this time was really *it*, he came, though minus the wife and kiddies. So also did all the other children come, a few minus some wives or husbands or children, too. At first the gaiety was a little strained, particularly when Nazario made a passing remark straight off the bat to Berta that he thought the old man looked a hell of a lot better than he had three years ago, and Berta and everyone else within hearing distance couldn't argue with that. But then they realized they were all home again, and Milagro was white and very beautiful, its juniper and piñon branches laden with a fresh snowfall, and the smell of piñon smoke on the air was almost like a drug making them high. The men rolled up their sleeves and passed around the ax, splitting wood, until Nazario sank the ax into his foot, whereupon they all drove laughing and drinking beer down to the Chamisaville Holy Cross Hospital where the doctor on call proclaimed the shoe a total loss, but only had to take two stitches between Nazario's toes. Later that same afternoon there was a piñata for the few little kids—some grandchildren, a pocketful of great-grandchildren—who had come, and, blindfolded, they pranced in circles swinging a wooden bat until the papier-mâché donkey burst, and everyone cheered and clapped as the youngsters trampled each other scrambling for the glittering goodies. Then the kids stepped up one after another to give Grandpa sticky candy kisses, and he embraced them all with tears in his eyes. Later the adults kissed Grandpa, giving him gentle abrazos so as not to cave in his eggshell chest. "God bless you" they whispered, and Amarante grinned, flashing his three teeth in woozy good-byes. "This was in place of coming to the funeral," he rasped to them in a quavering voice. "Nobody has to come to the funeral." Betita started to cry.

Out of the old man's earshot and eyesight his sons and daughters embraced each other, crossed themselves, crossed their fingers, and, casting their eyes toward heaven in supplication, murmured, not in a mean or nasty way, but with gentleness and much love for their father:

"Here's hoping . . ."

When, five years later, Jorge received the next letter from Sally, he wrote back furiously:

> NO! I just came for Mama's funeral!

On perfumed pink Safeway stationery she pleaded with him to reconsider, she begged him to come. For them all she outlined their father's pathetic condition. He'd had a heart attack after Betita's death. He had high blood pressure. His veins were clotted with cholesterol. His kidneys were hardly functioning. He had fallen and broken his hip. A tumor the size of an avocado had been removed from beside his other lung, and it was such a rare tumor they didn't know if it was malignant or benign. They thought, also, that he had diabetes. Then, most recently, a mild attack of pneumonia had laid him out for a couple of weeks. As an afterthought she mentioned that some lymph nodes had been cut from his neck for biopsies because they thought he had leukemia, but it turned out he'd had an infection behind his ears where the stems of his glasses were rubbing too hard.

Jorge wrote back:

> What is Papa trying to do to us all? I'm no spring chicken, Sally. *I* got a heart condition. *I'm* blind in one eye. *I* got bursitis so bad in one shoulder I can't lift my hand above my waist. And I've *got* diabetes!

He returned, though. He loved his father, he loved Milagro. Since the last time, Nadia had also died. The other surviving children came, but none of the grandchildren or great-grandchildren showed up. Times were a little tough, money hard to come by. And although maybe the old man was dying, he looked better than ever, better even than some of them. His cheeks seemed to have fleshed out a little, they were even a tiny bit rosy. Could it be their imagination, or was he walking less stooped over now? And his mind seemed sharper than before. When Jorge drove up the God damn old man was outside chopping wood!

They shared a quiet, subdued celebration. Most of them had arrived late and would leave early. And after they had all kissed their father good-bye again, and perhaps squeezed him a little harder than usual in their abrazos (hoping, maybe, to dislodge irrevocably something vital inside his body), the sons and daughters went for a walk on the mesa.

"I thought he said he was dying," Jorge complained, leaning heavily on a cane, popping glycerin tablets from time to time.

"I wrote you all what has happened," Sally sighed. "I told you what Papa said."

"How old is he now?" asked Berta.

"He was born in 1880, qué no?" Ricardo said.

"That makes him eighty-four," Billy said glumly. "And already I'm fifty."

"He's going to die," Sally said sadly. "I can feel it in my bones."

And those that didn't look at her with a mixture of hysteria and disgust solemnly crossed themselves. . . .

For the Christmas of 1970 only Jorge came. He bitched, ranted, and raved at Sally in a number of three-, four-, and five-page letters, intimating in no uncertain terms that he couldn't care less if his father *had* lost all the toes on one foot plus something related to his bladder, he wasn't flying across any more oceans for any more Christmases to say good-bye to the immortal son of a bitch.

But he came.

The airplane set down in the capital; he took the Trailways bus up. Ricardo, who was recovering from stomach surgery but slowly dying of bone cancer anyway, met him at Rael's store. Sally came up later. Jorge had one blind askew eye and poor vision in the other, he was bald, limping noticeably, haggard and frail and crotchety. He felt that for sure this trip was going to kill him, and did not understand why he kept making it against his will.

Then, when Jorge saw Amarante, his suspicions were confirmed. His father wasn't growing old: he had reached some kind of nadir ten or twelve years ago and now he was growing backward, aiming toward middle age, maybe youth. To be sure, when Amarante lifted his shirt to display the scars he looked like a banana that had been hacked at by a rampaging machete-wielding maniac, but the light in his twinkling old eyes, magnified by those glasses, seemed like something stolen from the younger generation.

The next day, Christmas Day, in the middle of Christmas dinner, Jorge suffered a heart attack, flipped over in his chair, his mouth full of candied sweet potato, and died.

Bunny Ortega, Bruce Maés, and the new man replacing Bernardo Medina (who had also died), Gilbert Otero, smiled sadly but with much sympathy when Sally and Ricardo accompanied the body to the Ortega Funeral Home in Chamisaville.

"Well, well," Bunny said solicitously. "So the old man finally passed away."

"No-no-no," Sally sobbed. "This is my brother . . . his son! . . ."

"*Ai, Chihuahua!*"

146

And here it was, two years later more or less, and Joe Mondragón had precipitated a crisis, and Amarante Córdova had never been so excited in his life.

One day, during his Doña Luz daughter's weekly visit, Amarante told her, "Hija, you got to write me a letter to all the family."

Sally burst into tears. "I can't. I won't. No. You can't make me."

"But we have to tell everyone about what José has done. They must see this thing and take part in it before they die. Tell them the shooting is about to start—"

So Sally dutifully advised her surviving siblings about what Joe Mondragón had done; she informed them that the shooting was about to start.

Maybe they read her letters, maybe they only looked at the postmark, but to a man jack they all replied: "Send us your next letter *after* Papa is dead!"

"That's the trouble with this younger generation," Amarante whined petulantly. "They don't give a damn about anything important anymore."

From *The Milagro Beanfield War*, 1974

RENA CORNETT (*American, b. 1919*)
AS TOLD TO WENDY EWALD (*American, b. 1951*)

[*Rena Cornett has always lived within five miles of her birthplace in Eastern Kentucky. She and her husband, Oliver Meade, had eight children and raised as many more from other families. Their home was a gathering place for adults and children alike. Now the children have grown, married, and have children of their own. Oliver and Rena lived alone in their house on the top of Pine Mountain, until Oliver died in October 1977. Now Rena stays there by herself, but her grandchildren come to visit with her as often as they can.*]

I was born right near the mouth of Ingram's Creek, October the third in Nineteen and Nineteen. I spent most of my childhood daydreaming. I must have been eight or nine when I started school. I know I never got to go as much as I would like to have.

*   *   *

I believe that great-grandparents are the roots of our souls. We're their offspring, and I think that once we learn to love them, we can reach out and touch them.

I learned from my great-grandparents that it takes determination and courage and a will power to face a wilderness life. And I think, if the world turned around today, and I met my great-great-grandparents, from what I found out from my Daddy and Grandpa about them, I could just pick up and walk with them.

Many times when I was young and walked to school alone, I felt my great-grandmother was with me. She would tell me what the name of this flower was and the name of that flower was. I told her yonder in that picture this morning that I'm so sick. I'm not worth a button. She seemed to say to me to get up and try to go on, so I did.

It's good to study anybody. My grandchildren, sometimes they astonish me. I can picture things in them that their parents can't see at all.

I wish parents now would sit down and tell their children where to find the bee tree, how to find the walnut tree that will bear, how to find the mulberry tree, and where to find the slippery elm tree. It would be so much better than criticizing people.

It's somewhat lonely not to have the children around, but I keep myself occupied. I think as Oliver and I grew older, we grew closer together. We had more time with each other, and we had more to talk about.

I think at meal time we each missed our children. I never eat without thinking of the time when eighteen sat down at the table. But then when we were alone, we could take our time and talk as we liked and stay calm as we liked.

I think the older we got, the more we needed each other, and there's nothing better than companionship with an older person.

Oliver was a logger man most of his life, and he loved the trees. Even after he was blind, he went into the woods with other people, and he would feel the trees and try to tell what kind they were.

He built things all the time and when he wasn't working, he was talking. Whatever he did, he enjoyed. He loved the mountains. He didn't want to go anyplace. He just wanted he and I together.

In some ways I'm getting used to Oliver's death and in ways I'm expecting him to come back. I feel like it's my responsibility to carry on from here, and I hope now that Oliver's gone my life can be healthier. I took care of him for eight years, and when he died I was exhausted. I would like to get strong enough to do the work I'd like to do.

I'd like my house to grow old and go down as I do. I'd like it to walk on a cane a while and say, 'Well done. I was made with love and I'm passing with love.'

From an autobiographical oral narrative given by Rena Cornett to Wendy Ewald, in *Appalachia: A Self-Portrait*, 1979

CHAPTER FOUR
SOLITUDE/LONELINESS

Solitude and loneliness are two different aspects, not always separable in experience, of being alone: the positive, reflective, meditative and the frightening, melancholy, sometimes tragic or pathetic. Growing old inevitably exposes our personal vulnerability as fragile beings, our physical and emotional dependence on others. After Shakespeare's old King Lear has abdicated his throne, the fool mocks him mercilessly: "Now thou art a Zero without a figure: I am better than thou art now; I am a fool, thou art nothing." Lear, who "has ever but slenderly known himself," has no effective response to this shocking reality.

Facing existential aloneness without the essential social masks and conventions that define our public selves, can be a terrifying experience. Yet it is filled with potential for deepening self-knowledge, cultivating loving relationships, and soulfully accepting mortality. This chapter is deliberately brief and perhaps a bit lonely in order to encourage readers to linger with ideas expressed and feelings evoked. Its three sections explore the strangeness and beauty of realizing one's separateness; anguished exhaustion, illness, or isolation and the accompanying yearning for love, meaning, and security; and loss of a spouse and search for spiritual growth.

The chapter begins with two short pieces by twentieth-century British writers. Siegfried Sassoon's poem "When I'm Alone" evokes the strangeness that often accompanies the recognition that one really is alone in the world—physically separate from all other beings, including those parental figures whose stable care and love provided the necessary illusions of security in childhood. John Cowper Powys's view—"the older we get *the lonelier we get*"—rests on an understanding that change (historical as well as biological and psychological) inevitably deprives us of what is familiar and comfortable, sometimes leaving a deep sense of dislocation and loss. He advises that we learn to enjoy loneliness, which is a foretaste of becoming inanimate.

The next series, ranging from the African Chaza legend "The Calabash Children" to the German artist Kaethe Kollwitz's description of her aged mother in 1924, explores varying responses to physical decline and disease. Like other "eldertales" from around the world, "The Calabash Children" is a story about a poor, isolated, and exhausted old person that aims to teach a lesson about character in old age. From this old African woman's prayers to the Great Spirit, we turn to Psalm 31 of the Hebrew Scriptures, where we hear a wrenching plea to God from an isolated old man beseiged by enemies and a failing body. The selection from Ellen Newton's *This Bed My Centre* is a savage indictment of a contemporary nursing home. Newton testifies eloquently to the need for nursing homes that are responsive to individuals and conducive to creative social engagement. "Where there is no love," Sir Francis Bacon's epigram suggests, we are likely to find many rooms of empty faces.

The final group of readings describes experiences of widowhood, from grieving over a recent death to living for many years without one's spouse. "An Old Woman and Her Cat," by the contemporary English writer Doris Lessing, depicts the deterioration of Hetty, a long-widowed, fiercely independent woman of the London slums, whose wild cat Tibby substitutes for children too embarrassed to be seen with the old woman. An excerpt from Italian writer Marco Lodoli's novel *The Ambassador* portrays the disorientation and longing of Lorenzo, who has recently lost his wife Caterina. In Alifa Rifaat's "Telephone Call," set in contemporary Cairo, we witness a grieving widow's struggle to submit to the will of Allah. The last selection is a short story, "The Open Cage," by the Russian Jewish immigrant writer Anzia Yezierska, now a U.S. citizen. Yezierska's story takes place in a dilapidated New York City apartment house where three hundred tenants cook their solitary meals in single rooms.

The selections in Solitude/Loneliness, then, acknowledge the possibilities of painful isolation and despair as well as opportunities for peaceful self-knowledge and smiling acceptance of fate—within lives as well as across cultures, eras, and social conditions. All individual human beings, no matter how powerful physically or socially, are sailing "down Time's quaint stream / Without an oar," to recall the Dickinson poem from chapter one. Taken together, this chapter's readings suggest that survival of the human spirit amidst life's lonely trials requires finding the faith and strength to persist along one's own tributary, letting go of what cannot be changed.

SIEGFRIED SASSOON (*English, 1886–1967*)

> '*When I'm alone*'—the words tripped off his tongue
> As though to be alone were nothing strange.
> '*When I was young,*' he said; '*when I was young. . . .*'

I thought of age, and loneliness, and change.
I thought how strange we grow when we're alone,
And how unlike the selves that meet, and talk,
And blow the candles out, and say good-night.
Alone . . . The word is life endured and known.
It is the stillness where our spirits walk
And all but inmost faith is overthrown.

"When I'm Alone," 1918

JOHN COWPER POWYS *(English, 1872–1963)*

The Stoics made a wise contribution to the idea of an unending education when they laid so much stress upon being in harmony with Nature; and it seems to me that from a contemplation of the habits of old dogs, old horses, old cats, and even *old trees*, many shrewd hints can be discovered for the skilful self-handling of our human old age. One thing we must surely accept as an axiom in this matter—the necessity for banking up, digging in, and narrowing down. . . .

But if by the time we're sixty we haven't learnt what a knot of paradox and contradiction life is, and how exquisitely the good and the bad are mingled in every action we take, and what a compromising hostess Our Lady of Truth is, we haven't grown old to much purpose.

I suppose the hardest of all things to learn and the thing that most distinguishes what is called a 'ripe old age' is the knowledge that while bold uncritical action is necessary if things are to move at all, we are only heading for fresh disaster if some portion of our interior soul doesn't function in critical detachment, while we commit ourselves to the tide, keeping a weather-eye upon both horizons! . . .

Where then is the escape? Where is the Truth? Where is the Reality? Where is Rest and Reassurance? In one direction only; in that inviolable Present which is not our age, nor our father's nor our children's, but is the ever-recurring *Moment* where all Pasts and all Futures and all Presents form and transform and meet and mix and resolve and dissolve; till sinking down with Time itself, their creator and sustainer and destroyer and restorer, into the solitary soul of every one of us, they become that sub-species of eternity which perhaps is the only eternity we shall ever know.

To enjoy old age is to enjoy in a few human years immense epochs of super-human and sub-human life-consciousness. Aeons of vegetative existence are in it following aeons of unrealizable godlike existence. The old cart-horse's husky-harsh breathing into the sunrise, the old carrion-crow's husky-harsh croaking into the sunset, have behind them millions of years of cosmogonic contentment. . . .

By far the largest part of the difference between a happy and unhappy old age depends on its power of adjusting itself to the Inanimate.

The older we get *the lonelier we get;* and this means an increase of happiness to those who like loneliness, and a proportionate decrease to those who detest it. The reason why so many old men—even powerful old men like Homer's Nestor—tend to grow so garrulous, is that they experience a rebellious distaste for the loneliness they feel closing in about them. Their garrulousness is like the whistling of a child when the road between school and home begins to darken. Nothing in the world is lonelier than the Inanimate; and between an old man enjoying himself in the sun and a fragment of granite enjoying *itself* in the sun there is an unutterable reciprocity.

The happiness of our old age, therefore, largely depends upon on how far we have carried the cult of enjoying the Inanimate before this final epoch begins.

From the introduction to *The Art of Growing Old,* 1944

TANGANYIKA/CHAZA LEGEND (*African*)

In a village at the foot of a high mountain, there lived a lonely woman. Her husband was dead and she had never had any children, so she looked forward with dread to a comfortless old age.

Day after day she swept the house, fetched water from the river, collected firewood from the forest and cooked her solitary meals. She had a large piece of land near the river where she grew her vegetables and tended her banana trees, spending most of her spare time weeding and hoeing and wishing she had sons and daughters to help her. The other women in the village were often unkind to her and mocked her when she was tired, saying that she must be a very bad woman since the gods had never sent her any children.

Now the people in this part of Africa believed that a powerful Spirit lived on the top of the mountain, and early in the morning and late at night they would look upwards to the snow-capped peak and pray. The lonely woman prayed too, every day asking for someone to help her with her labours, and at last the Spirit answered her prayers.

It happened like this. One morning she planted some gourd seeds on her farm by the river, and from the start the young plants seemed to be particularly healthy and quick to grow. Each morning she was amazed at the growth which had occurred during the night, until at last the flowers on the gourd plants turned into fruit. The woman weeded carefully around each plant, knowing that very soon she would be able to harvest the gourds, dry them, cut them and sell them in the market for bowls and ladles which were used by all the people round about.

As she was hoeing one day, she suddenly saw a stranger standing at the edge of her plot. She was surprised and wondered how he had come, for she had seen and heard no one on the path which led towards her. He was tall and handsome and had the bearing of a chief. He smiled at the woman and said:

'I am a messenger from the Great Spirit of the mountain. He has sent me to tell you that your prayers have been heard. Tend these gourds with all your skill and through them the Spirit will send you good luck.'

Then the man disappeared as suddenly as he had come.

The woman was amazed but deciding that what she had seen and heard was no dream, but had really happened, she worked even harder on her farm, wondering how the gourds would be able to bring her the good luck she had been promised.

A week or so later, the gourds were ready for harvesting and the woman cut the stems carefully and carried the fruit home. She scooped out the pulp from inside each one and then put them on the rafters inside her hut so that they would dry and become firm and strong. Then they would be called calabashes and people could use them for bowls, and for carrying water.

There was one particularly fine gourd, which the woman placed on the ground beside the fire inside her hut, where she did her cooking, hoping it would dry quickly so that she could soon use it herself.

The next morning the woman went early to her farm to weed the ground around her bananas, and while she was away the messenger from the Great Spirit came to her hut and laying his hand on the gourd by the fire, he changed it into a young boy. Then he touched the gourds up in the rafters and they, too, changed into children.

When the messenger had disappeared, the hut became full of childish voices calling:

'Kitete! Kitete, our oldest brother. Help us down!'

So the boy by the fire stood up and helped the other children clamber down from the rafters; but nobody in the village knew what had happened.

The children ran laughing from the hut. Some seized brooms and swept the house, others weeded the ground outside and fed the hens. Two of them filled the large water-pots which stood at the door with water from the river, while several little boys ran into the forest and came back with bundles of firewood. Only Kitete did not work. The Spirit had not made him into a clever child like the others, and he just sat smiling foolishly, by the side of the fire, listening to the talk and laughter of his companions as they worked.

When all was done, the children cried:

'Kitete! Kitete! Help us back to our places in the roof,' and one by one the eldest child lifted them up to the rafters, when they immediately turned back into gourds again, and as soon as Kitete resumed his place by the fire, he too became a gourd.

The woman trudged slowly home, burdened by a large bundle of grass she had cut for re-thatching her roof, but when she saw that all her work had been done she cried out in amazement. She looked in every corner of her hut and compound and finding nobody there, she went to her neighbours.

'Somebody has done all my work for me while I was at the farm,' she said. 'Do you know who it was?'

'We saw lots of children running about in your compound today,' answered the village women. 'We thought they were relations of yours, but we did not speak to them.'

The woman was greatly puzzled and went home to cook her evening meal, wondering what had happened in her absence. Suddenly she remembered the words of the messenger who had spoken to her by the river. He had said that the Great Spirit would send her good luck if she tended the gourd plants well. Could this be the luck he had spoken of, she wondered.

The next day, the same thing happened. The children called to Kitete, who helped them down from the rafters. Then they worked hard for the woman, some of them even repairing the weak spots on her roof with the grass she had brought home the day before.

The neighbours heard the young voices again, and creeping silently to the edge of the compound, they watched the children at work. Presently they saw the children go inside the hut and soon all was quiet and deserted again.

When the woman came home and saw what her helpers had done, she went outside, and gazing up at the mountain, prayed to the Great Spirit and thanked him for his kindness. But she still did not know how it had happened, for there was nothing to show her that it was the gourds which had turned into children.

However, the neighbours were getting more and more curious, and as soon as they saw the woman leave for her farm the next day, they crept up to the door of her hut and peered silently inside.

Suddenly the gourd by the fire changed into a boy, and voices were heard in the rafters calling:

'Kitete! Kitete, our eldest brother. Help us down.'

The peeping women were amazed to see the children clambering down from the roof and only just managed to get outside the compound before the children came laughing from the hut to begin their day's work.

That evening when the woman returned, the villagers were waiting for her and told her all that they had seen, but the foolish woman, instead of accepting the gift of the Great Spirit unquestioningly, decided to spy on the children herself.

She pretended to go to her farm the next morning, but soon turned and crept quietly up to the door of her hut, in time to see everything that went on. As the children burst out of the doorway in an excited group, they stopped short on finding the woman still there gazing at them in amazement.

'So you are the children who have been helping me,' she said. 'Thank you all very much.'

They stood still and said nothing, but presently they began their tasks as usual and only Kitete sat idle. When the work was done and the children asked Kitete to help them up into the rafters again, the woman would not let them go there.

'O no!' she exclaimed. 'You are my children now and I do not want you to change into gourds again. I will cook you your supper and then you will all lie down on the floor by the fire, as other women's children do.'

So the woman kept the children as her own and they helped her so much with the work in the farm and the compound that soon she became rich, with fields of vegetables, many banana trees, and flocks of sheep and goats.

Only Kitete did not work. He was a foolish child and spent his days sitting by the fire which he kept burning with the sticks brought into the compound by his brothers and sisters. They grew older and taller, and the woman thanked the Great Spirit each day for sending them to her, but as she grew richer she became more impatient with the witless Kitete and often abused him with her tongue for being so helpless.

One afternoon, while the other children were outside working at their various jobs, the woman came into the hut to begin cooking the evening meal. The shadows contrasted so greatly with the bright sunshine outside that she could not see, at first, where Kitete lay beside the fire. Tripping over his body, she dropped her pot of prepared vegetable stew, smashing it into fragments and spilling all the food.

Angrily she stood up, and wiping the food from her face she exclaimed:

'What a worthless creature you are! How many times have I told you not to lie near the doorway! But what can anyone expect from such a child as you. You're nothing but a worthless calabash anyway!' Then raising her voice even higher, as she heard the other children returning from the farm, she shouted:

'And they're only calabashes too! Why I bother to cook food for them I can't imagine.'

But her shout turned to a scream as she looked down at her feet, for Kitete had changed back into a gourd, and she screamed even louder in another moment, for as each child came into the hut, it dropped on to the ground and became a gourd again.

The woman knew why this had happened.

'Oh, what a fool I am!' she cried, wringing her hands. 'I called the children calabashes and now the spell is broken. The Great Spirit is angry with me and my children are no more.'

It was true. The children never appeared again and the woman lived alone in her hut, getting poorer and poorer until at last she died.

"The Calabash Children," as retold by Kathleen Arnott, 1962

PSALM 31:10–13, HEBREW SCRIPTURES

> Take pity on me, Yahweh,
> I am in trouble now.
> Grief wastes away my eye,
> my throat, my inmost parts.
>
> For my life is worn out with sorrow,
> my years with sighs;
> my strength yields under misery,
> my bones are wasting away.
> I am contemptible,
> Loathsome to my neighbours,
> to my friends a thing of fear.
>
> Those who see me in the street
> hurry past me;
> I am forgotten, as good as dead in their hearts,
> something discarded.

ELLEN NEWTON (*Australian, b. 1896*)

Sunday   No visitors today. Not many will come more than once. It is not simply that it is cold and comfortless. There's something aggressive about the room, even when you are used to it. A few, like Amanda and Rose, can make their own good weather, wherever they are. But only a few.

Because there is so little coming and going from outside, and no communication worth mentioning inside, living in a nursing home is an odd kind of segregation. It's like being lost in a fog that closes down more heavily, just as you think you can see your way out.

Bed as a residence is not a thing to cultivate. To wake at an acceptable hour, stretch your body, spring out of bed and draw in the breath of early morning from the garden—to spend the day among *people*, with not too much work and a little play—then go comfortably tired to bed: *that* is different. This bed I would like better if the mattress did not yield to me as easily. It sags with every movement, so that it seems that one day it must surely wrap itself completely around me. . . .

There's a hint of sun today in my small wedge of sky, but it does not touch my room. The sense of segregation is so palpable, you feel as if at any moment you will be tightly enclosed in a cocoon of isolation. Except for the milkman, before dawn there's no sound of traffic passing by. Everything is negative. You never hear young people singing, speeding recklessly home from late parties, or even the stereophonic calls of philandering tomcats. Never the sound of children's voices, laughing and calling to each other as they race down the street. Only spasmodic screeching a few doors away, that would send cold shivers down anyone's spine. Yet they tell me nobody here ever has severe pain. It's like living in space. But it has its own grim kind of permanence, for we are all here for the term of our unnatural lives. Unless you are 'away with the fairies', the lasting anguish of being uprooted from your own kind must destroy you. And there's no speaking of it to anyone.

Tuesday   A writer, whose beautifully perceptive essays and letters are cherished by people lucky enough to own them, once asked me if I kept a diary. My answer was 'No'.

'Begin today,' she said in her clipped, clear voice.

Often I've wished I had taken her advice long ago. A diary cannot blush. It will let you unwind—without audible comment. My present safety valve is this rather scruffy, well-used notebook complete with ballpoint pen. If you must search your heart, better to put in your time writing of what you find there, than wasting your days wallowing in wretchedness.

There are twenty-nine patients at Haddon and one shower recess. Both shower and recess are shabby and in need of repair. In the small enclosure, adjoining the unscreened shower, are two toilets. These are semi-enclosed, with half doors, like they have in stables. The National Trust might care to set its seal on these, and on the plumbing as well. Few of my fellow-travellers are toilet trained. Or they've forgotten the rudiments, poor dears.

*   *   *

Friday   This afternoon, in watery sunshine, five of us are wheeled out on to the grass and grouped in a tight half circle immediately opposite the front door. One is blind. Three are deaf, with modern hearing-aids, which they carefully keep out of action. All but one are unsmiling and completely withdrawn. My attempts at communication meet no response. Pity, and a sense of complete frustration wrack me. They have put me next to Miss Alice, with neatly coiled white hair and forget-me-not blue eyes. Sister says she is the last remnant of one of the very old pioneer families. She smiles at me. Perhaps she lip-reads a little. The sky has quickly clouded over. She looks up, smiles and says, 'The good Lord Jesus sends us the weather.' She repeats this phrase every few moments. Of them all, she alone seems to live happily in some unseen world of her own. She might even manage a simple jigsaw puzzle, or enjoy watching T.V. if there were room, or any opportunity for it. All the others stare, hard-eyed, into space. Well rugged-up as we are, within half an hour it is considered too cold to linger, and all five are soon wheeled inside again. Frankly, I don't think a good time has been had by anyone, though I would have been glad to stay in the fresh air for a while with only a book for company. The tragedy of this sad assortment at Haddon is that almost everyone has ceased to be a person. Nothing seems to touch the emptiness of lives so far astray from even the fringe of ordinary human values. If only one could do something about it. There's something so cold about mere passive acceptance. Probably the life-cycle of a flying beetle holds more interest and companionship than do the lives of the twenty-nine patients under this roof.

*   *   *

Friday   Helen to see me. She comes, bringing every comfort she can think of. But she need only bring herself. Which is everything. It's all very well to say 'no man is an island'. When man has no one to share a laugh with, a simple meal, or a glass of wine, no one to talk over a book, or a snippet of news with, he is indeed an island, and a ghost-infested one at that. Pain can be endured. But the laceration of one's spirit and senses in this place is quite another thing. Only a saint could bear this. A saint is what I'm not.

November

Monday   How quickly the weeks have slipped into November. Suddenly I'm aware that for a month I've not heard one pitiful, mindless cry. There are a few very old patients here, but not one illness is debited to the crime of being old. Here they take old age for what it is—a stage in transit. But not a disease. A fact of life.

Half my allotted time here has almost melted away. There are other men and women with terminal illness, too. Like me they can stay no longer than three months. They need expert care from time to time, but they can enjoy a game of chess, sometimes amble along a sunlit balcony or garden path, and pass the time of day with their peers. Or even carve a little wooden boat to delight some child. Environment is not everything. But this place is buoyant. It's a little world where, even if you will soon 'fear no more the heat o' the sun, Nor the furious winter's rages,' you are still a human being. You still have your own life beyond the limits of any casebook. Something seems to say you may not be immortal. But Life is.

*   *   *

Rose is back from Paris and Dublin. Looking well and very *soignée,* she comes to see me this afternoon. She brings me dewy violets and a print, already framed, of Cézanne's. It is mostly exquisite greens, a bridge you can almost walk through to the other side, still waters, and a few waterlilies. This light is not kind to it, but even so, it does my soul good, as Helen's youngest daughter said to me when she tasted her first slice of water-melon.

Rose talks about music and theatre in Paris, Dublin and London, and does it well. It's easy to understand why so many of this generation's gifted young can't get abroad quickly enough to try their wings. After she is gone something of her gift for living stays with me for a while.

But that gallery of faces in the lounge is still with me. Everyone wears the tragic mask of isolation that clings to unhappy old age. Much of it is tied up with situations that shouldn't be too difficult to change. A small, unregimented space—with no T.V.—to share a pot of tea and gossip with a friend who still calls you by your first name. There might be a quiet corner where you can play dominoes or draughts, do a jigsaw puzzle or smoke a pipe and talk about cricket and old times. There's no place for quiet talk, or even to write a letter here.

Some of these very people in the lounge may have small skills they could enjoy using. But in these places there's no design for living. Some old people have great wisdom, mellowed by time and long experience. Why not let them use it, meaningfully? Simply to exist is not living.

*   *   *

Sometimes it's a struggle to prevent my deep love of people from turning to hate. This is one of the pains that all but one or two of my twenty odd neighbours will never know. For me, there's no escape from fearful nights like this. I wonder if the time will come when families and physicians can understand the torture of spirit that must be lived through in places like this. Something that flays the senses. It is pain that is deep-seated, and enduring. Different, but not less, than the pain of a scald, or a crushed or twisted limb. And it must happen to any man or woman when terminal illness sentences them to life in a so-called geriatric hospital alongside the mentally ill.

From *This Bed My Centre,* 1979

SIR FRANCIS BACON *(English, 1561–1629)*

But little do men perceive what solitude is, and how far it extendeth. For a crowd is not company; and faces are but a gallery of pictures; and talk but a tinkling cymbal, where there is no love.

From "Of Friendship," in *The Essayes, or Counsels Civill and Morall,* 1625

STEPHEN VINCENT BENÉT *(American, 1898–1943)*

> . . . Wake at night and ease me
> But it does not please me,
> Sick I am, sick I am,
> Apple pared to quick I am.
> . . . A stone's a stone
> And a tree's a tree,
> But what was the sense
> of aging me?

From "Old Man Hoppergrass," 1936

ROBERT FROST *(American, 1874–1963)*

> All out-of-doors looked darkly in at him
> Through the thin frost, almost in separate stars,
> That gathers on the pane in empty rooms.
> What kept his eyes from giving back the gaze
> Was the lamp tilted near them in his hand.
> What kept him from remembering what it was
> That brought him to that creaking room was age.
> He stood with barrels round him—at a loss.
> And having scared the cellar under him
> In clomping here, he scared it once again
> In clomping off—and scared the outer night,
> Which has its sounds, familiar, like the roar
> Of trees and crack of branches, common things,
> But nothing so like beating on a box.
> A light he was to no one but himself
> Where now he sat, concerned with he knew what,
> A quiet light, and then not even that.
> He consigned to the moon—such as she was,
> So late-arising—to the broken moon,
> As better than the sun in any case
> For such a charge, his snow upon the roof,
> His icicles along the wall to keep;
> And slept. The log that shifted with a jolt
> Once in the stove, disturbed him and he shifted,
> And eased his heavy breathing, but still slept.

One aged man—one man—can't keep a house,
A farm, a countryside, or if he can,
It's thus he does it of a winter night.

"An Old Man's Winter Night," 1916

AIG HIGO *(Nigerian, b. 1942)*

I struck tomorrow square in the face
Yesterday groaned and said,
'Please mind your steps today.'
I left them swimming with today.

Hidesong
Birdsong
Unto my soul
What funeral pyre rejects your bones?

My spider soul is spinning
Spinning
Spinning endlessly.
Scarabwise I tow my days along
Alone I tow my death along.

"Hidesong," 1963

KAETHE KOLLWITZ *(German, 1917–1944)*

When I entered Mother's room today to bring her down to supper, I saw a
strange scene. Like something out of a fairy tale. Mother sat at the table,
under the lamp, in Grandfather's easy chair. In front of her were snapshots
she was looking through. Diagonally across her shoulders sat Frau
Klingelhof's big cat.

Mother used to be unable to stand cats. But now she likes to have the cat
on her lap. The cat warms her hands. Sometimes it seems to me that Mother
thinks the cat is a baby. When it wants to get down, Mother clasps it anxiously, as if she were afraid the baby will fall. Then her face is full of concern.
She actually struggles with the cat.

In the picture Helmy Hart took of Mother, which shows only the head,
Mother has a strange expression. The wisdom of great age is there. But it is
not the wisdom that thinks in thoughts; rather it operates through dim
feelings. These are not the "thoughts hitherto inconceivable" that Goethe
had, but the summation of eighty-seven years of living, which are now

161

unclearly felt. Mother muses. Yet even that is not quite it, for musing implies, after all, thinking. It is hard to say what the picture expresses. The features themselves do not definitely express one thing or another. Precisely because Mother no longer thinks, there is a unity about her. A very old woman who lives within herself in undifferentiated perception. Yes, that is right; but in addition: who lives within herself according to an order that is pure and harmonious. As Mother's nature always was.

It seems more and more evident to me that Mother does not recognize the cat for what it is, but thinks it is a baby. Often she wraps it up in a blanket and holds it just like a child. It is touching and sweet to see my old mother doing this.

Diary entry for 22 October 1924

DORIS LESSING (*English, b. 1919*)

Her name was Hetty, and she was born with the twentieth century. She was seventy when she died of cold and malnutrition. She had been alone for a long time, since her husband had died of pneumonia in a bad winter soon after the Second World War. He had not been more than middleaged. Her four children were now middleaged, with grown children. Of these descendants one daughter sent her Christmas cards, but otherwise she did not exist for them. For they were all respectable people, with homes and good jobs and cars. And Hetty was not respectable. She had always been a bit strange, these people said, when mentioning her at all.

When Fred Pennefather, her husband, was alive and the children just growing up, they all lived much too close and uncomfortable in a Council flat in that part of London which is like an estuary, with tides of people flooding in and out: they were not half a mile from the great stations of Euston, St. Pancras, and King's Cross. The blocks of flats were pioneers in that area, standing up grim, grey, hideous, among many acres of little houses and gardens, all soon to be demolished so that they could be replaced by more tall grey blocks. The Pennefathers were good tenants, paying their rent, keeping out of debt; he was a building worker, "steady," and proud of it. There was no evidence then of Hetty's future dislocation from the normal, unless it was that she very often slipped down for an hour or so to the platforms where the locomotives drew in and ground out again. She liked the smell of it all, she said. She liked to see people moving about, "coming and going from all those foreign places." She meant Scotland, Ireland, the North of England. These visits into the din, the smoke, the massed swirling people were for her a drug, like other people's drinking or gambling. Her husband teased her, calling her a gypsy. She was in fact part gypsy, for her

162

mother had been one, but had chosen to leave her people and marry a man who lived in a house. Fred Pennefather liked his wife for being different from the run of the women he knew, and had married her because of it, but her children were fearful that her gypsy blood might show itself in worse ways than haunting railway stations. She was a tall woman with a lot of glossy black hair, a skin that tanned easily, and dark strong eyes. She wore bright colours, and enjoyed quick tempers and sudden reconciliations. In her prime she attracted attention, was proud and handsome. All this made it inevitable that the people in those streets should refer to her as "that gypsy woman." When she heard them, she shouted back that she was none the worse for that.

After her husband died and the children married and left, the Council moved her to a small flat in the same building. She got a job selling food in a local store, but found it boring. There seem to be traditional occupations for middleaged women living alone, the busy and responsible part of their lives being over. Drink. Gambling. Looking for another husband. A wistful affair or two. That's about it. Hetty went through a period of, as it were, testing out all these, like hobbies, but tired of them. While still earning her small wage as a saleswoman, she began a trade in buying and selling secondhand clothes. She did not have a shop of her own, but bought clothes from householders, and sold these to stalls and the secondhand shops. She adored doing this. It was a passion. She gave up her respectable job and forgot all about her love of trains and travellers. Her room was always full of bright bits of cloth, a dress that had a pattern she fancied and did not want to sell, strips of beading, old furs, embroidery, lace. There were street traders among the people in the flats, but there was something in the way Hetty went about it that lost her friends. Neighbours of twenty or thirty years' standing said she had gone queer, and wished to know her no longer. But she did not mind. She was enjoying herself too much, particularly the moving about the streets with her old perambulator, in which she crammed what she was buying or selling. She liked the gossiping, the bargaining, the wheedling from house-holders. It was this last which—and she knew this quite well, of course—the neighbours objected to. It was the thin edge of the wedge. It was begging. Decent people did not beg. She was no longer decent.

Lonely in her tiny flat, she was there as little as possible, always prefer-ring the lively streets. But she had after all to spend some time in her room, and one day she saw a kitten lost and trembling in a dirty corner, and brought it home to the block of flats. She was on a fifth floor. While the kitten was growing into a large strong tom, he ranged about that conglom-eration of staircases and lifts and many dozens of flats, as if the building were a town. Pets were not actively persecuted by the authorities, only forbidden and then tolerated. Hetty's life from the coming of the cat became more sociable, for the beast was always making friends with somebody in the cliff that was the block of flats across the court, or not coming home for nights at a time, so that she had to go and look for him and knock on doors and ask, or returning home kicked and limping, or bleeding after a fight with his kind. She made scenes with the kickers, or the owners of the enemy cats, exchanged cat lore with cat lovers, was always having to bandage and nurse her poor Tibby. The cat was soon a scarred warrior with fleas, a torn ear, and a ragged look to him. He was a multicoloured cat and his eyes were small and yellow. He was a long way down the scale from the delicately coloured, elegantly shaped pedigree cats. But he was independent, and often caught himself pigeons when he could no longer stand the tinned cat food, or the bread and packet gravy Hetty fed him, and he purred and nestled when she grabbed him to her bosom at those times she suffered loneliness. This happened less and less. Once she had realised that her children were hoping that she would leave them alone because the old rag trader was an embarrassment to them, she accepted it, and a bitterness that always had wild humour in it only welled up at times like Christmas. She sang or chanted to the cat: "You nasty old beast, filthy old cat, nobody wants you, do they Tibby, no, you're just an alley tom, just an old stealing cat, hey Tibs, Tibs, Tibs."

The building teemed with cats. There were even a couple of dogs. They all fought up and down the grey cement corridors. There were sometimes dog and cat messes which someone had to clear up, but which might be left for days and weeks as part of neighbourly wars and feuds. There were many complaints. Finally an official came from the Council to say that the ruling about keeping animals was going to be enforced. Hetty, like others, would have to have her cat destroyed. This crisis coincided with a time of bad luck for her. She had had 'flu; had not been able to earn money, had found it hard to get out for her pension, had run into debt. She owed a lot of back rent, too. A television set she had hired and was not paying for attracted the visits of a television representative. The neighbours were gossiping that Hetty had "gone savage." This was because the cat had brought up the stairs and along the passageways a pigeon he had caught, shedding feathers and blood all the way; a woman coming in to complain found Hetty plucking the pigeon to stew it, as she had done with others, sharing the meal with Tibby.

"You're filthy," she would say to him, setting the stew down to cool in his dish. "Filthy old thing. Eating that dirty old pigeon. What do you think you are, a wild cat? Decent cats don't eat dirty birds. Only those old gypsies eat wild birds."

One night she begged help from a neighbour who had a car, and put into the car herself, the television set, the cat, bundles of clothes, and the pram. She was driven across London to a room in a street that was a slum because it was waiting to be done up. The neighbour made a second trip to bring her bed and her mattress, which were tied to the roof of the car, a chest of drawers, an old trunk, saucepans. It was in this way that she left the street in which she had lived for thirty years, nearly half her life.

She set up house again in one room. She was frightened to go near "them" to re-establish pension rights and her identity, because of the arrears of rent she had left behind, and because of the stolen television set. She started trading again, and the little room was soon spread, like her last, with a rainbow of colours and textures and lace and sequins. She cooked on a single gas ring and washed in the sink. There was no hot water unless it was boiled in saucepans. There were several old ladies and a family of five children in the house, which was condemned.

She was in the ground floor back, with a window which opened onto a derelict garden, and her cat was happy in a hunting ground that was a mile around this house where his mistress was so splendidly living. A canal ran close by, and in the dirty city-water were islands which a cat could reach by leaping from moored boat to boat. On the islands were rats and birds. There were pavements full of fat London pigeons. The cat was a fine hunter. He soon had his place in the hierarchies of the local cat population and did not have to fight much to keep it. He was a strong male cat, and fathered many litters of kittens.

In that place Hetty and he lived five happy years. She was trading well, for there were rich people close by to shed what the poor needed to buy cheaply. She was not lonely, for she made a quarrelling but satisfying friendship with a woman on the top floor, a widow like herself who did not see her children either. Hetty was sharp with the five children, complaining about their noise and mess, but she slipped them bits of money and sweets after telling their mother that "she was a fool to put herself out for them, because they wouldn't appreciate it." She was living well, even without her pension. She sold the television set and gave herself and her friend upstairs some day-trips to the coast, and bought a small radio. She never read books or magazines. The truth was that she could not write or read, or only so badly it was no pleasure to her. Her cat was all reward and no cost, for he fed himself, and continued to bring in pigeons for her to cook and eat, for which in return he claimed milk.

"Greedy Tibby, you greedy *thing*, don't think I don't know, oh yes I do, you'll get sick eating those old pigeons, I do keep telling you that, don't I?"

At last the street was being done up. No longer a uniform, long, disgraceful slum, houses were being bought by the middle-class people. While this meant more good warm clothes for trading—or begging, for she still could not resist the attraction of getting something for nothing by the use of her plaintive inventive tongue, her still-flashing handsome eyes—Hetty knew,

165

like her neighbours, that soon this house with its cargo of poor people would be bought for improvement.

In the week Hetty was seventy years old came the notice that was the end of this little community. They had four weeks to find somewhere else to live.

Usually, the shortage of housing being what it is in London—and everywhere else in the world, of course—these people would have had to scatter, fending for themselves. But the fate of this particular street was attracting attention, because a municipal election was pending. Homelessness among the poor was finding a focus in this street which was a perfect symbol of the whole area, and indeed the whole city, half of it being fine converted tasteful houses, full of people who spent a lot of money, and half being dying houses tenanted by people like Hetty.

As a result of speeches by councillors and churchmen, local authorities found themselves unable to ignore the victims of this redevelopment. The people in the house Hetty was in were visited by a team consisting of an unemployment officer, a social worker, and a rehousing officer. Hetty, a strong gaunt old woman wearing a scarlet wool suit she had found among her cast-offs that week, a black knitted teacosy on her head, and black buttoned Edwardian boots too big for her, so that she had to shuffle, invited them into her room. But although all were well used to the extremes of poverty, none wished to enter the place, but stood in the doorway and made her this offer: that she should be aided to get her pension—why had she not claimed it long ago?—and that she, together with the four other old ladies in the house, should move to a Home run by the Council out in the northern suburbs. All these women were used to, and enjoyed, lively London, and while they had no alternative but to agree, they fell into a saddened and sullen state. Hetty agreed too. The last two winters had set her bones aching badly, and a cough was never far away. And while perhaps she was more of an urban soul even than the others, since she had walked up and down so many streets with her old perambulator loaded with rags and laces, and since she knew so intimately London's texture and taste, she minded least of all the idea of a new home "among green fields." There were, in fact, no fields near the promised Home, but for some reason all the old ladies had chosen to bring out this old song of a phrase, as if it belonged to their situation, that of old women not far off death. "It will be nice to be near green fields again," they said to each other over cups of tea.

The housing officer came to make final arrangements. Hetty Pennefather was to move with the others in two weeks' time. The young man, sitting on the very edge of the only chair in the crammed room, because it was greasy and he suspected it had fleas or worse in it, breathed as lightly as he could because of the appalling stink: there was a lavatory in the house, but it had been out of order for three days, and it was just the other side of a thin wall. The whole house smelled.

The young man, who knew only too well the extent of the misery due to lack of housing, who knew how many old people abandoned by their children did not get the offer to spend their days being looked after by the authorities, could not help feeling that this wreck of a human being could count herself lucky to get a place in this "Home," even if it was—and he knew and deplored the fact—an institution in which the old were treated like naughty and dimwitted children until they had the good fortune to die.

But just as he was telling Hetty that a van would be coming to take her effects and those of the other four old ladies, and that she need not take anything more with her than her clothes "and perhaps a few photographs," he saw what he had thought was a heap of multicoloured rags get up and put its ragged gingery-black paws on the old woman's skirt. Which today was a cretonne curtain covered with pink and red roses that Hetty had pinned around her because she liked the pattern.

"You can't take that cat with you," he said automatically. It was something he had to say often, and knowing what misery the statement caused, he usually softened it down. But he had been taken by surprise.

Tibby now looked like a mass of old wool that has been matting together in dust and rain. One eye was permanently half-closed, because a muscle had been ripped in a fight. One ear was vestigial. And down a flank was a hairless slope with a thick scar on it. A cat-hating man had treated Tibby as he treated all cats, to a pellet from his airgun. The resulting wound had taken two years to heal. And Tibby smelled.

No worse, however, than his mistress, who sat stiffly still, bright-eyed with suspicion, hostile, watching the well-brushed tidy young man from the Council.

"How old is that beast?"

"Ten years, no, only eight years, he's a young cat about five years old," said Hetty, desperate.

"It looks as if you'd do him a favour to put him out of his misery," said the young man.

When the official left, Hetty had agreed to everything. She was the only one of the old women with a cat. The others had budgerigars or nothing. Budgies were allowed in the Home.

She made her plans, confided in the others, and when the van came for them and their clothes and photographs and budgies, she was not there, and they told lies for her. "Oh we don't know where she can have gone, dear," the old women repeated again and again to the indifferent van driver. "She was here last night, but she did say something about going to her daughter in Manchester." And off they went to die in the Home.

Hetty knew that when houses have been emptied for redevelopment they may stay empty for months, even years. She intended to go on living in this one until the builders moved in.

It was a warm autumn. For the first time in her life she lived like her gypsy forebears, and did not go to bed in a room in a house like respectable people. She spent several nights, with Tibby, sitting crouched in a doorway of an empty house two doors from her own. She knew exactly when the police would come around, and where to hide herself in the bushes of the overgrown shrubby garden.

As she had expected, nothing happened in the house, and she moved back in. She smashed a back windowpane so that Tibby could move in and out without her having to unlock the front door for him, and without leaving a window suspiciously open. She moved to the top back room and left it every morning early, to spend the day in the streets with her pram and her rags. At night she kept a candle glimmering low down on the floor. The lavatory was still out of order, so she used a pail on the first floor, instead, and secretly emptied it at night into the canal, which in the day was full of pleasure boats and people fishing.

Tibby brought her several pigeons during that time.

"Oh you are a clever puss, Tibby, Tibby! Oh you're clever, you are. You know how things are, don't you, you know how to get around and about."

The weather turned very cold; Christmas came and went. Hetty's cough came back, and she spent most of her time under piles of blankets and old clothes, dozing. At night she watched the shadows of the candle flame on floor and ceiling—the windowframes fitted badly, and there was a draught. Twice tramps spent the night in the bottom of the house and she heard them being moved on by the police. She had to go down to make sure the police had not blocked up the broken window the cat used, but they had not. A blackbird had flown in and had battered itself to death trying to get out. She plucked it, and roasted it over a fire made with bits of floorboard in a baking pan: the gas of course had been cut off. She had never eaten very much, and was not frightened that some dry bread and a bit of cheese was all that she had eaten during her sojourn under the heap of clothes. She was cold, but did not think about that much. Outside there was slushy brown snow everywhere. She went back to her nest thinking that soon the cold spell would be over and she could get back to her trading. Tibby sometimes got into the pile with her, and she clutched the warmth of him to her. "Oh you clever cat, you clever old thing, looking after yourself, aren't you? That's right my ducky, that's right my lovely."

And then, just as she was moving about again, with snow gone off the ground for a time but winter only just begun, in January, she saw a builder's van draw up outside, a couple of men unloading their gear. They did not

168

come into the house: they were to start work next day. By then Hetty, her cat, her pram piled with clothes and her two blankets, were gone. She also took a box of matches, a candle, an old saucepan and a fork and spoon, a tinopener, a candle and a rat-trap. She had a horror of rats.

About two miles away, among the homes and gardens of amiable Hampstead, where live so many of the rich, the intelligent and the famous, stood three empty, very large houses. She had seen them on occasion, a couple of years before, when she had taken a bus. This was a rare thing for her, because of the remarks and curious looks provoked by her mad clothes, and by her being able to appear at the same time such a tough battling old thing and a naughty child. For the older she got, this disreputable tramp, the more there strengthened in her a quality of fierce, demanding childishness. It was all too much of a mixture; she was uncomfortable to have near.

She was afraid that "they" might have rebuilt the houses, but there they still stood, too tumbledown and dangerous to be of much use to tramps, let alone the armies of London's homeless. There was no glass left anywhere. The flooring at ground level was mostly gone, leaving small platforms and juts of planking over basements full of water. The ceilings were crumbling. The roofs were going. The houses were like bombed buildings.

But on the cold dark of a late afternoon she pulled the pram up the broken stairs and moved cautiously around the frail boards of a second-floor room that had a great hole in it right down to the bottom of the house. Looking into it was like looking into a well. She held a candle to examine the state of the walls, here more or less whole, and saw that rain and wind blowing in from the window would leave one corner dry. Here she made her home. A sycamore tree screened the gaping window from the main road twenty yards away. Tibby, who was cramped after making the journey under the clothes piled in the pram, bounded down and out and vanished into neglected undergrowth to catch his supper. He returned fed and pleased, and seemed happy to stay clutched in her hard thin old arms. She had come to watch for his return after hunting trips, because the warm purring bundle of bones and fur did seem to allay, for a while, the permanent ache of cold in her bones.

Next day she sold her Edwardian boots for a few shillings—they were fashionable again—and bought a loaf and some bacon scraps. In a corner of the ruins well away from the one she had made her own, she pulled up some floorboards, built a fire, and toasted bread and the bacon scraps. Tibby had brought in a pigeon, and she roasted that, but not very efficiently. She was afraid of the fire catching and the whole mass going up in flames; she was afraid too of the smoke showing and attracting the police. She had to keep damping down the fire, and so the bird was bloody and unappetising, and in the end Tibby got most of it. She felt confused, and discouraged, but thought it was because of the long stretch of winter still ahead of her before spring could come. In fact, she was ill. She made a couple of attempts to trade and earn money to feed herself before she acknowledged she was ill. She knew she was not yet dangerously ill, for she had been that in her life, and would have been able to recognise the cold listless indifference of a real last-ditch illness. But all her bones ached, and her head ached, and she coughed more than she ever had. Yet she still did not think of herself as suffering particularly from the cold, even in that sleety January weather. She had never, in all her life, lived in a properly heated place, had never known a really warm home, not even when she lived in the Council flats. Those flats had electric fires, and the family had never used them, for the sake of economy, except in very bad spells of cold. They piled clothes onto themselves, or went to bed early. But she did know that to keep herself from dying now she could not treat the cold with her usual indifference. She knew she must eat. In the comparatively dry corner of the windy room, away from the gaping window through which snow and sleet were drifting, she made another nest—her last. She had found a piece of plastic sheeting in the rubble, and she laid that down first, so that the damp would not strike up. Then she spread her two blankets over that. Over them were heaped the mass of old clothes. She wished she had another piece of plastic to put on top, but she used sheets of newspaper instead. She heaved herself into the middle of this, with a loaf of bread near to her hand. She dozed, and waited, and nibbled bits of bread, and watched the snow drifting softly in. Tibby sat close to the old blue face that poked out of the pile and put up a paw to touch it. He miaowed and was restless, and then went out into the frosty morning and brought in a pigeon. This the cat put, still struggling and fluttering a little, close to the old woman. But she was afraid to get out of the pile in which the heat was being made and kept with such difficulty. She really could not climb out long enough to pull up more splinters of plank from the floors, to make a fire, to pluck the pigeon, to roast it. She put out a cold hand to stroke the cat.

"Tibby, you old thing, you brought it for me then, did you? You did, did you? Come here, come in here. . . ." But he did not want to get in with her. He miaowed again, pushed the bird closer to her. It was now limp and dead.

"You have it then. You eat it. I'm not hungry, thank you Tibby."

But the carcase did not interest him. He had eaten a pigeon before bringing this one up to Hetty. He fed himself well. In spite of his matted fur, and his scars and his half-closed yellow eye, he was a strong healthy cat.

At about four the next morning there were steps and voices downstairs. Hetty shot out of the pile and crouched behind a fallen heap of plaster and beams, now covered with snow, at the end of the room near the window. She could see through the hole in the floorboards down to the first floor, which had collapsed entirely, and through it to the ground floor. She saw a man in a thick overcoat and muffler and leather gloves holding a strong torch to illuminate a thin bundle of clothes lying on the floor. She saw that this bundle was a sleeping man or woman. She was indignant—*her* home was being trespassed upon. And she was afraid because she had not been aware of this other tenant of the ruin. Had he, or she, heard her talking to the cat? And where was the cat? If he wasn't careful he would be caught, and that would be the end of him. The man with a torch went off and came back with a second man. In the thick dark far below Hetty was a small cave of strong light, which was the torchlight. In this space of light two men bent to lift the bundle, carried it out across the dangertraps of fallen and rotting boards that made gangplanks over the water-filled basements. One man was holding the torch in the hand that supported the dead person's feet, and the light jogged and lurched over trees and grasses: the corpse was being taken through the shrubberies to a car.

There are men in London who, between the hours of two and five in the morning—when the real citizens are asleep, who should not be disturbed by such unpleasantness as the corpses of the poor—make the rounds of all the empty, rotting houses they know about, to collect the dead, and to warn the living that they ought not to be there at all, inviting them to one of the official Homes or lodgings for the homeless.

Hetty was too frightened to get back into her warm heap. She sat with the blankets pulled around her, and looked through gaps in the fabric of the house, making out shapes and boundaries and holes and puddles and mounds of rubble, as her eyes, like her cat's, became accustomed to the dark.

She heard scuffling sounds and knew they were rats. She had meant to set the trap, but the thought of her friend Tibby, who might catch his paw, had stopped her. She sat up until the morning light came in grey and cold, after nine. Now she did know herself to be very ill and in danger, for she had lost all the warmth she had huddled into her bones under the rags. She shivered violently. She was shaking herself apart with shivering. In between spasms she drooped limp and exhausted. Through the ceiling above her—but it was not a ceiling, only a cobweb of slats and planks—she could see into a dark cave which had been a garret, and through the roof above that, the grey sky, teeming with incipient rain. The cat came back from where he had been hiding, and sat crouched on her knees, keeping her stomach warm, while she thought out her position. These were her last clear thoughts. She told herself that she would not last out until spring unless she allowed "them" to find her, and take her to hospital. After that, she would be taken to a Home.

But what would happen to Tibby, her poor cat? She rubbed the old beast's scruffy head with the ball of her thumb and muttered: "Tibby, Tibby, they won't get you, no, you'll be all right, yes, I'll look after you."

Towards midday, the sun oozed yellow through miles of greasy grey cloud, and she staggered down the rotting stairs, to the shops. Even in those London streets, where the extraordinary has become usual, people turned to stare at a tall gaunt woman, with a white face that had flaming red patches on it, and blue compressed lips, and restless black eyes. She wore a tightly buttoned man's overcoat, torn brown woolen mittens, and an old fur hood. She pushed a pram loaded with old dresses and scraps of embroidery and torn jerseys and shoes, all stirred into a tight tangle, and she kept pushing this pram up against people as they stood in queues, or gossiped, or stared into windows, and she muttered: "Give me your old clothes darling, give me your old pretties, give Hetty something, poor Hetty's hungry." A woman gave her a handful of small change, and Hetty bought a roll filled with tomato and lettuce. She did not dare go into a cafe, for even in her confused state she knew she would offend, and would probably be asked to leave. But she begged a cup of tea at a street stall, and when the hot sweet liquid flooded through her she felt she might survive the winter. She bought a carton of milk and pushed the pram back through the slushy snowy street to the ruins.

Tibby was not there. She urinated down through the gap in the boards, muttering, "A nuisance, that old tea," and wrapped herself in a blanket and waited for the dark to come.

Tibby came in later. He had blood on his foreleg. She had heard scuffling and she knew that he had fought a rat, or several, and had been bitten. She poured the milk into the tilted saucepan and Tibby drank it all.

She spent the night with the animal held against her chilly bosom. They did not sleep, but dozed off and on. Tibby would normally be hunting, the night was his time, but he had stayed with the old woman now for three nights.

Early next morning they again heard the corpse removers among the rubble on the ground floor, and saw the beams of the torch moving on wet walls and collapsed beams. For a moment the torchlight was almost straight on Hetty, but no one came up: who could believe that a person could be desperate enough to climb those dangerous stairs, to trust those crumbling splintery floors, and in the middle of winter?

Hetty had now stopped thinking of herself as ill, of the degrees of her illness, of her danger—of the impossibility of her surviving. She had cancelled out in her mind the presence of winter and its lethal weather, and it was as if spring were nearly here. She knew that if it had been spring when she had had to leave the other house, she and the cat could have lived here for months and months, quite safely and comfortably. Because it seemed to her an impossible and even a silly thing that her life, or, rather, her death, could depend on something so arbitrary as builders starting work on a house in January rather than in April, she could not believe it: the fact would not stay in her mind. The day before she had been quite clearheaded. But today her thoughts were cloudy, and she talked and laughed aloud. Once she scrambled up and rummaged in her rags for an old Christmas card she had got four years before from her good daughter.

In a hard harsh angry grumbling voice she said to her four children that she needed a room of her own now that she was getting on. "I've been a good mother to you," she shouted to them before invisible witnesses—former neighbours, welfare workers, a doctor. "I never let you want for anything, never! When you were little you always had the best of everything! You can ask anybody; go on, ask them, then!"

She was restless and made such a noise that Tibby left her and bounded on to the pram and crouched watching her. He was limping, and his foreleg was rusty with blood. The rat had bitten deep. When the daylight came, he left Hetty in a kind of sleep, and went down into the garden where he saw a pigeon feeding on the edge of the pavement. The cat pounced on the bird, dragged it into the bushes, and ate it all, without taking it up to his mistress. After he had finished eating, he stayed hidden, watching the passing people. He stared at them intently with his blazing yellow eye, as if he were thinking, or planning. He did not go into the old ruin and up the crumbling wet stairs until late—it was as if he knew it was not worth going at all.

He found Hetty, apparently asleep, wrapped loosely in a blanket, propped sitting in a corner. Her head had fallen on her chest, and her quantities of white hair had escaped from a scarlet woollen cap, and concealed a face that was flushed a deceptive pink—the flush of coma from cold. She was not yet dead, but she died that night. The rats came up the walls and along the planks and the cat fled down and away from them, limping still, into the bushes.

Hetty was not found for a couple of weeks. The weather changed to warm, and the man whose job it was to look for corpses was led up the dangerous stairs by the smell. There was something left of her, but not much.

As for the cat, he lingered for two or three days in the thick shrubberies, watching the passing people and beyond them, the thundering traffic of the main road. Once a couple stopped to talk on the pavement, and the cat, seeing two pairs of legs, moved out and rubbed himself against one of the legs. A hand came down and he was stroked and patted for a little. Then the people went away.

The cat saw he would not find another home, and he moved off, nosing and feeling his way from one garden to another, through empty houses, finally into an old churchyard. This graveyard already had a couple of stray cats in it, and he joined them. It was the beginning of a community of stray cats going wild. They killed birds, and the field mice that lived among the grasses, and they drank from puddles. Before winter had ended the cats had had a hard time of it from thirst, during the two long spells when the ground froze and there was snow and no puddles and the birds were hard to catch because the cats were so easy to see against the clean white. But on the whole they managed quite well. One of the cats was female, and soon there were a swarm of wild cats, as wild as if they did not live in the middle of a city surrounded by streets and houses. This was just one of half a dozen communities of wild cats living in that square mile of London.

Then an official came to trap the cats and take them away. Some of them escaped, hiding till it was safe to come back again. But Tibby was caught. He was not only getting old and stiff—he still limped from the rat's bite—but he was friendly, and did not run away from the man, who had only to pick him up in his arms.

"You're an old soldier, aren't you?" said the man. "A real tough one, a real old tramp."

It is possible that the cat even thought that he might be finding another human friend and a home.

But it was not so. The haul of wild cats that week numbered hundreds, and while if Tibby had been younger a home might have been found for him, since he was amiable, and wished to be liked by the human race, he was really too old, and smelly and battered. So they gave him an injection and, as we say, "put him to sleep."

"An Old Woman and Her Cat," 1972

MARCO LODOLI (Italian, b. 1956)

Boredom is the worst feeling there is. Unfortunately, you don't sleep well, or much, when you're seventy, and afterward the day is long. I get up at dawn, wash up, give myself a nice, close shave, pick out a clean shirt, and that's it, I don't have anything else to do. So out I go, the way somebody would dive into the endless sea from a boat that's slowly sinking, and I head off in any direction, pounding my feet on the asphalt just to get away from the house, and from the thought of me, an old widower, sitting in an armchair. Sometimes I go as far as the overpass for the railroad tracks, wait for four or five trains to go by, try to read the plaques on the sides of the cars to see what cities they're rushing off to. Or else I deliberately get lost in neighborhoods I'm not familiar with, hoping that something exciting will happen to me, something new, that somebody will shout, "Lorenzo," and take me with him somewhere amusing. Because it's not true that when old people get old they become wise and look out at the world and all the confusing things that go on in it from some kind of high, heavenly balcony, full of flowers. I'm not like that, at least: I'd still like to be in the thick of things, grab on to what's passing by even if it's not going anywhere. It's just that nobody wants old people around, so they're forced into a corner to become wise and spit out empty sayings. Some mornings I feel like I did when I was twenty years old, hungry and full of love and stupid dreams, and going down to the senior citizens' center to play canasta and drink my fourth of a liter and cry over my past just isn't for me. Besides, I don't even know how to play canasta; you pick up, you discard, you squirm like a snake—what's so enjoyable about that? I'd rather go over to the bowling alley in the Acquacetosa complex and roll a few balls down the alley, I'd rather do that, though I never do, because I'm embarrassed, with all those kids running around wild. I stop in just to watch for a little bit, to breathe in that air crackling with youth, to envy certain girls when they knock down all ten pins with one roll and then laugh and throw their arms around their boyfriends. The thing is, the world's changing too fast and I can't keep up with it: There're things written on the walls I don't understand, names I never heard of before, though I suppose they must be important, considering all the love and hate they attract; I hear songs coming out of cars that don't say anything to me, in the bars it's as if the men were talking some other language. Sometimes I go to the show and, though I try to pay attention, to follow every scene, to stay awake, the story doesn't make one bit of sense to me. On the way out I hear people saying, "What a beautiful movie that was," and I'd like somebody to explain to me what parts and why, and where I was. After they finish with their cards, the old men in the senior citizens' center go take in the dirty movies in a theater down the street where they show three in a row. Everybody sits by himself, with his hat on his head, and keeps himself company with all that squashed flesh up on the screen. I tried it, too. Then I went back home with a lump in my throat and on the bed I laid out my Caterina's blouses and skirts, all big and light, like sails, and if a breeze would have blown through the house and if there were real justice in the world, the bed would have moved, flown, carried me away to her.

From *The Ambassador*, 1992

ALIFA RIFAAT (*Egyptian, b. 1930*)

From a nearby flat a telephone rings and rings, then stops, and the number is redialled and the ringing starts again, then stops, then starts again. What desperate contact is someone trying to make at this hour of the night? Is it a matter of life or death, or perhaps one of love? There is nothing like love to induce such a state of despair, no other reason to explain such obstinacy: a lover has been left and seeks the opportunity to plead to be allowed back. He must know that his beloved is at the other end and is refusing to pick up the receiver.

And here I am sitting for hours alone in my flat, knowing there is no one to ring, that there is no question of pleading or submitting to any terms, for there is no way of communicating from the grave. Does not everyone try to find some glimmer of hope even in the darkest situations? Does not the man standing on the scaffold hope that some miracle will, in the few seconds left, save him? Is not history full of such miracles? And yet I don't really ask for a miracle, nothing as tangible as that, just the very smallest of signs that he is there beyond the grave waiting for me. A small sign that I would understand and I would seek nothing further after that. Why, for instance, couldn't the vase of artificial flowers change its place from the small table by the window and I wake from sleep to find it on top of the bookcase? It is so little to ask.

The telephone has stopped ringing. Has the caller accepted his fate? Or has he sought temporary peace in sleep? It's late. The black head of night is being streaked with grey. These next few hours are the only ones during which Cairo knows a short period of quiet, a time when even the solitary cars that are about don't find it necessary to hoot. Outside the window the street is deserted except for the few cats that scavenge in peace at night and snatch their hours of sleep in the daytime.

Soon the call to dawn prayers will float like clouds of sound across the sleeping city. I shall hear it from three different mosques that surround our building. The calls will follow one another not quite synchronized, so that when one is pronouncing the *shahadah* [the doctrinal formula in Islam], another will be telling me that "prayer is better than sleep"—I who spend my nights awake.

The night around me is pregnant with a silence that speaks of memories. The familiar objects tell me of the life I lived so fully and which, with his death, has come to a sudden stop. Since then I have been waiting. Otherwise, what is the significance of the forty days after death? Has it not come down to us from the Pharaohs, those experts on death, that during these days the dead are still hovering around us and only later take themselves off elsewhere? If he is to communicate, then it must surely be during this period, for after that we shall truly be in two separate worlds.

I must try to stop myself from thinking of the terrible changes being wrought on that face and body I loved so much. How often had I prayed that I might die first and be spared the struggle to continue in life without him.

As usual I am waiting for the call to dawn prayers, after which I shall go to my bedroom and sleep for a few hours. The maid will let herself into the flat with her own key, clean up, bring in the necessities for life and put them in the fridge, take the money I leave for her, and depart. This is the only way to live at present, to turn life upside down, to sleep, with the aid of sleeping pills, during the hours when life is being led, and to be awake with my thoughts of him when the world around me is sleeping: to turn life upside down and thus to be partly dead to it.

The silence is torn apart by the ringing of the telephone. Ever since he died the telephone has been silent, except perhaps during the day when the maid would answer and tell the caller that her mistress was not available and did not want any calls. But who would ring at such an hour? As the noise bored into my ears I suddenly knew the significance of the call. No, it would not be his voice at the other end; things were done more subtly than that. I knew exactly what would happen.

I walked towards the little side table, the one we'd bought together, and with a steady hand raised the receiver to my ear. As I had expected, no voice broke the silence. I held it closer to my ear, thinking that maybe there would be the sound of breathing, but even this I told myself would not happen. What was happening demanded a high degree of faith on my part. Life and death were both a matter of faith. As I held the receiver tightly against my ear it was as though, like the Sufi image of the water taking on the colour of its container, I were being poured from a container of black despair into one of light-filled hope and confidence. And so I sat holding a soundless receiver to my ear for what might have been minutes or hours. In such circumstances, what is time? Then, suddenly, the spell was broken and the line went dead. I woke from my reverie to the first words of the call to prayer seeping through into the room.

I rose and made my ablutions, then returned to the living room, spread out my prayer carpet and performed the dawn prayer. As I sat with my prayer-beads, I was conscious of being enveloped in a cloak of contentment and gratitude. I knew for certain that all was right.

The all-pervading silence was shattered by the ringing of the telephone again, more blaring and insistent than the first time. I tried to will it to stop, for I felt an instinctive reluctance to answer it. After sitting for so long with my prayer-beads, my legs were stiff and shook with exhaustion as I walked across the room to the telephone. In trepidation I picked up the receiver and the voice of the operator immediately greeted me:

"Good morning, madam. I'm sorry for the call you had some minutes ago. It was a call from abroad and the call was put through to you by mistake. Please accept our apologies for waking you at this hour."

"It doesn't matter," I said and replaced the receiver.

I went back and sat down again on the prayer carpet. My hand was trembling as the prayer-beads ran through my fingers and I kept on asking pardon of the Almighty. Only now I was aware of the enormity of what I had sought from Him and which, in my simplicity, I had thought He had granted: a sign from the beyond. Then I was reminded of how when the

177

Prophet, on whom be the blessings and peace of God, died, the Muslims were plunged into consternation and disbelief by the news and of Abu Bakr's words to them: "For those of you who worship Muhammed, Muhammed is dead; and for those who worship Allah, Allah is alive and dies not."

Though the tears were running down my cheeks, I finally felt at peace with myself in submitting to what the Almighty had decreed.

"Telephone Call," in *Distant View of a Minaret*, 1983

TAJIHI (*Japanese, eighth century* c.e.)

The mallards call with evening from the reeds
And float with dawn midway on the water;
They sleep with their mates, it is said,
With white wings overlapping and tails asweep
Lest the frost should fall upon them.

As the stream that flows never returns,
And as the wind that blows is never seen,
My wife, of this world, has left me,
Gone I know not whither!
So here, on the sleeves of these clothes
She used to have me wear,
I sleep now all alone!

ENVOY

Cranes call flying to the reedy shore;
How desolate I remain
As I sleep alone!

From the *Man'yōshū*, Ancient Period, to 794 c.e.

ANZIA YEZIERSKA (*Russian American, 1885–1970*)

I live in a massive, outmoded apartment house, converted for roomers—a once fashionable residence now swarming with six times as many people as it was built for. Three hundred of us cook our solitary meals on two-burner gas stoves in our dingy furnished rooms. We slide past each other in the narrow hallways on our way to the community bathrooms, or up and down the stairs, without speaking.

But in our rooms, with doors closed, we are never really alone. We are invaded by the sounds of living around us; water gurgling in the sinks of neighboring rooms; the harsh slamming of a door, a shrill voice on the hall telephone, the radio from upstairs colliding with the television set next door. Worse than the racket of the radios are the smells—the smells of cooking mixing with the odors of dusty carpets and the unventilated accumulation left by the roomers who preceded us—these stale layers of smells seep under the closed door. I keep the window open in the coldest weather, to escape the smells.

Sometimes, after a long wait for the bathroom you get inside only to find that the last person left the bathtub dirty. And sometimes the man whose room is right next to the bath and who works nights, gets so angry with the people who wake him up taking their morning baths that he hides the bathtub stopper.

One morning I hurried to take my bath while the tub was still clean— only to find that the stopper was missing. I rushed angrily back to my room and discovered I had locked myself out. The duplicate key was downstairs in the office, and I was still in my bathrobe with a towel around my neck. I closed my eyes like an ostrich, not to be seen by anyone, and started down the stairway.

While getting the key, I found a letter in my mailbox. As soon as I was inside my room, I reached for my glasses on the desk. They weren't there. I searched the desk drawers, the bureau drawers, the shelf by the sink. Finally, in despair, I searched the pockets of my clothes. All at once, I realized that I had lost my letter, too.

In that moment of fury I felt like kicking and screaming at my failing memory—the outrage of being old! Old and feeble-minded in a house where the man down the hall revenges himself on his neighbors, where roomer hates roomer because each one hates himself for being trapped in this house that's not a home, but a prison where the soul dies long before the body is dead.

My glance, striking the mirror, fixed in a frightened stare at the absurd old face looking at me. I tore off the eyeshade and saw the narrowing slits where eyes had been. Damn the man who hid the bathtub stopper. Damn them all!

There was a tap at the door and I ignored it. The tapping went on. I kicked open the door at the intruder, but no one was there. I took my ready-made printed sign—Busy, Please do not disturb!—and hung it on the door.

The tapping began again—no, no, no one at the door. It was something stirring in the farthest corner of the molding. I moved toward it. A tiny bird, wings hunched together, fluttered helplessly.

I jumped back at the terrible fear of something alive and wild in my room. My God, I told myself, it's only a little bird! Why am I so scared? With a whirring of wings, the bird landed on the window frame. I wanted to push it out to freedom, but I was too afraid to touch it.

For a moment I couldn't move, but I couldn't bear to be in the same room with that frightened little bird. I rushed out to Sadie Williams.

A few times, when her door was open, I had seen parakeets flying freely about the room. I had often overheard her love-talk to her birds who responded to her like happy children to their mother.

"Mamma loves baby; baby loves mamma; come honey-bunch, come darling tweedle-dee-tweedle-dum! Bonny-boy dearest, come for your bath."

Her room was only a few doors away, and yet she had never invited me in. But now I banged on her door, begging for help.

"Who is it?" she shouted.

"For God's sake!" I cried, "A bird flew into my room, it's stuck by the window, it can't fly out!"

In an instant she had brushed past me into my room.

"Where's the bird?" she demanded.

"My God," I cried, "Where is it? Where is it? It must have flown out."

Sadie moved to the open window. "Poor darling," she said. "It must have fallen out. Why didn't you call me sooner?"

Before I could tell her anything, she was gone. I sat down, hurt by her unfriendliness. The vanished bird left a strange silence in my room. Why was I so terrified of the helpless little thing? I might have given it a drink of water, a few crumbs of bread. I might have known what to do if only I had not lost my glasses, if that brute of a man hadn't hid the bathtub stopper.

A sudden whirring of wings crashed into my thought. The bird peered at me from the molding. I fled to Sadie Williams, "Come quick," I begged, "the bird—the bird!"

Sadie burst into my room ahead of me. There it was peering at us from the farthest corner of the molding. "Chickadee, chickadee, dee, dee, dee!" Sadie crooned, cupping her hands toward the bird. "Come, fee, fee, darling! Come, honey." On tiptoes she inched closer, closer, closer, cooing in that same bird-voice—until at last, in one quick, deft movement, she cupped the frightened bird in her hands. "Fee, fee, darling!" Sadie caressed it with a finger, holding it to her large breast. "I'll put you into the guest cage. It's just been cleaned for you."

Without consulting me, she carried the bird to her room. A little cage with fresh water was ready. Shooing away her parakeets, she gently placed the bird on the swing and closed the cage. "Take a little water, fee, fee dear," she coaxed. "I'll get some seed you'll like."

With a nimble leap the bird alighted on the floor of the cage and dipped its tiny beak into the water.

"It drinks! It drinks!" I cried joyfully. "Oh, Sadie, you've saved my baby bird!"

"Shhh!" she admonished, but I went on gratefully. "You're wonderful! Wonderful!"

"Shut up! You're scaring the bird!"

"Forgive me," I implored in a lower voice. "So much has happened to me this morning. And the bird scared me—poor thing! I'll—But I'm not dressed. May I leave my baby with you for a while longer? You know so well how to handle it."

Back in my room, I dressed hurriedly. Why did I never dream that anything so wonderful as this bird would come to me? Is it because I never had a pet as a child that this bird meant so much to me in the loneliness of old age! This morning I did not know of its existence. And now it had become my only kin on earth. I shared its frightened helplessness away from its kind.

Suddenly I felt jealous of Sadie caring for my bird, lest it get fonder of her than of me. But I was afraid to annoy her by coming back too soon. So I set to work to give my room a thorough cleaning to insure a happy home for my bird. I swept the floor, and before I could gather up the sweepings in the dustpan, another shower of loose plaster came raining down. How could I clean up the dinginess, the dirt in the stained walls?

An overwhelming need to be near my bird made me drop my cleaning and go to Sadie. I knocked at the door. There was no answer, so I barged in. Sadie was holding the tiny thing in her cupped hands, breathing into it, moaning anxiously. "Fee, fee, darling!"

Stunned with apprehension I watched her slowly surrendering the bird into the cage.

"What's the matter?" I clutched her arm.

"It won't eat. It only took a sip of water. It's starving, but it's too frightened to eat. We'll have to let it go—"

"It's my bird!" I pleaded. "It came to *me*. I won't let it go—"

"It's dying. Do you want it to die?"

"Why is it dying?" I cried, bewildered.

"It's a wild bird. It has to be free."

I was too stunned to argue.

"Go get your hat and coat, we're going to Riverside Drive."

My bird in her cage, I had no choice but to follow her out into the park. In a grove full of trees, Sadie stopped and rested the cage on a thick bush. As she moved her hand, I grabbed the cage and had it in my arms before either of us knew what I had done.

"It's so small," I pleaded, tightening my arms around the cage. "It'll only get lost again. Who'll take care of it?"

"Don't be a child," she said, coldly. "Birds are smarter than you." Then in afterthought she added, "You know what you need? You need to buy yourself a parakeet. Afterwards I'll go with you to the pet store and help you pick a bird that'll talk to you and love you."

"A bought bird?" I was shocked. A bird bought to love me? She knew so much about birds and so little about my feelings. "My bird came to me from the sky," I told her. "It came to my window of all the windows of the neighborhood."

Sadie lifted the cage out of my arms and put it back on the bush. "Now, watch and see," she said. She opened the cage door and very gently took the bird out, holding it in her hand and looking down at it.

"You mustn't let it go!" I said, "You mustn't . . ."

She didn't pay any attention to me, just opened her finger slowly. I wanted to stop her, but instead I watched. For a moment, the little bird stayed where it was, then Sadie said something softly, lovingly, and lifted her hand with the bird on it.

There was a flutter, a spread of wings, and then the sudden strong freedom of a bird returning to its sky.

I cried out, "Look, it's flying!" My frightened baby bird soaring so sure of itself lifted me out of my body. I felt myself flying with it, and I stood there staring, watching it go higher and higher. I lifted my arms, flying with it. I saw it now, not only with sharpened eyesight, but with sharpened senses of love. Even as it vanished into the sky, I rejoiced in its power to go beyond me.

I said aloud, exulting, "It's free."

I looked at Sadie. Whatever I had thought of her, she was the one who had known what the little bird needed. All the other times I had seen her, she had remembered only herself, but with the bird she forgot.

Now, with the empty cage in her hand, she turned to go back to the apartment house we had left. I followed her. We were leaving the bird behind us, and we were going back into our own cage.

"The Open Cage," 1979

CHAPTER FIVE
WORKS

This chapter addresses both the work of living and lives devoted to work in the later years. We have used the term *works* to signify material products of labor (e.g., works of art, industry, or scholarship) as well as moral efforts or endeavors ("good works"). The chapter can be read as a series of meditations on the work involved in crafting and completing a good life. Selections by artists or about art are intended to evoke the fruitful analogy between crafting a life and making a work of art. The chapter's four groupings explore the difficult movement from vain wishes to ideals of a good life; work as a spiritual quest; psychological and economic dimensions of work; and living well as the real work of life.

The chapter opens with the famous passage from Ecclesiastes on the futility of all human endeavor:

> Vanity of vanity, saith Koheleth;
> Vanity of Vanities, all is vanity.
>
> . . . .
>
> All things toil to weariness;
> Man cannot utter it.

It may seem perverse to give such prominence to an ancient view, considered pessimistic or obsolete by so many modern folk. Yet the vanity of the usual human pursuits of pleasure, power, productivity, and wealth is a motif that runs through all genuine wisdom literature. Its harsh truths must be confronted directly by anyone seriously interested in the paradox of physical decline and spiritual growth. The problem is not that health and worldly goods are inherently bad, but that they are necessarily fleeting and can become false idols.

The first series of readings conveys several views on using one's limited time and abilities well. As an old man, the Renaissance painter and sculptor Michelangelo acknowledged that his own art had been a false idol; at age seventy-five, he wrote that his soul could only be calmed by "that divine love that opened his arms on the cross to take us in." In the Japanese folktale

"The Story of the Man Who Did Not Wish to Die," the wealthy Sentaro flies on a paper crane to a country of perpetual life—only to find that its immortal residents long for death as something good and desirable. It is best, he learns, to return home and "live a good and industrious life."

The next grouping explores work as a spiritual quest: the joyful work of maturing and gaining mastery of a craft, as well as work that enables one to endure oppression or adversity. Rudolf Arnheim, the American psychologist of art, describes how age and experience change the way artists make art. The historian Arnold Toynbee echoes Arnheim as he records changing attitudes toward his life's work of scholarship.

Ecclesiastes 3:9–22 offers a powerful rejoinder to its own bitter vanity motif that opens this chapter. The passage from the ancient Hindu Bhagavad-Gita speaks clearly of a self that does not die, but evolves and changes. Look to your duty is "Krishna's Counsel in Time of War," but have confidence that true peace comes with the renunciation of striving. In "Mother to Son," the African-American poet Langston Hughes speaks in the inspiring voice of a mother hard at work, urging her son to keep on climbing the material and spiritual stairs of life.

The fourth series of readings articulates psychological and economic dimensions of work and retirement. The German artist Kaethe Kollwitz and her contemporary Sigmund Freud both express the deep satisfactions of their work and convey a powerful need to continue working until death. Passages from Émile Zola's novel *Germinal* and from Paul Tournier's *Learn to Grow Old* emphasize the material conditions of aging workers and aged pensioners.

In the final grouping, various voices sing in counterpoint about work and rest, participation and disengagement. Alfred Tennyson's restless "Ulysses" and the French essayist Michel Eyquem de Montaigne seek noble work: "Old age hath yet his honour and his toil," writes Tennyson. Henry David Thoreau and the Hasidic rabbi Levi Isaac ben Meir offer reminders that rushing and striving for a livelihood are not one's true life work. Again the vanity note is sounded. Finally, Amy Lowell's poem about her onion-eating, flute-playing neighbor celebrates the transformative power of making art. By day, the neighbor is fat, bald, vulgar, and unprepossessing. By night, when he plays his flute, he creates beauty—and in the mind of the listening poet becomes beautiful.

ECCLESIASTES 1:1–18, HEBREW SCRIPTURES

The words of Koheleth, the son of
David, king in Jerusalem.
Vanity of vanities, saith Koheleth;
Vanity of vanities, all is vanity.
What profit hath man of all his labour
Wherein he laboureth under the sun?
One generation passeth away, and another generation cometh;
And the earth abideth for ever.
The sun also ariseth, and the sun goeth down,
And hasteth to his place where he ariseth.
The wind goeth toward the south,
And turneth about unto the north;
It turneth about continually in its circuit,
And the wind returneth again to its circuits.
All the rivers run into the sea,
Yet the sea is not full;
Unto the place whither the rivers go,
Thither they go again.
All things toil to weariness;
Man cannot utter it,
The eye is not satisfied with seeing,
Nor the ear filled with hearing.
That which hath been is that which shall be,
And that which hath been done is that which shall be done;
And there is nothing new under the sun.

Is there a thing whereof it is said: 'See, this is new'?—it hath been already, in the ages which were before us. There is no remembrance of them of former times; neither shall there be any remembrance of them of latter times that are to come, among those that shall come after.

I Koheleth have been king over Israel in Jerusalem. And I applied my heart to seek and to search out by wisdom concerning all things that are done under heaven; it is a sore task that God hath given to the sons of men to be exercised therewith. I have seen all the works that are done under the sun; and, behold, all is vanity and a striving after wind.

That which is crooked cannot be made straight;
And that which is wanting cannot be numbered.

I spoke with my own heart, saying: 'Lo, I have gotten great wisdom, more also than all that were before me over Jerusalem'; yea, my heart hath had great experience of wisdom and knowledge. And I applied my heart to know wisdom, and to know madness and folly—I perceived that this also was a striving after wind.

> For in much wisdom is much vexation;
> And he that increaseth knowledge increaseth sorrow.

MICHELANGELO *(Florentine/Italian, 1475–1564)*

> The voyage of my life at last has reached,
> across a stormy sea, in a fragile boat,
> the common port all must pass through, to give
> an accounting for every evil and pious deed.
> So now I recognize how laden with error
> was the affectionate fantasy
> that made art an idol and sovereign to me,
> like all things men want in spite of their best interests.
> What will become of all my thoughts of love,
> once gay and foolish, now that I'm nearing two deaths?
> I'm certain of one, and the other looms over me.
> Neither painting nor sculpture will be able any longer
> to calm my soul, now turned toward that divine love
> that opened his arms on the cross to take us in.

Sonnet, 1554

THE GOSPEL ACCORDING TO MATTHEW 25:14–30, THE NEW TESTAMENT

For the kingdom of heaven is as a man travelling into a far country, who called his own servants, and delivered unto them his goods.

And unto one he gave five talents, to another two, and to another one; to every man according to his several ability; and straightway took his journey.

Then he that had received the five talents went and traded with the same, and made them other five talents.

And likewise he that had received two, he also gained other two.

But he that had received one went and digged in the earth, and hid his lord's money.

After a long time the lord of those servants cometh, and reckoneth with them.

And so he that had received five talents came and brought other five talents, saying, Lord, thou deliveredst unto me five talents: behold, I have gained beside them five talents more.

His lord said unto him, Well done, thou good and faithful servant: thou hast been faithful over a few things, I will make thee ruler over many things: enter thou into the joy of thy lord.

He also that had received two talents came and said, Lord, thou deliveredst unto me two talents: behold, I have gained two other talents beside them.

His lord said unto him, Well done, good and faithful servant; thou hast been faithful over a few things, I will make thee ruler over many things: enter thou into the joy of thy lord.

Then he which had received the one talent came and said, Lord, I knew thee that thou art an hard man, reaping where thou hast not sown, and gathering where thou hast not strawed:

And I was afraid, and went and hid thy talent in the earth: lo, there thou hast that is thine.

His lord answered and said unto him, Thou wicked and slothful servant, thou knewest that I reap where I sowed not, and gather where I have not strawed:

Thou oughtest therefore to have put my money to the exchangers, and then at my coming I should have received mine own with usury.

Take therefore the talent from him, and give it unto him which hath ten talents.

For unto every one that hath shall be given, and he shall have abundance: but from him that hath not shall be taken away even that which he hath.

And cast ye the unprofitable servant into outer darkness: there shall be weeping and gnashing of teeth.

ALLAN B. CHINEN (*Japanese American, b. 1952*)

Once upon a time, an old man and his wife lived in a house overlooking the sea. Through the years, all their sons died, leaving the old couple to poverty and loneliness. The old man barely earned a living by gathering wood in the forest and selling it in the village. One day in the wilderness, he met a man with a long beard. "I know all about your troubles," the stranger said, "and I want to help." He gave the old man a small leather bag and when the old man looked in it, he fainted with surprise: the bag was filled with gold! By the time the old man came to, the stranger was gone. So the old man threw away his wood, and rushed home. But along the way, he began to think. "If I tell my wife about this money, she will waste it all," he told himself. And so when he arrived at home, he said nothing to his wife. Instead, he hid the money under a pile of manure.

The next day, the old man awoke to find that his wife had cooked a wonderful breakfast, with sausages and bread. "Where did you find the money for this?" he asked his wife.

"You did not bring any wood to sell yesterday," she said, "so I sold the manure to the farmer down the road." The old man ran out, shrieking with dismay. Then he glumly went to work in the forest, muttering to himself.

Deep in the woods, he met the stranger again. The man with the long beard laughed. "I know what you did with the money, but I still want to help." So he gave the old man another purse filled with gold. The old man rushed home, but along the way he started thinking again. "If I tell my wife, she will squander this fortune. . . ." And so he hid the money under the ashes in the fireplace. The next day he awoke to find his wife had cooked another hearty breakfast. "You did not bring back any firewood," she explained, "so I sold the ashes to the farmer up the road."

The old man ran into the forest, pulling out his hair in consternation. Deep in the wilderness, he met the stranger a third time. The man with the long beard smiled sadly. "It seems you are not destined to be rich, my friend," the stranger said. "But I still want to help." He offered the old man a large bag. "Take these two dozen frogs and sell them in the village. Then use the money to buy the largest fish you can find—not dried fish, shellfish, sausages, cakes, or bread. Just the largest fish!" With that the stranger vanished.

The old man hurried to the village and sold his frogs. Once he had the money in hand, he saw the wonderful things he could buy at the market, and he thought the stranger's advice odd. But the old man decided to follow the instructions, and bought the largest fish he could find. He returned home too late in the evening to clean the fish, so he hung it outside from the rafters. Then he and his wife went to bed.

That night, it stormed, and the old man and woman could hear the waves thundering on the rocks below their house. In the middle of the night, someone pounded on the door. The old man went to see who it might be, and found a group of young fishermen dancing and singing outside.

"Thank you for saving our lives!" they told the old man.

"What do you mean?" he asked. So the fishermen explained that they were caught at sea by the storm, and did not know which way to row until the old man put out a light for them. "A light?" he asked. So they pointed. And the old man saw his fish hanging from the rafters, shining with such a great light it could be seen for miles around.

From that day on, the old man hung out the shining fish each evening to guide the young fishermen home, and they shared their catch with him. And so he and his wife lived in comfort and honor the rest of their days.

From "The Shining Fish—The Elder Cycle Completed,"
adaptation of a traditional Italian folktale, 1989

SHUNSUI TAMENAGA (*Japanese, 1790–1843*)

Long, long ago there lived a man called Sentaro. His surname meant "Millionaire," but although he was not so rich as all that, he was still very far removed from being poor. He had inherited a small fortune from his father and lived on this, spending his time carelessly, without any serious thoughts of work, till he was about thirty-two years of age.

One day, without any reason whatsoever, the thought of death and sickness came to him. The idea of falling ill or dying made him very wretched.

"I should like to live," he said to himself, "till I am five or six hundred years old at least, free from all sickness. The ordinary span of a man's life is very short."

He wondered whether it were possible, by living simply and frugally henceforth, to prolong his life as long as he wished.

He knew there were many stories in ancient history of emperors who had lived a thousand years, and there was a Princess of Yamato, who it was said, lived to the age of five hundred. This was the latest story of a very long life on record.

Sentaro had often heard the tale of the Chinese King named Shin-no-Shiko. He was one of the most able and powerful rulers in Chinese history. He built all the large palaces, and also the famous great wall of China. He had everything in the world he could wish for, but in spite of all his happiness, and the luxury and splendour of his Court, the wisdom of his councillors and the glory of his reign, he was miserable because he knew that one day he must die and leave it all.

When Shin-no-Shiko went to bed at night, when he rose in the morning, as he went through his day, the thought of death was always with him. He could not get away from it. Ah—if only he could find the "Elixir of Life," he would be happy.

The Emperor at last called a meeting of his courtiers and asked them all if they could not find for him the "Elixir of Life" of which he had so often read and heard.

One old courtier, Jofuku by name, said that far away across the seas there was a country called Horaizan, and that certain hermits lived there who possessed the secret of the "Elixir of Life." Whoever drank of this wonderful draught lived for ever.

The Emperor ordered Jofuku to set out for the land of Horaizan, to find the hermits, and to bring him back a phial of the magic elixir. He gave Jofuku one of his best junks, fitted it out for him, and loaded it with great quantities of treasures and precious stones for Jofuku to take as presents to the hermits.

Jofuku sailed for the land of Horaizan, but he never returned to the waiting Emperor; but ever since that time Mount Fuji has been said to be the fabled Horaizan and the home of hermits who had the secret of the elixir, and Jofuku has been worshipped as their patron god.

Now Sentaro determined to set out to find the hermits, and if he could, to become one, so that he might obtain the water of perpetual life. He remembered that as a child he had been told that not only did these hermits live on Mount Fuji, but that they were said to inhabit all the very high peaks.

So he left his old home to the care of his relatives, and started out on his quest. He travelled through all the mountainous regions of the land, climbing to the tops of the highest peaks, but never a hermit did he find.

At last, after wandering in an unknown region for many days, he met a hunter.

"Can you tell me," asked Sentaro, "where the hermits live who have the Elixir of Life?"

"No," said the hunter; "I can't tell you where such hermits live, but there is a notorious robber living in these parts. It is said that he is chief of a band of two hundred followers."

This odd answer irritated Sentaro very much, and he thought how foolish it was to waste more time in looking for the hermits in this way, so he decided to go at once to the shrine of Jofuku, who is worshipped as the patron god of the hermits in the South of Japan.

Sentaro reached the shrine and prayed for seven days, entreating Jofuku to show him the way to a hermit who could give him what he wanted so much to find.

At midnight of the seventh day, as Sentaro knelt in the temple, the door of the innermost shrine flew open, and Jofuku appeared in a luminous cloud, and calling to Sentaro to come nearer, spoke thus:

"Your desire is a very selfish one and cannot be easily granted. You think that you would like to become a hermit so as to find the Elixir of Life. Do you know how hard a hermit's life is? A hermit is only allowed to eat fruit and berries and the bark of pine trees; a hermit must cut himself off from the world so that his heart may become as pure as gold and free from every earthly desire. Gradually after following these strict rules, the hermit ceases to feel hunger or cold or heat, and his body becomes so light that he can ride on a crane or a carp, and can walk on water without getting his feet wet.

"You, Sentaro, are fond of good living and of every comfort. You are not even like an ordinary man, for you are exceptionally idle, and more sensitive to heat and cold than most people. You would never be able to go barefoot or to wear only one thin dress in the winter time! Do you think that you would ever have the patience or the endurance to live a hermit's life?

"In answer to your prayer, however, I will help you in another way. I will send you to the country of Perpetual Life, where death never comes—where the people live for ever!"

Saying this, Jofuku put into Sentaro's hand a little crane made of paper, telling him to sit on its back and it would carry him there.

Sentaro obeyed wonderingly. The crane grew large enough for him to ride on it with comfort. It then spread its wings, rose high in the air, and flew away over the mountains right out to sea.

Sentaro was at first quite frightened; but by degrees he grew accustomed to the swift flight through the air. On and on they went for thousands of miles. The bird never stopped for rest or food, but as it was a paper bird it doubtless did not require any nourishment, and strange to say, neither did Sentaro.

After several days they reached an island. The crane flew some distance inland and then alighted.

As soon as Sentaro got down from the bird's back, the crane folded up of its own accord and flew into his pocket.

Now Sentaro began to look about him wonderingly, curious to see what the country of Perpetual Life was like. He walked first round about the country and then through the town. Everything was, of course, quite strange, and different from his own land. But both the land and the people seemed prosperous, so he decided that it would be good for him to stay there and took up lodgings at one of the hotels.

The proprietor was a kind man, and when Sentaro told him that he was a stranger and had come to live there, he promised to arrange everything that was necessary with the governor of the city concerning Sentaro's sojourn there. He even found a house for his guest, and in this way Sentaro obtained his great wish and became a resident in the country of Perpetual Life.

Within the memory of all the islanders no man had ever died there, and sickness was a thing unknown. Priests had come over from India and China and told them of a beautiful country called Paradise, where happiness and bliss and contentment fill all men's hearts, but its gates could only be reached by dying. This tradition was handed down for ages from generation to generation—but none knew exactly what death was except that it led to Paradise.

Quite unlike Sentaro and other ordinary people, instead of having a great dread of death, they all, both rich and poor, longed for it as something good and desirable. They were all tired of their long, long lives, and longed to go to the happy land of contentment called Paradise of which the priests had told them centuries ago.

All this Sentaro soon found out by talking to the islanders. He found himself, according to his ideas, in the land of *Topsyturvydom*. Everything was upside down. He had wished to escape from dying. He had come to the land of Perpetual Life with great relief and joy, only to find that the inhabitants themselves, doomed never to die, would consider it bliss to find death.

What he had hitherto considered poison these people ate as good food, and all the things to which he had been accustomed as food they rejected. Whenever any merchants from other countries arrived, the rich people rushed to them eager to buy poisons. These they swallowed eagerly hoping for death to come so that they might go to Paradise.

But what were deadly poisons in other lands were without effect in this strange place, and people who swallowed them with the hope of dying, only found that in a short time they felt better in health instead of worse.

Vainly they tried to imagine what death could be like. The wealthy would have given all their money and all their goods if they could but shorten their lives to two or three hundred years even. Without any change to live on for ever seemed to this people wearisome and sad.

In the chemist-shops there was a drug which was in constant demand, because after using it for a hundred years, it was supposed to turn the hair slightly grey and to bring about disorders of the stomach.

Sentaro was astonished to find that the poisonous globe-fish was served up in restaurants as a delectable dish, and hawkers in the streets went about selling sauces made of Spanish flies. He never saw anyone ill after eating these horrible things, nor did he ever see anyone with as much as a cold.

Sentaro was delighted. He said to himself that he would never grow tired of living, and that he considered it profane to wish for death. He was the only happy man on the island. For his part he wished to live thousands of years and to enjoy life. He set himself up in business, and for the present never even dreamed of going back to his native land.

As years went by, however, things did not go as smoothly as at first. He had heavy losses in business, and several times some affairs went wrong with his neighbours. This caused him great annoyance.

Time passed like the flight of an arrow for him, for he was busy from morning till night. Three hundred years went by in this monotonous way, and then at last he began to grow tired of life in this country, and he longed to see his own land and his old home. However long he lived here, life would always be the same, so was it not foolish and wearisome to stay on here for ever?

Sentaro, in his wish to escape from the country of Perpetual Life, recollected Jofuku, who had helped him before when he was wishing to escape from death—and he prayed to the saint to bring him back to his own land again.

No sooner did he pray than the paper crane popped out of his pocket. Sentaro was amazed to see that it had remained undamaged after all these years. Once more the bird grew and grew till it was large enough for him to mount it. As he did so, the bird spread its wings and flew swiftly out across the sea in the direction of Japan.

Such was the wilfulness of the man's nature that he looked back and regretted all he had left behind. He tried to stop the bird in vain. The crane held on its way for thousands of miles across the ocean.

Then a storm came on, and the wonderful paper crane got damp, crumpled up, and fell into the sea. Sentaro fell with it. Very much frightened at the thought of being drowned, he cried out loudly to Jofuku to save him. He looked round, but there was no ship in sight. He swallowed a quantity of seawater, which only increased his miserable plight. While he was thus struggling to keep himself afloat, he saw a monstrous shark swimming towards him. As it came nearer it opened its huge mouth ready to devour him. Sentaro was all but paralysed with fear now that he felt his end so near, and screamed out as loudly as ever he could to Jofuku to come and rescue him.

Lo, and behold, Sentaro was awakened by his own screams, to find that during his long prayer he had fallen asleep before the shrine, and that all his extraordinary and frightful adventures had been only a wild dream. He was in a cold perspiration with fright, and utterly bewildered.

Suddenly a bright light came towards him, and in the light stood a messenger. The messenger held a book in his hand, and spoke to Sentaro:

"I am sent to you by Jofuku, who in answer to your prayer, has permitted you in a dream to see the land of Perpetual Life. But you grew weary of living there, and begged to be allowed to return to your native land so that you might die. Jofuku, so that he might try you, allowed you to drop into the sea, and then sent a shark to swallow you up. Your desire for death was not real, for even at that moment you cried out loudly and shouted for help.

"It is also vain for you to wish to become a hermit, or to find the Elixir of Life. These things are not for such as you—your life is not austere enough. It is best for you to go back to your paternal home, and to live a good and industrious life. Never neglect to keep the anniversaries of your ancestors, and make it your duty to provide for your children's future. Thus will you live to a good old age and be happy, but give up the vain desire to escape death, for no man can do that, and by this time you have surely found out that even when selfish desires are granted they do not bring happiness.

"In this book I give you there are many precepts good for you to know—if you study them, you will be guided in the way I have pointed out to you."

The angel disappeared as soon as he had finished speaking, and Sentaro took the lesson to heart. With the book in his hand he returned to his old home, and giving up all his old vain wishes, tried to live a good and useful life and to observe the lessons taught him in the book, and he and his house prospered henceforth.

"The Story of the Man Who Did Not Wish to Die," c. 1800

RUDOLF ARNHEIM (*American, b. 1904*)

Our way of looking at the human seasons is determined by two conceptions. One of these conceptions is biological. It describes an arch rising from the weakness of the child to the unfolded powers of the mature person and then descending toward the infirmity of old age. In this view, the late style of life is that of the old man leaning on his cane—the three-legged creature, as the riddle of the sphinx describes him. It is the season of the "winter of pale misfeature," as Keats has it in his sonnet. The biological view considers not only the decline of physical strength but also the weakening of what one may call the practical powers of the mind. The acuity of vision and the range of auditory perception decline, memory begins to fail, reaction time lengthens, and the flexibility of intelligence gives way to a channeled concentration on particular established interests, knowledge, and connections. When these biological aspects determine the view of advanced age, people are afraid of getting old and look upon their capacity for productive achievement with doubt and irony.

There is another way of looking at the accomplishments of the aging mind. This second conception complements the first by finding in the passing of the years an ever continuing increase of wisdom. In our diagram, the symmetry of the biological arch is overlaid by a flight of steps leading from the limitations of the child to the high world view of those who have lived long and have seen it all. It is a conception that expresses itself socially and historically in the reverence for the ancient counselors, prophets, and rulers, and the respect for the older members of the traditional family. It accounts also for the attention paid to the late works of artists and thinkers. The curiosity of our modern theorists and historians about the particular character of late works is often coupled with the expectation of finding the highest achievements, the purest examples, the deepest insights in the final products of a life of search and labor.

Although reverence for the old exists probably in every mature culture, the theoretical interest in the motives, attitudes, and stylistic characteristics of late styles is limited presumably to periods that have reached a late phase of their own development. This is so not only because history and psychology are favorite occupations of late civilizations but also because generations discovering in their own conduct the symptoms of a declining age are naturally interested in the great examples of the corresponding stage of human development. It occurs to me, in fact, that we cannot go very far in a study of late styles without finding parallels to them in certain features of our present aesthetic and intellectual climate and perhaps also in our own personal way of life.

Inevitably we begin by looking at works created at the end of long careers. Longevity is one of our indispensable helpers, and only with hesitation do we consider also the late products of short careers. We dwell on the late works of a Michelangelo, Titian, Rembrandt, Cézanne, Goethe, or Beethoven, who all lived long lives, but it takes a special dispensation to include artists like Mozart, Van Gogh, or Franz Kafka, who died young. These short-lived geniuses can concern us only if we assume that death did not strike them blindly in the midst of a career that was structured for a longer duration. . . .

Be this as it may, we are not merely concerned with chronological age when we refer to the late works of artists. What we are interested in is a particular style, the expression of an attitude that is found often, but neither necessarily nor exclusively, in the end products of long careers. Some people, and some artists among them, live to what we call a ripe age without ever receiving the blessing of maturity.

Much of what is observed about the qualities of the typical aged mind concerns the relation of a person to his or her world. In this respect we may distinguish three phases of human development. An early attitude, found in young children and surviving in certain aspects of cultural and individual behavior, springs from a primary distance from outer experience. The world is perceived and understood only in broad generalities and contains neither much differentiation between the various facts of experience nor indeed any differentiation between the self and the other, the individual and his world. It is a state of mind in which the outer world is not yet segregated from the self and which Freud has described as the origin of the "oceanic feeling."

This primary lack of differentiation is followed by a second phase, a gradual conquest of reality. The self as an active and observant subject distinguishes itself from the objective world of people and things. This is the most important outcome of an increasing capacity for discrimination. The child learns to distinguish categories of things and to identify individual objects, places, and persons. An adult attitude develops, to which our Western culture offers a historical parallel in the new interest for the facts of outer reality, a curiosity that awoke first in the thirteenth century and created during the Renaissance the age of natural science, scientific exploration, and cultivation of individual persons, places, and events—a state of mind expressed in chronicles, in treatises on geography, botany, astronomy, anatomy, as well as in naturalistic painting and portraiture. This second phase of man's attitude toward reality has overcome the detachment of infancy. It is distinguished by a hearty worldliness that scrutinizes the environment in order to interact with it.

Perhaps that germinal age of the Renaissance contained already some features of a third and last phase, in which we recognize the symptoms of aging. But it is particularly in more recent times that the characteristically late attitude manifests itself clearly. I will mention some of these manifestations.

First, the interest in the nature and appearance of the world is no longer motivated primarily by the desire to interact with it. The paintings of the Impressionists, for example, are the products of a detached contemplation. The images depicting the natural and the man-made setting abandon the properties of texture, contour, and local color that report on the material particularity of the objects. The practical value of those material characteristics is not considered relevant. A similar attitude can be observed in the pursuit of pure science, as it develops especially in Europe.

Such a detachment of contemplation from practical application, however, is not simply negative. It goes with a worldview that transcends outer appearance in search of the underlying essentials, the basic laws that control the observable manifestations. This tendency is evident in the physical sciences and it also expresses itself recently in the exploration of deep-seated structure in anthropology, psychology, and linguistics.

As another symptom of what I call the late phase of the human attitude I will mention the shift from hierarchy to coordination. Instrumental here is the conviction that similarities are more important than differences and that organization should derive from the consensus among equals rather than from obedience to superordinate principles or powers. Socially, of course, this is democracy, the most mature and sophisticated type of human community, which presupposes the greatest human wisdom, although in practice, more often than not, it makes do with the least. In the arts, it involves, for example, the renunciation of governing compositional schemes, such as the triangular groupings of the Renaissance, in favor of a spread of coordinated units. These units, in turn, abandon their uniqueness, by which each element of a composition possesses an individual character and identifies its equally unique place and function in the composition or plot of the whole. Instead, in works of a late style the viewer or listener meets the same kind of thing or event in every area of the spatial pattern and in every phase of what in earlier style is narration or development in time. The sense of eventful action gives way, in space as well as in time, to a state or situation of pervasive aliveness. This structural uniformity in the late phase cannot but remind us of the earliest one, in which, as I suggested, discrimination between things as well as between the self and the world is still weak. However, a lifetime of difference separates a state of mind that cannot yet discriminate from one that no longer cares to.

*   *   *

I referred earlier to a second phase of development, which I called the phase of adulthood. In the composition of works of art, this attitude is visible when the dynamics of the total action originates in separate motivational centers. This is most easily seen in a figural work, where, let us say, the brutal aggression of a Sextus Tarquinius copes with a Lucretia vigorously defending her virtue. The same kind of dynamics activates the components of a musical conception typical of that active outlook on life, for example, in the interplay of the peasants' dance and the thunderstorm in Beethoven's *Pastoral* Symphony. One might say that the artist, from whose initiative all activity in the work ultimately springs, has delegated his resources of energy to the agents of his composition. And these agents behave as though they were acting on their own inherent impulses.

In late works, on the contrary, the dynamics moving the various characters is not of their own making. Rather they are subjected to this dynamics by a power that affects them all equally. Here again the artist, as he always does, has delegated his initiative to his creation, but this initiative no longer animates the individual motors of his characters. It is now manifest as the power of a fate pervading the entire world of the work. The living and the dead, the corpse of Christ and his mourning mother, all are now beings in the same state, equally active and inactive, aware and unaware, enduring and resisting.

This changed mechanism of energy generation and distribution in the late works manifests itself in a different handling of the formal means of expression, for example, in the role of light in painting. In an earlier style, light is produced by a well defined source, which, as a distinctive agent of its own, dispenses it to the recipients, to human figures or architecture, and they in turn display their individual reactions to it. But in a late Titian or Rembrandt, the entire scene has caught fire. The state of being inflamed is possessed and shared by all. One might describe this phenomenon more generally by saying that the imports from the world of reality, in which discrete forces act upon one another, have been consumed by the aging mind so fully as to be transformed into characteristics of the presentation as a whole, that is, into attributes of what we call style. The late style reduces the contribution of the objectively given to an almost totally metabolized matter, which sustains a unitary world view, the outcome of long and deep contemplation.

The differences of outlook accompanying the stages of life raise the problem of how productive and, then again, how problematic the relation between master and disciple might be in the arts. At times, these relations are

197

quite complex. One can think of examples in which the late works, although indigestible to the immediately following generation, powerfully affect a later one. This is true for the poetry of Hölderlin, the music of Wagner, or the Arles period of Van Gogh. Even more interesting are instances in which a new generation assimilates from a late style aspects it can accommodate to its own outlook. As a relatively recent example we remember the influence of the late works of Claude Monet on the American Abstract Expressionists. In Monet's last landscapes we see the final outcome of a lifelong development, during which the subject matter was gradually absorbed by an ever more conspicuous texture, fully realized in his water lilies, his footbridge paintings, and so forth. Essential to our appreciation of these works, however, is the fact that in spite of the radical transformation of the subject matter all the fulness and wealth of experienced reality remains present. The greatest possible range of artistic content reaches from the concreteness of the individual things of nature to the uniformity of the artist's all-encompassing view. This, we might say, is the final achievement of the human mind when it matures at an advanced age, and it is only natural that in the case of Claude Monet the influence he exerted on the painters of a later and younger generation could not reach to the depth he had attained himself.

"On the Late Style of Life and Art," 1978

ECCLESIASTES 3:9–22, HEBREW SCRIPTURES

What profit hath he that worketh in that he laboureth? I have seen the task which God hath given to the sons of men to be exercised therewith. He hath made every thing beautiful in its time; also He hath set the world in their heart, yet so that man cannot find out the work that God hath done from the beginning even to the end. I know that there is nothing better for them, than to rejoice, and to get pleasure so long as they live. But also that every man should eat and drink, and enjoy pleasure for all his labour, is the gift of God. I know that, whatsoever God doeth, it shall be for ever; nothing can be added to it, nor any thing taken from it; and God hath so made it, that men should fear before Him. That which is hath been long ago, and that which is to be hath already been; and God seeketh that which is pursued.

And moreover I saw under the sun, in the place of justice, that wickedness was there; and in the place of righteousness, that wickedness was there. I said in my heart: 'The righteous and the wicked God will judge; for there is a time there for every purpose and for every work.' I said in my heart: 'It is because of the sons of men, that God may sift them, and that they may see that they themselves are but as beasts.' For that which befalleth the sons of men befalleth beasts; even one thing befalleth them; as the one dieth, so dieth the other; yea, they have all one breath; so that man hath no pre-eminence above a beast; for all is vanity. All go unto one place; all are of the dust, and all return to dust. Who knoweth the spirit of man whether it goeth upward, and the spirit of the beast whether it goeth downward to the earth? Wherefore I perceived that there is nothing better, than that a man should rejoice in his works; for that is his portion; for who shall bring him to see what shall be after him?

ARNOLD TOYNBEE (*English, 1889–1975*)

What has made me work? When I was a child at school, the spur that I was first conscious of was anxiety. I was anxious always to be well ahead in puzzling out the meaning of passages of Greek and Latin that I might be called on to construe in class. I am still anxious to arrive well in time for catching trains and planes. This has its disadvantages. It uses up a lot of nervous energy that might be put to more positive use; and sometimes I carry my beforehandness to a point at which it catches me out. When I arrive at the station forty minutes ahead of my train's departure-time, the porter will not wait till the train comes into the station; so I have to put my luggage on board myself. Something like that happened to me once when I was called on to construe a difficult passage of Thucydides. I had prepared it carefully; but that had been several weeks ago; I had now far outshot the point that we had reached in class, and my mastery of this passage had grown rusty. If the master had not known my ways, he might have thought that I had not done my homework. I think he guessed the truth—which was that I had done it too far ahead of the date at which it was being re-quired.

Anxiety can be a bad thing if it goes to these extremes, and it is never a good thing in itself. It is, though, a powerful driving-force; so its drawbacks may be outweighed by its results.

A second spur that has pricked me on has been, and still is, conscience. In a previously published book, I have mentioned that my grandfather on my father's side came off a farm within sight of the tower of St. Botolph's church at Boston, England. The puritan conscience was perhaps part of my father's family's social heritage. In my attitude towards work I am Ameri-can-minded, not Australian-minded. To be always working, and this at full stretch, has been laid upon me by my conscience as a duty. This enslavement to work for work's sake is. I suppose, irrational; but thinking so would not liberate me. If I slacked, or even just slackened, I should be conscience-stricken and therefore uneasy and unhappy, so this spur seems likely to continue to drive me on so long as I have any working-power left in me.

Anxiety and conscience are a powerful pair of dynamos. Between them, they have ensured that I shall work hard, but they cannot ensure that one shall work at anything worthwhile. They are blind forces, which drive but do not direct. Fortunately, I have also been moved by a third motive: the wish to see and understand. I did not become conscious of this motive till some time after I had become aware of the other two; but I think that, before I became conscious of it, it must have been moving me, and this since an early stage of my life. Curiosity is a positive motive for action. It is also one of the distinctive characteristics of human nature as contrasted with the natures of non-human animals. All human beings have curiosity in some degree; and we also all have it about things that are of no practical use—or that seem, at least, to be of no practical use at the time when our curiosity is first excited by them. However, this universal human quality is stronger in some people than it is in others. This is one of the points in which human beings differ from each other markedly. The charge of curiosity with which I have been endowed happens to be high. This is a gift of the gods, and I am heartily grateful for it.

At school the anxiety that drove me into preparing my classwork far ahead of time had the fortunate effect of liberating my time for the pursuit of my curiosity. Just before a lesson in class for which I had prepared long ago, I would be free to work at what I liked, when some of the other boys were preparing for this next lesson at the last moment. 'What I liked' means 'what I chose', 'what I had set myself to work at.' The anxiety that had enslaved me to my work had also freed me to make myself my own director of studies. The prescribed work had become subordinate to the work that I mapped out for myself. In doing the prescribed work far ahead of time, I had taken it in my stride and had got it out of the way.

When I am asked, as I sometimes am asked, why I have spent my life on studying history, my answer is 'for fun'. I find this an adequate answer, and it is certainly a sincere one. If the questioner goes on to ask whether, if I could have my life over again, I would spend it in the same way again, I answer that I would, and I say this with conviction.

But why study history in particular? Curiosity is omnivorous. There are innumerable other things in the Universe, besides history, that can and do arouse curiosity in human beings. Why has my curiosity focused itself on history? The answer to this question is one that I know for certain. I am an historian because my mother was one. I cannot remember a time when I had not already taken it for granted that I was going to follow my mother's bent. When I had turned four, my father said that they could no longer afford a nurse for me. My mother asked if she might keep the nurse for a year longer, supposing that she earned the nurse's twelve-months' wage by writing a book; and my father agreed. I can remember vividly the excitement of seeing the proofs of *Tales from Scottish History* arrive. The fee was twenty pounds, and that was a nurse's wage for a year in England in 1893–4. When the year was up and the money was spent, the nurse went and my mother took over the job of putting me to bed. She kept me happy and good at bedtime by telling me the history of England, in instalments, from the beginning to 1895.

Certainly it was my mother who inspired me to become an historian, but I have followed my mother's bent in this rather general sense only. My mother, I think, loved the concrete facts of history for their own sake. I love them, too, of course. If one did not love them, one could never become an historian. Facts are an historian's stock in trade, and he has to acquire them in quantities that would be repellent if the facts did not fascinate him. I love the facts of history, but not for their own sake. I love them as clues to something beyond them—as clues to the nature and meaning of the mysterious Universe in which every human being awakes to consciousness. We wish to understand the Universe and our place in it. We know that our understanding of it will never be more than a glimmer, but this does not discourage us from seeking as much light as we can win.

Curiosity may be focused on anything in the Universe; but the spiritual reality behind the phenomena is, I believe, the ultimate objective of all curiosity; and it is in virtue of this that curiosity has something divine in it. Thanks to my mother's bent, my approach to this ultimate objective happens to be through the study of human affairs. Physics, botany, geology, or any other study that one can think of, offer alternative roads towards the same human goal. However, in the Jewish–Christian–Muslim *Weltanschauung*, history is set in a framework of theology. This traditional Western vista of history has been rejected by many Western historians—and by their non-Western disciples too—during the last two centuries and a half. Yet I believe that every student of human affairs does have a theology, whether he acknowledges this or not; and I believe that he is most at the mercy of his theology when he is most successful in keeping it repressed below the threshold of his consciousness.

Of course I can speak only for myself. I am sure that the reason why the study of human affairs has the hold on me that it has is because it is the window on the Universe that is open for me. A geologist or a botanist, travelling through a landscape that has not been the scene of any important events in human history, will see in it the hand of God, as vividly as I see this at, say, Bodh Gaya or Jerusalem. But, since my own approach to the presence behind the phenomena happens to lie in the field of human affairs, unhumanized non-human nature does not speak to me movingly. I am moved by Mount Cynthus more than by Mount Everest, and by the Jordan more than by the Amazon.

Why work, and why at history? Because, for me, this is the pursuit that leads, however haltingly, towards the *Visio Beatifica*.

From "Why and How I Work," in *Experiences*, 1969

THE BHAGAVAD-GITA (*Hindu, c. fourth century* B.C.E.)

Sanjaya

Arjuna sat dejected,
filled with pity,
his sad eyes blurred by tears.
Krishna gave him counsel.

Lord Krishna

Why this cowardice
in time of crisis, Arjuna?
The coward is ignoble, shameful,
foreign to the ways of heaven.

Don't yield to impotence!
It is unnatural in you!
Banish this petty weakness from your heart.
Rise to the fight, Arjuna!

Arjuna

Krishna, how can I fight
against Bhishma and Drona
with arrows
when they deserve my worship?

It is better in this world
to beg for scraps of food
than to eat meals
smeared with the blood
of elders I killed
at the height of their power
while their goals
were still desires.

We don't know which weight
is worse to bear—

our conquering them
or their conquering us.
We will not want to live
if we kill
the sons of Dhritarashtra
assembled before us.

The flaw of pity
blights my very being;
conflicting sacred duties
confound my reason.
I ask you to tell me
decisively—Which is better?
I am your pupil.
Teach me what I seek!

I see nothing
that could drive away
the grief
that withers my senses;
even if I won kingdoms
of unrivaled wealth
on earth
and sovereignty over gods.

Sanjaya

Arjuna told this
to Krishna—then saying,
"I shall not fight,"
he fell silent.

Mocking him gently,
Krishna gave this counsel
as Arjuna sat dejected,
between the two armies.

Lord Krishna

You grieve for those beyond grief,
and you speak words of insight;
but learned men do not grieve
for the dead or the living.

Never have I not existed,
nor you, nor these kings;
and never in the future
shall we cease to exist.

Just as the embodied self
enters childhood, youth, and old age,
so does it enter another body;
this does not confound a steadfast man.

Contacts with matter make us feel
heat and cold, pleasure and pain.
Arjuna, you must learn to endure
fleeting things—they come and go!

When these cannot torment a man,
when suffering and joy are equal
for him and he has courage,
he is fit for immortality.

Nothing of nonbeing comes to be,
nor does being cease to exist;
the boundary between these two
is seen by men who see reality.

Indestructible is the presence
that pervades all this;
no one can destroy
this unchanging reality.

Our bodies are known to end,
but the embodied self is enduring,
indestructible, and immeasurable;
therefore, Arjuna, fight the battle!

He who thinks this self a killer
and he who thinks it killed,
both fail to understand;
it does not kill, nor is it killed.

It is not born,
it does not die;
having been,
it will never not be;
unborn, enduring,
constant, and primordial,

it is not killed
when the body is killed.

Arjuna, when a man knows the self
to be indestructible, enduring, unborn,
unchanging, how does he kill
or cause anyone to kill?

As a man discards
worn-out clothes
to put on new
and different ones,
so the embodied self
discards
its worn-out bodies
to take on other new ones.

Weapons do not cut it,
fire does not burn it,
waters do not wet it,
wind does not wither it.

It cannot be cut or burned;
it cannot be wet or withered;
it is enduring, all-pervasive,
fixed, immovable, and timeless.

It is called unmanifest,
inconceivable, and immutable;
since you know that to be so,
you should not grieve!

If you think of its birth
and death as ever-recurring,
then too, Great Warrior,
you have no cause to grieve!

Death is certain for anyone born,
and birth is certain for the dead;
since the cycle is inevitable,
you have no cause to grieve!

Creatures are unmanifest in origin,
manifest in the midst of life,
and unmanifest again in the end.
Since this is so, why do you lament?

Rarely someone
sees it,
rarely another
speaks it,
rarely anyone
hears it—
even hearing it,
no one really knows it.

The self embodied in the body
of every being is indestructible;
you have no cause to grieve
for all these creatures, Arjuna!

Look to your own duty;
do not tremble before it;
nothing is better for a warrior
than a battle of sacred duty.

The doors of heaven open
for warriors who rejoice
to have a battle like this
thrust on them by chance.

If you fail to wage this war
of sacred duty,
you will abandon your own duty
and fame only to gain evil.

People will tell
of your undying shame,
and for a man of honor
shame is worse than death.

The great chariot warriors will think
you deserted in fear of battle;
you will be despised
by those who held you in esteem.

Your enemies will slander you,
scorning your skill
in so many unspeakable ways—
could any suffering be worse?

If you are killed, you win heaven;
if you triumph, you enjoy the earth;

therefore, Arjuna, stand up
and resolve to fight the battle!

Impartial to joy and suffering,
gain and loss, victory and defeat,
arm yourself for the battle,
lest you fall into evil.

Understanding is defined in terms of philosophy;
now hear it in spiritual discipline.
Armed with this understanding, Arjuna,
you will escape the bondage of action.

No effort in this world
is lost or wasted;
a fragment of sacred duty
saves you from great fear.

This understanding is unique
in its inner core of resolve;
diffuse and pointless are the ways
irresolute men understand.

Undiscerning men who delight
in the tenets of ritual lore
utter florid speech, proclaiming,
"There is nothing else!"

Driven by desire, they strive after heaven
and contrive to win powers and delights,
but their intricate ritual language
bears only the fruit of action in rebirth.

Obsessed with powers and delights,
their reason lost in words,
they do not find in contemplation
this understanding of inner resolve.

Arjuna, the realm of sacred lore
is nature—beyond its triad of qualities,
dualities, and mundane rewards,
be forever lucid, alive to your self.

For the discerning priest,
all of sacred lore
has no more value than a well
when water flows everywhere.

Be intent on action,
not on the fruits of action;
avoid attraction to the fruits
and attachment to inaction!

Perform actions, firm in discipline,
relinquishing attachment;
be impartial to failure and success—
this equanimity is called discipline.

Arjuna, action is far inferior
to the discipline of understanding;
so seek refuge in understanding—pitiful
are men drawn by fruits of action.

Disciplined by understanding,
one abandons both good and evil deeds;
so arm yourself for discipline—
discipline is skill in actions.

Wise men disciplined by understanding
relinquish the fruit born of action;
freed from these bonds of rebirth,
they reach a place beyond decay.

When your understanding passes beyond
the swamp of delusion,
you will be indifferent to all
that is heard in sacred lore.

When your understanding turns
from sacred lore to stand fixed,
immovable in contemplation,
then you will reach discipline.

Arjuna

Krishna, what defines a man
deep in contemplation whose insight
and thought are sure? How would he speak?
How would he sit? How would he move?

Lord Krishna

When he gives up desires in his mind,
is content with the self within himself,

then he is said to be a man
whose insight is sure, Arjuna.

When suffering does not disturb his mind,
when his craving for pleasures has vanished,
when attraction, fear, and anger are gone,
he is called a sage whose thought is sure.

When he shows no preference
in fortune or misfortune
and neither exults nor hates,
his insight is sure.

When, like a tortoise retracting
its limbs, he withdraws his senses
completely from sensuous objects,
his insight is sure.

Sensuous objects fade
when the embodied self abstains from food;
the taste lingers, but it too fades
in the vision of higher truth.

Even when a man of wisdom
tries to control them, Arjuna,
the bewildering senses
attack his mind with violence.

Controlling them all,
with discipline he should focus on me;
when his senses are under control,
his insight is sure.

Brooding about sensuous objects
makes attachment to them grow;
from attachment desire arises,
from desire anger is born.

From anger comes confusion;
from confusion memory lapses;
from broken memory understanding is lost;
from loss of understanding, he is ruined.

But a man of inner strength
whose senses experience objects
without attraction and hatred,
in self-control, finds serenity.

In serenity, all his sorrows
dissolve;
his reason becomes serene,
his understanding sure.

Without discipline,
he has no understanding or inner power;
without inner power, he has no peace;
and without peace where is joy?

If his mind submits to the play
of the senses,
they drive away insight,
as wind drives a ship on water.

So, Great Warrior, when withdrawal
of the senses
from sense objects is complete,
discernment is firm.

When it is night for all creatures,
a master of restraint is awake;
when they are awake, it is night
for the sage who sees reality.

As the mountainous depths
of the ocean
are unmoved when waters
rush into it,
so the man unmoved
when desires enter him
attains a peace that eludes
the man of many desires.

When he renounces all desires
and acts without craving,
possessiveness,
or individuality, he finds peace.

This is the place of the infinite spirit;
achieving it, one is freed from delusion;
abiding in it even at the time of death,
one finds the pure calm of infinity.

LANGSTON HUGHES (*African American, 1902–1967*)

> Well, son, I'll tell you:
> Life for me ain't been no crystal stair.
> It's had tacks in it,
> And splinters,
> And boards torn up,
> And places with no carpet on the floor—
> Bare.
> But all the time
> I'se been a-climbin' on,
> And reachin' landin's,
> And turnin' corners,
> And sometimes goin' in the dark
> Where there ain't been no light.
> So boy, don't you turn back.
> Don't you set down on the steps
> 'Cause you finds it's kinder hard.
> Don't you fall now—
> For I'se still goin', honey,
> I'se still climbin',
> And life for me ain't been no crystal stair.

"Mother to Son," 1926

KAETHE KOLLWITZ (*German, 1867–1945*)

July 20, 1917

Dear Frau Hasse!

Of all the letters I received for my fiftieth birthday, your letter stands out. My heartfelt thanks. When you wish that all the good spirits of creative joy, love and peace of mind may be at my side, I must say a hearty Amen to that. Such wishes bring new strength, and I need strength. Everyone needs it. And people can help one another a great deal through their sympathy, through their thinking of one another.

I dearly wish that my health may stand up for a long time to come. Primarily in order to finish the work—to finish it well—which I am doing for my boy who fell in battle. But beyond that I have in mind many other things still to be done. Growing old is fine if one keeps strong and well. Today we celebrated Liebermann's birthday. At seventy he is wholly unbent; his last works are perhaps his best. May the same be granted to me.

But not to grow old and be an invalid. . . .

211

October 1923

I am reading Emil Ludwig's account of Goethe's last years. How he gathered his forces and shut away all alien influences in order to fulfil himself in his work, to produce it out of himself to the last, to bring the pyramid of his life to its ultimate apex. What a splendid figure, this very old Goethe: wrathful, powerful, essential, concentrated to the utmost. How he presents the justifications of violence and all that follows from it. He is full of irony and impatience and intolerance. He overcomes Age, which in kind and thoughtful people usually produces tolerance, an attitude of "children, love one another." Leaving that state far behind, in his great age Goethe begins to blaze anew. He says of Death: "My conviction of our continuance after death springs from the concept of activity. For if I go on indefatigably doing my work to the end, nature is obliged to assign me another form of existence when the present form is no longer able to contain my spirit."

October 1923

A great response from my show. How happy I am!

November 1936

I am gradually realizing now that I have come to the end of my working life. Now that I have had the group cast in cement, I do not know how to go on. There is really nothing more to say. I thought of doing another small sculpture, *Age*, and I had some vague ideas about a relief. But whether I do them or not is no longer important. Not for the others and not for myself. Also there is this curious silence surrounding the expulsion of my work from the Academy show, and in connection with the Kronprinzenpalais. Scarcely anyone had anything to say to me about it. I thought people would come, or at least write—but no. Such a silence all around us.—That too has to be experienced. Well, Karl is still here. I see him every day and we talk and show one another our love. But how will it be when he too is gone?

One turns more and more to silence. All is still. I sit in Mother's chair by the stove, evenings, when I am alone.

Nordhausen, June 13, 1944

My dear children

Hans' letter has just come and Josef Faasen has just left. Do not misunderstand what I am writing today and do not think me ungrateful; but I must say this to you: My deepest desire is no longer to live. I know that many people grow older than I, but everyone knows when the desire to lay aside his life has come to him. For me it has come. The fact that I may or may not be able to stay here a while does not change that. Leaving you two, you and your children, will be terribly hard for me. But the unquenchable longing for death remains. If only you could make up your minds to take me in your arms once more, and then let me go. How grateful I would be. Do not be frightened and do not try to talk me out of it. I bless my life, which has given me such an infinitude of good along with all its hardships. Nor have I wasted it; I have used what strength I had to the best of my ability. All I ask of you now is to let me go—my time is up. I could add much more to this, and no doubt you will say that I am not yet done for, that I can write quite well and my memory is still clear. Nevertheless, the longing for death remains. . . . The desire, the unquenchable longing for death remains.—I shall close now, dear children. I thank you with all my heart.

From diary entries and letters of 20 July 1917, October 1923, November 1936, and 13 June 1944

SIGMUND FREUD (*Austrian, 1856–1939*)

Bergasse 19, Vienna IX, 6.3.1910

. . . I cannot face with comfort the idea of life without work; work and the free play of the imagination are for me the same thing, I take no pleasure in anything else. That would be a recipe for happiness but for the appalling thought that productivity is entirely dependent on a sensitive disposition. What would one do when ideas failed or words refused to come? It is impossible not to shudder at the thought. Hence, in spite of all the acceptance of fate which is appropriate to an honest man, I have one quite secret prayer: that I may be spared any wasting away and crippling of my ability to work because of physical deterioration.

In the words of King Macbeth, let us die in harness.

With cordial greetings,

Yours,

Freud

From a letter to Dr. Oskar Pfister, 6 March 1910

WILLIAM STAFFORD (*American, 1914–1993*)

They will give you a paperweight
carved out of heavy wood with black letters
that say everyone likes you and will miss
so steady and loyal a worker.

You carry it home and look at the nice message.
Not always have people allowed you even
a quiet exit—catcalls from that woman
who once appeared kind, plenty of lectures.

And oh the years of hovering anger
all around when each day reluctantly
opened and then followed like some dedicated,
stealthy, calculating, teasing assassin.

Now you can walk into the evening.
Walls where people live lean
on each side. You feel your mother by you
again, and your father has taken your hand.

Sister Peg skips ahead and looks back
that way we all loved and said, "Ours—
how eager she is! Beautiful!" We didn't
stay true, Peg. We didn't, we didn't.

The road bends gradually, then aims
straight at sunset. People are streaming
where all the sky opens on a bluff
and the sea drops off, blue and bright.

Suddenly this moment is worth all the rest.
Never has the sweetness arched so near
and overwhelming. They say a green flash
comes if you are lucky right at the end.

Now you see it was always there.

"Toward the End," 1991

ÉMILE ZOLA (French, 1840–1902)

The workman, after having emptied the trams, had seated himself on the earth, glad of the accident, maintaining his savage silence; he had simply lifted his large, dim eyes to the carman, as if annoyed by so many words. The latter, indeed, did not usually talk at such length. The unknown man's face must have pleased him that he should have been taken by one of these itchings for confidence which sometimes make old people talk aloud even when alone.

"I belong to Montsou," he said, "I am called Bonnemort."

"Is it a nickname?" asked Étienne, astonished.

The old man made a grimace of satisfaction and pointed to the Voreux:

"Yes, yes; they have pulled me three times out of that, torn to pieces, once with all my hair scorched, once with my gizzard full of earth, and another time with my belly swollen with water, like a frog. And then, when they saw that nothing would kill me, they called me Bonnemort for a joke."

His cheerfulness increased, like the creaking of an ill-greased pulley, and ended by degenerating into a terrible spasm of coughing. The fire basket now clearly lit up his large head, with its scanty white hair and flat, livid face, spotted with bluish patches. He was short, with an enormous neck, projecting calves and heels, and long arms, with massive-hands falling to his knees. For the rest, like his horse, which stood immovable, without suffering from the wind, he seemed to be made of stone; he had no appearance of feeling either the cold or the gusts that whistled at his ears. When he coughed his throat was torn by a deep rasping; he spat at the foot of the basket and the earth was blackened.

Étienne looked at him and at the ground which he had thus stained.

"Have you been working long at the mine?"

Bonnemort flung open both arms.

"Long? I should think so. I was not eight when I went down into the Voreux and I am now fifty-eight. Reckon that up! I have been everything down there; at first trammer, then putter, when I had the strength to wheel, then pikeman for eighteen years. Then, because of my cursed legs, they put me into the earth cutting, to bank up and patch, until they had to bring me up, because the doctor said I should stay there for good. Then, after five years of that, they made me carman. Eh? that's fine—fifty years at the mine, forty-five down below."

While he was speaking, fragments of burning coal, which now and then fell from the basket, lit up his pale face with their red reflection.

"They tell me to rest," he went on, "but I'm not going to; I'm not such a fool. I can get on for two years longer, to my sixtieth, so as to get the pension of one hundred and eighty francs. If I wish them good-evening to-day they would give me a hundred and fifty at once. They are cunning, the beggars. Besides, I am sound, except my legs. You see, it's the water which has got under my skin through being always wet in the cuttings. There are days when I can't move a paw without screaming."

A spasm of coughing interrupted him again.

"And that makes you cough so," said Étienne.

But he vigorously shook his head. Then, when he could speak:

"No, no! I got cold a month ago. I never used to cough; now I can't get rid of it. And the queer thing is that I spit, that I spit ——"

The rasping was again heard in his throat, followed by the black expectoration.

"Is it blood?" asked Étienne, at last venturing to question him.

Bonnemort slowly wiped his mouth with the back of his hand.

"It's coal. I've got enough in my carcase to warm me till I die. And it's five years since I put a foot down below. I stored it up, it seems, without knowing it. Bah, it keeps you!"

From *Germinal*, c. 1885

PAUL TOURNIER (*Swiss, 1898–1986*)

Popular wisdom is right when it asserts that money is not everything. The doctor has enough experience of people to realize that. He sees very unhappy people among those who are very wealthy, and others who suffer terribly from boredom amidst their expensive amusements. All the same, there is a threshold below which the condition of the pensioner is deplorable. Everything that one can write on the problems of retirement will be no more than words in the wind or 'a cymbal clashing' (I Cor. 13.1), in St Paul's words, if a radical change is not made in the financial situation of the low-income pensioner.

From *Learning to Grow Old*, 1971

ALFRED TENNYSON (*English, 1809–1892*)

It little profits that an idle king,
By this still hearth, among these barren crags,
Match'd with an aged wife, I mete and dole
Unequal laws unto a savage race,
That hoard, and sleep, and feed, and know not me.
I cannot rest from travel: I will drink
Life to the lees: all times I have enjoy'd
Greatly, have suffer'd greatly, both with those
That loved me, and alone; on shore, and when
Thro' scudding drifts the rainy Hyades
Vext the dim sea: I am become a name;
For always roaming with a hungry heart
Much have I seen and known; cities of men
And manners, climates, councils, governments,
Myself not least, but honour'd of them all;
And drunk delight of battle with my peers,
Far on the ringing plains of windy Troy.
I am a part of all that I have met;

Yet all experience is an arch wherethro'
Gleams that untravell'd world, whose margin fades
For ever and for ever when I move.
How dull it is to pause, to make an end,
To rust unburnish'd, not to shine in use!
As tho' to breathe were life. Life piled on life
Were all too little, and of one to me
Little remains: but every hour is saved
From that eternal silence, something more,
A bringer of new things; and vile it were
For some three suns to store and hoard myself,
And this gray spirit yearning in desire
To follow knowledge like a sinking star,
Beyond the utmost bound of human thought.
    This is my son, mine own Telemachus,
To whom I leave the sceptre and the isle—
Well-loved of me, discerning to fulfil
This labour, by slow prudence to make mild
A rugged people, and thro' soft degrees
Subdue them to the useful and the good.
Most blameless is he, centred in the sphere
Of common duties, decent not to fail
In offices of tenderness, and pay
Meet adoration to my household gods,
When I am gone. He works his work, I mine.
    There lies the port; the vessel puffs her sail:
There gloom the dark broad seas. My mariners,
Souls that have toil'd, and wrought, and thought with me—
That ever with a frolic welcome took
The thunder and the sunshine, and opposed
Free hearts, free foreheads—you and I are old;
Old age hath yet his honour and his toil;
Death closes all: but something ere the end,
Some work of noble note, may yet be done,
Not unbecoming men that strove with Gods.
The lights begin to twinkle from the rocks:
The long day wanes: the slow moon climbs: the deep
Moans round with many voices. Come, my friends,
'Tis not too late to seek a newer world.
Push off, and sitting well in order smite
The sounding furrows; for my purpose holds
To sail beyond the sunset, and the baths

Of all the western stars, until I die.
It may be that the gulfs will wash us down:
It may be we shall touch the Happy Isles,
And see the great Achilles, whom we knew.
Tho' much is taken, much abides; and tho'
We are not now that strength which in old days
Moved earth and heaven; that which we are, we are;
One equal temper of heroic hearts,
Made weak by time and fate, but strong in will
To strive, to seek, to find, and not to yield.

"Ulysses," 1842

HENRY DAVID THOREAU *(American, 1817–1862)*

. . . My Good Genius seemed to say,— Go fish and hunt far and wide day by day,—farther and wider,—and rest thee by many brooks and hearth-sides without misgiving. Remember thy Creator in the days of thy youth. Rise free from care before the dawn, and seek adventures. Let the noon find thee by other lakes, and the night overtake thee everywhere at home. There are no larger fields than these, no worthier games than may here be played. Grow wild according to thy nature, like these sedges and brakes, which will never become English hay. Let the thunder rumble; what if it threaten ruin to farmers' crops? that is not its errand to thee. Take shelter under the cloud, while they flee to carts and sheds. Let not to get a living be thy trade, but thy sport. Enjoy the land, but own it not. Through want of enterprise and faith men are where they are, buying and selling, and spending their lives like serfs.

O Baker Farm!

"Landscape where the richest element
Is a little sunshine innocent." . . .

"No one runs to revel
On thy rail-fenced lea." . . .

"Debate with no man hast thou,
With questions art never perplexed,
As tame at the first sight as now,
In thy plain russet gabardine dressed." . . .

"Come ye who love,
And ye who hate,
Children of the Holy Dove,

> And Guy Faux of the state,
> And hang conspiracies
> From the tough rafters of the trees!"

Men come tamely home at night only from the next field or street, where their household echoes haunt, and their life pines because it breathes its own breath over again; their shadows, morning and evening, reach farther than their daily steps. We should come home from far, from adventures, and perils, and discoveries every day, with new experience and character.

From "Baker Farm," in *Walden, or Life in the Woods,* 1854

HASIDIC TALE (*c. 1740–1810*)

The rabbi of Berdichev saw a man hurrying along the street, looking neither right nor left.

"Why are you rushing so much?" he asked the man.

"I'm rushing after my livelihood," the man answered.

"And how do you know," said the rabbi, "that your livelihood is running on before you so that you have to rush after it? Perhaps it's behind you, and all you need to do is stand still."

Tale about Rabbi Levi Isaac ben Meir of Berdichev

ADOLF GUGGENBÜHL-CRAIG (*Swiss, b. 1923*)

Today there is too much corruption and artificial sweetness in the picture of the wise man. The image has worn out and turned saccharine. Let us bury the wise old man and instead be inspired and guided by the old fool. An old person who accepts mental and physical deterioration, illness, death, and dying is closer to wisdom than one who rejects it. This seems paradoxical: if the old person can confront the terrible aspects of aging—including the psychological, mental, and physical deficits and the fear of becoming senile and demented—he will gain a special psychological quality which is much more precious than trivial wisdom. This includes accepting that one has lost contact with the collective unconscious and that one is now merely a historical figure. There is potential spiritual significance here, too: when one accepts the folly of old age and rejects the projection of wisdom onto it, one has become fully individuated.

What is the origin of the myth of the old fool? Is it my invention? I do not think so. Old people are often described as strange and foolish, and unfortunately they are often ridiculed by others. On the other hand, the *fool* is an old mythological figure who was often very highly regarded. It is unfortu-

219

nate that folly has been separated from old age in recent times. We have gone to great lengths to assure ourselves that there is nothing foolish about old age. The old fool is not a new myth. I am attempting to recover an old myth which is well-known, but has been repressed. The acceptance of the mythology of the old fool may be a blessing for the old person. His role in society improves. The old fool rejects being regarded as intelligent and wise and refuses the projection of wisdom. This means that he rids himself of positions of power and frees himself from responsibility. He leaves life's battlefield and allows himself to be the fool that he really is. I once saw a bus full of old women who had returned from an excursion. They giggled and teased each other and behaved very foolishly. They did not try to impress anyone or talk intelligently, but merely behaved as they wished. The sight was genuinely refreshing.

I am not suggesting that old people not work, only that they need not be driven by a purpose. Their purpose should not be to make money, to boost the economy, or to maintain power. Rather, they should simply enjoy. It is often said that old people have talents and abilities that are wasted, in that they do not serve the country's economy. I believe old age should play a useless role in society—the role of the fool—and thus warrant a unique freedom. Therefore, any social welfare system for the old is a great blessing. It permits them to turn to their true selves. No longer forced to make a living, they can enjoy the freedom of fools. They can live outside economic restrictions and simply "waste their time," be it with grandchildren or just sitting doing nothing. Above all, they no longer need a thorough grasp of that which is going on around them. Nothing is more embarrassing than an old person who continually attempts to show that she remains mentally alert, that she is still "with it," connected to the modern collective conscious and unconscious.

The association of wisdom and old age has caused much damage. For example, Albert Schweitzer, the jungle doctor, was an unusually talented and idealistic man. He was an organist who specialized in Johann Sebastian Bach. A philanthropist, he helped the sick in Africa and founded the hospital in Lambarene in Cameroon. Nevertheless, this genius fell victim to the corrupt mythology of the wise old man. In his old age he became a vain, tyrannical, negatively conservative racist. According to his colleagues of that period, he was completely unable to tolerate criticism of any kind. He believed he knew how the hospital should be run and refused advice. He thought that only he could treat the "blacks." He believed that his outdated, patriarchal attitude was the only correct approach. Not only was Schweitzer being led by the myth of the wise old man, it was being projected onto him. How much better if he could have accepted the myth of the old fool. He could have displayed greatness by accepting the role of the fool instead of becoming a righteous, vain old man.

*   *   *

The image of the old fool takes the horror away from the deficit model of aging. Growing old becomes rewarding again. In old age, we can rid ourselves of our power, but also of our responsibility. We can admit to ourselves as well as to our environment that, in God's name, we are not completely in control any more. By this we old people—I am saying *we* old people since I myself am standing at the threshold of old age—should not be prevented from participating in conversations. Our opinions and memories can still be very valuable for the world if they are accepted for what they are: comments or speculations by a person who belongs to a time gone by, who is devoid of all power, and whose intellectual abilities may even have declined. There must be something to the saying that "Children and fools speak the truth."

From "Long-Live the Old Fool" in *The Old Fool and the Corruption of Myth*, 1991

RABBI ELEAZAR ᴮᴱᴺ AZARIAH *(Hebrew, late first century–second century c.e.)*

He whose wisdom exceeds his works, to what may he be likened? To a tree whose branches are numerous but whose roots are few. The wind comes along and uproots it and sweeps it down. . . .

But he whose works exceed his wisdom, to what can he be likened? To a tree whose branches are few but whose roots are numerous. Then even if all the winds of the world come along and blow against it, they cannot stir it from its place.

As it is said: "He shall be like a tree planted by waters, sending forth its roots by a stream; it does not sense the coming of heat; its leaves are ever fresh; it has no care in a year of drought; it does not cease to yield fruit" (Jeremiah 17:8).

From *Ethics of the Fathers*

MICHEL EYQUEM DE MONTAIGNE *(French, 1533–1592)*

I cannot accept the way in which we establish the duration of our life. I see that the sages, as compared with popular opinion, make it a great deal shorter. "What," said the younger Cato to those who wanted to keep him from killing himself, "am I now at an age where I can be reproached for abandoning life too soon?" Yet he was only forty-eight. He regarded that age as quite ripe and quite advanced, considering how few men reach it. And

221

those who delude themselves with the idea that some course or other which they call natural promises a few years beyond, might do so properly if they had a privilege to exempt them from the many accidents to which we are all naturally subject, and which can interrupt this course that they promise themselves.

What an idle fancy it is to expect to die of a decay of powers brought on by extreme old age, and to set ourselves this term for our duration, since that is the rarest of all deaths and the least customary! We call it alone natural, as if it were contrary to nature to see a man break his neck by a fall, be drowned in a shipwreck, or be snatched away by the plague or a pleurisy, and as if our ordinary condition did not expose us to all these mishaps. Let us not flatter ourselves with these fine words: we ought perhaps rather to call natural what is general, common, and universal.

Death of old age is a rare, singular, and extraordinary death, and hence less natural than the others; it is the last and ultimate sort of death; the further it is from us, the less it is to be hoped for. It is indeed the bourn beyond which we shall not go, and which the law of nature has prescribed as not to be passed; but it is a very rare privilege of hers to make us last that long. It is an exemption which she grants by special favor to a single person in the space of two or three centuries, relieving him of the misfortunes and difficulties that she has cast in the way of others during this long period.

Thus my idea is to consider the age we have reached as one few people reach. Since in the ordinary course of things men do not come thus far, it is a sign that we are well along. And since we have passed the customary limits which are the true measure of our life, we must not hope to go much further. Having escaped so many occasions of dying, at which we see everyone stumble, we must recognize that an extraordinary fortune, and one out of the usual, like the one that is keeping us going, is not due to last much longer.

It is a defect in the very laws to hold this false idea: they have it that a man is not capable of the management of his estate until he is twenty-five, whereas he will hardly keep the management of his life that long. Augustus cut off five years from the ancient Roman ordinances, and declared that it was enough for those assuming the office of judge to be thirty. Servius Tullius released the knights who had passed forty-seven from service in war; Augustus set this back to forty-five. To send men back into retirement before the age of fifty-five or sixty seems not very reasonable to me. I should be of the opinion that our employment and occupation should be extended as far as possible, for the public welfare; I find the fault in the other direction, that of not putting us to work soon enough. Augustus had been universal judge of the world at nineteen, and yet would have a man be thirty in order to pass judgment on the position of a gutter.

As for me, I think our souls are as developed at twenty as they are ever to be, and give the promise of all they ever can do. No soul which at that age has not given very evident earnest of its strength has given proof of it later. The natural qualities and virtues give notice within that term, or never, of whatever vigor or beauty they possess:

> If the thorn will not prick at birth,
> It never will prick on earth,

they say in Dauphiné.

If I were to enumerate all the beautiful human actions, of whatever kind, that have come to my knowledge, I should think I would find that the greater part were performed, both in ancient times and in our own, before the age of thirty, rather than after. Yes, often even in the lives of the same men.

May I not say that with all assurance about those of Hannibal and of Scipio, his great adversary? They lived a good half of their life on the glory acquired in their youth: great men afterward in comparison with all others, but by no means in comparison with themselves.

As for me, I hold it as certain that since that age my mind and my body have rather shrunk than grown, and gone backward rather than forward. It is possible that in those who employ their time well, knowledge and experience grow with living; but vivacity, quickness, firmness, and other qualities much more our own, more important and essential, wither and languish.

> When age had crushed the body with its might,
> The limbs collapse with weakness and decay,
> The judgment limps, and mind and speech give way.
>
> Lucretius

Sometimes it is the body that first surrenders to age, sometimes, too, it is the mind; and I have seen enough whose brains were enfeebled before their stomach and lets; and inasmuch as this is a malady hardly perceptible to the sufferer and obscure in its symptoms, it is all the more dangerous. For the time, I complain of the laws, not that they leave us at work too long, but that they set us to work too late. It seems to me that considering the frailty of our life and how many ordinary natural reefs it is exposed to, we should not allot so great a part of it to birth, idleness, and apprenticeship.

"On Age," c. 1580

AMY LOWELL (*American, 1874–1925*)

> The neighbour sits in his window and plays the flute.
> From my bed I can hear him,
> And the round notes flutter and tap about the room,

And hit against each other,
Blurring to unexpected chords.
It is very beautiful,
With the little flute-notes all about me,
In the darkness.

In the daytime,
The neighbour eats bread and onions with one hand
And copies music with the other.
He is fat and has a bald head,
So I do not look at him,
But run quickly past his window.
There is always the sky to look at,
Or the water in the well!

But when night comes and he plays his flute,
I think of him as a young man,
With gold seals hanging from his watch,
And a blue coat with silver buttons.
As I lie in my bed
The flute-notes push against my ears and lips,
And I go to sleep, dreaming.

"Music," 1914

CHAPTER SIX
EROS/THANATOS

Eros and Thanatos—the names of the Greek gods of love and death—refer
to physical love and physical death, certainly. But they also encompass a
wider range of feelings and energies: the urge to create and the desire to
destroy; the instinct to go forth into the world and the desire for home; the
yearning for immortality and the drive for extinction. Moving from Eros to
Thanatos, the selections in this chapter illustrate these energies and explore
the complex relations between them in the second half of life. Several groupings articulate grief over the loss of erotic power; forms of solace or compensation for loss; the metamorphosis of love over time; long-devoted couples
facing the loss of one another; reflections on the necessity of one's own
death, including rage against it; and confrontations with death itself, encompassing hope, comfort, and transcendence.

The first series begins with another powerful passage from Ecclesiastes
and concludes with an elegy by the sixth-century Roman poet Maximianus.
As in the reference to Ecclesiastes in chapter five, Koheleth sounds the vanity
motif, this time warning against reliance on the pleasures of youthful
beauty: "And the dust returneth to the earth as it was; and the spirit
returneth unto God who gave it." But before the spirit departs, the aged
flesh decays, and may no longer draw the delighted gaze of another. Must
one then be reconciled to the loss of erotic joys, or become an object of
derision—a "dirty old man" or woman—like the butt of Chaucer's "Miller's
Tale"?

The next group of readings opens with an implicit response to these
questions from Plato's *Republic*. Speaking to Socrates, the aged Cephalus argues that the loss of sexual passion is actually a blessing and that
virtue is the key to a good old age. The Chinese poet Po Chü-i speaks of
the great comfort of long friendship. Yet the body and soul continue
to "burn," as Goethe and Muriel Rukeyser remind us. Is there a higher
yearning? a transformation of Eros? The section ends with the contemporary Kurdish poet Buland al-Haydari's longing for a loving glance, a warm
touch.

225

May Sarton's poem "A Farewell" opens a series of reflections on the ways that love dissolves, stagnates, transforms, or renews itself over a long period of time. Love, physical and spiritual, may continue to flourish even as the lovers' bodies lose their youthful beauty. The contemporary American novelist Mary Gordon draws a lesson from the Gospel story of Mary anointing the feet of Jesus. "We must not deprive ourselves, our loved ones, of the luxury of extravagant affections," she writes. "We must not try to second-guess death by refusing to love the ones we loved." Mona Van Duyn uses Gordon's words to launch her poem, "Late Loving." This series concludes with "Late Love," by the nineteenth-century Russian poet Fyodor Ivanovitch Tyutchev.

The fourth grouping bridges Eros and Thanatos. Beginning with Archibald MacLeish's "The Old Grey Couple," these readings express the poignant experiences of long-married couples avoiding, facing, or choosing death and mourning loss. "Alas, she is no more, whose soul was bent to mine like bending seaweed," wrote the seventh-century Japanese poet Kakinomoto Hitamoro.

The next series—from a poem by the early-twentieth century Tunisian poet Abu al-Qasim al-Shabbi to a passage from the contemporary Columbian novelist Gabriel García Márquez's *One Hundred Years of Solitude*—contains various reflections on the inevitability of one's own death. For some, life seems too long. "The magic of life is dry" mourns al-Shabbi. Death steals upon others unawares. The relatives of Márquez's Amaranta Ursula see that she is dead before she herself knows it: "'My God,' she exclaimed in a low voice. 'So this is what it's like to be dead.'"

But death is not an easy job to accomplish. Nor does everyone believe in renouncing the fight against it. Dylan Thomas's famous poem "Do not go gentle into that good night" opens a longer series on struggle and submission, the tensions between longing to be at rest and the desire to live forever, between fear of death and yearning for reconciliation with the inevitable. "The philosopher does not fear death," wrote the French philosopher Charles Renouvier, "it is the old man. The old man has not the courage to submit, yet I have to submit to the inevitable."

The last section on confronting death itself opens with the sixteenth-century French poet Pierre de Ronsard's witty, rueful farewell to his friends. The comforting Twenty-Third Psalm is included, along with thoughts from the Dalai Lama on the importance of the moment of death. John Donne's poetic affirmation of his Christian faith in eternal life closes the chapter: "Death, thou shalt die."

ECCLESIASTES 12:1–8, HEBREW SCRIPTURES

Remember then thy Creator in the days of thy youth,
Before the evil days come,
And the years draw nigh, when thou shalt say:
'I have no pleasure in them';

Before the sun, and the light, and the moon,
And the stars, are darkened,
And the clouds return after the rain;

In the day when the keepers of the house shall tremble,
And the strong men shall bow themselves,
And the grinders cease because they are few,
And those that look out shall be darkened in the windows,

And the doors shall be shut in the street,
When the sound of the grinding is low;
And one shall start up at the voice of a bird,
And all the daughters of music shall be brought low;

Also when they shall be afraid of that which is high,
And terrors shall be in the way;
And the almond-tree shall blossom,
And the grasshopper shall drag itself along,
And the caperberry shall fail;
Because man goeth to his long home,
And the mourners go about the streets;

Before the silver cord is snapped asunder,
And the golden bowl is shattered,
And the pitcher is broken at the fountain,
And the wheel falleth shattered into the pit;

And the dust returneth to the earth as it was,
And the spirit returneth unto God who gave it.

Vanity of vanities, saith Koheleth;
All is vanity.

MIMNERMUS (*Greek, known 650–600 B.C.E.*)

O Golden Love, what life, what joy but yours?
    Come death when you are gone and make an end.
When gifts and presents are no longer mine,

     Nor the sweet intimacies of a loved one.
These are the flowers of youth. But painful old age,
     The bane of beauty, following swiftly on,
Wearies the heart of man with sad foreboding
     And removes his pleasure in the sun.
Hateful is he to maiden and to boy
     And moulded by the gods to our sorrow.

"Oh, Golden Love"

SAPPHO *(Greek, fl. c. 610–580 B.C.E.)*

     You slight the fair gifts of the
          deep-bosomed Muses, children,
          when you say 'We will crown
          you, dear [Sappho], as first of
          singers with the clear sweet
          voice'.
     Do you not realise that age has
          wrinkled all my skin, that my
          hair has become white from
          being black, and that I have
          hardly any teeth left; or that my
          knees can no longer carry my body back
          again to the old days when
          I joined in the dance, like
          the fawns, the nimblest
          of living things?
     But what can I do? Not even
          God himself can do what
          cannot be done. And, for us, as
          unfailingly as starry
          night follows rosy-armed
          morning, and brings darkness to the
          furthest ends of the earth, so
          death tracks down and
          overtakes every living thing;
          and as he himself would not
          give Orpheus his dearest wife,
          so is he ever used to keep
          prisoner every woman whom
          he overtakes, even if he should

make her follow her spouse with
    his singing and piping.
But listen now—I love
    delicate living, and for me
    brightness and beauty and a longing
    for the sunlight have been
    given me as a protection.
    And, therefore, I have no
    intention of departing to the
    Grace of God before I need,
    but will lovingly pursue my
    life with you who love me.
And now this is enough
    for me that I have your
    love, and I desire no more.

"To Her Pupils"

GEOFFREY CHAUCER (*English, c. 1344–1400*)

She was a girl of eighteen years of age
Jealous he was and kept her in the cage,
For he was old and she was wild and young;
He thought himself quite likely to be stung.
He might have known, were Cato on his shelf,
A man should marry someone like himself.
A man should pick an equal for his mate.
Youth and age are often in debate.
His wits were dull, he'd fallen in the snare
And had to bear his cross as others bear.

From "The Miller's Tale," in *Canterbury Tales*, c. 1380

MAXIMIANUS (*Tuscan/Roman, c. 460–c. 530 C.E.*)

Jealous old age, reluctant to hasten my end,
Why come a laggard in this my worn-out body?
Set free my wretched life from such a prison:
Death is my peace and life a punishment.
What I was once, I am not: the best has perished;
Illness and fear possess what's left of me.
Life is a bore in my grief, though once it was happy,

And what is worse than dying is my wish to die.
While young and handsome, while mind and sense remained,
I was a speaker renowned throughout the world.
Often I fashioned the lying songs of a poet,
And often my fictions brought real glory to me.
Often I won the decision in cases at law,
Deserving the tribute awarded my nimble tongue.
What can be deathless now when my body's failing,
Alas, what portion of life remains to the old!
Not less than these talents was the grace of my sublime beauty;
When it is absent there's nothing else can please,
Not even virtue, more precious than tawny gold. . . .

From his first elegy, Age of Justinian, sixth century

PLATO (*Greek, 427–347 B.C.E.*)

[Aged Cephalus speaks:]

"I will tell you, Socrates, what I think of old age. Men of my age flock together. We are birds of a feather, as the old proverb has it; and at our reunions the constant story of my companions runs, 'I cannot eat; I cannot drink; youth's pleasures, sex, and love are gone. Life is no longer worth living.' Some complain of the slights that they must endure from relatives, and they will tell you over and over again how many evils old age causes. But to me, Socrates, these complainers seem to blame that which is really not the cause. For if old age were at fault, I too as an old man, and every other old man also, would have felt as they do. This is not my own experience nor that of many others whom I have known. I remember well the old poet Sophocles, when in answer to the question, 'How are you when it comes to sex, Sophocles? Can you still make love to a woman?' 'Peace,' he replied, 'most gladly have I escaped from this mad and furious tyrant.' His words have frequently come to my mind since, and they seem as good to me now as when he first uttered them. For a great peace and freedom from these things comes with old age. After the passions relax their grip, then, as Sophocles says, we are freed from the hold not of one mad master only, but of many. As regards both sex and complaints about relatives, there is but one cause, Socrates. It is not old age but men's characters and temperaments; for the man who has a calm and happy disposition will scarcely feel the pressure of age. The man who is of the opposite disposition finds that both youth and old age are equally troublesome." I listened in admiration, and wanting him to go on and expatiate, I said, "Yes, Cephalus, but I rather suspect that people generally are not convinced by your statement. I rather suspect that people generally think old age sits lightly upon your shoulders, not because of your cheerful disposition, but because you are rich. Wealth is known to be a great comforter."

"You are correct," he answered. "They are not convinced. There is something in what they claim; not, however, so much as they think. I might answer them as Themistocles answered the Seriphian who was abusing him and saying that he was famous, not on account of his own merits but because he was an Athenian: 'If you had been a native of my country or I of yours, neither of us would have been famous.' And to those who are not rich and are impatient of old age, the same answer may be given. For to the good poor man old age cannot be a light burden, nor can a bad rich man ever find peace with himself."

*   *   *

"Let me tell you, Socrates, that when a man thinks himself to be near death, fears and cares enter into his mind that he never had before. The tales of a world below and the punishment that is demanded there for what one has done here once constituted something to laugh about. But now he is tormented with the thought that they may be true, either from the weakness of age or because he is now approaching that far place—for these reasons he enjoys a clearer view of such things. Suspicions and alarms crowd quickly upon such a man, and he begins to reflect and ponder what wrongs he has done to others. When he finds that the total of his transgressions is large, he will often like a child start up in his sleep out of fear. He is overwhelmed with dark fears. To the man who is conscious of no sins, sweet hope, as Pindar beautifully says, is the kind nurse of his old age: 'Hope cherishes,' he says, 'the soul of the man who lives in justice and holiness, and is the nurse of his age and the companion of his journey; hope that is mightiest to sway the restless soul of man.' How admirable are his words!"

From *The Republic*, book 1, last half of the fourth century B.C.E.

PO CHÜ-I (*Chinese, 772–846 C.E.*)

> We are growing old together, you and I;
> Let us ask ourselves, what is age like?
> The dull eye is closed ere night comes;
> The idle head, still uncombed at noon.
> Propped on a staff, sometimes a walk abroad;
> Or all day sitting with closed doors.
> One dares not look in the mirror's polished face;
> One cannot read small-letter books.

231

Deeper and deeper, one's love of old friends;
Fewer and fewer, one's dealings with young men.
One thing only, the pleasure of idle talk,
Is great as ever, when you and I meet.

"Old Age," 835 C.E.

JOHANN WOLFGANG VON GOETHE (*German, 1749–1832*)

Tell a wise person, or else keep silent,
because the massman will mock it right away.
I praise what is truly alive,
what longs to be burned to death.

In the calm water of the love-nights,
where you were begotten, where you have begotten,
a strange feeling comes over you
when you see the silent candle burning.

Now you are no longer caught
in the obsession with darkness,
and a desire for higher love-making
sweeps you upward.

Distance does not make you falter,
now, arriving in magic, flying,
and, finally, insane for the light,
you are the butterfly and you are gone.

And so long as you haven't experienced
this: to die and so to grow,
you are only a troubled guest
on the dark earth.

"The Holy Longing," 1814

MURIEL RUKEYSER (*American, 1913–1980*)

The randy old
woman said
Tickle me up
I'll be
dead very soon—
Nothing will

touch me then
but the clouds
of the sky
and the bone-
white light
off the moon
Touch me
before I go
down
among the bones
My dear one
alone
to the night—
I said
I know I know
But all I know
tonight
Is that the sun
and the moon
they burn
with the one
one light.

In her burning
signing
what does the
white moon say?
The moon says
The sun
is shining.

"In Her Burning," 1944

BULAND AL-HAYDARI (*Kurdish/Iraqi, b. 1926*)

Another winter,
And here am I,
By the side of the stove,
Dreaming that a woman might dream of me,
That I might bury in her breast
A secret she would not mock;
Dreaming that in my fading years
I might spring forth as light,

And she would say:
This light is mine;
Let no woman draw near it.
> Here by the side of the stove,
> Another winter,
> And here am I,
> Spinning my dreams and fearing them,
> Afraid her eyes would mock
> My bald, idiotic head,
> My greying, aged soul,
> Afraid her feet would kick
> My love,
> And here, by the side of the stove,
> I would be lightly mocked by woman.
Alone,
Without love, or dreams, or a woman,
And tomorrow I shall die of the cold within,
Here, by the side of the stove.

"Old Age," 1974

MAY SARTON (*American, b. 1912*)

For a while I shall still be leaving,
Looking back at you as you slip away
Into the magic islands of the mind.
But for a while now all alive, believing
That in a single poignant hour
We did say all that we could ever say
In a great flowing out of radiant power.
It was like seeing and then going blind.

After a while we shall be cut in two
Between real islands where you live
And a far shore where I'll no longer keep
The haunting image of your eyes, and you,
As pupils widen, widen to deep black
And I able neither to love or grieve
Between fulfillment and heartbreak.
The time will come when I can go to sleep.

But for a while still, centered at last,
Contemplate a brief amazing union,

234

Then watch you leave and then let you go.
I must not go back to the murderous past
Nor force a passage through to some safe landing,
But float upon this moment of communion
Entranced, astonished by pure understanding—
Passionate love dissolved like summer snow.

"A Farewell," 1981

W. B. YEATS *(Irish, 1865–1939)*

When you are old and grey and full of sleep,
And nodding by the fire, take down this book,
And slowly read, and dream of the soft look
Your eyes had once, and of their shadows deep;

How many loved your moments of glad grace,
And loved your beauty with love false or true,
But one man loved the pilgrim soul in you,
And loved the sorrows of your changing face;

And bending down beside the glowing bars,
Murmur, a little sadly, how Love fled
And paced upon the mountains overhead
And hid his face amid a crowd of stars.

"When You Are Old," 1893

JOHN CIARDI *(American, 1916–1986)*

Why would they want one another,
those two old crocks of habit
up heavy from the stale bed?

Because we are not visible where we dance,
though a word none hears can call us
to the persuasion of kindness, and there sing.

"The Aging Lovers," 1989

ETHAN CANIN *(American, b. 1960)*

Where are we going? Where, I might write, is this path leading us? Francine is asleep and I am standing downstairs in the kitchen with the door closed and the light on and a stack of mostly blank paper on the counter in front of me.

My dentures are in a glass by the sink. I clean them with a tablet that bubbles in the water, and although they were clean already I just cleaned them again because the bubbles are agreeable and I thought their effervescence might excite me to action. By action, I mean I thought they might excite me to write. But words fail me.

This is a love story. However, its roots are tangled and involve a good bit of my life, and when I recall my life my mood turns sour and I am reminded that no man makes truly proper use of his time. We are blind and small-minded. We are dumb as snails and as frightened, full of vanity and misinformed about the importance of things. I'm an average man, without great deeds except maybe one, and that has been to love my wife.

I have been more or less faithful to Francine since I married her. There has been one transgression—leaning up against a closet wall with a red-haired purchasing agent at a sales meeting once in Minneapolis twenty years ago; but she was buying auto upholstery and I was selling it and in the eyes of judgment this may bear a key weight. Since then, though, I have ambled on this narrow path of life bound to one woman. This is a triumph and a regret. In our current state of affairs it is a regret because in life a man is either on the uphill or on the downhill, and if he isn't procreating he is on the downhill. It is a steep downhill indeed. These days I am tumbling, falling headlong among the scrub oaks and boulders, tearing my knees and abrading all the bony parts of the body. I have given myself to gravity.

Francine and I are married now forty-six years, and I would be a bamboozler to say that I have loved her for any more than half of these. Let us say that for the last year I haven't; let us say this for the last ten, even. Time has made torments of our small differences and tolerance of our passions. This is our state of affairs. Now I stand by myself in our kitchen in the middle of the night; now I lead a secret life. We wake at different hours now, sleep in different corners of the bed. We like different foods and different music, keep our clothing in different drawers, and if it can be said that either of us has aspirations, I believe that they are to a different bliss. Also, she is healthy and I am ill. And as for conversation—that feast of reason, that flow of the soul— our house is silent as the bone yard.

Last week we did talk. "Frank," she said one evening at the table, "there is something I must tell you."

The New York game was on the radio, snow was falling outside, and the pot of tea she had brewed was steaming on the table between us. Her medicine and my medicine were in little paper cups at our places.

"Frank," she said, jiggling her cup, "what I must tell you is that someone was around the house last night."

I tilted my pills onto my hand. "Around the house?"

"Someone was at the window."

On my palm the pills were white, blue, beige, pink: Lasix, Diabinese, Slow-K, Lopressor. "What do you mean?"

She rolled her pills onto the tablecloth and fidgeted with them, made them into a line, then into a circle, then into a line again. I don't know her medicine so well. She's healthy, except for little things. "I mean," she said, "there was someone in the yard last night."

"How do you know?"

"Frank, will you really, please?"

"I'm asking how you know."

"I heard him," she said. She looked down. "I was sitting in the front room and I heard him outside the window."

"You heard him?"

"Yes."

"The front window?"

She got up and went to the sink. This is a trick of hers. At that distance I can't see her face.

"The front window is ten feet off the ground," I said.

"What I know is that there was a man out there last night, right outside the glass." She walked out of the kitchen.

"Let's check," I called after her, I walked into the living room, and when I got there she was looking out the window.

"What is it?"

She was peering out at an angle. All I could see was snow, blue-white.

"Footprints," she said.

I built the house we live in with my two hands. That was forty-nine years ago, when, in my foolishness and crude want of learning, everything I didn't know seemed like a promise. I learned to build a house and then I built one. There are copper fixtures on the pipes, sanded edges on the struts and queen posts. Now, a half-century later, the floors are flat as a billiard table but the man who laid them needs two hands to pick up a woodscrew. This is the diabetes. My feet are gone also. I look down at them and see two black shapes when I walk, things I can't feel. Black clubs. No connection with the ground. If I didn't look, I could go to sleep with my shoes on.

Life takes its toll, and soon the body gives up completely. But it gives up the parts first. This sugar in the blood: God says to me: "Frank Manlius—codger, man of prevarication and half-truth—I shall take your life from you, as from all men. But first—" But first! Clouds in the eyeball, a heart that makes noise, feet cold as uncooked roast. And Francine, beauty that she was—now I see not much more than the dark line of her brow and the intersections of her body: mouth and nose, neck and shoulders. Her smells have changed over the years so that I don't know what's her own anymore and what's powder.

We have two children, but they're gone now too, with children of their own. We have a house, some furniture, small savings to speak of. How Francine spends her day I don't know. This is the sad truth, my confession. I am gone past nightfall. She wakes early with me and is awake when I return, but beyond this I know almost nothing of her life.

I myself spend my days at the aquarium. I've told Francine something else, of course, that I'm part of a volunteer service of retired men, that we spend our days setting young businesses afoot: "Immigrants," I told her early on, "newcomers to the land." I said it was difficult work. In the evenings I could invent stories, but I don't, and Francine doesn't ask.

I am home by nine or ten. Ticket stubs from the aquarium fill my coat pocket. Most of the day I watch the big sea animals—porpoises, sharks, a manatee—turn their saltwater loops. I come late morning and move a chair up close. They are waiting to eat then. Their bodies skim the cool glass, full of strange magnifications. I think, if it is possible, that they are beginning to know me: this man—hunched at the shoulder, cataractic of eye, breathing through water himself—this man who sits and watches. I do not pity them. At lunchtime I buy coffee and sit in one of the hotel lobbies or in the cafeteria next door, and I read poems. Browning, Whitman, Eliot. This is my secret. It is night when I return home. Francine is at the table, four feet across from my seat, the width of two dropleaves. Our medicine is in cups. There have been three Presidents since I held her in my arms.

The cafeteria moves the men along, old or young, who come to get away from the cold. A half-hour for a cup, they let me sit. Then the manager is at my table. He is nothing but polite. I buy a pastry then, something small. He knows me—I have seen him nearly every day for months now—and by his slight limp I know he is a man of mercy. But business is business.

"What are you reading?" he asks me as he wipes the table with a wet cloth. He touches the saltshaker, nudges the napkins in their holder. I know what this means.

"I'll take a cranberry roll," I say. He flicks the cloth and turns back to the counter.

This is what:

> *Shall I say, I have gone at dusk through narrow streets*
> *And watched the smoke that rises from the pipes*
> *Of lonely men in shirt-sleeves, leaning out of windows?*

Through the magnifier glass the words come forward, huge, two by two. With spectacles, everything is twice enlarged. Still, though, I am slow to read it. In a half-hour I am finished, could not read more, even if I bought another roll. The boy at the register greets me, smiles when I reach him. "What are you reading today?" he asks, counting out the change.

The books themselves are small and fit in the inside pockets of my coat. I put one in front of each breast, then walk back to see the fish some more. These are the fish I know: the gafftopsail pompano, sixgill shark, the starry flounder with its upturned eyes, queerly migrated. He rests half-submerged in sand. His scales are platey and flat-hued. Of everything upward he is wary, of the silvery seabass and the bluefin tuna that pass above him in the region of light and open water. For a life he lies on the bottom of the tank. I look at him. His eyes are dull. They are ugly and an aberration. Above us the bony fishes wheel at the tank's corners. I lean forward to the glass. "*Platichthys stellatus,*" I say to him. The caudal fin stirs. Sand moves and resettles, and I see the black and yellow stripes. "Flatfish," I whisper, "we are, you and I, obervers of this life."

"A man on our lawn," I say a few nights later in bed.

"Not just that."

I breathe in, breathe out, look up at the ceiling. "What else?"

"When you were out last night he came back."

"He came back."

"Yes."

"What did he do?"

"Looked in at me."

Later, in the early night, when the lights of cars are still passing and the walked dogs still jingle their collar chains out front, I get up quickly from bed and step into the hall. I move fast because this is still possible in short bursts and with concentration. The bed sinks once, then rises. I am on the landing and then downstairs without Francine waking. I stay close to the staircase joists.

In the kitchen I take out my almost blank sheets and set them on the counter. I write standing up because I want to take more than an animal's pose. For me this is futile, but I stand anyway. The page will be blank when I finish. This I know. The dreams I compose are the dreams of others, remembered bits of verse. Songs of greater men than I. In months I have written few more than a hundred words. The pages are stacked, sheets of different sizes.

If I could

one says.

It has never seemed

says another. I stand and shift them in and out. They are mostly blank, sheets from months of nights. But this doesn't bother me. What I have is patience.

Francine knows nothing of the poetry. She's a simple girl, toast and butter. I myself am hardly the man for it: forty years selling (anything—steel piping, heater elements, dried bananas). Didn't read a book except one on sales. Think victory, the book said. Think *sale*. It's a young man's bag of apples, though; young men in pants that nip at the waist. Ten years ago I left the Buick in the company lot and walked home, dye in my hair, cotton rectangles in the shoulders of my coat. Francine was in the house that afternoon also, the way she is now. When I retired we bought a camper and went on a trip. A traveling salesman retires, so he goes on a trip. Forty miles out of town the folly appeared to me, big as a balloon. To Francine, too. "Frank," she said in the middle of a bend, a prophet turning to me, the camper pushing sixty and rocking in the wind, trucks to our left and right big as trains—"Frank," she said, "these roads must be familiar to you."

So we sold the camper at a loss and a man who'd spent forty years at highway speed looked around for something to do before he died. The first poem I read was in a book on a table in a waiting room. My eyeglasses made half-sense of things.

> *THESE*
> *are the desolate, dark weeks*

I read

> *when nature in its barrenness*
> *equals the stupidity of man.*

Gloom, I thought, and nothing more, but then I reread the words, and suddenly there I was, hunched and wheezing, bald as a trout, and tears were in my eye. I don't know where they came from.

In the morning an officer visits. He has muscles, mustache, skin red from the cold. He leans against the door frame.

"Can you describe him?" he says.

"It's always dark," says Francine.

"Anything about him?"

"I'm an old woman. I can see that he wears glasses."

"What kind of glasses?"

"Black."

"Dark glasses?"

"Black glasses."

"At a particular time?"

"Always when Frank is away."

"Your husband has never been here when he's come?"

"Never."

"I see." He looks at me. This look can mean several things, perhaps that he thinks Francine is imagining. "But never at a particular time?"

"No."

"Well," he says. Outside on the porch his partner is stamping his feet. "Well," he says again. "We'll have a look." He turns, replaces his cap, heads out to the snowy steps. The door closes. I hear him say something outside.

"Last night—" Francine says. She speaks in the dark. "Last night I heard him on the side of the house."

We are in bed. Outside, on the sill, snow has been building since morning.

"You heard the wind."

"Frank." She sits up, switches on the lamp, tilts her head toward the window. Through a ceiling and two walls I can hear the ticking of our kitchen clock.

"I heard him climbing," she says. She has wrapped her arms about her own waist. "He was on the house. I heard him. He went up the drainpipe." She shivers as she says this. "There was no wind. He went up the drainpipe and then I heard him on the porch roof."

"Houses make noise."

"I heard him. There's gravel there."

I imagine the sounds, amplified by hollow walls, rubber heels on timber. I don't say anything. There is an arm's length between us, cold sheet, a space uncrossed since I can remember.

"I have made the mistake in my life of not being interested in enough people," she says then. "If I'd been interested in more people, I wouldn't be alone now."

"Nobody's alone," I say.

"I mean that if I'd made more of an effort with people I would have friends now. I would know the postman and the Giffords and the Kohlers, and we'd be together in this, all of us. We'd sit in each other's living rooms on rainy days and talk about the children. Instead we've kept to ourselves. Now I'm alone."

"You're not alone," I say.

"Yes, I am." She turns the light off and we are in the dark again. "You're alone, too."

My health has gotten worse. It's slow to set in at this age, not the violent shaking grip of death; instead—a slow leak, nothing more. A bicycle tire: rimless, thready, worn treadless already and now losing its fatness. A war of attrition. The tall camels of the spirit steering for the desert. One morning I realized I hadn't been warm in a year.

And there are other things that go, too. For instance, I recall with certainty that it was on the 23rd of April, 1945, that, despite German counter-offensives in the Ardennes, Eisenhower's men reach the Elbe; but I cannot remember whether I have visited the savings and loan this week. Also, I am unable to produce the name of my neighbor, though I greeted him yesterday in the street. And take, for example, this: I am at a loss to explain whole decades of my life. We have children and photographs, and there is an understanding between Francine and me that bears the weight of nothing less than half a century, but when I gather my memories they seem to fill no more than an hour. Where has my life gone?

It has gone partway to shoddy accumulations. In my wallet are credit cards, a license ten years expired, twenty-three dollars in cash. There is a photograph but it depresses me to look at it, and a poem, half-copied and folded into the billfold. The leather is pocked and has taken on the curve of my thigh. The poem is from Walt Whitman. I copy only what I need.

But of all things to do last, poetry is a barren choice. Deciphering other men's riddles while the world is full of procreation and war. A man should go out swinging an axe. Instead, I shall go out in a coffee shop.

But how can any man leave this world with honor? Despite anything he does, it grows corrupt around him. It fills with locks and sirens. A man walks into a store now and the microwaves announce his entry; when he leaves, they make electronic peeks into his coat pockets, his trousers. Who doesn't feel like a thief? I see a policeman now, any policeman, and I feel a fright. And the things I've done wrong in my life haven't been crimes. Crimes of the heart perhaps, but nothing against the state. My soul may turn black but I can wear white trousers at any meeting of men. Have I loved my wife? At one time, yes—in rages and torrents. I've been covered by the pimples of ecstasy and have rooted in the mud of despair; and I've lived for months, for whole years now, as mindless of Francine as a tree of its mosses.

And this is what kills us, this mindlessness. We sit across the tablecloth now with our medicines between us, little balls and oblongs. We sit, sit. This has become our view of each other, a tableboard apart. We sit.

"Again?" I say.
"Last night."
We are at the table. Francine is making a twisting motion with her fingers. She coughs, brushes her cheek with her forearm, stands suddenly so that the table bumps and my medicines move in the cup.
"Francine," I say.
The half-light of dawn is showing me things outside the window: silhouettes, our maple, the eaves of our neighbor's garage. Francine moves and stands against the glass, hugging her shoulders.

"You're not telling me something," I say.

She sits and makes her pills into a circle again, then into a line. Then she is crying.

I come around the table, but she gets up before I reach her and leaves the kitchen. I stand there. In a moment I hear a drawer open in the living room. She moves things around, then shuts it again. When she returns she sits at the other side of the table. "Sit down," she says. She puts two folded sheets of paper onto the table. "I wasn't hiding them," she says.

"What weren't you hiding?"

"These," she says. "He leaves them."

"He leaves them?"

"They say he loves me."

"Francine."

"They're inside the windows in the morning." She picks one up, unfolds it. Then she reads:

> *Ah, I remember well (and how can I*
> *But evermore remember well) when first*

She pauses, squint-eyed, working her lips. It is a pause of only faint understanding. Then she continues:

> *Our flame began, when scarce we knew what was*
> *The flame we felt.*

When she finishes she refolds the paper precisely. "That's it," she says. "That's one of them."

At the aquarium I sit, circled by glass and, behind it, the senseless eyes of fish. I have never written a word of my own poetry but can recite the verse of others. This is the culmination of a life. *Coryphaena hippurus,* says the plaque on the dolphin's tank, words more beautiful than any of my own. The dolphin circles, circles, approaches with alarming speed, but takes no notice of, if he even sees, my hands. I wave them in front of his tank. What must he think has become of the sea? He turns and his slippery proboscis nudges the glass. I am every part sore from life.

> *Ah, silver shrine, here will I take my rest*
> *After so many hours of toil and quest,*
> *A famished pilgrim—saved by miracle.*

There is nothing noble for either of us here, nothing between us, and no miracles. I am better off drinking coffee. Any fluid refills the blood. The counter boy knows me and later at the café he pours the cup, most of a dollar's worth. Refills are free but my heart hurts if I drink more than one. It hurts no different from a bone, bruised or cracked. This amazes me.

Francine is amazed by other things. She is mystified, thrown beam ends by the romance. She reads me the poems now at breakfast, one by one. I sit. I roll my pills. "Another came last night," she says, and I see her eyebrows rise. "Another this morning." She reads them as if every word is a surprise. Her tongue touches teeth, shows between lips. These lips are dry. She reads:

> Kiss me as if you made believe
> You were not sure, this eve,
> How my face, your flower, had pursed
> Its petals up

That night she shows me the windowsill, second story, rimmed with snow, where she finds the poems. We open the glass. We lean into the air. There is ice below us, sheets of it on the trellis, needles hanging from the drainwork.

"Where do you find them?"

"Outside," she says. "Folded, on the lip."

"In the morning?"

"Always in the morning."

"The police should know about this."

"What will they be able to do?"

I step away from the sill. She leans out again, surveying her lands, which are the yard's-width spit of crusted ice along our neighbor's chain link and the three maples out front, now lost their leaves. She peers as if she expects this man to appear. An icy wind comes inside. "Think," she says. "Think. He could come from anywhere."

One night in February, a month after this began, she asks me to stay awake and stand guard until the morning. It is almost spring. The earth has reappeared in patches. During the day, at the borders of yards and driveways, I see glimpses of brown—though I know I could be mistaken. I come home early that night, before dusk, and when darkness falls I move a chair by the window downstairs. I draw apart the outer curtain and raise the shade. Francine brings me a pot of tea. She turns out the light and pauses next to me, and as she does, her hand on the chair's backbrace, I am so struck by the proximity of elements—of the night, of the teapot's heat, of the sounds of water outside—that I consider speaking. I want to ask her what has become of us, what has made our breathed air so sorry now, and loveless. But the timing is wrong and in a moment she turns and climbs the stairs. I look out into the night. Later, I hear the closet shut, then our bed creak.

There is nothing to see outside, nothing to hear. This I know. I let hours pass. Behind the window I imagine fish moving down to greet me: broom-tail grouper, surfperch, sturgeon with their prehistoric rows of scutes. It is almost possible to see them. The night is full of shapes and bits of light. In it the moon rises, losing the colors of the horizon, so that by early morning it is high and pale. Frost has made a ring around it.

A ringed moon above, and I am thinking back on things. What have I regretted in my life? Plenty of things, mistakes enough to fill the car showroom, then a good deal of the back lot. I've been a man of gains and losses. What gains? My marriage, certainly, though it has been no knee-buckling windfall but more like a split decision in the end, a stock risen a few points since bought. I've certainly enjoyed certain things about the world, too. These are things gone over and over again by the writers and probably enjoyed by everybody who ever lived. Most of them involve air. Early morning air, air after a rainstorm, air through a car window. Sometimes I think the cerebrum is wasted and all we really need is the lower brain, which I've been told is what makes the lungs breathe and the heart beat and what lets us smell pleasant things. What about the poetry? That's another split decision, maybe going the other way if I really made a tally. It's made me melancholy in old age, sad when if I'd stuck with motor homes and the national league standings I don't think I would have been rooting around in regret and doubt at this point. Nothing wrong with sadness, but this is not the real thing—not the death of a child but the feelings of a college student reading *Don Quixote* on a warm afternoon before going out to the lake.

Now, with Francine upstairs, I wait for a night prowler. He will not appear. This I know, but the window glass is ill-blown and makes moving shadows anyway, shapes that change in the wind's rattle. I look out and despite myself am afraid.

Before me, the night unrolls. Now the tree leaves turn yellow in moonshine. By two or three, Francine sleeps, but I get up anyway and change into my coat and hat. The books weigh against my chest. I don gloves, scarf, galoshes. Then I climb the stairs and go into our bedroom, where she is sleeping. On the far side of the bed I see her white hair and beneath the blankets the uneven heave of her chest. I watch the bedcovers rise. She is probably dreaming at this moment. Though we have shared this bed for most of a lifetime I cannot guess what her dreams are about. I step next to her and touch the sheets where they lie across her neck.

"Wake up," I whisper. I touch her cheek, and her eyes open. I know this though I cannot really see them, just the darkness of their sockets.

"Is he there?"

"No."

"Then what's the matter?"

"Nothing's the matter," I say. "But I'd like to go for a walk."

"You've been outside," she says. "You saw him, didn't you?"

"I've been at the window."

"Did you see him?"

"No. There's no one there."

"Then why do you want to walk?" In a moment she is sitting aside the bed, her feet in slippers. "We don't ever walk," she says.

I am warm in all my clothing. "I know we don't," I answer. I turn my arms out, open my hands toward her. "But I would like to. I would like to walk in air that is so new and cold."

She peers up at me. "I haven't been drinking," I say. I bend at the waist, and though my head spins, I lean forward enough so that the effect is of a bow. "Will you come with me?" I whisper. "Will you be queen of this crystal night?" I recover from my bow, and when I look up again she has risen from the bed, and in another moment she has dressed herself in her wool robe and is walking ahead of me to the stairs.

Outside, the ice is treacherous. Snow had begun to fall and our galoshes squeak and slide, but we stay on the plowed walkway long enough to leave our block and enter a part of the neighborhood where I have never been. Ice hangs from the lamps. We pass unfamiliar houses and unfamiliar trees, street signs I have never seen, and as we walk the night begins to change. It is becoming liquor. The snow is banked on either side of the walk, plowed into hillocks at the corners. My hands are warming from the exertion. They are the hands of a younger man now, someone else's fingers in my gloves. They tingle. We take ten minutes to cover a block but as we move through this neighborhood my ardor mounts. A car approaches and I wave, a boatman's salute, because here we are together on these rare and empty seas. We are nighttime travelers. He flashes his headlamps as he passes, and this fills me to the gullet with celebration and bravery. The night sings to us. I am Bluebeard now, Lindbergh, Genghis Khan.

No, I am not.

I am an old man. My blood is dark from hypoxia, my breaths singsong from disease. It is only the frozen night that is splendid. In it we walk, stepping slowly, bent forward. We take steps the length of table forks. Francine holds my elbow.

I have mean secrets and small dreams, no plans greater than where to buy groceries and what rhymes to read next, and by the time we reach our porch again my foolishness has subsided. My knees and elbows ache. They ache with a mortal ache, tired flesh, the cartilage gone sandy with time. I don't have the heart for dreams. We undress in the hallway, ice in the ends of our hair, our coats stiff from cold. Francine turns down the thermostat. Then we go upstairs and she gets into her side of the bed and I get into mine.

It is dark. We lie there for some time, and then, before dawn, I know she is asleep. It is cold in our bedroom. As I listen to her breathing I know my life is coming to an end. I cannot warm myself. What I would like to tell my wife is this:

> What the
> imagination
> seizes
> as beauty must be truth. What holds you
> to what you see of me is
> that grasp alone.

But I do not say anything. Instead I roll in the bed, reach across, and touch her, and because she is surprised she turns to me.

When I kiss her the lips are dry, cracking against mine, unfamiliar as the ocean floor. But then the lips give. They part. I am inside her mouth, and there, still, hidden from the world, as if ruin had forgotten a part, it is wet— Lord! I have the feeling of a miracle. Her tongue comes forward. I do not know myself then, what man I am, whom I lie with in embrace. I can barely remember her beauty. She touches my chest and I bite lightly on her lip, spread moisture to her cheek and then kiss there. She makes something like a sigh. "Frank," she says. "Frank." We are lost now in seas and deserts. My hand finds her fingers and grips them, bone and tendon, fragile things.

"We Are Nighttime Travelers," 1988

THE GOSPEL ACCORDING TO JOHN 12:3, THE NEW TESTAMENT

Then took Mary a pound of ointment of spikenard, very costly, and anointed the feet of Jesus, and wiped his feet with her hair: and the house was filled with the odour of the ointment.

MONA VAN DUYN (American, b. 1921)

"What Christ was saying, what he meant [in the story of Mary and Martha] was that the pleasures of that hair, that ointment, must be taken. Because the accidents of death would deprive us soon enough. We must not deprive ourselves, our loved ones, of the luxury of our extravagant affections. We must not try to second-guess death by refusing to love the ones we loved. . . ."

—Mary Gordon, final payments

> If in my mind I marry you every year
> it is to calm an extravagance of love
> with dousing custom, for it flames up fierce

and wild whenever I forget that we live
in double rooms whose temperature's controlled
by matrimony's turned-down thermostat.
I need the mnemonics, now that we are old,
of oath and law in re-memorizing that.
Our dogs are dead, our child never came true.
I might use up, in my weak-mindedness,
the whole human supply of warmth on you
before I could think of others and digress.
"Love" is finding the familiar dear.
"In love" is to be taken by surprise.
Over, in the shifty face you wear,
and over, in the assessments of your eyes,
you change, and with new sweet or barbed word
find out new entrances to my inmost nerve.
When you stand at the stove it's I who am most stirred.
When you finish work I rest without reserve.
Daytimes, sometimes, our three-legged race seems slow.
Squabbling onward, we chafe from being so near.
But all night long we lie like crescents of Velcro,
turning together till we re-adhere.
Since you, with longer stride and better vision,
more clearly see the finish line, I stoke
my hurrying self, to keep it in condition,
with light and life-renouncing meals of smoke.
As when a collector scoops two Monarchs in
at once, whose fresh flights to and from each other
are netted down, so in vows I re-imagine
I re-invoke what keeps us stale together.
What you try to give is more than I want to receive,
yet each month when you pick up scissors for our appointment
and my cut hair falls and covers your feet I believe
that the house is filled again with the odor of ointment.

"Late Loving," 1990

FYODOR IVANOVICH TYUTCHEV (*Russian, 1803–1873*)

How much more superstitiously
And fondly we love in declining years.
Shine on, shine on, farewell light
Of this last love, this light of sunset!

The shadows have spread across the sky
And only westward does radiance wander.
Linger, linger, evening-day,
Lengthen, lengthen, O enchantment.
Let blood run thin in veins, our fondness

Does not run thin within our hearts.
O you, O you, O my last love!
You are my bliss and my despair.

"Last Love," 1854

ARCHIBALD MacLEISH *(American, 1892–1982)*

They have only to look at each other to laugh—
no one knows why, not even they:
something back in the life they lived,
something they both remember but no words can say.

They go off at an evening's end to talk
but they don't, or to sleep but they lie awake—
hardly a word, just a touch, just near,
just listening but not to hear.

Everything they know they know together—
everything, that is, but one:
their lives they've learned like secrets from each other;
their deaths they think of in the nights alone.

"The Old Gray Couple (1)," 1976

ARNA BONTEMPS *(African American, 1903–1973)*

Old Jeff Patton, the black share farmer, fumbled with his bow tie. His fingers trembled and the high stiff collar pinched his throat. A fellow loses his hand for such vanities after thirty or forty years of simple life. Once a year, or maybe twice if there's a wedding among his kinfolks, he may spruce up; but generally fancy clothes do nothing but adorn the wall of the big room and feed the moths. That had been Jeff Patton's experience. He had not worn his stiff-bosomed shirt more than a dozen times in all his married life. His swallow-tailed coat lay on the bed beside him, freshly brushed and pressed, but it was as full of holes as the overalls in which he worked on weekdays. The moths had used it badly. Jeff twisted his mouth into a hideous toothless

249

grimace as he contended with the obstinate bow. He stamped his good foot and decided to give up the struggle.

"Jennie," he called.

"What's that, Jeff?" His wife's shrunken voice came out of the adjoining room like an echo. It was hardly bigger than a whisper.

"I reckon you'll have to he'p me wid this heah bow tie, baby," he said meekly. "Dog if I can hitch it up."

Her answer was not strong enough to reach him, but presently the old woman came to the door, feeling her way with a stick. She had a wasted, dead-leaf appearance. Her body, as scrawny and gnarled as a string bean, seemed less than nothing in the ocean of frayed and faded petticoats that surrounded her. These hung an inch or two above the tops of her heavy unlaced shoes and showed little grotesque piles where the stockings had fallen down from her negligible legs.

"You oughta could do a heap mo' wid a thing like that'n me—beingst as you got yo' good sight."

"Looks like I oughta could," he admitted. "But ma fingers is gone democrat on me. I get all mixed up in the looking glass an' can't tell wicha way to twist the devilish thing."

Jennie sat on the side of the bed and old Jeff Patton got down on one knee while she tied the bow knot. It was a slow and painful ordeal for each of them in this position. Jeff's bones cracked, his knee ached, and it was only after a half dozen attempts that Jennie worked a semblance of a bow into the tie.

"I got to dress maself now," the old woman whispered. "These is ma old shoes an' stockings, and I ain't so much as unwrapped ma dress."

"Well, don't worry 'bout me no mo', baby," Jeff said. "That 'bout finishes me. All I gotta do now is slip on that old coat 'n ves' an' I'll be fixed to leave."

Jennie disappeared again through the dim passage into the shed room. Being blind was no handicap to her in that black hole. Jeff heard the cane placed against the wall beside the door and knew that his wife was on easy ground. He put on his coat, took a battered top hat from the bedpost and hobbled to the front door. He was ready to travel. As soon as Jennie could get on her Sunday shoes and her old black silk dress, they would start.

Outside the tiny log house, the day was warm and mellow with sunshine. A host of wasps were humming with busy excitement in the trunk of a dead sycamore. Gray squirrels were searching through the grass for hickory nuts and blue jays were in the trees, hopping from branch to branch. Pine woods stretched away to the left like a black sea. Among them were scattered scores of log houses like Jeff's, houses of black share farmers. Cows and pigs wandered freely among the trees. There was no danger of loss. Each farmer knew his own stock and knew his neighbor's as well as he knew his neighbor's children.

Down the slope to the right were the cultivated acres on which the colored folks worked. They extended to the river, more than two miles away, and they were today green with the unmade cotton crop. A tiny thread of a road, which passed directly in front of Jeff's place, ran through these green fields like a pencil mark.

Jeff, standing outside the door, with his absurd hat in his left hand, surveyed the wide scene tenderly. He had been forty-five years on these acres. He loved them with the unexplained affection that others have for the countries to which they belong.

The sun was hot on his head, his collar still pinched his throat, and the Sunday clothes were intolerably hot. Jeff transferred the hat to his right hand and began fanning with it. Suddenly the whisper that was Jennie's voice came out of the shed room.

"You can bring the car round front whilst you's waitin'," it said feebly. There was a tired pause; then it added, "I'll soon be fixed to go."

"A'right, baby," Jeff answered. "I'll get it in a minute."

But he didn't move. A thought struck him that made his mouth fall open. The mention of the car brought to his mind, with new intensity, the trip he and Jennie were about to take. Fear came into his eyes; excitement took his breath. Lord, Jesus!

"Jeff . . . O Jeff," the old woman's whisper called.

He awakened with a jolt. "Hunh, baby?"

"What you doin'?"

"Nuthin. Jes studyin'. I jes been turnin' things round'n round in ma mind."

"You could be gettin' the car," she said.

"Oh yes, right away, baby."

He started round to the shed, limping heavily on his bad leg. There were three frizzly chickens in the yard. All his other chickens had been killed or stolen recently. But the frizzly chickens had been saved somehow. That was fortunate indeed, for these curious creatures had a way of devouring "Poison" from the yard and in that way protecting against conjure and black luck and spells. But even the frizzly chickens seemed now to be in a stupor. Jeff thought they had some ailment; he expected all three of them to die shortly.

The shed in which the old T-model Ford stood was only a grass roof held up by four corner poles. It had been built by tremulous hands at a time when the little rattletrap car had been regarded as a peculiar treasure. And, miraculously, despite wind and downpour it still stood.

Jeff adjusted the crank and put his weight upon it. The engine came to life with a sputter and bang that rattled the old car from radiator to taillight.

Jeff hopped into the seat and put his foot on the accelerator. The sputtering and banging increased. The rattling became more violent. That was good. It was good banging, good sputtering and rattling, and it meant that the aged car was still in running condition. She could be depended on for this trip.

Again, Jeff's thought halted as if paralyzed. The suggestion of the trip fell into the machinery of his mind like a wrench. He felt dazed and weak. He swung the car out into the yard, made a half turn and drove around to the front door. When he took his hands off the wheel, he noticed that he was trembling violently. He cut off the motor and climbed to the ground to wait for Jennie.

A few minutes later she was at the window, her voice rattling against the pane like a broken shutter.

"I'm ready, Jeff."

He did not answer, but limped into the house and took her by the arm. He led her slowly through the big room, down the step and across the yard.

"You reckon I'd oughta lock the do'?" he asked softly.

They stopped and Jennie weighed the question. Fina!', she shook her head.

"Ne' mind the do'," she said. "I don't see no cause to lock up things."

"You right," Jeff agreed. "No cause to lock up."

Jeff opened the door and helped his wife into the car. A quick shudder passed over him. Jesus! Again he trembled.

"How come you shaking so?" Jennie whispered.

"I don't know," he said.

"You mus' be scairt, Jeff."

"No, baby, I ain't scairt."

He slammed the door after her and went around to crank up again. The motor started easily. Jeff wished that it had not been so responsive. He would have liked a few more minutes in which to turn things around in his head. As it was, with Jennie chiding him about being afraid, he had to keep going. He swung the car into the little pencil-mark road and started off toward the river, driving very slowly, very cautiously.

Chugging across the green countryside, the small battered Ford seemed tiny indeed. Jeff felt a familiar excitement, a thrill, as they came down the first slope to the immense levels on which the cotton was growing. He could not help reflecting that the crops were good. He knew what that meant, too; he had made forty-five of them with his own hands. It was true that he had worn out nearly a dozen mules, but that was the fault of old man Stevenson, the owner of the land. Major Stevenson had the odd notion that one mule was all a share farmer needed to work a thirty-acre plot. It was an expensive notion, the way it killed mules from overwork, but the old man held to it. Jeff thought it killed a good many share farmers as well as mules, but he had no sympathy for them. He had always been strong, and he had been taught to have no patience with weakness in men. Women or children might be tolerated if they were puny, but a weak man was a curse. Of course, his own children—

Jeff's thought halted there. He and Jennie never mentioned their dead children any more. And naturally he did not wish to dwell upon them in his mind. Before he knew it, some remark would slip out of his mouth and that would make Jennie feel blue. Perhaps she would cry. A woman like Jennie could not easily throw off the grief that comes from losing five grown children within two years. Even Jeff was still staggered by the blow. His memory had not been much good recently. He frequently talked to himself. And, although he had kept it a secret, he knew that his courage had left him. He was terrified by the least unfamiliar sound at night. He was reluctant to venture far from home in the daytime. And that habit of trembling when he felt fearful was now far beyond his control. Sometimes he became afraid and trembled without knowing what had frightened him. The feeling would just come over him like a chill.

The car rattled slowly over the dusty road. Jennie sat erect and silent, with a little absurd hat pinned to her hair. Her useless eyes seemed very large, very white in their deep sockets. Suddenly Jeff heard her voice, and he inclined his head to catch the words.

"Is we passed Delia Moore's house yet?" she asked.

"Not yet," he said.

"You must be drivin' mighty slow, Jeff."

"We might just as well take our time, baby."

There was a pause. A little puff of steam was coming out of the radiator of the car. Heat wavered above the hood. Delia Moore's house was nearly half a mile away. After a moment Jennie spoke again.

"You ain't really scairt, is you, Jeff?"

"Nah, baby, I ain't scairt."

"You know how we agreed—we gotta keep on goin'."

Jewels of perspiration appeared on Jeff's forehead. His eyes rounded, blinked, became fixed on the road.

"I don't know," he said with a shiver. "I reckon it's the only thing to do."

"Hm."

A flock of guinea fowls, pecking in the road, were scattered by the passing car. Some of them took to their wings; others hid under bushes. A blue jay, swaying on a leafy twig, was annoying a roadside squirrel. Jeff held an even speed till he came near Delia's place. Then he slowed down noticeably.

Delia's house was really no house at all, but an abandoned store building converted into a dwelling. It sat near a crossroads, beneath a single black cedar tree. There Delia, a cattish old creature of Jennie's age, lived alone. She had been there more years than anybody could remember, and long ago had won the disfavor of such women as Jennie. For in her young days Delia had been gayer, yellower and saucier than seemed proper in those parts. Her ways with menfolks had been dark and suspicious. And the fact that she had had as many husbands as children did not help her reputation.

"Yonder's old Delia," Jeff said as they passed.

"What she doin'?"

"Jes sittin' in the do'," he said.

"She see us?"

"Hm," Jeff said. "Musta did."

That relieved Jennie. It strengthened her to know that her old enemy had seen her pass in her best clothes. That would give the old she-devil something to chew her gums and fret about, Jennie thought. Wouldn't she have a fit if she didn't find out? Old evil Delia! This would be just the thing for her. It would pay her back for being so evil. It would also pay her, Jennie thought, for the way she used to grin at Jeff—long ago when her teeth were good.

The road became smooth and red, and Jeff could tell by the smell of the air that they were nearing the river. He could see the rise where the road turned and ran along parallel to the stream. The car chugged on monotonously. After a long silent spell, Jennie leaned against Jeff and spoke.

"How many bale o' cotton you think we got standin'?" she said.

Jeff wrinkled his forehead as he calculated.

"'Bout twenty-five, I reckon."

"How many you make las' year?"

"Twenty-eight," he said. "How come you ask that?"

"I's jes thinkin'," Jennie said quietly.

"It don't make a speck o' difference though," Jeff reflected. "If we get much or if we get little, we still gonna be in debt to old man Stevenson when he gets through counting up agin us. It's took us a long time to learn that."

Jennie was not listening to these words. She had fallen into a trance-like meditation. Her lips twitched. She chewed her gums and rubbed her gnarled hands nervously. Suddenly she leaned forward, buried her face in the nervous hands and burst into tears. She cried aloud in a dry cracked voice that suggested the rattle of fodder on dead stalks. She cried aloud like a child, for she had never learned to suppress a genuine sob. Her slight old frame shook heavily and seemed hardly able to sustain such violent grief.

"What's the matter, baby?" Jeff asked awkwardly. "Why you cryin' like all that?"

"I's jes thinkin'," she said.

"So you the one what's scairt now, hunh?"

"I ain't scairt, Jeff. I's jes thinkin' 'bout leavin' eve'thing like this—eve'thing we been used to. It's right sad-like."

Jeff did not answer, and presently Jennie buried her face again and cried.

The sun was almost overhead. It beat down furiously on the dusty wagon-path road, on the parched roadside grass and the tiny battered car. Jeff's hands, gripping the wheel, became wet with perspiration; his forehead sparkled. Jeff's lips parted. His mouth shaped a hideous grimace. His face suggested the face of a man being burned. But the torture passed and his expression softened again.

"You mustn't cry, baby," he said to his wife. "We gotta be strong. We can't break down."

Jennie waited a few seconds, then said, "You reckon we oughta do it, Jeff? You reckon we oughta go 'head an' do it, really?"

Jeff's voice choked; his eyes blurred. He was terrified to hear Jennie say the thing that had been in his mind all morning. She had egged him on when he had wanted more than anything in the world to wait, to reconsider, to think things over a little longer. Now she was getting cold feet. Actually there was no need of thinking the question through again. It would only end in making the same painful decision once more. Jeff knew that. There was no need of fooling around longer.

"We jes as well to do like we planned," he said. "They ain't nothin' else for us now—it's the bes' thing."

Jeff thought of the handicaps, the near impossibility, of making another crop with his leg bothering him more and more each week. Then there was always the chance that he would have another stroke, like the one that had made him lame. Another one might kill him. The least it could do would be to leave him helpless. Jeff gasped—Lord, Jesus! He could not bear to think of being helpless, like a baby, on Jennie's hands. Frail, blind Jennie.

The little pounding motor of the car worked harder and harder. The puff of steam from the cracked radiator became larger. Jeff realized that they were climbing a little rise. A moment later the road turned abruptly and he looked down upon the face of the river.

"Jeff."

"Hunh?"

"Is that the water I hear?"

"Hm. Tha's it."

"Well, which way you goin' now?"

"Down this-a way," he said. "The road runs 'long 'side o' the water a lil piece."

She waited a while calmly. Then she said, "Drive faster."

"A'right, baby," Jeff said.

The water roared in the bed of the river. It was fifty or sixty feet below the level of the road. Between the road and the water there was a long smooth slope, sharply inclined. The slope was dry, the clay hardened by prolonged summer heat. The water below, roaring in a narrow channel, was noisy and wild.

"Jeff."

"Hunh?"

"How far you goin'?"

"Jes a lil piece down the road."

"You ain't scairt, is you, Jeff?"

"Nah, baby," he said trembling. "I ain't scairt."

"Remember how we planned it, Jeff. We gotta do it like we said. Brave-like."

"Hm."

Jeff's brain darkened. Things suddenly seemed unreal, like figures in a dream. Thoughts swam in his mind foolishly, hysterically, like little blind fish in a pool within a dense cave. They rushed, crossed one another, jostled, collided, retreated and rushed again. Jeff soon became dizzy. He shuddered violently and turned to his wife.

"Jennie, I can't do it. I can't." His voice broke pitifully.

She did not appear to be listening. All the grief had gone from her face. She sat erect, her unseeing eyes wide open, strained and frightful. Her glossy black skin had become dull. She seemed as thin, as sharp and bony, as a starved bird. Now, having suffered and endured the sadness of tearing herself away from beloved things, she showed no anguish. She was absorbed with her own thoughts, and she didn't even hear Jeff's voice shouting in her ear.

Jeff said nothing more. For an instant there was light in his cavernous brain. The great chamber was, for less than a second, peopled by characters he knew and loved. They were simple, healthy creatures, and they behaved in a manner that he could understand. They had quality. But since he had already taken leave of them long ago, the remembrance did not break his heart again. Young Jeff Patton was among them, the Jeff Patton of fifty years ago who went down to New Orleans with a crowd of country boys to the Mardi Gras doings. The gay young crowd, boys with candy-striped shirts and rouged-brown girls in noisy silks, was like a picture in his head. Yet it did not make him sad. On that very trip Slim Burns had killed Joe Beasley—the crowd had been broken up. Since then Jeff Patton's world had been the Greenbriar Plantation. If there had been other Mardi Gras carnivals, he had not heard of them. Since then there had been no time; the years had fallen on him like waves. Now he was old, worn out. Another paralytic stroke (like the one he had already suffered) would put him on his back for keeps. In that condition, with a frail blind woman to look after him, he would be worse off than if he were dead.

Suddenly Jeff's hands became steady. He actually felt brave. He slowed down the motor of the car and carefully pulled off the road. Below, the water of the stream boomed, a soft thunder in the deep channel. Jeff ran the car onto the clay slope, pointed it directly toward the stream and put his foot heavily on the accelerator. The little car leaped furiously down the steep incline toward the water. The movement was nearly as swift and direct as a fall. The two old black folks, sitting quietly side by side, showed no excitement. In another instant the car hit the water and dropped immediately out of sight.

A little later it lodged in the mud of a shallow place. One wheel of the crushed and upturned little Ford became visible above the rushing water.

"A Summer Tragedy," 1933

KAKINOMOTO HITAMORO (*Japanese, fl. c. 680–710 C.E.*)

> Since in Karu lived my wife,
> I wished to be with her to my heart's content;
> But I could not visit her constantly
> Because of the many watching eyes—
> Men would know of our troth,
> Had I sought her too often.
> So our love remained secret like a rock-pent pool;
> I cherished her in my heart,
> Looking to aftertime when we should be together,
> And lived secure in my trust
> As one riding a great ship.
> Suddenly there came a messenger
> Who told me she was dead—
> Was gone like a yellow leaf of autumn.
> Dead as the day dies with the setting sun,
> Lost as the bright moon is lost behind the cloud,
> Alas, she is no more, whose soul
> Was bent to mine like bending seaweed!
>
> When the word was brought to me
> I knew not what to do nor what to say;
> But restless at the mere news,
> And hoping to heal my grief
> Even a thousandth part,

I journeyed to Karu and searched the market place
Where my wife was wont to go!

There I stood and listened,
But no voice of her I heard,
Though the birds sang in the Unebi Mountain;
None passed by who even looked like my wife.
I could only call her name and wave my sleeve.

ENVOYS

In the autumn mountains
The yellow leaves are so thick.
Alas, how shall I seek my love
Who has wandered away?
I know not the mountain track.

I see the messenger come
As the yellow leaves are falling.
Oh, well I remember
How on such a day we used to meet—
My wife and I!

In the days when my wife lived,
We went out to the embankment near by—
We two, hand in hand—
To view the elm trees standing there
With their outspreading branches

Thick with spring leaves. Abundant as their greenery
Was my love. On her leaned my soul.
But who evades mortality?
One morning she was gone, flown like an early bird.
Clad in a heavenly scarf of white,
To the wide fields where the shimmering *kagerō* rises
She went and vanished like the setting sun.

"Since in Karu lived my wife," in the *Man'yōshū*, Ancient Period, to 794 C.E.

ABU AL-QASIM AL-SHABBI (*Arabic/Tunisian, 1909–1934*)

We walk, as all round walks on creation . . . yet, to what goal?
With the birds we sing to the sun; as the spring plays on its flute;
We read out to Death the tale of Life . . . yet, how ends that tale?

Thus I spoke to the winds, and thus they answered: ask of Being itself how it began.

Covered over in mist, in bitter weariness cried out my soul: Whither shall I go?

I said: walk on with life; it replied: what reaped I as I walked before?

Collapsed like a parched and withered plant I cried: Where, o heart, is my rake?

Bring it, that I may trace my grave in the dark silence, bury myself,

Bring it, for darkness is dense around me, and the mists of sorrow are settled on high.

Dawn fills the goblets of passion, yet they shatter in my hands;

Proud youth has fled into the past, and left on my lips a lament.

Come, o heart! We are two strangers who made of life an art of sorrow;

We have fed long on life, sung long with youth.

And now with night go barefooted over the rocky paths—and bleed.

We are satiated with dust, our thirst quenched with tears,

Left and right we have scattered dreams, love, pain and sorrow,

And then? I, remote from the joy of the world and its song,

In the darkness of death bury the days of my life, cannot even mourn their passing,

And the flowers of life, in grievous, troubling silence, fall at my feet.

The magic of life is dry: come, o my weeping heart, let us now try death. Come!

"In the Shadow of the Valley of Death," c. 1930

TRADITIONAL HAUSA TALE (*African, tenth century*)

There were two old men who journeyed together. The name of one was Life, and the other was called Death. They came to a place where a spring flowed, and the man who owned the spring greeted them. They asked him for permission to drink. He said: "Yes, drink. But let the elder drink first, because that is the custom."

Life said, "I, indeed, am the elder."

Death said, "No, I am the elder."

Life answered: "How can that be? Life came first. Without living things to die, Death does not exist."

Death said: "On the contrary, before Life was born everything was Death. Living things come out of Death, go on a while, and then return to Death."

Life replied: "Surely that is not the way it is. Before Life there was no Death, merely that which is not seen. The Creator made this world out of the unseen substances. When the first person died, that was the beginning of Death. Therefore you, Death, are the younger."

Death argued: "Death is merely what we do not know. When the Creator created, he molded everything out of what we do not know. Therefore Death is like a father to Life."

They disputed this way, standing beside the spring. And at last they asked the owner of the water to judge the dispute. He said: "How can one speak of Death without Life, from which it proceeds? And how can one speak of Life without Death, to which all living things go? Both of you have spoken eloquently. Your words are true. Neither can exist without the other. Neither of you is senior. Neither of you is junior. Life and Death are merely two faces [masks] of the Creator. Therefore you are of equal age. Here is a gourd of water. Drink from it together."

They received the gourd of water. They drank. And after that they continued their journey. What say you of these two travellers? They go from one place to another in each other's company. Can one be the elder and the other the younger? If you do not know, let us consider other things.

"Life and Death"

GABRIEL GARCÍA MÁRQUEZ (*Colombian, b. 1928*)

Although she was already a hundred years old and on the point of going blind from cataracts, she still had her physical dynamism, her integrity of character, and her mental balance intact. No one would be better able than she to shape the virtuous man who would restore the prestige of the family, a man who would never have heard talk of war, fighting cocks, bad women, or wild undertakings, four calamities that, according to what Ursula thought, had determined the downfall of their line.

That woman has been your ruination, Ursula would shout at her greatgrandson when she saw him coming into the house like a sleepwalker. She's got you so bewitched that one of these days I'm going to see you twisting around with colic and with a toad in your belly.

. . . . .

The years nowadays don't pass the way the old ones used to, she would say, feeling that everyday reality was slipping through her hands. In the past, she thought, children took a long time to grow up.

. . . . .

The truth was that Ursula resisted growing old even when she had already lost count of her age and she was a bother on all sides as she tried to meddle in everything and as she annoyed strangers with her questions as to whether they had left a plaster Saint Joseph to be kept until the rains were over during the days of the war. No one knew exactly when she had begun to lose her sight. Even in her later years, when she could no longer get out of bed, it seemed that she was simply defeated by decrepitude, but no one discovered that she was blind. She had noticed it before the birth of José Arcadio. At first she thought it was a matter of a passing debility and she secretly took marrow syrup and put honey in her eyes, but quite soon she began to realize that she was irrevocably sinking into the darkness. . . . She did not tell anyone about it because it would have been a public recognition of her uselessness. Even though the trembling of her hands was more and more noticeable and the weight of her feet was too much for her, her small figure was never seen in so many places at the same time. She was almost as diligent as when she had the whole weight of the house on her shoulders. Nevertheless, in the impenetrable solitude of decrepitude, she had such clairvoyance as she examined the most insignificant happenings in the family that for the first time she saw clearly the truths that her busy life in former times had prevented her from seeing.

· · · · ·

It was then that it occurred to her that her clumsiness was not the first victory of decrepitude and darkness but a sentence passed by time.

· · · · ·

Ursula cried in lamentation when she discovered that for more than three years she had been a plaything for the children.

· · · · ·

She finally mixed up the past with the present in such a way that in the two or three waves of lucidity that she had before she died, no one knew for certain whether she was speaking about what she felt or what she remembered. Little by little she was shrinking, turning into a fetus. . . . One Palm Sunday they went into the bedroom while Fernanda was in church and carried Ursula out by the neck and ankles.

Poor great-great-grandmother, Amaranta Ursula said. She died of old age.

Ursula was startled.

I'm alive! she said.

You can see, Amaranta Ursula said, suppressing her laughter, that she's not even breathing.

I'm talking! Ursula shouted.

She can't even talk, Aureliano said. She died like a little cricket.

Then Ursula gave into the evident. My God, she exclaimed in a low voice. So this is what it's like to be dead.

From *One Hundred Years of Solitude*, 1967

DYLAN THOMAS (*Welsh, 1914–1953*)

Do not go gentle into that good night,
Old age should burn and rave at close of day;
Rage, rage against the dying of the light.

Though wise men at their end know dark is right,
Because their words had forked no lightning they
Do not go gentle into that good night.

Good men, the last wave by, crying how bright
Their frail deeds might have danced in a green bay,
Rage, rage against the dying of the light.

Wild men who caught and sang the sun in flight,
And learn, too late, they grieved it on its way,
Do not go gentle into that good night.

Grave men, near death, who see with blinding sight
Blind eyes could blaze like meteors and be gay,
Rage, rage against the dying of the light.

And you, my father, there on the sad height,
Curse, bless, me now with your fierce tears, I pray.
Do not go gentle into that good night.
Rage, rage against the dying of the light.

"Do not go gentle into that good night," 1952

THOM JONES (*American, b. 1945*)

She wondered how many times a week he had to do this. Plenty, no doubt.
At least every day. Maybe twice . . . three times. Maybe, on a big day, five
times. It was the ultimate bad news, and he delivered it dryly, like Sergeant
Joe Friday. He was a young man, but his was a tough business and he had
gone freeze-dried already. Hey, the bad news wasn't really a surprise!
She . . . *knew*. Of course, you always hope for the best. She heard but she
didn't hear.

"What?" she offered timidly. She had hoped . . . for better. Geez! Give
me a break! What was he saying? Breast and uterus? Double trouble! She
knew it would be the uterus. There had been the discharge. The bloating, the
cramps. The fatigue. But it was common and easily curable provided you got
it at stage one. Eighty percent cure. But the breast—that one came out of the
blue and that could be really tricky—that was fifty-fifty. Strip out the lymph
nodes down your arm and guaranteed chemo. God! Chemo. The worst thing

in the world. Good-bye hair—there'd be scarves, wigs, a prosthetic breast, crying your heart out in "support" groups. Et cetera.

"Mrs. Wilson?" The voice seemed to come out of a can. Now the truth was revealed and all was out in the open. Yet how—tell me this—how would it ever be possible to have a life again? The voice from the can had chilled her. To the core.

"Mrs. Wilson, your last CA 125 hit the ceiling," he said. "I suspect that this could be an irregular kind of can . . . cer."

Some off-the-wall kind of can . . . cer? A kind of wildfire cancer! Not the easygoing, 80 percent cure, tortoise, as-slow-as-molasses-in-January cancer!

January. She looked past the thin oncologist, wire-rimmed glasses, white coat, inscrutable. Outside, snowflakes tumbled from the sky, kissing the pavement—each unique, wonderful, worth an hour of study, a microcosm of the Whole: awe-inspiring, absolutely fascinating, a gift of divinity gratis. Yet how abhorrent they seemed. They were white, but the whole world had lost its color for her now that she'd heard those words. The shine was gone from the world. Had she been Queen of the Universe for a million years and witnessed glory after glory, what would it have mattered now that she had come to this?

She . . . came to . . . went out, came back again . . . went out. There was this . . . wonderful show. Cartoons. It was the best show. This wasn't so bad. True, she had cancer but . . . these wonderful cartoons. Dilaudid. On Dilaudid, well, you live, you die—that's how it is . . . life in the Big City. It happens to everyone. It's part of the plan. Who was she to question the plan?

The only bad part was her throat. Her throat was on fire. "Intubation." The nurse said she'd phone the doctor and maybe he'd authorize more dope.

"Oh, God, please. Anything."

"Okay, let's just fudge a little bit, no one needs to know," the nurse said, twisting a knob on Tube Control Central. Dilaudid. Cartoons. Oh, God, thank God, Dilaudid! Who invented that drug? Write him a letter. Knight him. Award the Nobel Prize to Dilaudid Man. Where was that knob? A handy thing to know. Whew! Whammo! Swirling, throbbing ecstasy! And who was that nurse? Florence Nightingale, Mother Teresa would be proud . . . oh, boy! It wasn't just relief from the surgery; she suddenly realized how much psychic pain she had been carrying and now it was gone with one swoop of a magic wand. The cartoons. Bliss . . .

His voice wasn't in a can, never had been. It was a normal voice, maybe a little high for a man. Not that he was effeminate. The whole problem with him was that he didn't seem real. He wasn't a flesh-and-blood kinda guy.

Where was the *empathy?* Why did he get into this field if he couldn't empathize? In this field, empathy should be your stock-in-trade.

"The breast is fine, just a benign lump. We brought a specialist in to get it, and I just reviewed the pathology report. It's nothing to worry about. The other part is not . . . so good. I'm afraid your abdomen . . . it's spread throughout your abdomen . . . it looks like little Grape-Nuts, actually. It's exceedingly rare and it's . . . it's a rapid form of . . . can . . . cer. We couldn't really take any of it out. I spent most of my time in there untangling adhesions. We're going to have to give you cisplatin . . . if it weren't for the adhesions, we could pump it into your abdomen directly—you wouldn't get so sick that way—but those adhesions are a problem and may cause problems further along." Her room was freezing, but the thin oncologist was beginning to perspire. "It's a shame," he said, looking down at her chart. "You're in such perfect health . . . otherwise."

She knew this was going to happen yet she heard herself say, "Doctor, do you mean . . . I've got to take—"

"Chemo? Yeah. But don't worry about that yet. Let's just let you heal up for a while." He slammed her chart shut and . . . whiz, bang, he was outta there.

Good-bye, see ya.

The guessing game was over and now it was time for the ordeal. She didn't want to hear any more details—he'd said something about a 20 percent five-year survival rate. Might as well bag it. She wasn't a fighter, and she'd seen what chemo had done to her husband, John. This was it. Finis!

She had to laugh. Got giddy. It was like in that song—*Freedom's just another word for nothing left to lose* . . . When you're totally screwed, nothing can get worse, so what's to worry? Of course she could get lucky . . . it would be a thousand-to-one, but maybe . . .

The ovaries and uterus were gone. The root of it all was out. Thank God for that. Those befouled organs were gone. Where? Disposed of. Burned. In a dumpster? Who cares? The source was destroyed. Maybe it wouldn't be so bad. How could it be that bad? After all, the talk about pain from major abdominal surgery was overdone. She was walking with her little cart and tubes by the third day—a daily constitutional through the ward.

Okay, the Dilaudid was permanently off the menu, but morphine sulfate wasn't half bad. No more cartoons but rather a mellow glow. Left, right, left, right. Hup, two, three, four! Even a journey of a thousand miles begins with the first step. On the morphine she was walking a quarter of an inch off the ground and everything was . . . softer, mercifully so. Maybe she could hack it for a thousand miles.

But those people in the hospital rooms, gray and dying, that was her.

Could such a thing be possible? To die? Really? Yes, at some point she guessed you did die. But her? Now? So soon? With so little time to get used to the idea?

No, this was all a bad dream! She'd wake up. She'd wake up back in her little girl room on the farm near Battle Lake, Minnesota. There was a Depression, things were a little rough, but big deal. What could beat a sun-kissed morning on Battle Lake and a robin's song? There was an abundance of jays, larks, bluebirds, cardinals, hummingbirds, red-winged blackbirds in those days before acid rain and heavy-metal poisoning, and they came to her yard to eat from the cherry, apple, plum, and pear trees. What they really went for were the mulberries.

Ah, youth! Good looks, a clean complexion, muscle tone, a full head of lustrous hair—her best feature, although her legs were pretty good, too. Strength. Vitality. A happy kid with a bright future. Cheerleader her senior year. Pharmacy scholarship at the college in Fergus Falls. Geez, if her dad hadn't died, she could have been a pharmacist. Her grades were good, but hard-luck stories were the order of the day. It was a Great Depression. She would have to take her chances. Gosh! It had been a great, wide, wonderful world in those days, and no matter what, an adventure lay ahead, something marvelous—a handsome prince and a life happily ever after. Luck was with her. Where had all the time gone? How had all the dreams . . . fallen away? Now she was in the Valley of the Shadow. The morphine sulfate was like a warm and friendly hearth in Gloom City, her one and only consolation.

He was supposed to be a good doctor, one of the best in the field, but he had absolutely no bedside manner. She really began to hate him when he took away the morphine and put her on Tylenol 3. Then it began to sink in that things might presently go downhill in a hurry.

They worked out a routine. If her brother was busy, her daughter drove her up to the clinic and then back down to the office, and the thin oncologist is . . . called away, or he's . . . running behind, or he's . . . *something.* Couldn't they run a business, get their shit together? Why couldn't they anticipate? It was one thing to wait in line at a bank when you're well, but when you've got cancer and you're this cancer patient and you wait an hour, two hours, or they tell you to come back next week . . . come back for something that's worse than anything, the very worst thing in the world! Hard to get up for that. You really had to brace yourself. Cisplatin, God! Metal mouth, restlessness, pacing. Flop on the couch, but that's no good; get up and pace, but you can't handle that, so you flop on the couch again. Get up and pace. Is this really happening to me? *I can't believe this is really happening to me!* How can such a thing be possible?

Then there were the episodes of simultaneous diarrhea and vomiting that sprayed the bathroom from floor to ceiling! Dry heaves and then dry heaves with bile and then dry heaves with blood. You could drink a quart of tequila and then a quart of rum and have some sloe gin too and eat pink birthday cakes and five pounds of licorice, Epsom salts, a pint of kerosene, some Southern Comfort—and you're on a Sunday picnic compared to cisplatin. Only an archfiend could devise a dilemma where to maybe *get well* you first had to poison yourself within a whisker of death, and in fact if you didn't die, you wished that you had.

There were visitors in droves. Flowers. Various intrusions at all hours. Go away. Leave me alone . . . please, God, leave me . . . alone.

Oh, hi, thanks for coming. Oh, what a lovely—such beautiful flowers . . .

There were moments when she felt that if she had one more episode of diarrhea, she'd jump out of the window. Five stories. Would that be high enough? Or would you lie there for a time and die slowly? Maybe if you took a header right onto the concrete. Maybe then you wouldn't feel a thing. Cisplatin: she had to pace. But she had to lie down, but she was squirrelly as hell and she couldn't lie down. TV was no good—she had double vision, and it was all just a bunch of stupid shit, anyhow. Soap operas—good grief! What absolute crap. Even her old favorites. You only live once, and to think of all the time she pissed away watching soap operas.

If only she could sleep. God, couldn't they give her Dilaudid? No! Wait! Hold that! Somehow Dilaudid would make it even worse. Ether then. Put her out. Wake me up in five days. Just let me sleep. She *had* to get up to pace. She *had* to lie down. She *had* to vomit. *Oh, hi, thanks for coming. Oh, what a lovely—such beautiful flowers.*

The second treatment made the first treatment seem like a month in the country. The third treatment—oh, damn! The whole scenario had been underplayed. Those movie stars who got it and wrote books about it were stoics, valiant warriors compared to her. She had no idea anything could be so horrible. Starving in Bangladesh? No problem, I'll trade. Here's my MasterCard and the keys to the Buick—I'll pull a rickshaw, anything! Anything but this. HIV-positive? Why just sign right here on the dotted line and you've got a deal! I'll trade with anybody! Anybody.

The thin oncologist with the Bugs Bunny voice said the CA 125 number was still up in the stratosphere. He said it was up to her if she wanted to go on with this. What was holding her up? She didn't know, and her own voice came from a can now. She heard herself say, "Doctor, what would you do . . . if you were me?"

He thought it over for a long time. He pulled off his wire rims and pinched his nose, world-weary. "I'd take the next treatment."

It was the worst by far—square root to infinity. Five days: no sleep, pacing, lying down, pacing. Puke and diarrhea. The phone. She wanted to tear it off the wall. Who invented it?—did they have shit for brains or what? *Oh, hi, well . . . just fine. Just dandy. Coming by on Sunday? With the kids? Well . . . no, I feel great. No. No. No. I'd love to see you . . .*

And then one day the thin-timbre voice delivered good news. "Your CA 125 is almost within normal limits. It's working!"

Hallelujah! Oh my God, let it be so! A miracle. Hurrah!

"It is a miracle," he said. He was almost human, Dr. Kildare, Dr. Ben Casey, Marcus Welby, M.D.—take your pick. "Your CA is down to rock bottom. I think we should do one, possibly two more treatments and then go back inside for a look. If we do too few, we may not kill it all but if we do too much—you see, it's toxic to your healthy cells as well. You can get cardiomyopathy in one session of cisplatin and you can die."

"One more is all I can handle."

"Gotcha, Mrs. Wilson. One more and in for a look."

"I hate to tell you this," he said. Was he making the cartoons go away? "I'll be up front about it, Mrs. Wilson, we've still got a problem. The little Grape-Nuts—fewer than in the beginning, but the remaining cells will be resistant to cisplatin, so our options are running thin. We could try a month of an experimental form of hard chemotherapy right here in the hospital—very, very risky stuff. Or we could resume the cisplatin, not so much aiming for a cure but rather as a holding action. Or we could not do anything at all . . ."

Her voice was flat. She said, "What if I don't do anything?"

"Dead in three months, maybe six."

She said, "Dead how?"

"Lungs, liver, or bowel. Don't worry, Mrs. Wilson, there won't be a lot of pain. I'll see to that."

Bingo! He flipped the chart shut and . . . whiz, bang, he was outta there!

She realized that when she got right down to it, she wanted to live, more than anything, on almost any terms, so she took more cisplatin. But the oncologist was right, it couldn't touch those resistant rogue cells; they were like roaches that could live through atomic warfare, grow and thrive. Well then, screw it! At least there wouldn't be pain. What more can you do? She shouldn't have let him open her up again. That had been the worst sort of folly. She'd let him steamroll her with Doctor Knows Best. Air had hit it. No wonder it was a wildfire. A conflagration.

Her friends came by. It was an effort to make small talk. How could they know? How could they *know* what it was like? They loved her, they said, with liquor on their breath. They had to get juiced before they could stand to come by! They came with casseroles and cleaned for her, but she had to sweat out her nights alone. Dark nights of the soul on Tylenol 3 and Xanax. A lot of good that was. But then when she was in her loose, giddy *freedom's just another word for nothing left to lose* mood, about ten days after a treatment, she realized her friends weren't so dumb. They knew that they couldn't really *know.* Bugs Bunny told her there was no point in going on with the cisplatin. He told her she was a very brave lady. He said he was sorry.

A month after she was off that poison, cisplatin, there was a little side benefit. She could see the colors of the earth again and taste food and smell flowers—it was a bittersweet pleasure, to be sure. But her friends took her to Hawaii, where they had this great friend ("You gotta meet him!") and he . . . he made a play for her and brought her flowers every day, expensive roses, et cetera. She had never considered another man since John had died from can . . . cer ten years before. How wonderful to forget it all for a moment here and there. A moment? Qualify that—make that ten, fifteen seconds. How can you forget it? Ever since she got the news she could . . . not . . . forget . . . it.

Now there were stabbing pains, twinges, flutterings—maybe it was normal everyday stuff amplified by the imagination or maybe it was real. How fast would it move, this wildfire brand? Better not to ask.

Suddenly she was horrible again. Those nights alone—killers. Finally one night she broke down and called her daughter. Hated to do it, throw in the towel, but this was the fifteenth round and she didn't have a prayer.

"Oh, hi. I'm just fine"—*blah blah blah*—"but I was thinking maybe I could come down and stay, just a while. I'd like to see Janey and—"

"We'll drive up in the morning."

At least she was with blood. And her darling granddaughter. What a delight. Playing with the little girl, she could forget. It was even better than Hawaii. After a year of sheer hell, in which all of the good stuff added up to less than an hour and four minutes total, there was a way to forget. She helped with the dishes. A little light cleaning. Watched the game shows, worked the *Times* crossword, but the pains grew worse. Goddamn it, it felt like nasty little yellow-tooth rodents or a horde of translucent termites— thousands of them, chewing her guts out! Tylenol 3 couldn't touch it. The new doctor she had been passed to gave her Dilaudid. She was enormously relieved. But what she got was a vial of little pink tablets and after the first dose she realized it wasn't much good in the pill form; you could squeeze by on it but they'd *promised*—no pain! She was losing steam. Grinding down.

They spent a couple of days on the Oregon coast. The son-in-law— somehow it was easy to be with him. He didn't pretend that things were other than they were. He could be a pain in the bun, like everyone, bitching over trivialities, smoking Kool cigarettes, strong ones—jolters! A pack a day easy, although he was considerate enough to go outside and do it. She wanted to tell him, "Fool! Your health is your greatest fortune!" But she was the one who'd let six months pass after that first discharge.

The Oregon coast was lovely, although the surf was too cold for actual swimming. She sat in the hotel whirlpool and watched her granddaughter swim a whole length of the pool all on her own, a kind of dog-paddle thing but not bad for a kid going on seven. They saw a show of shooting stars one night but it was exhausting to keep up a good front and not to be morbid, losing weight big time. After a shower, standing at the mirror, scars zigzagging all over the joint like the Bride of Frankenstein, it was just awful. She was bald, scrawny, ashen, yet with a bloated belly. She couldn't look. Sometimes she would sink to the floor and just lie there, too sick to even cry, too weak to even get dressed, yet somehow she did get dressed, slapped on that hot, goddamn wig, and showed up for dinner. It was easier to do that if you pretended that it wasn't real, if you pretended it was all on TV.

She felt like a naughty little girl sitting before the table looking at meals her daughter was killing herself to make—old favorites that now tasted like a combination of forty-weight Texaco oil and sawdust. It was a relief to get back to the couch and work crossword puzzles. It was hell imposing on her daughter but she was frightened. Terrified! They were her blood. They *had* to take her. Oh, to come to this!

The son-in-law worked swing shift and he cheered her in the morning when he got up and made coffee. He was full of life. He was real. He was authentic. He even interjected little pockets of hope. Not that he pushed macrobiotics or any of that foolishness, but it was a fact—if you were happy, if you had something to live for, if you loved life, you lived. It had been a mistake for her to hole up there in the mountains after John died. The Will to Live was more important than doctors and medicines. You had to reinvigorate the Will to Live. The granddaughter was good for that. She just couldn't go the meditation-tape route, imagining microscopic, ravenous, good-guy little sharks eating the bad cancer cells, et cetera. At least the son-in-law didn't suggest that or come on strong with a theology trip. She noticed he read the King James Bible, though.

She couldn't eat. There was a milk-shake diet she choked down. Vanilla, chocolate fudge, strawberry—your choice. Would Madame like a bottle of wine with dinner? Ha, ha, ha.

Dilaudid. It wasn't working, there was serious pain, especially in her chest, dagger thrusts—*Et tu, Brute?* She watched the clock like a hawk and had her pills out and ready every four hours—and that last hour was getting to be murder, a morbid sweat began popping out of her in the last fifteen minutes. One morning she caved in and timidly asked the son-in-law, "Can I take three?"

269

He said, "Hell, take four. It's a safe drug. If you have bad pain, take four." Her eyes were popping out of her head. "Here, drink it with coffee and it will kick in faster."

He was right. He knew more than the doctor. You just can't do everything by the book. Maybe that had been her trouble all along—she was too compliant, one of those "cancer" personalities. She believed in the rules. She was one of those kind who wanted to leave the world a better place than she found it. She had been a good person, had always done the right thing—this just wasn't right. It wasn't fair. She was so . . . angry!

The next day, over the phone, her son-in-law bullied a prescription of methadone from the cancer doctor. She heard one side of a lengthy heated exchange while the son-in-law made a persuasive case for methadone. He came on like Clarence Darrow or F. Lee Bailey. It was a commanding performance. She'd never heard of anyone giving a doctor hell before. God bless him for not backing down! On methadone tablets a warm orange glow sprung forth and bloomed like a glorious, time-lapse rose in her abdomen and then rolled through her body in orgasmic waves. The sense of relief shattered all fear and doubt though the pain was still there to some extent. It was still there but—so what? And the methadone tablets lasted a very long time—no more of that *every four hours* bullshit.

Purple blotches all over her skin, swollen ankles. Pain in her hips and joints. An ambulance trip to the emergency room. "Oh," they said, "it's nothing . . . vascular purpura. Take aspirin. Who's next?"

Who's next? Why hadn't she taken John's old .38 revolver the very day she heard that voice in the can? Stuck it in the back of her mouth and pulled the trigger? She had no fear of hellfire. She was a decent, moral person but she did not believe. Neither was she the Hamlet type—what lies on the other side? It was probably the same thing that occurred before you were born—zilch. And zilch wasn't that bad. What was wrong with zilch?

One morning she waited overlong for the son-in-law to get up, almost smashed a candy dish to get him out of bed. Was he going to sleep forever? Actually, he got up at his usual time.

"I can't. Get. My breath," she told him.

"You probably have water in your lungs," the son-in-law said. He knew she didn't want to go to the clinic. "We've got some diuretic. They were Boxer's when she had congestive heart failure—dog medicine, but it's the same thing they give humans. Boxer weighed fifty-five pounds. Let me see . . . take four, no, take three. To be cautious. Do you feel like you have to cough?"

"Yes." Kaff, kaff, kaff.

"This might draw the water out of your lungs. It's pretty safe. Try to eat a banana or a potato skin to keep your potassium up. If it doesn't work, we can go over to the clinic."

How would he know something like that? But he was right. It worked like magic. She had to pee like crazy but she could breathe. The panic to end all panics was over. If she could only go . . . number two. Well, the methadone slows you down. "Try some Metamucil," the son-in-law said.

It worked. Kind of, but it sure wasn't anything to write home about. "I can't breathe. The diuretics aren't working."

The son-in-law said they could tap her lung. It would mean another drive to the clinic, but the procedure was almost painless and provided instantaneous relief. It worked but it was three days of exhaustion after that one. The waiting room. Why so long? Why couldn't they anticipate? You didn't have to be a genius to know which way the wildfire was spreading. Would the methadone keep that internal orange glow going or would they run out of ammo? Was methadone the ultimate or were there bigger guns? Street heroin? She'd have to put on her wig and go out and score China White.

The little girl began to tune out. Gramma wasn't so much fun anymore; she just lay there and she gave off this smell. There was no more dressing up; it was just the bathrobe. In fact, she felt the best in her old red-and-black tartan pattern, flannel, ratty-ass bathrobe, not the good one. The crosswords—forget it, too depressing. You could live the life of Cleopatra but if it came down to this, what was the point?

The son-in-law understood. Of all the people to come through. It's bad and it gets worse and so on until the worst of all. "I don't know how you can handle this," he'd say. "What does it feel like? Does it feel like a hangover? Worse than a hangover? Not like a hangover. Then what? Like drinking ten pots of boiled coffee? Like that? Really? Jittery! Oh, God, that must be awful. How can you stand it? Is it just like drinking too much coffee or is there some other aspect? Your fingers are numb? Blurred vision? It takes eight years to watch the second hand sweep from twelve to one? Well, if it's like that, how did you handle *five days?* I couldn't—I'd take a bottle of pills, shoot myself. Something. What about the second week? Drained? Washed out? Oh, brother! I had a three-day hangover once—I'd rather die than do that again. I couldn't ride out that hangover again for money. I know I couldn't handle chemo . . ."

One afternoon after he left for work, she found a passage circled in his well-worn copy of Schopenhauer: "In early youth, as we contemplate our coming life, we are like children in a theater before the curtain is raised, sitting there in high spirits and eagerly waiting for the play to begin. It is a blessing that we do not know what is really going to happen." Yeah! She gave up the crosswords and delved into *The World As Will and Idea*. This Schopenhauer was a genius! Why hadn't anyone told her? She was a reader, she had waded through some philosophy in her time—you just couldn't make any sense out of it. The problem was the terminology! She was a crossword ace, but words like *eschatology*—hey! Yet Schopenhauer got right into the heart of all the important things. The things that really mattered. With Schopenhauer she could take long excursions from the grim specter of impending death. In Schopenhauer, particularly in his aphorisms and reflections, she found an absolute satisfaction, for Schopenhauer spoke the truth and the rest of the world was disseminating lies!

Her son-in-law helped her with unfinished business: will, mortgage, insurance, how shall we do this, that, and the other? Cremation, burial plot, et cetera. He told her the stuff that her daughter couldn't tell her. He waited for the right moment and then got it all in—for instance, he told her that her daughter loved her very much but that it was hard for her to say so. She knew she cringed at this revelation, for it was ditto with her, and she knew that he could see it. Why couldn't she say to her own daughter three simple words, "I love you"? She just couldn't. Somehow it wasn't possible. The son-in-law didn't judge her. He had to be under pressure, too. Was she bringing everyone in the house down? Is that why he was reading Schopenhauer? No, Schopenhauer was his favorite. "Someone had to come out and tell it like it is," he would say of the dour old man with muttonchops whose picture he had pasted on the refrigerator. From what she picked up from the son-in-law, Schopenhauer wrote his major work by his twenty-sixth birthday—a philosophy that was ignored almost entirely in his lifetime and even now, in this day and age, it was thought to be more of a work of art than philosophy in the truest sense. A work of art? Why, it seemed irrefutable! According to the son-in-law, Schopenhauer spent the majority of his life in shabby rooms in the old genteel section of Frankfurt, Germany, that he shared with successions of poodles to keep him company while he read, reflected, and wrote about life at his leisure. He had some kind of small inheritance, just enough to get by, take in the concerts, do a little traveling now and then. He was well versed in several languages. He read virtually everything written from the Greeks on upward, including the Eastern writers, a classical scholar, and had the mind to chew things over and make something of the puzzle of life. The son-in-law, eager to discourse, said Freud called Schopenhauer one of the six greatest men who ever lived. Nietzsche, Thomas Mann, and Richard Wagner all paid tribute to this genius who had been written off with one word—pessimist. The son-in-law lamented that his works were going out of print, becoming increasingly harder to find. He was planning a trip to Frankfurt, where he hoped to find a little bust of his hero. He had written to officials in Germany making inquiries.

They had given him the brush-off. He'd have to fly over himself. And she, too, began to worry that the works of this writer would no longer be available . . . she, who would be worms' meat any day.

Why? Because the *truth* was worthwhile. It was more important than anything, really. She'd had ten years of peaceful retirement, time to think, wonder, contemplate, and had come up with nothing. But new vistas of thought had been opened by the curiously ignored genius with the white muttonchops, whose books were harder and harder to get and whom the world would consider a mere footnote from the nineteenth century—a crank, a guy with an ax to grind, a hypochondriac, a misogynist, an alarmist who slept with pistols under his pillow, a man with many faults. Well, check anyone out and what do you find?

For God's sake, how were you supposed to make any sense out of this crazy-ass shit called life? If only she could simply push a button and never have been born.

The son-in-law took antidepressants and claimed to be a melancholiac, yet he always seemed upbeat, comical, ready with a laugh. He had a sense of the absurd that she had found annoying back in the old days when she liked to pretend that life was a stroll down Primrose Lane. If she wasn't walking down the "sunny side of the street" at least she was "singin' in the rain." Those were the days.

What a fool!

She encouraged the son-in-law to clown and philosophize, and he flourished when she voiced a small dose of appreciation or barked out a laugh. There was more and more pain and discomfort, but she was laughing more too. Schopenhauer: "No rose without a thorn. But many a thorn without a rose." The son-in-law finessed all of the ugly details that were impossible for her. Of all the people to come through!

With her lungs temporarily clear and mineral oil enemas to regulate her, she asked her daughter one last favor. Could they take her home just once more?

They made an occasion of it and drove her up into the mountains for her granddaughter's seventh birthday party. Almost everyone in the picturesque resort town was there, and if they were appalled by her deterioration they did not show it. She couldn't go out on the sun porch, had to semi-recline on the couch, but everyone came in to say hello and all of the bad stuff fell away for . . . an entire afternoon! She was deeply touched by the warm affection of her friends. There were . . . so many of them. My God! They loved her, truly they did. She could see it. You couldn't bullshit her anymore; she could see deep into the human heart; she knew what people were. What wonderful friends. What a perfect afternoon. It was the last . . . good thing.

When she got back to her daughter's she began to die in earnest. It was in the lungs and the bowel, much as the doctor said it would be. Hell, it was probably in the liver even. She was getting yellow, not just the skin but even the whites of her eyes. There was a week in the hospital, where they tormented her with tests. That wiped out the last of her physical and emotional stamina.

She fouled her bed after a barium lower G.I. practically turned to cement and they had to give her a powerful enema. Diarrhea in the bed. The worst humiliation. "Happens all the time, don't worry," the orderly said.

She was suffocating. She couldn't get the least bit of air. All the main players were in the room. She knew this was it! Just like that. Bingo! There were whispered conferences outside her room. Suddenly the nurses, those heretofore angels of mercy, began acting mechanically. They could look you over and peg you, down to the last five minutes. She could see them give her that *anytime now* look. A minister dropped in. There! That was the tip-off—the fat lady was singing.

When the son-in-law showed up instead of going to work she looked to him with panic. She'd been fighting it back but now . . . he was there, he would know what to do without being asked, and in a moment he was back with a nurse. They cranked up the morphine sulfate, flipped it on full-bore. Still her back hurt like hell. All that morphine and a backache . . . just give it a minute . . . ahhh! Cartoons.

Someone went out to get hamburgers at McDonald's. Her daughter sat next to her holding her hand. She felt sorry for them. They were the ones who were going to have to stay behind and play out their appointed roles. Like Schopenhauer said, the best they would be able to do for themselves was to secure a little room as far away from the fire as possible, for Hell was surely in the here-and-now, not in the hereafter. Or was it?

She began to nod. She was holding onto a carton of milk. It would spill. Like diarrhea-in-the-bed all over again. Another mess. The daughter tried to take the carton of milk away. She . . . held on defiantly. Forget the Schopenhauer—what a lot of crap that was! She did not want to cross over. She wanted to live! She wanted to live!

The daughter wrenched the milk away. The nurse came back and cranked up the morphine again. They were going for "comfort." Finally the backache . . . the cartoons . . . all of that was gone.

(She was back on the farm in Battle Lake, Minnesota. She was nine years old and she could hear her little red rooster, Mr. Barnes, crowing at first light. Then came her brother's heavy work boots clomping downstairs and the vacuum swoosh as he opened up the storm door, and then his boots crunch-crunching through the frozen snow. Yes, she was back on the farm all right. Her brother was making for the outhouse and presently Barnes would go after him, make a divebomb attack. You couldn't discourage Mr. Barnes. She heard her brother curse him and the thwap of the tin feed pan hitting the bird. Mr. Barnes's frontal assaults were predictable. From the sound of it, Fred walloped him good. As far as Mr. Barnes was concerned, it was his barnyard. In a moment she heard the outhouse door slam shut and another tin thwap. That Barnes—he was something. She should have taken a lesson. Puffed out her chest and walked through life—"I want the biggest and the best and the most of whatever you've got!" There were people who pulled it off. You really could do it if you had the attitude.

Her little red rooster was a mean little scoundrel, but he had a soft spot for her in his heart of steel and he looked out for her, cooed for her and her alone. Later, when young men came to see her, they soon arranged to meet her thereafter at the drugstore soda fountain uptown. One confrontation with Barnes, even for experienced farm boys, was one too many. He was some kind of rooster all right, an eccentric. Yeah, she was back on the farm. She . . . could feel her sister shifting awake in the lower bunk. It was time to get up and milk the cows. Her sister always awoke in good humor. Not her. She was cozy under a feather comforter and milking the cows was the last thing she wanted to do. Downstairs she could hear her mother speaking cheerfully to her brother as he came back inside, cursing the damn rooster, threatening to kill it. Her mother laughed it off; she didn't have a mean bone in her body.

She . . . could smell bacon in the pan, the coffee pot was percolating, and her grandmother was up heating milk for her Ovaltine. She hated Ovaltine, particularly when her grandmother overheated the milk—burned it—but she pretended to like it, insisted that she needed it for her bones, and forced it down so she could save up enough labels to get a free decoder ring to get special messages from Captain Cody, that intrepid hero of the airwaves. She really wanted to have that ring, but there was a Great Depression and money was very dear, so she never got the decoder or the secret messages or the degree in pharmacology. Had she been more like that little banty rooster, had she been a real go-getter . . . Well—it was all but over now.)

The main players were assembled in the room. She . . . was nodding in and out but she could hear. There she was, in this apparent stupor, but she was more aware than anyone could know. She heard someone say somebody at McDonald's put "everything" on her hamburger instead of "cheese and ketchup only." They were making an issue out of it. One day, when they were in her shoes, they would learn to ignore this kind of petty stuff, but you couldn't blame them. That was how things were, that's all. Life. That was it. That was what it was. And here she lay . . . dying.

Suddenly she realized that the hard part was all over now. All she had to do was . . . let go. It really wasn't so bad. It wasn't . . . anything special. It just was. She was trying to bring back Barnes one last time—that little memory of him had been fun, why not go out with a little fun? She tried to remember his coloring—orange would be too bright, rust too drab, scarlet too vivid. His head was a combination of green, yellow, and gold, all blended, and his breast and wings a kind of carmine red? No, not carmine. He was just a little red rooster, overly pugnacious, an ingrate. He could have been a beautiful bird if he hadn't gotten into so many fights. He got his comb ripped off by a raccoon he'd caught stealing eggs in the henhouse, a big bull raccoon that Barnes had fought tooth and nail until Fred ran into the henhouse with his .410 and killed the thieving intruder. Those eggs were precious. They were income. Mr. Barnes was a hero that day. She remembered how he used to strut around the barnyard. He always had his eye on all of the hens; they were his main priority, some thirty to forty of them, depending. They were his harem and he was the sheik. Boy, was he ever. She remembered jotting down marks on a pad of paper one day when she was home sick with chicken pox. Each mark represented an act of rooster fornication. In less than a day, Mr. Barnes had committed the sexual act forty-seven times that she could see—and she didn't have the whole lay of the land from her window by any means. Why, he often went out roving and carousing with hens on other farms. There were bitter complaints from the neighbors. Barnes really could stir things up. She had to go out on her bicycle and round him up. Mr. Barnes was a legend in the county. Mr. Barnes thought the whole world belonged to him and beyond that—the suns, the stars, and the Milky Way—all of it! Did it feel good or was it torment? It must have been a glorious feeling, she decided. Maybe that was what Arthur Schopenhauer was driving at in his theory about the Will to Live. Mr. Barnes was the very personification of it.

Of course it was hard work being a rooster, but Barnes seemed the happiest creature she had ever known. Probably because when you're doing what you really want to do, it isn't work. No matter how dull things got on the farm, she could watch Barnes by the hour. Barnes could even redeem a hot, dog-day afternoon in August. He wasn't afraid of anything or anybody. Did he ever entertain a doubt? Some kind of rooster worry? Never! She tried to conjure up one last picture of him. He was just a little banty, couldn't have weighed three pounds. Maybe Mr. Barnes would be waiting for her on the other side and would greet her there and be her friend again.

She nodded in and out. In and out. The morphine was getting to be too much. Oh, please God. She hoped she wouldn't puke . . . So much left unsaid, undone. Well, that was all part of it. If only she could see Barnes strut his stuff one last time. "Come on, Barnes. Strut your stuff for me." Her brother, Fred, sitting there so sad with his hamburger. After a couple of beers, he could do a pretty good imitation of Mr. Barnes. Could he . . . would he . . . for old time's sake? Her voice was too weak, she couldn't speak. Nowhere near. Not even close. Was she dead already? Fading to black? It was hard to tell. "Don't feel bad, my darling brother. Don't mourn for me. I'm okay" . . . and . . . one last thing—"Sarah, I do love you, darling! Love you! Didn't you know that? Didn't it show? If not, I'm so, so very sorry . . ." But the words wouldn't come—couldn't come. She . . . was so sick. You can only get so sick and then there was all that dope. Love! She should have shown it to her daughter instead of . . . assuming. She should have been more demonstrative, more forthcoming . . . That's what it was all about. *Love your brother as yourself* and *love the Lord God almighty with all your heart and mind and soul.* You were sent here to love your brother. Do your best. Be kind to animals, obey the Ten Commandments, stuff like that. Was that it? Huh? Or was that all a lot of horseshit?

She . . . nodded in and out. Back and forth. In and out. She went back and forth. In and out. Back and forth . . . in and out. There wasn't any tunnel or white light or any of that. She just . . . died.

"I Want to Live!," 1992

JUNICHIRO TANIZAKI *(Japanese, 1886–1965)*

JUNE 19

. . . Until I was in my fifties there was nothing I dreaded so much as premonitions of death, but now that is no longer true. Perhaps I am already tired of life—I feel as if it makes no difference when I die. The other day at the Toranomon Hospital when they told me it might be cancer, my wife and Miss Sasaki seemed to turn pale, but I was quite calm. It was surprising that I could be calm even at such a moment. I almost felt relieved, to think that my long, long life was finally coming to an end. And so I haven't the slightest desire to cling to life, yet as long as I live I cannot help feeling attracted to the opposite sex. I am sure I'll be like this until the moment of my death. I don't have the vigor of a man like Kuhara Fusanosuke who managed to father a child at ninety, I'm already completely impotent. Even so, I can enjoy sexual stimulation in all kinds of distorted, indirect ways. At present I am living for that pleasure, and for the pleasure of eating. Satsuko alone seems to have a vague notion of what is in my mind. She's the only one in the house who has even the faintest idea. She seems to be making little experiments, subtly and indirectly, to see how I react.

I know very well that I am an ugly, wrinkled old man. When I look in the mirror at bedtime after taking out my false teeth, the face I see is really weird. I don't have a tooth of my own in either jaw. I hardly even have gums. If I clamp my mouth shut, my lips flatten together and my nose hangs down to my chin. It astonishes me to think that this is my own face. Not even monkeys have such hideous faces. How could anyone with a face like this ever hope to appeal to a woman? Still, there is a certain advantage in the fact that it puts people off guard, convinces them that you are an old man who knows he can't claim that sort of favor. But although I am neither entitled nor able to exploit my advantage, I can be near a beautiful woman without arousing suspicion. And to make up for my own inability, I can get her involved with a handsome man, plunge the whole household into turmoil, and take pleasure in *that*.

From *Dairy of a Mad Old Man*, 1965

ÉLIE METCHNIKOFF (*Russian, 1845–1916*)

Physiology of Taste Brillat-Savarin relates as follows:—"A great-aunt of mine died at the age of 93. Although she had been confined to bed for some time her faculties were still well preserved, and the only evidence of her condition was the decrease in appetite and weakening of her voice. She had always been very friendly to me, and once when I was at her bedside, ready to tend her affectionately, although that did not hinder me from seeing her with the philosophical eye that I always turned on everything about me, 'Is it you, my nephew?' she said in her feeble voice. 'Yes, Aunt, I am here at your service, and I think you will do very well to take a drop of this good old wine.' 'Give it me, my dear; I can always take a little wine.' I made ready at once, and gently supporting her, gave her half a glass of my best wine. She brightened up at once, and turning on me her eyes which used to be so beautiful, said: 'Thank you very much for this last kindness; if you ever reach my age you will find that one wants to die just as one wants to sleep.' These were her last words, and in half an hour she fell into her last sleep." . . .

It is a well-known saying that the longer a man has lived the more he wishes to live. Charles Renouvier, a French philosopher who died a few years ago, has left a definite proof of the truth of the saying. When he was eighty-eight years old, and knew that he was dying, he recorded his impressions in his last days. Let me quote from what he wrote four days before his death. "I have no illusions about my condition; I know quite well that I am going to die, perhaps in a week, perhaps in a fortnight. And I have still so much to say on my subject." "At my age I have no longer the right to hope: my days are numbered, and perhaps my hours. I must resign myself." "I do not die without regrets. I regret that I cannot foresee in any way the fate of my views." "And I am leaving the world before I have said my last word. A

278

man always dies before he has finished his work, and that is the saddest of the sorrows of life." "But that is not the whole trouble, when a man is old, very old, and accustomed to life, it is very difficult to die. I think that young men accept the idea of dying more easily, perhaps more willingly than old men. When one is more than eighty years old, one is cowardly and shrinks from death. And when one knows and can no longer doubt that death is coming near, deep bitterness falls on the soul." "I have faced the question from all sides in the last few days; I turn the one idea over in my mind; I *know* that I am going to die, but I cannot *persuade* myself that I am going to die. It is not the philosopher in me that protests. The philosopher does not fear death; it is the *old man*. The old man has not the courage to submit, and yet I have to submit to the inevitable."

From "Natural Death," in *The Prolongation of Life*, 1908

ALICE WALKER (*African American, b. 1944*)

Mr. Sweet was a diabetic and an alcoholic and a guitar player and lived down the road from us on a neglected cotton farm. My older brothers and sisters got the most benefit from Mr. Sweet, for when they were growing up he had quite a few years ahead of him and so was capable of being called back from the brink of death any number of times—whenever the voice of my father reached him as he lay expiring. "To hell with dying, man," my father would say, pushing the wife away from the bedside (in tears although she knew the death was not necessarily the last one unless Mr. Sweet really wanted it to be). "These children want Mr. Sweet!" And they did want him, for at a signal from Father they would come crowding around the bed and throw themselves on the covers, and whoever was the smallest at the time would kiss him all over his wrinkled brown face and begin to tickle him so that he would laugh all down in his stomach, and his mustache, which was long and sort of straggly, would shake like Spanish moss and was also that color.

Mr. Sweet had been ambitious as a boy, wanted to be a doctor or lawyer or sailor, only to find that black men fare better if they are not. Since he could become none of these things he turned to fishing as his one earnest career and playing the guitar as his sole claim to doing anything extraordinarily well. His son, the only one that he and his wife, Miss Mary, had, was shiftless as the day is long and spent money as if he were trying to see the bottom of the mint, which Mr. Sweet would tell him was the clean brown palm of his hand. Miss Mary loved her "baby," however, and worked hard to get him the "li'l necessaries" of life, which turned out mostly to be women.

279

Mr. Sweet was a tall, thinnish man with thick kinky hair going dead white. He was dark brown, his eyes were very squinty and sort of bluish, and he chewed Brown Mule tobacco. He was constantly on the verge of being blind drunk, for he brewed his own liquor and was not in the least a stingy sort of man, and was always very melancholy and sad, though frequently when he was "feelin' good" he'd dance around the yard with us, usually keeling over just as my mother came to see what the commotion was.

Toward all of us children he was very kind, and had the grace to be shy with us, which is unusual in grown-ups. He had great respect for my mother for she never held his drunkenness against him and would let us play with him even when he was about to fall in the fireplace from drink. Although Mr. Sweet would sometimes lose complete or nearly complete control of his head and neck so that he would loll in his chair, his mind remained strangely acute and his speech not too affected. His ability to be drunk and sober at the same time made him an ideal playmate, for he was as weak as we were and we could usually best him in wrestling, all the while keeping a fairly coherent conversation going.

We never felt anything of Mr. Sweet's age when we played with him. We loved his wrinkles and would draw some on our brows to be like him, and his white hair was my special treasure and he knew it and would never come to visit us just after he had had his hair cut off at the barbershop. Once he came to our house for something, probably to see my father about fertilizer for his crops because, although he never paid the slightest attention to his crops, he liked to know what things would be best to use on them if he ever did. Anyhow, he had not come with his hair since he had just had it shaved off at the barbershop. He wore a huge straw hat to keep off the sun and also to keep his head away from me. But as soon as I saw him I ran up and demanded that he take me up and kiss me with his funny mustache, which smelled so strongly of tobacco. Looking forward to burying my small fingers into his woolly hair I threw away his hat only to find he had done something to his hair, that it was no longer there! I let out a squall which made my mother think that Mr. Sweet had finally dropped me in the well or something and from that day I've been wary of men in hats. However, not long after, Mr. Sweet showed up with his hair grown out and just as white and kinky and impenetrable as it ever was.

Mr. Sweet used to call me his princess, and I believed it. He made me feel pretty at five and six, and simply outrageously devastating at the blazing age of eight and a half. When he came to our house with his guitar the whole family would stop whatever they were doing and sit around him and listen to him play. He liked to play "Sweet Georgia Brown," that was what he called me sometimes, and also he liked to play "Caldonia" and all sorts of sweet, sad, wonderful songs which he sometimes made up. It was from one of these songs that I learned that he had had to marry Miss Mary when he had in fact loved somebody else (now living in Chi-ca-go, or De-stroy, Michigan). He was not sure that Joe Lee, her "baby," was also his baby. Sometimes he would cry and that was an indication that he was about to die again. And so we would all get prepared, for we were sure to be called upon.

I was seven the first time I remember actually participating in one of Mr. Sweet's "revivals"—my parents told me I had participated before, I had been the one chosen to kiss him and tickle him long before I knew the rite of Mr. Sweet's rehabilitation. He had come to our house, it was a few years after his wife's death, and was very sad, and also, typically, very drunk. He sat on the floor next to me and my older brother; the rest of the children were grown up and lived elsewhere, and began to play his guitar and cry. I held his woolly head in my arms and wished I could have been old enough to have been the woman he loved so much and that I had not been lost years and years ago.

When he was leaving, my mother said to us that we'd better sleep light that night for we'd probably have to go over to Mr. Sweet's before daylight. And we did. For soon after we had gone to bed one of the neighbors knocked on our door and called my father and said that Mr. Sweet was sinking fast and if he wanted to get in a word before the crossover he'd better shake a leg and get over to Mr. Sweet's house. All the neighbors knew to come to our house if something was wrong with Mr. Sweet, but they did not know how we always managed to make him well, or at least stop him from dying, when he was often so near death. As soon as we heard the cry we got up, my brother and I and my mother and father, and put on our clothes. We hurried out of the house and down the road, for we were always afraid that we might someday be too late and Mr. Sweet would get tired of dallying.

When we got to the house, a very poor shack really, we found the front room full of neighbors and relatives and a man met us at the door and said that it was all very sad that old Mr. Sweet Little (for Little was his family name, although we mostly ignored it) was about to kick the bucket. He advised my parents not to take my brother and me into the "death room," seeing we were so young and all, but we were so much more accustomed to the death room than he that we ignored him and dashed in without giving his warning a second thought. I was almost in tears, for these deaths upset me fearfully, and the thought of how much depended on me and my brother (who was such a ham most of the time) made me very nervous.

The doctor was bending over the bed and turned back to tell us for at least the tenth time in the history of my family that, alas, old Mr. Sweet Little was dying and that the children had best not see the face of implacable death (I didn't know what "implacable" was, but whatever it was, Mr. Sweet was not!). My father pushed him rather abruptly out of the way saying, as he always did and very loudly, for he was saying it to Mr. Sweet, "To hell with dying, man, these children want Mr. Sweet"—which was my cue to throw myself upon the bed and kiss Mr. Sweet all around his whiskers and under the eyes and around the collar of his nightshirt where he smelled so strongly of all sorts of things, mostly liniment.

I was very good at bringing him around, for as soon as I saw that he was struggling to open his eyes I knew he was going to be all right, and so could finish my revival sure of success. As soon as his eyes were open he would begin to smile and that way I knew that I had surely won. Once, though, I got a tremendous scare, for he could not open his eyes and later I learned that he had had a stroke and that one side of his face was stiff and hard to get into motion. When he began to smile I could tickle him in earnest because I was sure that nothing would get in the way of his laughter, although once he began to cough so hard that he almost threw me off his stomach, but that was when I was very small, little more than a baby, and my bushy hair had gotten in his nose.

When we were sure he would listen to us we would ask him why he was in bed and when he was coming to see us again and could we play with his guitar, which more than likely would be leaning against his bed. His eyes would get all misty and he would sometimes cry out loud, but we never let it embarrass us, for he knew that we loved him and that we sometimes cried too for no reason. My parents would leave the room to just the three of us; Mr. Sweet, by that time, would be propped up in bed with a number of pillows behind his head and with me sitting and lying on his shoulder and along his chest. Even when he had trouble breathing he would not ask me to get down. Looking into my eyes he would shake his white head and run a scratchy old finger all around my hairline, which was rather low down, nearly to my eyebrows, and make some people say I looked like a baby monkey.

My brother was very generous in all this, he let me do all the revivaling— he had done it for years before I was born and so was glad to be able to pass it on to someone new. What he would do while I talked to Mr. Sweet was pretend to play the guitar, in fact pretend that he was a young version of Mr. Sweet, and it always made Mr. Sweet glad to think that someone wanted to be like him—of course, we did not know this then, we played the thing by ear, and whatever he seemed to like, we did. We were desperately afraid that he was just going to take off one day and leave us.

It did not occur to us that we were doing anything special; we had not learned that death was final when it did come. We thought nothing of triumphing over it so many times, and in fact became a trifle contemptuous of people who let themselves be carried away. It did not occur to us that if our own father had been dying we could not have stopped it, that Mr. Sweet was the only person over whom we had power.

When Mr. Sweet was in his eighties I was studying in the university many miles from home. I saw him whenever I went home, but he was never on the verge of dying that I could tell and I began to feel that my anxiety for his health and psychological well-being was unnecessary. By this time he not only had a mustache but was beginning to grow a beard. He was very peaceful, fragile, gentle, and the only jarring note about him was his old guitar, which he still played in the old sad, sweet, down-home blues way.

On Mr. Sweet's ninetieth birthday I was finishing my doctorate in Massachusetts and had been making arrangements to go home for several weeks' rest. That morning I got a telegram telling me that Mr. Sweet was dying again and could I please drop everything and come home. Of course I could. My dissertation could wait and my teachers would understand when I explained to them after I got back. I ran to the phone, called the airport, and within four hours I was speeding along the dusty road to Mr. Sweet's.

The house was more dilapidated than when I was last there, but it was overgrown with yellow roses which my family had planted many years ago. The air was heavy and sweet and very peaceful. I felt strange walking through the gate and up the old rickety steps. But the strangeness left me as I caught sight of the thin body I loved so well beneath the familiar quilt coverlet. Mr. Sweet!

His eyes were closed tight and his hands, crossed over his stomach, were thin and delicate, no longer scratchy. I remembered how as a small child I had run and jumped up on him just anywhere; now I knew he would not be able to support my weight. I looked around at my parents, and was surprised to see that my father and mother also looked old and frail. My father, his own hair very gray, leaned over the quietly sleeping old man, who, incidentally, smelled still of wine and tobacco, and said, as he'd done so many times, "To hell with dying, man! My daughter is home to see Mr. Sweet!" My brother hadn't been able to come, as he was in the war in Asia. I bent down and gently stroked the closed eyes and gradually they began to open. The closed, wine-stained lips twitched a little, then parted in a warm, slightly embarrassed smile. Mr. Sweet could see me and he recognized me and his eyes looked very spry and twinkly for a moment. I put my head down on the pillow next to his and we just looked at each other for a long time. Then he began to trace my peculiar hairline with a thin, smooth finger. I closed my eyes when his finger halted above my ear (he used to rejoice at the dirt in my ears when I was little), his hand stayed cupped around my cheek. When I opened my eyes, sure that I had reached him in time, his were closed.

Even at twenty-four how could I believe that I had failed? that Mr. Sweet was really gone? He had never gone before. But when I looked up at my parents I saw that they were holding back tears. They had loved him dearly. He was like a piece of rare and delicate china which was always being saved from breaking and which finally fell. I looked long at the old face, the wrinkled forehead, the red lips, the hands that still reached out to me. Soon I felt my father pushing something cool into my hands. It was Mr. Sweet's guitar. He had asked him months before to give it to me; he had known that even if I came next time he would not be able to respond in the old way. He did not want me to feel that my trip had been for nothing.

The old guitar! I plucked the strings, hummed "Sweet Georgia Brown." The magic of Mr. Sweet lingered still in the smooth wooden box. Through the window I could catch the fragrant delicate scent of tender yellow roses. The man on the high old-fashioned bed with the quilt coverlet and the glowing white hair had been my first love.

"To Hell with Dying," 1967

OGDEN NASH (*American, 1902–1971*)

> People expect old men to die,
> They do not really mourn old men.
> Old men are different. People look
> At them with eyes that wonder when . . .
> People watch with unshocked eyes;
> But the old men know when an old man dies.

"Old Men," in *Many Long Years Ago*, 1954

BERNARD BERENSON (*American, 1865–1959*)

June 26th, Venice

At 6:30 Emma bringing my tea reminded me with her congratulations that this is my birthday. Yes, I am eighty-six today, and I wonder how long this adventure will go on. It is an adventure keeping alive against all the invading powers of destruction that beset me. I get dead-tired after every exertion. I sweat hot and cold when I sneeze and cough, and literally expectorate, I doze every couple of hours all the waking hours and invariably after three or four hours of sleep. I ooze sleep and tend to doze continually. And yet between attacks I still have pleasure in my body, I still dream of fair women—*il lupo sogna agnello*—I still enjoy conversation. I still take pleasure in good-looking people old and young I pass in the street, and above all I get ecstatic over the beauty of nature and the splendours of art. While I have these I want to hold the fort till the last moment. What I pray to avoid is to go on existing when I am no longer alive.

May 6th, I Tatti

At my age what is it to be happy? Nothing spiritual or even mental. I fear it consists in one's bowels not troubling, but being warm, quiet, and comfortable. That first and foremost. Then of being relatively free from burning toes and finger tips, from a feeling of bloatedness, from stabbing aches and pains anywhere, from nausea and a disgusting taste in the mouth, from difficulties with bladder and intestine—in short, to be free from every kind of physical *malaise*. All negative, except perhaps the peace of the bowels, which does seem positive, and not mere alleviation, or even removal of pain. Shall I end that way, happy in my bowels and satisfied, all else of the infinitely detailed universe forgotten, ignored as in infancy—to which indeed extreme old age may be the complete return?

Why, what, whither? The mere joy of living, of having enjoyed bodily pleasure, satisfaction of the intellect, ecstasies, and transubstantiation of erotic impulses into visions, distant prospects of a freedom from animality that would transfigure. Is it not enough? More is unconceivable, mere verbiage.

Diary entries from 26 June 1951 and 6 May 1957

FLORIDA SCOTT-MAXWELL *(American, 1883–1979)*

My only fear about death is that it will not come soon enough. Life still interests and occupies me. Happily I am not in such discomfort that I wish for death, I love and am loved, but please God I die before I lose my independence. I do not know what I believe about life after death; if it exists then I burn with interest, if not—well, I am tired. I have endured the flame of living and that should be enough. . . .

I don't like to write this down, yet it is much in the minds of the old. We wonder how much older we have to become, and what degree of decay we may have to endure. We keep whispering to ourselves, "Is this age yet? How far must I go?" For age can be dreaded more than death. "How many years of vacuity? To what degree of deterioration must I advance?" Some want death now, as release from old age, some say they will accept death willingly, but in a few years. I feel the solemnity of death, and the possibility of some form of continuity. Death feels a friend because it will release us from the deterioration of which we cannot see the end. It is waiting for death that wears us down, and the distaste for what we may become.

From *The Measure of My Days*, 1968

JARED ANGIRA (*African, contemporary*)

The country of the dead
I speak
no answer
I weep
no pity
I watch
no colour
I listen
no sound
the country of the dead

I shout, the echo strikes
the dead rock
I kick, my toe mutilates
on dry stump
I weep, no pity
the country of the dead

I've searched the exit
but heard no owls
no parrots, the waves beat afar
on wrecks of ships
the sand stares with me
the country of the dead.

"The Country of the Dead"

PSALM 23, HEBREW SCRIPTURES

The Lord is my shepherd; I shall
not want.

He maketh me to lie down in green
pastures;
He leadeth me beside the still
waters.

He restoreth my soul;
He guideth me in straight paths
for His name's sake.

Yea, though I walk through the
valley of the shadow of death,

I will fear no evil,
For Thou art with me;
Thy rod and Thy staff, they com-
    fort me.

Thou preparest a table before me
    in the presence of mine enemies;
Thou hast anointed my head with
    oil; my cup runneth over.

Surely goodness and mercy shall
    follow me all the days of my life;
And I shall dwell in the house of
    the LORD for ever.

PIERRE DE RONSARD *(French, 1524–1585)*

I've no more than my bones, a skeleton I seem,
Unfleshed, unnerved, unmuscled, unpulped,
Whom the arrow of Death without pardon has struck.
I daren't look at my arms for fear I shall tremble.
Apollo and his son [Aesculapius], two great masters combined
Wouldn't know how to cure me; their medicines deceive me.
Farewell, pleasant sun; my eye's all stopped up.
My body is going where things disassemble.
What friend, seeing me stripped to this degree,
Will not bring back home a sad and tearful eye,
Consoling me in bed and kissing my face.
While wiping my eyes which Death has put to rest.
Farewell, dear companions, farewell my dear friends.
I'm going down first to prepare you a place.

From "Pièces posthumes," 1550s

DIANA O HEHIR *(American, b. 1929)*

Inch by inch along the bed,
Growing more compact, his arms pulled up like bird's wings
(My father is almost ninety),
I love you, I say over and over,
Until I read in *Time* Magazine that saying this holds the dying
  back;

They get polite, they hang around to thank you.
I love you, I say,
Under my breath.

In Bangkok you can buy a bird in front of the temple
For twenty cents. It's not to eat
Nor to listen to nor to admire but to
Set free.
Spring the door with your plastic diner's card, wait for the
    scrabble, the
Head poked out the door, air by your face,
And up he goes.

"Home Free," 1988

THE DALAI LAMA (*Tibetan, b. 1935*)

Death is a natural part of life, which we will all surely have to face sooner or later. To my mind, there are two ways we can deal with it while we are alive. We can either choose to ignore it or we can confront the prospect of our own death and, by thinking clearly about it, try to minimise the suffering that it can bring. However, in neither of these ways can we actually overcome it.

As a Buddhist, I view death as a normal process, a reality that I accept will occur as long as I remain in this earthly existence. Knowing that I cannot escape it, I see no point in worrying about it. I tend to think of death as being like changing your clothes when they are old and worn out, rather than as some final end. Yet death is unpredictable: We do not know when or how it will take place. So it is only sensible to take certain precautions before it actually happens.

Naturally, most of us would like to die a peaceful death, but it is also clear that we cannot hope to die peacefully if our lives have been full of violence, or if our minds have mostly been agitated by emotions like anger, attachment, or fear. So if we wish to die well, we must learn how to live well: Hoping for a peaceful death, we must cultivate peace in our mind, and in our way of life.

. . . From the Buddhist point of view, the actual experience of death is very important. Although how or where we will be reborn is generally dependent on karmic forces, our state of mind at the time of death can influence the quality of our next rebirth. So at the moment of death, in spite of the great variety of karmas we have accumulated, if we make a special effort to generate a virtuous state of mind, we may strengthen and activate a virtuous karma, and so bring about a happy rebirth.

The actual point of death is also when the most profound and beneficial inner experiences can come about. Through repeated acquaintance with the processes of death in meditation, an accomplished meditator can use his or her actual death to gain great spiritual realization. This is why experienced practitioners engage in meditative practices as they pass away. An indication of their attainment is that often their bodies do not begin to decay until long after they are clinically dead.

No less significant than preparing for our own death is helping others to die well. As newborn babies each of us was helpless and, without the care and kindness we received then, we would not have survived. Because the dying also are unable to help themselves, we should relieve them of discomfort and anxiety, and assist them, as far as we can, to die with composure.

Here the most important point is to avoid anything which will cause the dying person's mind to become more disturbed than it may already be. Our prime aim in helping a dying person is to put them at ease, and there are many ways of doing this. A dying person who is familiar with spiritual practice may be encouraged and inspired if they are reminded of it, but even kindly reassurance on our part can engender a peaceful, relaxed attitude in the dying person's mind.

Foreword to *The Tibetan Book of Living and Dying*, 1993

JOHN DONNE (*English, 1572–1631*)

> Death, be not proud, though some have calléd thee
> Mighty and dreadful, for thou art not so;
> For those whom thou think'st thou dost overthrow
> Die not, poor Death, nor yet canst thou kill me.
> From rest and sleep, which but thy pictures be,
> Much pleasure; then from thee much more must flow,
> And soonest our best men with thee do go,
> Rest of their bones, and soul's delivery.
> Thou art slave to fate, chance, kings, and desperate men,
> And dost with poison, war, and sickness dwell,
> And poppy or charms can make us sleep as well
> And better than thy stroke; why swell'st thou then?
> One short sleep past, we wake eternally
> And death shall be no more; Death, thou shalt die.

"Death, be not proud," 1633

CHAPTER SEVEN

CELEBRATION/LAMENT

Like most other chapters in this collection, Celebration/Lament is fashioned from the juxtaposition of seemingly opposite or contradictory ideas. In one sense, of course, celebration and lament involve the expression of very different emotions: joy and sorrow. Yet there is much wisdom in the popular phrase "How can you be glad if you've never been sad?" Celebration and lament are each other's teachers. As we get older, we learn to grieve for what time inexorably devours while taking pleasure in moments of love or beauty or work or wonder. In fact, celebration often emerges from the experience of grief.

This chapter explores several configurations of celebration and lament: appreciation of the beauty of the old, especially the beauty of old women; earnest and satirical responses to the passing of time; laments for the past and the role of faith in accepting what cannot be changed; and lyrical selections in which dark melodies mingle evocatively with bright harmonies.

We begin with appreciation. From the poet Hilda Morley to the psychiatrist and writer Robert Coles, we are given new eyes to see. In recent years, Jenny Joseph's "Warning" has become a favorite among readers who share her defiance of the very conventional images that Hilda Morley finds beautiful. In "miss rosie," the contemporary African-American poet Lucille Clifton celebrates a poor woman who used to be the "best looking gal in georgia," but is now a "wet brown bag of a woman."

The excerpts from Robert Coles's *The Old Ones of New Mexico* introduce us to Domingo and Dolores Garcia, a couple interviewed in rural New Mexico in 1972. Most of the inspiring words are spoken by Dolores, who at age eighty-three chases away her own questions about why she is still alive. "One lives. One dies. To ask questions with no good answers to them is to waste time that belongs to others." Domingo speaks only briefly, honoring his wife of fifty-eight years: "She wears old age like a bunch of fresh-cut flowers." His great respect for Dolores is expressed in the Spanish phrase *una anciana*, a venerable old woman.

The four selections by Archibald MacLeish, Mark Twain, Robert Browning, and Ogden Nash alternate between celebration and satire. Twain's remarks on the occasion of his seventieth birthday parody pompous testimonials of aged wisdom and poke fun at regimens designed to promote longevity. "We can't reach old age by another man's road," is Twain's only advice. The excerpts from Browning's famous "Rabbi Ben Ezra" reflect a fervent belief in the soulful possibilities of the second half of life. The nineteenth-century English poet's images of reminiscence and the stages of life are woven into a religious vision of what transcends the ravages of time. In "Old Is for Books," the twentieth-century American writer Ogden Nash mercilessly lampoons "Rabbi Ben Ezra" as the product of an idealistic young man in his thirties.

The passage from Walther von der Vogelweide's "Elegy" opens a series of laments for the past. Feelings of disorientation, of inexplicable loss and sadness are offset by acceptance, as in Rūdakī's early Islamic "Lament in Old Age": "Now the times have changed,—and I too, changed and altered must succumb." Selections from the Koran, Cotton Mather, and Olive Ann Burns reveal the role of religious faith in acceptance of life's changes. In the Koran, the aged Abraham learns that the mercy of Allah depends on absolute submission to His will. As an old man, the Colonial American preacher Cotton Mather thanks God for sparing him the pain and disease that Puritans considered an inevitable punishment for humans' sinful nature.

The last selections give lyrical voice to tones of darkness and light. In the passage from Sophocles' *Oedipus at Colonus*, the Chorus of Elders laments the plight of old Oedipus, reduced to the status of a wandering beggar. Even as they express the ancient Greek pessimism about old age and preference for early death, they admire the power of this "blind and ruined old man." In contrast, the contemporary American poet May Sarton feels new warmth and growth while musing on her life's oncoming winter. Shakespeare's seventy-third sonnet remains an incomparable celebration of love and aging. In his depiction of a holy death, Anathasius, a fourth-century bishop of Alexandria, pays tribute to St. Anthony. W. B. Yeats's "Sailing to Byzantium" contains the poet's famous answer to his depressing image of old age as a "paltry thing." The chapter concludes, in turn, with evocations of "heroic helplessness," wonder, and a prophetic yearning for a faithful community of all ages.

HILDA MORLEY (*American, b. 1920*)

> I begin to love the beauty
> of the old more than the beauty of
> the young—the old lady shielding
> her face from the hot sun with a black
> lace fan and the exquisite
> old man with the white beard & the old man pushing
> the car of the young man dying
> of dystrophy & the elderly
> woman in black holding the hand of a little
> child in an apricot smock

"I Begin to Love," 1988

JENNY JOSEPH (*English, b. 1932*)

> When I am an old woman I shall wear purple
> With a red hat which doesn't go, and doesn't suit me.
> And I shall spend my pension on brandy and summer gloves
> And satin sandals, and say we've no money for butter.
> I shall sit down on the pavement when I'm tired
> And gobble up samples in shops and press alarm bells
> And run my stick along the public railings
> And make up for the sobriety of my youth.
> I shall go out in my slippers in the rain
> And pick the flowers in other people's gardens
> and learn to spit.
>
> You can wear terrible shirts and grow more fat
> And eat three pounds of sausages at a go
> Or only bread and pickle for a week
> And hoard pens and pencils and beermats and things in boxes.
>
> But now we must have clothes that keep us dry
> And pay our rent and not swear in the street
> And set a good example for the children.
> We must have friends to dinner and read the papers.
>
> But maybe I ought to practise a little now?
> So people who know me are not too shocked and surprised
> When suddenly I am old, and start to wear purple.

"Warning," 1975

LUCILLE CLIFTON (*African American, b. 1936*)

> when I watch you
> wrapped up like garbage
> sitting, surrounded by the smell
> of too old potato peels
> or
> when I watch you
> in your old man's shoes
> with the little toe cut out
> sitting, waiting for your mind
> like next week's grocery
> i say
> when I watch you
> you wet brown bag of a woman
> who used to be the best looking gal in georgia
> used to be called the Georgia Rose
> i stand up
> through your destruction
> i stand up

"miss rosie," 1969

HARRIET BEECHER STOWE (*American, 1811–1890*)

She might be fifty-five or sixty; but hers was one of those faces that time seems to touch only to brighten and adorn. The snowy lisse crape cap, made after the strait Quaker pattern,—the plain white muslin handkerchief, lying in placid folds across her bosom,—the drab shawl and dress,—showed at once the community to which she belonged. Her face was round and rosy, with a healthful downy softness, suggestive of a ripe peach. Her hair, partially silvered by age, was parted smoothly back from a high placid forehead, on which time had written no inscription, except peace on earth, good will to men, and beneath shone a large pair of clear, honest, loving brown eyes; you only needed to look straight into them, to feel that you saw to the bottom of a heart as good and true as ever throbbed in woman's bosom. So much has been said and sung of beautiful young girls, why don't somebody wake up to the beauty of old women? If any want to get up an inspiration under this head, we refer them to our good friend Rachel Halliday, just as she sits there in her little rocking-chair.

From "The Quaker Settlement," in *Uncle Tom's Cabin*, 1852

ROBERT COLES (*American, b. 1929*)

He is eighty-three years old. Once he was measured as exactly six feet tall, but that was a half a century ago. He is sure that he has lost at least an inch or two. Sometimes, when his wife has grown impatient with his slouch, and told him to straighten up, he does her suggestion one better and tilts himself backward. Now are you happy? he seems to be asking her, and she smiles indulgently. His wife is also eighty-three. She always defers to her husband. She will not speak until he has had his say. She insists that he be introduced first to strangers. As the two of them approach a door, she makes a quick motion toward it, holds it patiently, and sometimes, if he is distracted by a conversation and slow to move through, one of her hands reaches for his elbow, while the other points: Go now, is the unstated message, so that I can follow.

They were born within a mile and within two months of one another in Cordova, New Mexico, in the north central part of the state. They are old Americans not only by virtue of age but by ancestry. For many generations their ancestors have lived in territory that is now part of the United States. Before the Declaration of Independence was written there were people not so far away from Cordova named Garcia living as they do, off the land. They are not, however, model citizens of their country. They have never voted, and no doubt the men who framed the Declaration of Independence would not be impressed by the boredom or indifference these New Mexicans demonstrate when the subject of politics comes up. They don't even make an effort to keep abreast of the news, though they do have a television set in their small adobe house. When Walter Cronkite or John Chancellor appears, neither of the Garcias listens very hard. For that matter, no programs really engage their undivided attention—and at first one is tempted to think them partially deaf. But the issue is taste, not the effects of age. Mrs. Garcia does like to watch some afternoon serials, but without the sound. She takes an interest in how the people dress and what the furniture in the homes looks like. The actors and actresses are company of sorts when Mr. Garcia is outside tending the crops or looking after the horses and cows. Nor is language the problem; they both prefer to speak Spanish, but they can make themselves understood quite well in English. They have had to, as Mrs. Garcia explains, with no effort to conceal her longstanding sense of resignation: "You bend with the wind. And Anglo people are a strong wind. They want their own way; they can be like a tornado, out to pass over everyone as they go somewhere. I don't mean to talk out of turn. There are Anglos who don't fit my words. But we are outsiders in a land that is ours. We are part of an Anglo country and that will not change. I had to teach the facts of life to my four sons, and in doing so I learned my own lesson well."

*   *   *

She stops and serves bread. She pours coffee. It is best black, she says in a matter of fact way, but the visitor will not be judged for his weak stomach or poor taste. She again apologizes for her failure to tell a brief, pointed, coherent story. Her mother was "sunny," was "very sunny" until the end, but she worries about "clouds" over her own thinking. The two Domingos in her life scoff at the idea, though. After the coffee she wants to go on. She likens herself to a weathered old tree that stands just outside, within sight. It is autumn and the tree is bare. She likens the coffee to a God-given miracle: suddenly one feels as if spring has come, one is budding and ready to go through another round of things. But she is definitely short of breath, coffee or no coffee, and needs no one to point it out. "Tomorrow then."

In the morning she is far stronger and quicker to speak out than later in the day. "Every day is like a lifetime," she says—immediately disavowing ownership of the thought. Her husband has said that for years, and to be honest, she has upon occasion taken issue with him. Some days start out bad, and only in the afternoon does she feel in reasonably good spirits. But she does get up at five every morning, and most often she is at her best when the first light appears. By the time her visitor arrives, early in the morning by his standards, she has done enough to feel a little tired and somewhat nostalgic: "Each day for me is a gift. My mother taught us to take nothing for granted. We would complain, or beg, as children do before they fall asleep, and she would remind us that if we are *really* lucky we will have a gift presented to us in the morning: a whole new day to spend and try to do something with. I suppose we should ask for more than that, but it's too late for me to do so.

"I prefer to sit here on my chair with my eyes on the mountains. I prefer to think about how the animals are doing; many of them have put themselves to sleep until spring. God has given them senses, and they use them. Things are not so clear for us—so many pushes and pulls, so many voices; I know what Babel means. I go in town shopping and there is so much argument: everyone has an opinion on something. The only time people lower their heads these days is on Sunday morning, for an hour, and even then they are turning around and paying attention to others. What is she wearing? How is he doing with his business? Do we any longer care what the Lord wants us to know and do?

"I am sorry. I am like a sheep who disobeys and has to be given a prod. I don't lose my thoughts when they're crossing my mind; it's when they have to come out as words that I find trouble. We should be careful with our thoughts, as we are with the water. When I'm up and making breakfast I watch for changes in the light. Long before the sun appears it has forewarned us. Nearer and nearer it comes, but not so gradually that you don't notice.

It's like one electric light going on after another. First there is dark. Then the dark lifts ever so little. Still, it might be a full moon and midnight. Then, like Domingo's knife with chickens, the night is cut up; it becomes a shadow of what it was, and Domingo will sometimes stop for a minute and say: 'Dolores, she is gone, but do not worry, she will be back.' He has memories like mine: his mother lived to be eighty-seven, and all her life she spoke like mine: 'Domingo, be glad,' she would tell him. Why should he be glad? His mother knew: 'God has chosen you for a trial here, so acquit yourself well every day, and never mind about yesterday or tomorrow.' We both forget her words, though. As the sun comes out of hiding and there is no longer any question that those clouds will go away, we thank dear God for his generosity, but we think back sometimes. We can't seem to help ourselves. We hold on and try to keep in mind the chores that await us, but we are tempted, and soon we will be slipping. There is a pole in our fire station. Once the men are on it, there is no stopping. Like them with a crash we land on those sad moments. We feel sorry for ourselves. We wish life had treated us more kindly. The firemen have a job to do, and I wonder what would happen to us if we didn't have ours to do. We might never come back to this year of 1972. We would be the captives of bad memories. But no worry; we are part of this world here; the sun gets stronger and burns our consciences; the animals make themselves known; on a rainy day the noise of the water coming down the side of the house calls to me—why am I not moving, too?"

She moves rather quickly, so quickly that she seems almost ashamed when someone takes notice, even if silently. Back in her seat she folds her arms, then unfolds them, putting her hands on her lap, her left hand over her right hand. Intermittently she breaks her position to reach for her coffee and her bread: "Domingo and I have been having this same breakfast for over fifty years. We are soon to be married fifty-five years, God willing. We were married a month after the Great War ended; it was a week before Christmas, 1918. The priest said he hoped our children would always have enough food and never fight in a war. I haven't had a great variety of food to give my family, but they have not minded. I used to serve the children eggs in the morning, but Domingo and I have stayed with hot bread and coffee. My fingers would die if they didn't have the dough to work over. I will never give up my oven for a new one. It has been here forty years, and is an old friend. I would stop baking bread if it gave out. My sons once offered to buy me an electric range, they called it, and I broke down. It was a terrible thing to do. The boys felt bad. My husband said I should be more considerate. I meant no harm, though. I don't deliberately say to myself: Dolores Garcia, you have been hurt, so now go and cry. The tears came and I was helpless before them. Later my husband said they all agreed I was in the right; the stove has been so good to us, and there is nothing wrong—the bread is as tasty as ever, I believe. It is a sickness, you know: being always dissatisfied with what you have and eager for a change."

She stops here and looks lovingly around the room. She is attached to every piece of furniture. Her husband made them: a round table, eight chairs, with four more in their bedroom, the beds there, the bureau there. She begins to tell how good Domingo is at carving wood: "That is what I would like to say about Domingo: he plants, builds, and harvests, he tries to keep us alive and comfortable with his hands. We sit on what he has made, eat what he has grown, sleep on what he has put together. We have never had a spring on our bed, but I have to admit, we bought our mattress. Buying, that is the sickness. I have gone to the city and watched people. They are hungry, but nothing satisfies their hunger. They come to stores like flies to sticky paper: they are caught. I often wonder who is better off. The fly dies. The people have to pay to get out of the store, but soon they are back again, the same look in their eyes. I don't ask people to live on farms and make chairs and tables; but when I see them buying things they don't need, or even want—except to make a purchase, to get something—then I say there is a sickness."

*   *   *

She stops to open the window and summon her husband. Maybe *he* should say exactly what he told his boys a long time ago about Santa Claus. But no, it is hopeless; he will not come in until he has finished his work. He is like a clock, so-and-so-many minutes to do one thing, then another. The cows know the difference between him and anyone else. He is quick. They get fast relief. When one of her sons tries to help, or she, or a grandchild, it is no good. The animals are restless, make a lot of noise, and Domingo pleads: leave him his few jobs, then when he goes, sell the animals. As for Santa Claus, forgotten for a moment, the gist of Domingo's speech is given by his wife: "My children, a saint is in chains, locked up somewhere, while all these stores have their impostors. Will you contribute to a saint's suffering? Santa Claus was meant to bring good news: the Lord's birthday is in the morning, so let us all celebrate by showing each other how much love we feel. Instead we say, I want, I want, I want. We say, More, more, more. We say Get this, then the next thing, and then the next. We lose our heads. We lose our souls. And somewhere that saint must be in hiding, may be in jail for all we know. If not, he is suffering. I tell you this not to make you feel bad. It is no one's fault. We are all to blame. Only let us stop. If we stop, others will not, I know. But that will be their sorrow, not ours to share with them."

She is not ready to guarantee every word as his. He is a man of few words, and she readily admits that she tends to carry on. Then, as if to confess something that is not a sin, and so not meant for a priest, yet bothers

297

her, she goes further, admits to talking out loud when no one is around. She is sure her husband doesn't do so, and she envies him his quiet self-assurance, his somewhat impassive temperament: "He is silent not because he has nothing to say. He is silent because he understands the world, and because he knows enough to say to himself: what will words and more words do to make the world any better? I have wished for years that I could be like him, but God makes each of us different."

*   *   *

. . . "I pray. I thank God for the time he has given me here, and ask Him to take me when He is ready, and I tell Him I will have no regrets. I think of all I have seen in this long life: the people, the changes. Even up here, in this small village, the world makes its presence felt. I remember when the skies had no planes in them, houses no wires sticking up, trying to catch television programs. I never wanted a refrigerator. I never needed one. But I have one. It is mostly empty. I have one weakness: ice cream. I make it, just as I make butter. I used to make small amounts and Domingo and I would finish what was there. Now I can make and store up butter or ice cream and give presents of them to my sons and their children. No wonder they bought us the refrigerator! As I lie on our bed and stare at the ceiling I think how wonderful it is: eighty-three, and still able to make ice cream. We need a long rest afterwards, but between the two of us we can do a good job. The man at the store has offered to sell any extra we have; he says he can get a good price. I laugh. I tell him he's going to turn me into a thief. It would be dishonest to sell food you make in your home for profit at a store. That's the way I feel. My husband gets angry: What do you mean 'dishonest?' he will say. I answer back: my idea of what is dishonest is not his. So we cannot go on about this. It is in my heart where the feeling is, not in my head. 'Oh, you are a woman!' he says, and he starts laughing. Later he will tell me that he was picking weeds, or taking care of our flowers, and he thought to himself: She is right, because to make food is part of our life as a family, and to start selling that is to say that we have nothing that is *ours*. It is what he always comes back to: better to have less money and feel we own ourselves, than more and feel at the mercy of so many strangers."

. . . The body has its seasons. I am in the last one; winter is never without pain and breakdowns. I don't want to spend my last years waiting on myself and worrying about myself. I have already lived over twice as long as our Savior. How greedy ought one be for life? God has his purposes. I wake up and feel those aches and I notice how wrinkled my skin is, and I wonder what I'm still doing alive. I believe it is wrong, to ask a question like that. One lives. One dies. To ask questions with no good answers to them is to waste time that belongs to others. I am here to care for my husband, to care for this house, to be here when my sons and my grandchildren come. The young have to see what is ahead. They have to know that there is youth and middle age and old age. My grandson Domingo asked me a while ago what it is like to be one hundred. He is ten. I told him to be one hundred is to live ten of his lifetimes. He seemed puzzled, so I knew I had been thoughtless. I took him around. I put my hand besides his and we compared skins. I said it is good to be young and it is good to be old. He didn't need any more explanations. He said when you're young you have a lot of years before you, but when you're old you have your children and your grandchildren and you love them and you're proud of them. I took him around again and hugged him tightly, and in a second he was out there with his father and his grandfather looking at the cows."

*   *   *

She stops abruptly, as if this is one conversation she doesn't want to pursue. Anyway, she has been dusting and sweeping the floor as she talks and now she is finished. Next come the plants, a dozen or so of them; they need to be watered and moved in or out of the sun. She hovers over them for a minute, doing nothing, simply looking. She dusts them, too. She prunes one: "I've been waiting for a week or so to do this. I thought to myself: that plant won't like it, losing so much. I dread cutting my toenails and fingernails. I am shaky with scissors. But I go after the plants with a surer touch. They are so helpless, yet they are so good to look at. They seem to live forever. Parts die, but new parts grow. I have had them so long—I don't remember the number of years. I know each one's needs, and I try to take care of them the same time each day. Maybe it is unnecessary nonsense, the amount of attention I give. I know that is what Domingo would say. Only once did he put his belief into words, and then I reminded him that he has his habits, too. No one can keep him from starting in one corner of his garden and working his way to the other, and with such care. I asked him years ago why not change around every once in a while and begin on the furthest side, and go faster. 'I couldn't do it,' he said, and I told him I understood. Habits are not crutches; habits are roads we have paved for ourselves. When we are old, and if we have done a good job, the roads last and make the remaining time useful: we get where we want to go, and without the delays we used to have when we were young. How many plants died on me when I was first learning! How often I forgot to water them, or watered them too much because I wanted to do right. Or I would expose them to the sun and forget that, like us, they need the shade, too. I was treating them as if they needed a dose of this, a trial of that. But they have been removed from God's forests, from Nature it is; and they need consideration. When we were young my husband also used to forget chores;

299

he'd be busy doing one thing, and he'd overlook the other. But slowly we built up our habits, and now I guess we are protected from another kind of forgetfulness: the head tires easily when you are our age, and without the habits of the years you can find yourself at a loss to answer the question: what next?''

*   *   *

One morning, in the midst of a conversation, she scolds herself for talking too much. She falls silent. She glances up at the picture of Christ at the Last Supper. Her face loses its tension. She slumps a bit, but not under the weight of pain or even age. She feels relaxed. There are a few dishes to wash. There is a curtain that needs mending. There is not only bread to make, but pies. Her grandchildren love her pies, and she loves seeing them eaten. "Children eat so fast," she says with a sigh of envy. She begins talking again. She resumes her activity. She has to pick at her food now. "When one is over eighty the body needs less," she observes—but immediately afterwards she looks a little shy, a little apprehensive: "I have no business talking like a doctor. Once the priest told me I talk like him. I told him: I have raised children; it is necessary at times to give them sermons, and hear their confessions. He smiled. If I had another life I would learn to be a nurse. In my day, few of our people could aim so high—not a woman like me, anyway. It is different today. My sons say their children will finish high school and my Domingo in Los Alamos says *his* Domingo does so well in school he may go on to a college. I laugh with my husband: a Domingo Garcia in a college. Maybe the boy will be a doctor. Who knows? He likes to take care of his dog. He has a gentle side to him. He is popular with the girls, so I don't think he's headed for the priesthood. He tells me he'd like to be a scientist, like the men his father looks after in the laboratories. I worry that he would make those bombs, though. I wouldn't want that on his conscience. My son told me they do other things there in the laboratories, not just make bombs. I said, 'Thank God!'

"Of course all of that is for the future. I don't know if I will be around to see my grandchildren have children of their own. One cannot take anything for granted. The priest laughed at Domingo and me last Sunday, and said, 'You two will outlast me; you will be coming here when you are both over one hundred.' I said, 'Thank you father, but that is a long way off, to be a hundred, and much can happen.' 'Have faith,' he said, and he is right: one must.''

She pauses for a few seconds, as if to think about her own admonition. Then she is back on her train of thought: "Sometimes after church Domingo and I walk through the cemetery. It is a lovely place, small and familiar. We pay our respects to our parents, to our aunts and uncles, to our children. A

300

family is a river; some of it has passed on and more is to come, and nothing is still, because we all move along, day by day, toward our destination. We both feel joy in our hearts when we kneel on the grass before the stones and say a prayer. At the edge of the cemetery near the gate is a statue of the Virgin Mary, larger than all the other stones. She is kneeling and on her shoulder is the Cross. She is carrying it—the burden of her Son's death. She is sad, but she has not given up. We know that she has never lost faith. It is a lesson to keep in mind. We always leave a little heavy at the sight of our Lord's mother under such a heavy obligation. But my husband never fails to hold my arm, and each Sunday his words are the same: 'Dolores, the Virgin will be an example to us this week.' It is as if each Sunday he is taking his vows—and me, too, because I say back to him, 'Yes, Domingo, she will be an example to us.' Now, mind you, an hour later one of us, or both of us, will have stumbled. I become cranky. Domingo has a temper. I hush him, and he explodes. He is inconsiderate, and I sulk. That is the way with two people who have lived together so long: the good and the bad are always there, and they have become part of one life, lived together.''

She hears his footsteps coming and quickens her activity a bit. She will not be rushed, but he needs his coffee and so does she. Often she doesn't so much need it as need to drink it because he is drinking it. He lifts his cup, she follows; he puts his down, and soon enough hers is also on the table. Always they get through at the same time. This particular morning Domingo is more expansive and concerned than usual—a foal has just been born. "Well, enough. I must go check on the mother and her infant." He is up and near the door when he turns around to say goodbye: "These days one never knows when the end will come. I know our time is soon up. But when I look at that mother horse and her child in the barn, or at my children and their children, I feel lucky to have been permitted for a while to be part of all this life here on earth." His hand is on the door, and he seems a little embarrassed to have spoken so. But he has to go on: "I am talking like my wife now! After all these years she sometimes falls into my silences and I carry on as she does. She is not just an old woman, you know. She wears old age like a bunch of fresh-cut flowers. She is old, advanced in years, *vieja*, but in Spanish we have another word for her, a word which tells you that she has grown with all those years. I think that is something one ought hope for and pray for and work for all during life: to grow, to become not only older but a bigger person. She is old, all right, *vieja*, but I will dare say this in front of her: she is *una anciana;* with that I declare my respect and have to hurry back to the barn.''

From "Una Anciana," in *The Old Ones of New Mexico,* 1973

ARCHIBALD MacLEISH (*American, 1892–1982*)

> At twenty, stooping round about,
> I thought the world a miserable place,
> Truth a trick, faith in doubt,
> Little beauty, less grace.
>
> Now at sixty what I see,
> Although the world is worse by far,
> Stops my heart in ecstasy.
> God, the wonders that there are!

"With Age Wisdom," c. 1952

MARK TWAIN (*American, 1835–1910*)

[*Introduction by William Dean Howells at a celebration for Twain's seventieth birthday*]

"Now, ladies and gentlemen, and Colonel Harvey, I will try to be greedy on your behalf in wishing the health of our honored and, in view of his great age, our revered guest. I will not say, 'O King, live forever!' but 'O King, live as long as you like!'" [Amid great applause and waving of napkins all rose and drank to Mark Twain.]

Well, if I had made that joke, it would be the best one I ever made, and in the prettiest language, too. I never can get quite to that height. But I appreciate that joke, and I shall remember it—and I shall use it when occasion requires.

I have had a great many birthdays in my time. I remember the first one very well, and I always think of it with indignation; everything was so crude, unaesthetic, primeval. Nothing like this at all. No proper appreciative preparation made; nothing really ready. Now, for a person born with high and delicate instincts—why, even the cradle wasn't whitewashed—nothing ready at all. I hadn't any hair, I hadn't my teeth, I hadn't any clothes, I had to go to my first banquet just like that. Well, everybody came swarming in. It was the merest little bit of a village—hardly that, just a little hamlet, in the backwoods of Missouri, where nothing ever happened, and the people were all interested, and they all came; they looked me over to see if there was anything fresh in my line. Why, nothing ever happened in that village—I— why, I was the only thing that had really happened there for months and months and months; and although I say it myself that shouldn't, I came the nearest to being a real event that had happened in that village in more than two years. Well, those people came, they came with that curiosity which is so provincial, with that frankness which also is so provincial, and they examined me all around and gave their opinion. Nobody asked them, and I shouldn't have minded if anybody had paid me a compliment, but nobody did. Their opinions were all just green with prejudice, and I feel those opinions to this day. Well, I stood that as long as—you know I was courteous, and I stood it to the limit. I stood it an hour, and then the worm turned. I was the worm; it was my turn to turn, and I turned. I knew very well the strength of my position; I knew that I was the only spotlessly pure and innocent person in that whole town, and I came out and said so. And they could not say a word. It was so true. They blushed; they were embarrassed. Well, that was the first after-dinner speech I ever made. I think it was after dinner.

It's a long stretch between that first birthday speech and this one. That was my cradle song, and this is my swan song, I suppose. I am used to swan songs; I have sung them several times.

This is my seventieth birthday, and I wonder if you all rise to the size of that proposition, realizing all the significance of that phrase, seventieth birthday.

The seventieth birthday! It is the time of life when you arrive at a new and awful dignity; when you may throw aside the decent reserves which have oppressed you for a generation and stand unafraid and unabashed upon your seven-terraced summit and look down and teach—unrebuked. You can tell the world how you got there. It is what they all do. You shall never get tired of telling by what delicate arts and deep moralities you climb up to that great place. You will explain the process and dwell on the particulars with senile rapture. I have been anxious to explain my own system this long time, and now at last I have the right.

I have achieved my seventy years in the usual way: by sticking strictly to a scheme of life which would kill anybody else. It sounds like an exaggeration, but that is really the common rule for attaining old age. When we examine the programme of any of these garrulous old people we always find that the habits which have preserved them would have decayed us; that the way of life which enabled them to live upon the property of their heirs so long, as Mr. Choate says, would have put us out of commission ahead of time. I will offer here, as a sound maxim, this: That we can't reach old age by another man's road.

I will now teach, offering my way of life to whomsoever desires to commit suicide by the scheme which has enabled me to beat the doctor and the hangman for seventy years. Some of the details may sound untrue, but they are not. I am not here to deceive; I am here to teach.

We have no permanent habits until we are forty. Then they begin to harden, presently they petrify, then business begins. Since forty I have been regular about going to bed and getting up—and that is one of the main things. I have made it a rule to go to bed when there wasn't anybody left to sit up with; and I have made it a rule to get up when I had to. This has resulted in an unswerving regularity of irregularity. It has saved me sound, but it would injure another person.

In the matter of diet—which is another main thing—I have been persistently strict in sticking to the things which didn't agree with me until one or the other of us got the best of it. Until lately I got the best of it myself. But last spring I stopped frolicking with mince pie after midnight; up to then I had always believed it wasn't loaded. For thirty years I have taken coffee and bread at eight in the morning, and no bite nor sup until seven-thirty in the evening. Eleven hours. That is all right for me, and is wholesome, because I have never had a headache in my life, but headachy people would not reach seventy comfortably by that road, and they would be foolish to try it. And I wish to urge upon you this—which I think is wisdom—that if you find you can't make seventy by any but an uncomfortable road, don't you go. When they take off the Pullman and retire you to the rancid smoker, put on your things, count your checks, and get out at the first way station where there's a cemetery.

I have made it a rule never to smoke more than one cigar at a time. I have no other restriction as regards smoking. I do not know just when I began to smoke, I only know that it was in my father's lifetime, and that I was discreet. He passed from this life early in 1847, when I was a shade past eleven; ever since then I have smoked publicly. As an example to others, and not that I care for moderation myself, it has always been my rule never to smoke when asleep, and never to refrain when awake. It is a good rule. I mean, for me; but some of you know quite well that it wouldn't answer for everybody that's trying to get to be seventy.

I smoke in bed until I have to go to sleep; I wake up in the night, sometimes once, sometimes twice, sometimes three times, and I never waste any of these opportunities to smoke. This habit is so old and dear and precious to me that I would feel as you, sir, would feel if you should lose the only moral you've got—meaning the chairman—if you've got one: I am making no charges. I will grant, here, that I have stopped smoking now and then, for a few months at a time, but it was not on principle, it was only to show off; it was to pulverize those critics who said I was a slave to my habits and couldn't break my bonds.

To-day it is all of sixty years since I began to smoke the limit. I have never bought cigars with life belts around them. I early found that those were too expensive for me. I have always bought cheap cigars—reasonably cheap, at any rate. Sixty years ago they cost me four dollars a barrel, but my taste has improved, latterly, and I pay seven now. Six or seven. Seven, I think. Yes, it's seven. But that includes the barrel. I often have smoking parties at my house; but the people that come have always just taken the pledge. I wonder why that is?

As for drinking, I have no rule about that. When the others drink I like to help; otherwise I remain dry, by habit and preference. This dryness does not hurt me, but it could easily hurt you, because you are different. You let it alone.

Since I was seven years old I have seldom taken a dose of medicine, and have still seldomer needed one. But up to seven I lived exclusively on allopathic medicines. Not that I needed them, for I don't think I did; it was for economy; my father took a drug store for a debt, and it made cod-liver oil cheaper than the other breakfast foods. We had nine barrels of it, and it lasted me seven years. Then I was weaned. The rest of the family had to get along with rhubarb and ipecac and such things, because I was the pet. I was the first Standard Oil Trust. I had it all. By the time the drug store was exhausted my health was established and there has never been much the matter with me since. But you know very well it would be foolish for the average child to start for seventy on that basis. It happened to be just the thing for me, but that was merely an accident; it couldn't happen again in a century.

I have never taken any exercise, except sleeping and resting, and I never intend to take any. Exercise is loathsome. And it cannot be any benefit when you are tired; and I was always tired. But let another person try my way, and see whence he will come out.

I desire now to repeat and emphasize that maxim: We can't reach old age by another man's road. My habits protect my life, but they would assassinate you.

I have lived a severely moral life. But it would be a mistake for other people to try that, or for me to recommend it. Very few would succeed: you have to have a perfectly colossal stock of morals; and you can't get them on a margin; you have to have the whole thing, and put them in your box. Morals are an acquirement—like music, like a foreign language, like piety, poker, paralysis—no man is born with them. I wasn't myself, I started poor. I hadn't a single moral. There is hardly a man in this house that is poorer than I was then. Yes, I started like that—the world before me, not a moral in the slot. Not even an insurance moral. I can remember the first one I ever got. I can remember the landscape, the weather, the—I can remember how everything looked. It was an old moral, an old second-hand moral, all out of repair, and didn't fit, anyway. But if you are careful with a thing like that, and keep it in a dry place, and save it for processions, and Chautauquas, and World's Fairs, and so on, and disinfect it now and then, and give it a fresh coat of whitewash once in a while, you will be surprised to see how well she will last and how long she will keep sweet, or at least inoffensive. When I got that mouldy old moral, she had stopped growing, because she hadn't any exercise; but I worked her hard, I worked her Sundays and all. Under this cultivation she waxed in might and stature beyond belief, and served me well and was my pride and joy for sixty-three years; then she got to associating with insurance presidents, and lost flesh and character, and was a sorrow to look at and no longer competent for business. She was a great loss to me. Yet not all loss. I sold her—ah, pathetic skeleton, as she was—I sold her to Leopold, the pirate King of Belgium; he sold her to our Metropolitan Museum, and it was very glad to get her, for without a rag on, she stands 57 feet long and 16 feet high and they think she's a brontosaur. Well, she looks it. They believe it will take nineteen geological periods to breed her match.

Morals are of inestimable value, for every man is born crammed with sin microbes, and the only thing that can extirpate these sin microbes is morals. Now you take a sterilized Christian—I mean, you take *the* sterilized Christian, for there's only one. Dear sir, I wish you wouldn't look at me like that.

Threescore years and ten!

It is the Scriptural statute of limitations. After that, you owe no active duties; for you the strenuous life is over. You are a time-expired man, to use Kipling's military phrase: You have served your term, well or less well, and you are mustered out. You are become an honorary member of the republic, you are emancipated, compulsions are not for you, nor any bugle call but "lights out." You pay the time-worn duty bills if you choose, or decline if you prefer—and without prejudice—for they are not legally collectable.

The previous-engagement plea, which in forty years has cost you so many twinges, you can lay aside forever; on this side of the grave you will never need it again. If you shrink at thought of night, and winter, and the late home-coming from the banquet and the lights and the laughter through the deserted streets—a desolation which would not remind you now, as for a generation it did, that your friends are sleeping, and you must creep in a-tiptoe and not disturb them, but would only remind you that you need not tiptoe, you can never disturb them more—if you shrink at thought of these things, you need only reply, "Your invitation honors me, and pleases me because you still keep me in your remembrance, but I am seventy; seventy, and would nestle in the chimney corner, and smoke my pipe, and read my book, and take my rest, wishing you well in all affection, and that when you in your turn shall arrive at pier No. 70 you may step aboard your waiting ship with a reconciled spirit, and lay your course toward the sinking sun with a contented heart."

Address given at a dinner in New York City on 5 December 1905.

ROBERT BROWNING *(English, 1812–1889)*

> Grow old along with me!
> The best is yet to be,
> The last of life, for which the first was made:

Our times are in his hand
Who saith, "A whole I planned,
Youth shows but half; trust God: see all, nor
  be afraid!"

*   *   *

Rejoice we are allied
To that which doth provide
And not partake, effect and not receive!
A spark disturbs our clod;
Nearer we hold of God
Who gives, than of his tribes that take, I must
  believe.

Then welcome each rebuff
That turns earth's smoothness rough,
Each sting that bids nor sit nor stand but go!
Be our joys three-parts pain!
Strive, and hold cheap the strain;
Learn, nor account the pang; dare, never
  grudge the throe!

For thence,—a paradox
Which comforts while it mocks,—
Shall life succeed in that it seems to fail:
What I aspired to be,
And was not, comforts me:
A brute I might have been, but would not sink
  i' the scale

*   *   *

Let us not always say,
"Spite of this flesh to-day
I strove, made head, gained ground upon the
  whole!"
As the bird wings and sings,
Let us cry, "All good things
Are ours, nor soul helps flesh more, now, than
  flesh helps soul!"

Therefore I summon age
To grant youth's heritage,
Life's struggle having so far reached its term:
Thence shall I pass, approved
A man, for aye removed

307

From the developed brute; a God though in
   the germ.

And I shall thereupon
Take rest, ere I be gone
Once more on my adventure brave and new:
Fearless and unperplexed,
When I wage battle next,
What weapons to select, what armor to indue.

Youth ended, I shall try
My gain or loss thereby;
Leave the fire-ashes, what survives is gold:
And I shall weigh the same,
Give life its praise or blame:
Young, all lay in dispute; I shall know, being old.

For note, when evening shuts,
A certain moment cuts
The deed off, calls the glory from the gray:
A whisper from the west
Shoots—"Add this to the rest,
Take it and try its worth: here dies another day."

So, still within this life,
Though lifted o'er its strife,
Let me discern, compare, pronounce at last,
"This rage was right i' the main,
That acquiescence vain:
The Future I may face now I have proved the Past."

       *   *   *

As it was better, youth
Should strive, through acts uncouth,
Toward making, than repose on aught found made:
So, better, age, exempt
From strife, should know, than tempt
Further. Thou waitedst age: wait death nor be afraid!

Enough now, if the Right
And Good and Infinite
Be named here, as thou callest thy hand thine own,
With knowledge absolute,
Subject to no dispute
From fools that crowded youth, nor let thee feel alone.

Be there, for once and all,
Severed great minds from small,
Announced to each his station in the Past!
Was I, the world arraigned,
Were they, my soul disdained,
Right? Let age speak the truth and give us peace at last!

Now, who shall arbitrate?
Ten men love what I hate,
Shun what I follow, slight what I receive;
Ten, who in ears and eyes
Match me: we all surmise,
They this thing, and I that: whom shall my soul believe?

    * * *

Thoughts hardly to be packed
Into a narrow act,
Fancies that broke through language and escaped;
All I could never be,
All, men ignored in me,
This, I was worth to God, whose wheel the pitcher shaped.

Ay, note that Potter's wheel,
That metaphor! and feel
Why times spins fast, why passive lies our clay,—
Thou, to whom fools propound,
When the wine makes its round,
"Since life fleets, all is change; the Past gone, seize to-day!"

Fool! All that is, at all,
Lasts ever, past recall;
Earth changes, but thy soul and God stand sure:
What entered into thee,
That was, is, and shall be:
Time's wheel runs back or stops: Potter and clay endure.

    * * *

But I need, now as then,
Thee, God, who mouldest men;
And since, not even while the whirl was worst,
Did I—to the wheel of life
With shapes and colors rife,
Bound dizzily—mistake my end, to slake Thy thirst:

So, take and use Thy work:
Amend what flaws may lurk,

What strain o' the stuff, what warpings past the aim!
My times be in Thy hand!
Perfect the cup as planned!
Let age approve of youth, and death complete the same!

From "Rabbi Ben Ezra," 1864

OGDEN NASH (*American, 1902–1971*)

A poet named Robert Browning eloped with a poetess named Eliz-
  abeth Barrett,
And since he had an independent income they lived in an Italian
  villa instead of a London garret.
He created quite a furor
With his elusive caesura.
He also created a youthful sage,
A certain Rabbi Ben Ezra who urged people to hurry up and age.
This fledgling said, Grow old along with me,
The best is yet to be.
I term him fledgling because such a statement, certes,
Could emanate only from a youngster in his thirties.
I have a friend named Ben Azzara who is far from a fledgling,
Indeed he is more like from the bottom of the sea of life a barna-
  cled dredgling.
He tells me that as the years have slipped by
His has become utterly dependent on his wife because he has for-
  gotten how to tie his tie.
He says he sleeps after luncheon instead of at night.
And he hates to face his shaving mirror because although his re-
  maining hair is brown his mustache comes out red and his
  beard comes out white.
Furthermore, he says that last week he was stranded for thirty-six
  hours in his club
Because he couldn't get out of the tub.
He says he was miserable, but when he reflected that the same
  thing probably eventually happened to Rabbi Ben Ezra
It relieved his mizra.

"Old Is for Books," 1931

WALTHER VON DER VOGELWEIDE *(German, c. 1170–1230)*

Alas, where have they vanished, all the years I knew!
Was all my life a vision, or can it be true?
What'er I thought existed, was that reality?
Since then methinks I've slept, though unbeknown to me.
Now once again awake, in ignorance I stand
Of all that was familiar as my either hand.
The folk, and land where I from childhood's years was reared,
Have grown to me as strange as falsehood e'er appeared.
And those who played with me are sluggish now and old;
The planted lands are waste, the trees cut down and sold.
Were not the river flowing as it used to flow,
In truth I think there were no limits to my woe.
I get a listless nod from men who knew me well;
When I recall the bygone days so full of glee,
Now just as lost as if I'd tried to punch the sea—Evermore,
 alas!

From "Elegy," 1227

ROLF JACOBSEN *(Norwegian, b. 1907)*

The girls whose feet moved so fast, where did they go?
Those with knees like small kisses and sleeping hair?

In the far reaches of time when they've become silent,
old women with narrow hands climb up stairs slowly

with huge keys in their bags and they look around
and chat with small children at cemetery gates.

In that big and bewildering country where winters are so long
and no one understands their expressions any more.

Bow clearly to them and greet them with respect
because they still carry everything with them,
 like a fragrance,

a secret bite-mark on the cheek, a nerve in
the palm of the hand somewhere betraying who they are.

"The Old Women," 1977

RŪDAKĪ (*Islamic/Persian, tenth century* c.e.)

Every tooth, ah me! has crumbled, dropped and fallen in decay!
Tooth it was not, nay say rather, 'twas a brilliant lamp's bright ray;
Each was white and silvery-flashing, pearl and coral in the light,
Glistening like the stars of morning or the raindrop sparkling bright;
Not a one remaineth to me, lost through weakness and decay.

Many a desert waste existeth where was once a garden glad;
And a garden glad existeth where was once a desert sad.
    Ah, thou moon-faced, musky-tressed one, how canst thou e'er know or
    deem
What was once thy poor slave's station,—how once held in high esteem?
On him now thy curling tresses, coquettish thou dost bestow,
In those days thou didst not see him, when his own rich curls did flow.
Time there was when he in gladness, happy did himself disport,
Pleasure in excess enjoying, though his silver store ran short;
Always bought he in the market, countless-priced above the rest,
Every captive Turki damsel with a round pomegranate breast.

Ever was my keen eye open for a maid's curled tresses long,
Ever alert my ear to listen to the word-wise man of song.
House I had not, wife nor children, no, nor female family ties,
Free from these and unencumbered have I been in every wise.

Those the times when mine was fortune, fortune good in plenteous store.
    Now the times have changed,—and I, too, changed and altered must
    succumb,
Bring the beggar's staff here to me; time for staff and scrip has come!

"Lament in Old Age," Age of the Caliphs, 632–1050 c.e.

SURA 15:54, THE KORAN

[Abraham] said, 'What,
do you give me good tidings, though
old age has smitten me? Of what do you
give me good tidings?' They said, 'We
give thee good tidings of truth. Be not
of those that despair.' He said, 'And who
despairs of the mercy of his Lord,
excepting those that are astray?'

COTTON MATHER (*American, 1663–1728*)

Cap. LXV. *Liberatus.*
or,
The Thanksgiving
of One
Advanced in Years,
and
præserved from grievous and painful Diseases.

. . . "O my God, why am I not *feeble and Sore broken, and roaring by reason of the Disquietness of my Heart,* under those *Terrible Distempers,* which Defy the *Physicians,* and which Torture the *Patients,* and under which *all the Days of the Afflicted are Evil Days? Lord,* It is not because I have *deserved* any such Exemption, any such Immunity. No, If I had my Desert, I should be *delivered up unto the Tormentors;* and *broken sore in the place of Dragons.*—It is thy *Free-Grace* that has Released me. My SAVIOUR who suffered Exquisite *Anguish* for me, has also pleaded for my Release from Deserved Anguish. And, O my SAVIOUR, Thou art *the keeper of my Soul!*

But, *What shall I Render to the Lord?*

Oh! Lett a *Life* thus at Liberty for the *Service* of God, be industriously Employ'd in it; and be fill'd with *Devotions* and *Benignities,* from which I have not Such Things as many miserables have, to take me off.

Oh! Lett me be full of Compassion for Such as I see Languishing in the dreadful Circumstances, which I who have *Sinned as much as they,* have never tasted of. With a Bleeding *Heart,* and an Ardent *Prayer* for them, Lett me Look upon them. And Lett me study all the Ways I can, to Releeve and Comfort them.

For more particular Maladies:—

Am I free from the STONE? *Lord,* Lett there be nothing allowed in the *Lower Parts of the Earth* with me, which thou mayst be offended at.

Am I free from the GOUT? *Lord,* Lett my *Feet* carry me cheerfully to the Places of my Duty, and *go about still doing of Good.* And Lett my *Hands* be full of *Good Works,* and never be applied unto any Evil Purposes.

Am I free from the CANCER? *Lord,* Lett my spirit be kept clear from all the Corrosions of *Envy,* and *Malice,* and Every Evil Frame towards my Neighbour. And Lett a *Sweetness of Temper* be always Conspicuous in me.

Am I free from the *PALSEY? Lord,* Lett me be Ready and Nimble in all the *Motions* of PIETY. And Lett me be One of Suitable *Activities,* in what I have to do for God, and His Kingdome, and my Neighbour.

Have I never felt the Anguish of *Broken Bones? All my Bones now shall*

313

Say, O Lord, who is like unto thee, which deliverest the poor from the Accidents, which I have been times without Number Expos'd unto! And, oh! Lett me beware of those *Falls into Sin,* which may bring the Anguish of *Broken Bones* upon me.''

Psal. CIII. 1, 2, 3, 4, 10.

"O my awakened Soul, Do thou / / Bless the ETERNAL GOD: / / And all my Inward Powers the Name / / of His pure Holiness. / /

O my awakened Soul, Do thou / / Bless the ETERNAL GOD; and O forget not any One / / of all His Benefits. / /

Tis He who gives a Pardon to / / all thy Iniquities; / / Tis He who gives an Healing to / / all thy Infirmities. / /

Tis He who doth Redeem thy Life / / from the Corrupting Pitt; / / Tis He who thee with Mercy doth / / and with Compassions Crown. / /

His Dealings have not been with us / / according to our Sins: / / Nor has He recompensed us / / according to our Crimes.

From "Liberatus," In *The Angel of Bethesda,* 1724

OLIVE ANN BURNS (1925–1990)

Miss Love broke in. "In the Bible, Jesus only healed the people who asked Him to—and believed He could. If Jesus could heal, can't God? If we pray and have faith?"

"Well'm, faith ain't no magic wand or money-back gar'ntee, either one. Hit's jest a way a-livin'. Hit means you don't worry th'ew the days. Hit means you go'n be holdin' on to God in good or bad times, and you accept whatever happens. Hit means you respect life like it is—like God made it—even when it ain't what you'd order from the wholesale house. Faith don't mean the Lord is go'n make lions lay down with lambs jest cause you ast him to, or make fire not burn. Some folks, when they pray to git well and don't even git better, they say God let'm down. But I say thet warn't even what Jesus was a-talkin' bout. When Jesus said ast and you'll git it, He was givin' a gar'ntee a-spiritual healin', not body healin'. He was sayin' thet if'n you git beat down—scairt to death you cain't do what you got to, or scairt you go'n die, or scairt folks won't like you—why, all you got to do is put yore hand in God's and He'll lift you up. I know it for a fact, Love. I can pray, 'Lord, hep me not be scairt,' and I don't know how, but it's like a eraser wipes the fears away. And I found out long time ago, when I look on what I got to stand as a dang hardship or a burden, it seems too heavy to carry. But when I look on the same dang thang as a challenge, why, standin' it or acceptin' it is like you

314

done entered a contest. Hit even gits excitin', waitin' to see how everthang's go'n turn out."

Grandpa stopped to move a little and his face twisted with pain. But he went on. "Jesus meant us to ast God to hep us stand the pain, not beg Him to take the pain away. We can ast for comfort and hope and patience and courage, and to be gracious when thangs ain't goin' our way, and we'll git what we ast for. They ain't no gar'ntee thet we ain't go'n have no troubles and ain't go'n die. But shore as frogs croak and cows bellow, God'll forgive us if'n we ast Him to."

From *Cold Sassy Tree,* 1984

PAULE MARSHALL (*African American, b. 1929*)

Slowly Avey Johnson stood up. She unhurriedly picked up her chair and, holding it easily with one hand against her side, began walking over to where the musicians were playing, away from the voice in her ear.

Once there, she set the chair down close to the bottle-and-spoon boys standing beside the drummers.

And then she did an odd thing. Instead of sitting down she turned and slowly retraced her steps to her old place beside the tree, and stood there. Her face was expressionless, her body still and composed, but her bottom lip had unfolded to bare the menacing sliver of pink.

The dancers in their loose, ever-widening ring were no more than a dozen feet away now. She could feel the reverberation of their powerful tread in the ground under her, and the heat from their bodies reached her in a strong yeasty wave. Soon only a mere four or five feet remained between them, yet she continued to stand there. Finally, just as the moving wall of bodies was almost upon her, she too moved—a single declarative step forward. At the same moment, what seemed an arm made up of many arms reached out from the circle to draw her in, and she found herself walking amid the elderly folk on the periphery, in their counterclockwise direction.

For a time she did nothing more than follow along in their midst. So as not to throw those behind her out of step, she was careful to move at their pace, although she did not attempt their little rhythmic tramp. She was content to simply be among them and to return the smiles and approving nods that came her way. By the time she had completed one full turn of the yard though and was back near the tree, she had slipped without being conscious of it into a step that was something more than just walking.

Her feet of their own accord began to glide forward, but in such a way they scarcely left the ground. Only the broad heels of her low-heeled shoes rose slightly and then fell at each step. She moved cautiously at first, each foot edging forward as if the ground under her was really water—

315

muddy river water—and she was testing it to see if it would hold her weight.

After a while, by the time in fact she reached the tree again, she was doing the flatfooted glide and stamp with aplomb. And she was smiling to herself, her eyes screened over.

"Ah, din' I say she wasn't the kind to let a little rough water get the better of her!" Lebert Joseph. Jubilant. A proud father.

"And look, she's doing the 'Carriacou Tramp' good as somebody been doing it all their life!" Rosalie Parvay exclaiming in astonishment as the two of them discovered her among the dancers.

Avey Johnson smiled but she neither heard nor saw them clearly. Because it was a score of hot August nights again in her memory, and she was standing beside her great-aunt on the dark road across from the church that doubled as a school. And under cover of the darkness she was performing the dance that wasn't supposed to be dancing, in imitation of the old folk shuffling in a loose ring inside the church. And she was singing along with them under her breath: *"Who's that ridin' the chariot/Well well well . . ."* The Ring Shout. Standing there she used to long to give her great-aunt the slip and join those across the road.

She had finally after all these decades made it across. The elderly Shouters in the person of the out-islanders had reached out their arms like one great arm and drawn her into their midst.

And for the first time since she was a girl, she felt the threads, that myriad of shiny, silken, brightly colored threads (like the kind used in embroidery) which were thin to the point of invisibility yet as strong as the ropes at Coney Island. Looking on outside the church in Tatem, standing waiting for the *Robert Fulton* on the crowded pier at 125th Street, she used to feel them streaming out of everyone there to enter her, making her part of what seemed a far-reaching, wide-ranging confraternity.

Now, suddenly, as if she were that girl again, with her entire life yet to live, she felt the threads streaming out from the old people around her in Lebert Joseph's yard. From their seared eyes. From their navels and their cast-iron hearts. And their brightness as they entered her spoke of possibilities and becoming even in the face of the bare bones and the burnt-out ends.

She began to dance then. Just as her feet of their own accord had discovered the old steps, her hips under the linen shirtdress slowly began to weave from side to side on their own, stiffly at first and then in a smooth wide arc as her body responded more deeply to the music. And the movement in her hips flowed upward, so that her entire torso was soon swaying. Arms bent, she began working her shoulders in the way the Shouters long ago used to do, thrusting them forward and then back in a strong casting-off motion. Her weaving head was arched high. All of her moving suddenly with a vigor and passion she hadn't felt in years, and with something of the stylishness and sass she had once been known for. *"Girl, you can out-jangle Bojangles."* Jay saying it with amazement at the Saturday night pretend dances when he would turn the floor over to her.

Yet for all the sudden unleashing of her body she was being careful to observe the old rule: Not once did the soles of her feet leave the ground. Even when the Big Drum reached its height in a tumult of voices, drums and the ringing iron, and her arms rose as though hailing the night, the darkness that is light, her feet held to the restrained glide-and-stamp, the rhythmic trudge, the Carriacou Tramp, the shuffle designed to stay the course of history. Avey Johnson could not have said how long she kept her arms raised or how many turns she made in the company of these strangers who had become one and the same with people in Tatem. Until suddenly Lebert Joseph did something which caused her arms to drop and her mind to swing back to the yard and the present moment. He had remained at her side all along, watching her dance with the smile that was at once triumphant and fatherly, and dancing himself, the slow measured tramp. But as her arms went up and her body seemed about to soar off into the night, his smile faded, and was replaced by the gaze that called to mind a jeweler's loupe or a laser beam in its ability to penetrate to her depth. His eyes probing deep, he went to stand facing her in front. His oversized hands went out, bringing to a halt for a moment the slow-moving tide around them. And then he bowed, a profound, solemn bow that was like a genuflection.

Rosalie Parvay nearby quickly followed her father's example. Taking his place in front of Avey Johnson she swept down before her in an exact copy of his gesture.

To her utter bewilderment others in the crowd of aged dancers, taking their cue from him also, began doing the same. One after another of the men and women trudging past, who were her senior by years, would pause as they reached her and, turning briefly in her direction, tender her the deep, almost reverential bow. Then, singing, they would continue on their way.

One elderly woman not only bowed but stepped close and took her hand. Cataracts dimmed her gaze. The face she raised to Avey Johnson was a ravaged landscape of dark hollows and caves where her wrinkled flesh had collapsed in on the bone. Her chin displayed the beginning of a beard: a few wispy white hairs that curled in on themselves. An old woman who was at once an old man. Tiresias of the dried dugs.

"Bercita Edwards of Smooth Water Bay, Carriacou," she said, and holding on to Avey Johnson's hand she peered close, searching for whatever it was she possessed that required her to defer despite her greater age. "And who you is?" she asked.

317

And as a mystified Avey Johnson gave her name, she suddenly remembered her great-aunt Cuney's admonition long ago. The old woman used to insist, on pain of a switching, that whenever anyone in Tatem, even another child, asked her her name she was not to say simply "Avey," or even "Avey Williams." But always "Avey, short for Avatara."

From *Praisesong for the Widow*, 1983

SOPHOCLES (*Greek/Athenian, c. 496–406 B.C.E.*)

CHORUS:
Show me a man who longs to live a day beyond his time
    who turns his back on a decent length of life,
I'll show the world a man who clings to folly.
For the long, looming days lay up a thousand things
closer to pain than pleasure, and the pleasures disappear,
    you look and know not where
when a man's outlived his limit, plunged in age
and the good comrade comes who comes at last to all,
not with a wedding-song, no lyre, no singers dancing—
the doom of the Deathgod comes like lightning
    always death at the last.

                    Not to be born is best
when all is reckoned in, but once a man has seen the light
    the next best thing, by far, is to go back
back where he came from, quickly as he can.
For once his youth slips by, light on the wing
lightheaded . . . what mortal blows can he escape
    what griefs won't stalk his days?
Envy and enemies, rage and battles, bloodshed
and last of all despised old age overtakes him,
stripped of power, companions, stripped of love—
the worst this life of pain can offer,
    old age our mate at last.

This is the grief he faces—I am not alone—
like some great headland fronting the north
hit by the winter breakers beating down
from every quarter—so he suffers,
terrible blows crashing over him
head to foot, over and over

318

down from every quarter—
now from the west, the dying sun
now from the first light rising
now from the blazing beams of noon
now from the north engulfed in endless night.

From *Oedipus at Colonus,* produced posthumously, 401 B.C.E.

MAY SARTON *(American, b. 1912)*

On a winter night
I sat alone
In a cold room,
Feeling old, strange
At the year's change,
In fire light.

Last fire of youth,
All brilliance burning,
And my year turning—
One dazzling rush,
Like a wild wish
Or blaze of truth.

First fire of age,
And the soft snow
Of ash below—
For the clean wood
The end was good;
For me, an image.

For then I saw
That fires, not I,
Burn down and die;
That flare of gold
Turns old, turns cold.
Not I. I grow.

Nor old, nor young,
The burning sprite
Of my delight,
A salamander
In fires of wonder,
Gives tongue, gives tongue!

"On a Winter Night," c. 1952

319

WILLIAM SHAKESPEARE (*English, 1564–1616*)

That time of year thou mayst in me behold
When yellow leaves, or none, or few, do hang
Upon those boughs which shake against the cold,
Bare ruined choirs where late the sweet birds sang.
In me thou seest the twilight of such day
As after sunset fadeth in the west,
Which by and by black night doth take away,
Death's second self, that seals up all in rest.
In me thou seest the glowing of such fire
That on the ashes of his youth doth lie,
As the deathbed whereon it must expire,
Consumed with that which it was nourished by.
 This thou perceiv'st, which makes thy love more strong,
 To love that well which thou must leave ere long.

Sonnet 73, 1592

ST. ATHANASIUS (*Egyptian, c. 295–373 c.e.*)

It is worthwhile for me to recall, and for you to hear (as you wish) what the end of his [Antony's] life was like, for even his death has become something imitable.

He came, as he customarily did, to inspect the monks who resided in the outer mountain, and when he learned from providence about his death, he spoke to the brothers, saying: "This is the last visitation I shall make to you, and I wonder if we shall see each other again in this life. Now it is time for me to perish, for I am nearly a hundred and five years old." When they heard him, they wept and embraced and kissed the old man. But he, like one sailing from a foreign city to his own, talked cheerfully and exhorted them not to lose heart in their labors nor to grow weary in the discipline, but to live as though dying daily. He told them, "Be zealous in protecting the soul from foul thoughts, as I said before, and compete with the saints, but do not approach the Meletian schismatics, for you know their evil and profane reputation. Nor are you to have any fellowship with the Arians, for their impiety is evident to everyone. And should you see the judges advocating their cause, do not be troubled, for this will end—their fantacizing posture is something perishable and ephemeral. Rather, keep yourselves pure from contact with them and guard both the tradition of the fathers and especially the holy faith in our Lord Jesus Christ, which you have learned from the Scriptures and have often had recalled to you by me."

When the brothers pressed him to stay with them and die there, he refused for a number of reasons, as he indicated even while remaining silent, but because of one in particular. The Egyptians love to honor with burial rites and to wrap in linens the bodies of their worthy dead, and especially of the holy martyrs, not burying them in the earth, but placing them on low beds and keeping them with them inside, and they intend by this practice to honor the deceased. Antony frequently asked a bishop to instruct the people on this matter, and he similarly corrected laymen and chastised women, saying, "It is neither lawful nor at all reverent to do this. The bodies of the patriarchs and the prophets are preserved even to this day in tombs, and the Lord's own body was put in a tomb, and a stone placed there hid it until he rose on the third day." And in saying these things he showed that the person violates the Law who does not, after death, bury the bodies of the deceased, even though they are holy. For what is greater or holier than the Lord's body? The many who heard him thereafter buried their dead, and gave thanks to the Lord that they had been taught well.

But Antony, aware of this practice and afraid that they might perform it for his body, pressed on, departing from the monks in the outer mountain. He entered the inner mountain to stay there as usual and in a few months became ill. He called those who were with him (they were two men who had also remained within, practicing the discipline fifteen years and assisting him on account of his age) and said to them, "I am going the way of the fathers, as it is written, for I see myself being summoned by the Lord. Be watchful and do not destroy your lengthy discipline, but as if you were making a beginning now, strive to preserve your enthusiasm. You know the treacherous demons—you know how savage they are, even though weakened in strength. Therefore, do not fear them, but rather draw inspiration from Christ always, and trust in him. And live as though dying daily, paying heed to yourselves and remembering what you heard from my preaching. And let there be no fellowship between you and the schismatics, and certainly none with the heretical Arians. For you know how I too have shunned them because of their Christ-battling and heterodox teaching. Rather, strive always to be bound to each other as allies, first of all in the Lord, and then in the saints, so that after death *they may receive you into the eternal habitations* as friends and companions. Consider these things and turn your minds to them, and if you care for me and remember me as a father, do not permit anyone to take my body to Egypt, lest they set it in the houses. It was for this reason that I went to the mountain and came here. You know how I always corrected the ones who practiced this and ordered them to stop that custom. Therefore, perform the rites for me yourselves, and bury my body in the earth. And let my word be kept secret by you, so that no one knows the place but you alone. For in the resurrection of the dead I shall

321

receive my body incorruptible once again from the Savior. Distribute my clothing. To Bishop Athanasius give the one sheepskin and the cloak on which I lie, which he gave to me new, but I have by now worn out. And to Bishop Serapion give the other sheepskin, and you keep the hair garment. And now God preserve you, children, for Antony is leaving and is with you no longer."

When he had said this, and they embraced him, he lifted his feet, and as if seeing friends who had come to him and being cheered by them (for as he lay there, his face seemed bright), he died and was taken to the fathers. Then they, in accordance with the commands he had given them, making preparations and wrapping his body, buried it in the earth, and to this day no one knows where it has been hidden except those two. And each of those who received the blessed Antony's sheepskin, and the cloak worn out by him, keeps it safe like some great treasure. For even seeing these is like beholding Antony, and wearing them is like bearing his admonitions with joy.

From *Life of Antony,* 361 C.E.

FLORIDA SCOTT-MAXWELL (*American, 1883–1979*)

We who are old know that age is more than a disability. It is an intense and varied experience, almost beyond our capacity at times, but something to be carried high. If it is a long defeat it is also a victory, meaningful for the initiates of time, if not for those who have come less far.

*   *   *

Age is truly a time of heroic helplessness. One is confronted by one's own incorrigibility. I am always saying to myself, "Look at you, and after a lifetime of trying." I still have the vices that I have known and struggled with—well it seems like since birth. Many of them are modified, but not much. I can neither order nor command the hubbub of my mind. Or is it my nervous sensibility? This is not the effect of age; age only defines one's boundaries. Life has changed me greatly, it has improved me greatly, but it has also left me practically the same. I cannot spell, I am over critical, egocentric and vulnerable. I cannot be simple. In my effort to be clear I become complicated. I know my faults so well that I pay them small heed. They are stronger than I am. They are me.

*   *   *

. . . I am awareness at the mercy of multiplicity. Ideas drift in like bright clouds, arresting, momentary, but they come as visitors. A shaft of insight can enter the back of my mind and when I turn to greet it, it is gone. I did not have it, it had me. My mood is light and dancing, or it is leaden. It is not I who choose my moods; I accept them, but from whom?

From *The Measure of My Days*, 1968

FRANCES, A NURSING-HOME RESIDENT (*American, twentieth century*)

"I've been told that I must not succumb to the facts of my age. But why shouldn't I? I am now in my 91st year and I doubt that my activity for example, in civic affairs, could restore my spirits to a state of bouncing bouyancy. Lack of physical strength alone keeps me inactive and often silent. I've been called senile. Senility is a convenient peg on which to hang nonconformity . . . A new set of faculties seems to be coming into operation. I seem to be awakening to a larger world of wonderment—to catch little glimpses of the immensity and diversity of creation. More than at any other time in my life, I seem to be aware of the beauties of our spinning planet and the sky above. I feel that old age sharpens my awareness."

Cited in *Wisdom and Age*, 1981

W. B. YEATS (*Irish, 1865–1939*)

That is no country for old men. The young
In one another's arms, birds in the trees
—Those dying generations—at their song,
The salmon-falls, the mackerel-crowded seas,
Fish, flesh, or fowl, commend all summer long
Whatever is begotten, born, and dies.
Caught in that sensual music all neglect
Monuments of unageing intellect.

An aged man is but a paltry thing,
A tattered coat upon a stick, unless
Soul clap its hands and sing, and louder sing
For every tatter in its mortal dress,
Nor is there singing school but studying
Monuments of its own magnificence;
And therefore I have sailed the seas and come
To the holy city of Byzantium.

323

O sages standing in God's holy fire
As in the gold mosaic of a wall,
Come from the holy fire, perne in a gyre,
And be the singing-masters of my soul.
Consume my heart away; sick with desire
And fastened to a dying animal
  It knows not what it is; and gather me
  Into the artifice of eternity.

Once out of nature I shall never take
My bodily form from any natural thing,
But such a form as Grecian goldsmiths make
Of hammered gold and gold enamelling
To keep a drowsy Emperor awake;
Or set upon a golden bough to sing
To lords and ladies of Byzantium
Of what is past, or passing, or to come.

"Sailing to Byzantium," 1927

ZECHARIAH 8:4–8, HEBREW SCRIPTURES

Thus says the LORD of hosts: Old men and old women shall again sit in the streets of Jerusalem, each with staff in hand for very age. And the streets of the city shall be full of boys and girls playing in its streets. Thus says the LORD of hosts: If it is marvelous in the sight of the remnant of this people in these days, should it also be marvelous in my sight, says the LORD of hosts? Thus says the LORD of hosts: Behold, I will save my people from the east country and from the west country; and I will bring them to dwell in the midst of Jerusalem; and they shall be my people and I will be their God, in faithfulness and in righteousness.

CHAPTER EIGHT
BODY/SPIRIT

This chapter addresses a fundamental human conflict that intensifies as one grows older: the tension between infinite dreams, wishes, ideas, and hopes on the one hand, and limited, vulnerable, fleeting physical existence on the other. While wrestling with this paradox, some writers celebrate the spirituality of the human body, others emphasize the embodiment of the human spirit, and still others articulate visions of transcendence. This chapter's groupings explore the relationship between age and beauty; affirmation in the face of physical decline and death; aspects of health, disease, and medicine; and spiritual maturity, death, and transcendence.

"When your youth goes, your beauty will go with it, and then you will suddenly discover that there are no triumphs left for you," writes Oscar Wilde in *The Picture of Dorian Gray*. While the physical perfection of youthful bodies remains our culture's dominant ideal, there are other kinds of beauty. The American novelist Annie Dillard's meditation on her mother's hands, M. F. K. Fisher's hilarious yet dignified self-description, and poet Marjorie Agosin's "My Belly" suggest that bodies conventionally considered unlovely become transfigured through affection and delight.

The next group of selections—whose authors range from the nineteenth-century American physician and author Oliver Wendell Holmes to the contemporary Russian poet Alexander Kushner—probes the experience of physical decline and the realization of one's own mortality. Bernard Berenson, American connoisseur of art and lover of beauty, writes of his "leaking, crumbling earthly tabernacle." And the Russian novelist Leo Tolstoy muses in his diary about the great mystery: "We know best of all what we do not understand at all, our soul, and one may say, God." The Greek writer Nikos Kazantzakis pays homage to his grandfather: "You taught me that our inner flame, contrary to the nature of the flesh, is able to flare up with ever-increasing intensity over the years. That was why (I saw this in you and admired you for it) you became continually fiercer as you aged, continually braver as you arrived ever closer to the abyss."

The next series touches on medical aspects of aging and death. From the

English physician Sir Anthony Carlisle to the Russian scientist Élie Metchnikoff, writers inquire: What are the causes of death in old age? Why does the body whither? Should we try to prolong life? The tenth-century Muslim physician Avicenna offers a regimen of physical health as a means of spiritual development. The early-twentieth-century French physician J. Bandaline endorses modern science's struggle to conquer the debilitating aspects of old age.

The final segment of this chapter contains a series of meditations on loss and transcendence. The first-century Roman poet Ovid tells the fable of Philemon and Baucis, an old couple whose enduring faithfulness and hospitality become the sacraments that secure them an eternal marriage. Except in myth and fable, however, marriages end, and loved ones part. The seventh-century Japanese poet Yamanoue Okura clings to life in spite of great pain: "And though I would rather die, / I cannot, and leave my children / Noisy like the flies of May."

Selections from several religious traditions articulate diverse perspectives on spirituality and death. Sometimes they disagree. The Native American Lame Deer, for example, challenges the ideas of Martin Luther when arguing against the Christian notion of vicarious redemptive suffering: "Insight does not come cheaply, and we want no angel or saint to gain it for us and give it to us secondhand." The famous Hebrew Psalm 71 follows an excerpt from The Tibetan Book of the Dead, a rhythmic prayer for fearless self-knowledge and bliss.

Having begun with a desire for eternal physical beauty, the chapter concludes with desire for transcendence over the physical. After exploring various expressions of beauty, truth, and redemption, the chapter's last words are from the Apostle Paul's letter to the Christian community in Corinth. Bodily afflictions, he writes, are only a momentary preparation for "an eternal weight of glory beyond all comparison."

OSCAR WILDE (*Irish, 1854–1900*)

'No, you don't feel it now. Some day, when you are old and wrinkled and ugly, when thought has seared your forehead with its lines, and passion branded your lips with its hideous fires, you will feel it, you will feel it terribly. Now, wherever you go, you charm the world. Will it always be so? . . . You have a wonderfully beautiful face, Mr. Gray. Don't frown. You have. And Beauty is a form of Genius—is higher, indeed, than Genius, as it needs no explanation. It is of the great facts of the world, like sunlight, or spring-time, or the reflection in dark waters of that silver shell we call the moon. It cannot be questioned. It has its divine right of sovereignty. It makes princes of those who have it. You smile? Ah! when you have lost it you won't smile. . . . People say sometimes that Beauty is only superficial. That may be so. But at least it is not so superficial as Thought is. To me, Beauty is the wonder of wonders. It is only shallow people who do not judge by appearances. The true mystery of the world is the visible, not the invisible. . . . Yes, Mr. Gray, the gods have been good to you. But what the gods give they quickly take away. You have only a few years in which to live really, perfectly, and fully. When your youth goes, your beauty will go with it, and then you will suddenly discover that there are no triumphs left for you, or have to content yourself with those mean triumphs that the memory of your past will make more bitter than defeats. Every month as it wanes brings you nearer to something dreadful. Time is jealous of you, and wars against your lilies and your roses. You will become sallow, and hollow-cheeked, and dull-eyed. You will suffer horribly. . . . Ah! realize your youth while you have it. Don't squander the gold of your days, listening to the tedious, trying to improve the hopeless failure, or giving away your life to the ignorant, the common, and the vulgar. These are the sickly aims, the false ideals, of our age. Live! Live the wonderful life that is in you! Let nothing be lost upon you. Be always searching for new sensations. Be afraid of nothing. . . . A new Hedonism—that is what our century wants. You might be its visible symbol. With your personality there is nothing you could not do. The world belongs to you for a season. . . . The moment I met you I saw that you were quite unconscious of what you really are, of what you really might be. There was so much in you that charmed me that I felt I must tell you something about yourself. I thought how tragic it would be if you were wasted. For there is such a little time that your youth will last—such a little time. The common hill-flowers wither, but they blossom again. The laburnum will be as yellow next June as it is now. In a month there will be purple stars on the clematis, and year after year the green night of its leaves will hold its purple stars. But we never get back our youth. The pulse of joy that beats in us at twenty, becomes sluggish. Our limbs fail, our senses rot. We degenerate into hideous puppets, haunted by the memory of the passions of which we were too much afraid, and the exquisite temptations that we had not the courage to yield to. Youth! Youth! There is absolutely nothing in the world but youth!'

From *The Picture of Dorian Gray*, 1890

M. F. K. FISHER (*American, 1908–1992*)

Outwardly, I think I put up a pretty good show. My hair is fine and I take care of my skin. And I like to wear a little makeup. I stand up straight, even though right now I hobble a bit because I have Parkinson's disease. I suppose that for the past ten years I've walked in a rather stiff, gingerly way, but I walk standing straight up. I have a certain dignity in my presence, I think. And I like to smile and laugh, although I don't do it unless I think that something is worth it. I'm curious. I have good manners. I know how to be polite and thoughtful to people older than I, if there are any around.

My husband told me that every self-respecting woman must have a full-length mirror in her house to see herself from top to bottom clearly. My full-length mirror is facing me at about a distance of ten feet from my bed when I get up in the morning. For decades I've slept without any pajamas or a nightie on, except in hotels and stuff. And about a year ago I suddenly realized that I could not face walking toward myself again in the morning because here is this strange, uncouth, ugly, kind of toadlike woman . . . long thin legs, long thin arms, and a shapeless little toadlike torso and this head at the top with great staring eyes. And I thought, Jesus, why do I have to do this? So I bought some nightgowns. I felt like an idiot, you know. [Laughs.] But I couldn't face it in the mornings. And I got some rather nice-looking gowns. My sister, Nora, has always worn beautiful lingerie, and she thinks my nighties are just abominable. If I'm going to hide myself, I want long-sleeved, high-necked, to-the-ground granny gowns. [Laughs.] I'd much rather not have to wear them, but I will not face that strange kind of half-humanoid, half-toad walking toward me in the morning. [Laughs.]

I don't mean to compromise with the gowns and all, and I don't think I'm a compromising person, but I certainly do know that there are certain facts of life that you've got to accept. I know some women who refuse to be old and they are like zombies walking around. They are lifted here and lifted there; you know, altered in the nose and eyes and chin, and they can't smile because it would ruin their latest do. In Japan there are a great many women who have their eyes unslanted. It's okay if they feel better, but I think they are compromising their fate and I refuse to do that. That's all, I refuse.

From an interview in *The Ageless Spirit*, 1992

ANNIE DILLARD (*American, b. 1945*)

Our parents and grandparents, and all their friends, seemed insensible to their own prominent defect, their limp, coarse skin.

We children had, for instance, proper hands; our fluid, pliant fingers joined their skin. Adults had misshapen, knuckly hands loose in their skin like bones in bags; it was a wonder they could open jars. They were loose in their skins all over, except at the wrists and ankles, like rabbits.

We were whole, we were pleasing to ourselves. Our crystalline eyes shone from firm, smooth sockets; we spoke in pure, piping voices through dark, tidy lips. Adults were coming apart, but they neither noticed nor minded. My revulsion was rude, so I hid it. Besides, we could never rise to the absolute figural splendor they alone could on occasion achieve. Our beauty was a mere absence of decrepitude; their beauty, when they had it, was not passive but earned; it was grandeur; it was a party to power, and to artifice, even, and to knowledge. Our beauty was, in the long run, merely elfin. We could not, finally, discount the fact that in some sense they owned us, and they owned the world.

Mother let me play with one of her hands. She laid it flat on a living-room end table beside her chair. I picked up a transverse pinch of skin over the knuckle of her index finger and let it drop. The pinch didn't snap back; it lay dead across her knuckle in a yellowish ridge. I poked it; it slid over intact. I left it there as an experiment and shifted to another finger. Mother was reading *Time* magazine.

Carefully, lifting it by the tip, I raised her middle finger an inch and released it. It snapped back to the tabletop. Her insides, at least, were alive. I tried all the fingers. They all worked. Some I could lift higher than others.

"That's getting boring."

"Sorry, Mama."

I refashioned the ridge on her index-finger knuckle; I made the ridge as long as I could, using both my hands. Moving quickly, I made parallel ridges on her other fingers—a real mountain chain, the Alleghenies; Indians crept along just below the ridgetops, eyeing the frozen lakes below them through the trees.

From *An American Childhood,* 1987

MARJORIE AGOSIN   (*Hispanic American, b. 1955*)

> Naked and as if in silence
> I approach my belly
> it has gone on changing like summer
> withdrawing from the sea
> or like a dress that expands with the hours
> My belly
> is more than round
> because when I sit down
> it spreads like a brush fire
> then,
> I touch it to recall
> all the things inside it:

salt and merriment
the fried eggs of winter breakfasts
the milk that strangled me in my youth
the coca-cola that stained my teeth
the nostalgia for the glass of wine
we discovered in *La Isla*
or french fries and olive oil
And as I remember
I feel it growing
and bowing down more and more ceremoniously to the ground
until it caresses my feet, my toes
that never could belong to a princess,

I rejoice
that my belly is as wide as Chepi's old sombrero—
Chepi was my grandmother—
and I pamper it no end
when it complains or has bad dreams
from eating too much.

Midsummer, at seventy years of age,
this Sunday the seventh
my belly is still with me
and proudly goes parading along the shore
some say I am already old and ugly
that my breasts are entangled with my guts
but my belly is here at my side a good companion
and don't say it's made of fat
rather tender morsels of meat toasting in the sun.

"Mi Estómago (My Belly)," 1986

e. e. cummings (*American, 1894–1962*)

why

do the
fingers

of the lit
tle once beau
tiful la

dy (sitting sew
ing at an o

pen window this
fine morning) fly

instead of dancing
are they possibly
afraid that life is
running away from
them (i wonder) or

isn't she a
ware that life (who
never grows old)
is always beau

tiful and
that nobod
y beauti

ful ev
er hur

ries

"why/do the," 1958

OLIVER WENDELL HOLMES (*American, 1809–1894*)

There is no doubt when old age begins. The human body is a furnace which keeps in blast three-score years and ten, more or less. It burns about three hundred pounds of carbon a year (besides other fuel), when in fair working order, according to a great chemist's estimate. When the fire slackens, life declines; when it goes out, we are dead.

It has been shown by some noted French experimenters, that the amount of combustion increases up to about the thirtieth year, remains stationary to about forty-five, and then diminishes. This last is the point where old age starts from. The great fact of physical life is the perpetual commerce with the elements, and the fire is the measure of it.

About this time of life, if food is plenty where you live—for that, you know, regulates matrimony,—you may be expecting to find yourself a grandfather some fine morning; a kind of domestic felicity which gives one a cool shiver of delight to think of, as among the not remotely possible events.

I don't mind much those slipshod lines Dr. Johnson wrote to Mrs. Thrale, telling her about life's declining from *thirty-five;* the furnace is in full blast for ten years longer, as I have said. The Romans came very near the mark; their age of enlistment reached from seventeen to forty-six years.

331

What is the use of fighting against the seasons, or the tides, or the movements of the planetary bodies, or this ebb in the wave of life that flows through us? We are old fellows from the moment the fire begins to go out. Let us always behave like gentlemen when we are introduced to new acquaintances.

Incipit Allegoria Senectutis

Old Age, this is Mr. Professor; Mr. Professor, this is Old Age.

Old Age.—Mr. Professor, I hope to see you well. I have known you for some time, though I think you did not know me. Shall we walk down the street together?

Professor (drawing back a little).—We can talk more quietly, perhaps, in my study. Will you tell me how it is you seem to be acquainted with everybody you are introduced to, though he evidently considers you an entire stranger?

Old Age.—I make it a rule never to force myself upon a person's recognition until I have known him at least *five years*.

Professor.—Do you mean to say that you have known me so long as that?

Old Age.—I do. I left my card on you longer ago than that, but I am afraid you never read it; yet I see you have it with you.

Professor.—Where?

Old Age.—There, between your eyebrows,—three straight lines running up and down; all the probate courts know that token,—'Old Age, his mark.' Put your forefinger on the inner end of one eyebrow, and your middle finger on the inner end of the other eyebrow; now separate the fingers, and you will smooth out my sign-manual; that's the way you used to look before I left my card on you.

Professor.—What message do people generally send back when you first call on them?

Old Age.—*Not at home.* Then I leave a card and go. Next year I call; get the same answer; leave another card. So for five or six,—sometimes ten years or more. At last, if they don't let me in, I break in through the front door or the windows.

We talked together in this way some time. Then Old Age said again,— Come, let us walk down the street together,—and offered me a cane, an eyeglass, a tippet, and a pair of over-shoes.—No, much obliged to you, said I. I don't want those things, and I had a little rather talk with you here, privately, in my study. So I dressed myself up in a jaunty way and walked out alone;—got a fall, caught a cold, was laid up with a lumbago, and had time to think over this whole matter.

From "The Professor's Paper," in *The Autocrat of the Breakfast Table*, 1858

LEO TOLSTOY *(Russian, 1828–1910)*

January 15, 1910

I remembered very vividly that I am conscious of myself in exactly the same way now, at eighty-one, as I was conscious of myself, my "I," at five or six years of age. Consciousness is immovable. Due to this alone there is the movement which we call "time." If time *moves on,* then there must be something that stands still. The consciousness of my "I" stands still. I would like to say the same of matter and space: if something exists in space, then there must be something that is non-material, non-spatial. I do not know as yet to what extent the latter may be asserted.

Am going to dinner. Nothing special this evening.

July 1, 1910

Our life is a quest for gratification. There is physical gratification in health, in satisfying the lusts of the body, in wealth, sexual love, fame, honor, power. All these gratifications 1) are outside our control, 2) may be taken away from us at any moment by death, and 3) are not accessible to everyone. But there is another kind of gratification, the spiritual, the love for others, which 1) is always in our control, 2) is not taken from us by death, as we can die loving, and 3) not only is accessible to all, but the more people live for it, the more joy there will be. . . .

4) Isn't it a strange thing that we understand least of all what we know best of all, or rather: we know best of all what we do not understand at all, our soul, and, one may say, God.

From diary entries for 15 January and 1 July 1910

BERNARD BERENSON *(American, 1865–1959)*

December 31st, I Tatti

My earthly tabernacle is too uncomfortable to live in. It leaks, it crumbles, it breaks away, now part of the roof and now a bit of the wall. The air blows through and yet it smokes and smells. It is no longer habitable. But where to go if I leave this wreck of a body of mine? And do I exist at all outside of this miserable carcass?

. . . How has it come about that I take it as a matter of course that I am a tenant only of this shack of a body, and not merely and wholly a function of this body? And how that I cannot conceive of my *itness* having another material body, little as I can believe that I must end with this one. "Enveloped in mystery," a problem that cannot so much as be stated, let alone solved. It is not a dialectical matter, what survival after the death of the body would be like, and where and for how long—no end!

333

Another year whirled away, leaving little but a blur in memory. Curious how dim and even veiled my remembrance of the past, no matter how recent. I seem to consume life as I live it, without much to recollect. Or is it that I have a poor memory? Or is my memory like a clouded night sky with a star here or there piercing the duskiness? What has happened to me in the year? I have been to Ischia and Naples, to Turin, Milan, and Venice, I have summered at Vallombrosa, returned to Ischia, settled down here, never quite unpacked after various moves, "hay fever" getting worse and worse, nose cauterized. My sisters paid us a long visit and parted on board the *Bianca Mano* at Naples. All like spokes of a wheel moving fast enough to seem one whirl. And now I face another year, 1952, my eighty-seventh. I scarcely ask what it will bring; I expect so little except creature comforts.

From a diary entry for 31 December 1951

HOWARD NEMEROV (*American, 1920–1991*)

The people on the avenue at noon,
Sharing the sparrows and the wintry sun,
The turned-off fountain with its basin drained
And cement benches etched with checkerboards,

Are old and poor, most every one of them
Wearing some decoration of his damage,
Bandage or crutch or cane; and some are blind,
Or nearly, tap-tapping along with white wands.

When they open their mouths, there are no teeth.
All the same, they keep on talking to themselves
Even while bending to hawk up spit or blood
In gutters that will be there when they are gone.

Some have the habit of getting hit by cars
Three times a year; the ambulance comes up
And away they go, mumbling even in shock
The many secret names they have for God.

"Near the Old Peoples' Home," 1975

W. H. AUDEN (*American, 1907–1973*)

All are limitory, but each has her own
    nuance of damage. The elite can dress and decent themselves,
        are ambulant with a single stick, adroit

334

to read a book all through, or play the slow movements of
    easy sonatas. (Yet, perhaps their very
carnal freedom is their spirit's bane: intelligent
    of what has happened and why, they are obnoxious
to a glum beyond tears.) Then come those on wheels, the average
    majority, who endure T.V. and, led by
lenient therapists, do community-singing, then
    the loners, muttering in Limbo, and last
the terminally incompetent, as improvident,
    unspeakable, impeccable as the plants
they parody. (Plants may sweat profusely but never
    sully themselves.) One tie, though, unites them: all
appeared when the world, though much was awry there, was more
    spacious, more comely to look at, its Old Ones
with an audience and secular station. Then a child,
    in dismay with Mamma, could refuge with Gran
to be revalued and told a story. As of now,
    we all know what to expect, but their generation
is the first to fade like this, not at home but assigned
    to a numbered frequent ward, stowed out of conscience
as unpopular luggage.
                As I ride the subway
    to spend half-an-hour with one, I revisage
who she was in the pomp and sumpture of her hey-day,
    when week-end visits were a presumptive joy,
not a good work. Am I cold to wish for a speedy
    painless dormition, pray, as I know she prays,
that God or Nature will abrupt her earthly function?

                                    "Old People's Home," 1970

NIKOS KAZANTZAKIS *(Greek, 1883–1957)*

I kiss your hand, beloved grandfather. I kiss your right shoulder, I kiss your left shoulder. My confession is over; now you must judge. I did not recount the details of daily life. Rinds they were. You tossed them into the garbage of the abyss and I did the same. With its large and small sorrows, large and small joys, life sometimes wounded me, sometimes caressed me. These habitual everyday affairs left us, and we left them. It was not worth the trouble to turn back and haul them out of the abyss. The world will lose nothing if the people I knew remain in oblivion. Contact with my contemporaries had very little influence on my life. I did not love many men, either because I failed to understand them or because I looked upon them with contempt; perhaps, also, because I did not chance to meet many who deserved being loved. I did not hate anyone, however, even though I harmed several people without desiring to. They were sparrows and I wished to turn them into eagles. I set about to deliver them from mediocrity and routine, pushed them without taking their endurance into account, and they crashed to the ground. Only the immortal dead enticed me, the great Sirens Christ, Buddha, and Lenin. From my early years I sat at their feet and listened intently to their seductive love-filled song. I struggled all my life to save myself from each of these Sirens without denying any one of them, struggled to unite these three clashing voices and transform them into harmony.

Women I loved. I was fortunate in chancing to meet extraordinary women along my route. No man ever did me so much good or aided my struggle so greatly as these women—and one above all, the last. But over this love-smitten body I throw the veil which the sons of Noah threw over their drunken father. I like our ancestors' myth about Eros and Psyche; surely you liked it too, grandfather. It is both shameful and dangerous to light a lamp, dispel the darkness, and see two bodies locked in an embrace. You knew this, you who hid your beloved helpmate Jeronima de las Cuevas in love's divine obscurity. I do the same with my Jeronima. Intrepid fellow athlete, cool fountain in our inhuman solitude, great comfort! Poverty and nakedness—yes, the Cretans are right in saying that poverty and nakedness are nothing, provided you have a good wife. We had good wives; yours was named Jeronima, mine Helen. What good fortune this was, grandfather! How many times did we not say to ourselves as we looked at them, Blessed the day we were born!

But we did not allow women, even the dearest, to lead us astray. We did not follow their flower-strewn road, we took them with us. No, we did not take them, these dauntless companions followed our ascents of their own free will.

One thing only we pursued all our lives: a harsh, carnivorous, indestructible vision—the essence. For its sake what venom we were given to drink by both gods and men, what tears we shed, what blood, how much sweat! Our whole lives, a devil (devil? or angel?) refused to leave us in peace. He leaned over, glued himself to us and hissed in our ears, "In vain! In vain! In vain!" He thought he would make us freeze in our tracks, but we repulsed him with a toss of our heads, clenched our teeth, and answered, "Just what we want! We're not working for pay, we have no desire for a daily wage. We are warring in the empty air, beyond hope, beyond paradise!"

This essence went by many names; it kept changing masks all the while we pursued it. Sometimes we called it supreme hope, sometimes supreme despair, sometimes summit of man's soul, sometimes desert mirage, and sometimes blue bird and freedom. And sometimes, finally, it seemed to us like an integral circle with the human heart as center and immortality as circumference, a circle which we arbitrarily assigned a heavy name loaded with all the hopes and tears of the world: "God."

Every integral man has inside him, in his heart of hearts, a mystic center around which all else revolves. This mystic whirling lends unity to his thoughts and actions; it helps him find or invent the cosmic harmony. For some this center is love, for others kindness or beauty, others the thirst for knowledge or the longing for gold and power. They examine the relative value of all else and subordinate it to this central passion. Alas for the man who does not feel himself governed inside by an absolute monarch. His ungoverned, incoherent life is scattered to the four winds.

Our center, grandfather, the center which swept the visible world into its whirl and fought to elevate it to the upper level of valor and responsibility, was the battle with God. Which God? The fierce summit of man's soul, the summit which we are ceaselessly about to attain and which ceaselessly jumps to its feet and climbs still higher. "Does man battle with God?" some acquaintances asked me sarcastically one day. I answered them, "With whom else do you expect him to battle?" Truly, with whom else?

That was why the whole of our lives was an ascent, grandfather—ascent, precipice, solitude. We set out with many fellow strugglers, many ideas, a great escort. But as we ascended and as the summit shifted and became more remote, fellow strugglers, ideas, and hopes kept bidding us farewell; out of breath, they were neither willing nor able to mount higher. We remained alone, our eyes riveted upon the Moving Monad, the shifting summit. We were swayed neither by arrogance nor by the naïve certainty that one day the summit would stand still and we would reach it; nor yet, even if we should reach it, by the belief that there on high we would find happiness, salvation, and paradise. We ascended because the very act of ascending, for us, was happiness, salvation, and paradise.

I marvel at the human soul; no power in heaven and earth is so great. Without being aware of it, we carry omnipotence within us. But we crush our souls beneath a weight of flesh and lard, and die without having learned what we are and what we can accomplish. What other power on earth is able to look the world's beginning and end straight in the eye without being blinded? In the beginning was not the Word (as is preached by the souls crushed beneath lard and flesh) nor the Act, nor the Creator's hand filled with life-receiving clay. In the beginning was Fire. And in the end is neither immortality nor recompense, paradise nor the inferno. In the end is Fire. Between these two fires, dear grandfather, we traveled; and we fought, by following Fire's commandment and working with it, to turn flesh into flame, thought into flame—hope, despair, honor, dishonor, glory, into flame. You

337

went in the lead and I followed. You taught me that our inner flame, contrary to the nature of the flesh, is able to flare up with ever-increasing intensity over the years. That was why (I saw this in you and admired you for it) you became continually fiercer as you aged, continually braver as you arrived ever closer to the abyss. Tossing the bodies of saints, rulers, and monks into the crucible of your glance, you melted them down like metals, purged away their rust, and refined out the pure gold: their soul. What soul? The flame. This you united with the conflagration that engendered us and the conflagration which shall devour us.

From the epilogue to *Report to Greco*, 1965

ALEXANDER KUSHNER *(Russian, b. 1936)*

What is so still
As an old man staring
At a bird through his final
Hospital window?
. . . Seeing the bushes
Against a kiosk,
Wearing the hospital
Striped pyjamas.
Was he a clerk?
A builder or what?
Whatever, already
He has forgot.
A domino fan?
Stereo tinker?
This window the last
Toy he has got.

"The Old Man," c. 1965

SIR ANTHONY CARLISLE *(English, 1768–1840)*

Experience has fully convinced me that the later stages of human life are often abridged by unsuitable Diet, or prematurely ended by Disorders which are not treated with sufficient attention. . . . It seems little more than a vulgar error, to consider the termination of advanced life as the inevitable consequence of time, when the immediate cause of death in old persons is generally known to be some well-marked disease.

338

*   *   *

Diseases, not the mere exhaustion of Age, are the ordinary causes of death in old persons.

From "An Essay on the Disorders of Old Age and on the Means for Prolonging Life," 1819

HIPPOCRATES   (*Greek, c. 460–377 B.C.E*)

Growing bodies have the most innate heat; they therefore require the most food, for otherwise their bodies are wasted. In old persons the heat is feeble, and therefore they require little fuel, as it were, to the flame, for it would be extinguished by much. On this account, also, fevers in old persons are not equally acute, because their bodies are cold.

Old people, on the whole, have fewer complaints than young; but those chronic diseases which do befall them generally never leave them.

Those things which one has been accustomed to for a long time, although worse than things which one is not accustomed to, usually give less disturbance; but a change must sometimes be made to things one is not accustomed to.

From *Aphorisms,* mid-fifth/early fourth century B.C.E.

AVICENNA   (*Persian/Muslim, 980–1037*)

The dryness (of the body) is increased in two ways: by lessening of the power of receiving "matter"; by lessening of the native moisture resulting from dispersal of the (innate) heat. The heat becomes more feeble because dryness predominates in the substance of the members, and because the innate moisture becomes relatively less. The innate moisture is to the innate heat as the oil of a lamp is to the flame. For there are two forms of moisture in the flame: water, which holds its own, and oil, which is used up. So, in a corresponding manner, the innate heat holds its own in respect of the innate moisture, but is used up *pari passu* with increase of extraneous heat, due, e.g., to defective digestion, which is comparable with the aqueous moisture of the flame. As the dryness increases, the innate heat lessens, and the result is natural death.

For the reason why the (human) body does not live any longer than it does lies in the fact that the initial innate moisture holds out against being dispersed both by the alien heat and by the heat in the body itself (both that which is innate and that derived from bodily movement). And this resistance is maintained as long as the one is weaker than the other, and as long as something is provided to replace that which has been thus dispersed—to wit, from the aliment. Furthermore, as we have already stated, the power or faculty which operates upon the aliment in order to render it useful in this way only does so up to the end of life.

Therefore we may say that the art of maintaining the health is not the art of averting death, or of averting extraneous injuries from the body; or of securing the utmost longevity possible to the human being. It is concerned with two other things—(*a*) the prevention of putrefactive breakdown; (*b*) the safeguarding of innate moisture from too rapid dissipation, and maintaining it at such a degree of strength that the original type of constitution peculiar to the person shall not change even up to the last moment of life.

This is secured by a suitable regimen, namely (*a*) one which will ensure the replacement of the innate heat and moisture which are dispersed from the body as exactly as possible; and (*b*) a regimen which will prevent any agents which would lead to a rapid desiccation from gaining the upper hand—excluding agents which produce a normal desiccation; (*c*) one which safeguards the body from the development of putrefactive processes within it and from the influence of alien heat (whether extraneous or intrinsic).

For all bodies have not the same degree of innate moisture and innate heat. There is a great diversity in regard to them.

*   *   *

The real object of conserving the energies of the body lies in the attainment of spiritual development. The actual bodily occupation is itself, if we will it so, the practical means of that attainment. The energy of will to associate this means of worship with the subjugation of the vices inherent in our frailty must be employed during the early years if we are not to find ourselves in old age powerless to advance along the critical stages of the journey to the only true Goal. This principle underlies the idea of "right Regimen."

From "On the Causes of Health and Disease; the Necessity of Death" and "The Regimen Proper for the Physically Matured," in *The Canon of Medicine of Avicenna,* late tenth or early eleventh century

PABLO NERUDA (*Chilean, 1904–1973*)

How long does a man live, after all?

Does he live a thousand days, or one only?

A week, or several centuries?

How long does a man spend dying?

What does it mean to say 'for ever'?

Lost in these preoccupations,
I set myself to clear things up.

I sought out knowledgeable priests,
I waited for them after their rituals,
I watched them when they went their ways
to visit God and the Devil.

They wearied of my questions.
They on their part knew very little;
they were no more than administrators.

Medical men received me
in between consultations,
a scalpel in each hand,
saturated in aureomycin,
busier each day.
As far as I could tell from their talk,
the problem was as follows:
It was not so much the death of a microbe—
they went down by the ton—
but the few which survived
showed signs of perversity.

They left me so startled
that I sought out the grave-diggers.
I went to the rivers where they burn
enormous painted corpses,
tiny bony bodies,
emperors with an aura
of terrible curses,
women snuffed out at a stroke
by a wave of cholera.
There were whole beaches of dead
and ashy specialists.

When I got the chance
I asked them a slew of questions.
They offered to burn me;
it was the only thing they knew.

In my own country the undertakers
answered me, between drinks:

341

'Get yourself a good woman
and give up this nonsense.'

I never saw people so happy.

Raising their glasses they sang,
toasting health and death
They were huge fornicators.

I returned home, much older
after crossing the world.

Now I question nobody.

But I know less every day.

"And How Long?," 1958

J. BANDALINE, M.D. (*French, n.d.*)

And modern humanity, upsetting all its idols, turned its eyes toward science, expecting it to vanquish suffering, old age, death. What a charming illusion, what a sweet dream to think of the freshness and the joys of the first twenty years of our life being added to the experience and the wisdom of mature age!

We all, however, know the inevitable approach of old age, and are ready, like Faust, to give our soul to the devil, if he will free us from the burden of our years, and but few people obediently subordinate themselves to this inexorable law.

But however burdensome and tedious life may be, in spite of all the suffering and adversity it may bring, man and every living being in general clings to it and loves it. To live! To live! this cry comes from every heart.

And just as the love of living is the most profound and insuperable instinct of man, from times immemorial the desire to keep and prolong it has been paramount in scientific investigations: the short time of youth, this period of beauty and development of force, the age of highest earthly happiness they have tried to prolong indefinitely.

From "The Struggle of Science with Old Age," in *Medical Record*, 18 July 1903

ÉLIE METCHNIKOFF (*Russian, 1845–1916*)

Ought we to listen to the cry of humanity that life is too short and that it would be well to prolong it? Would it really be for the good of the human race to extend the duration of the life of man beyond its present limits?

Already it is complained that the burden of supporting old people is too heavy, and statesmen are perturbed by the enormous expense which will be entailed by State support of the aged. . . .

If the question were merely one of prolonging the life of old people without modifying old age itself, such considerations would be justified. It must be understood, however, that the prolongation of life would be associated with the preservation of intelligence and of the power to work. In the earlier parts of this book I have given many examples which show the possibility of useful work being done by persons of advanced years. When we have reduced or abolished such causes of precocious senility as intemperance and disease, it will no longer be necessary to give pensions at the age of sixty or seventy years. The cost of supporting the old, instead of increasing, will diminish progressively. . . .

It has long been a charge against medicine and hygiene that they tend to weaken the human race. By scientific means unhealthy people, or those with inherited blemishes, have been preserved so that they can give birth to weak offspring. . . . It is clear that a valuable existence of great service to humanity is compatible with a feeble constitution and precarious health. . . . I need only instance the names of Fresnel, Leopardi, Weber, Schumann and Chopin. It does not follow that we ought to cherish diseases and leave to natural selection the duty of preserving the individuals which can resist them. On the other hand, it is indispensable to try to blot out the diseases themselves, and, in particular, the evils of old age, by the methods of hygiene and therapeutics. . . . We must use all our endeavours to allow men to complete their normal course of life, and to make it possible for old men to play their parts as advisers and judges, endowed with their long experience of life.

From "Should We Try to Prolong Human Life?," in *The Prolongation of Life,* 1908

OVID *(Roman, 43 B.C.E.–17 or 18 C.E.)*

> "Power of heaven is immense, has no bounds:
> whatever gods want is accomplished; this will show you:
> in Phrygian hills, oak borders linden, surrounded
> by a mid-sized wall: I've seen the place myself:
> Pittheus sent me to the country where his father, Pelops,
> once reigned; not far off is marsh,
> once habitable, now crowded with coots and swamp birds;
> Jupiter comes here in mortal shape with son,
> Mercury, carrying wand but wings off;
> they go to a thousand houses seeking rest:

343

bolts lock a thousand houses: but one
receives them: small, roofed with thatch and swamp reeds,
but good old Baucis and Philemon, the same age,
married in that cottage in youth, aged there
together; they admit poverty, bear it level-headedly,
and thus lighten it; no matter if you ask there
for master or servant, the whole house is just two:
those ordering serve

so, heaven-tenants come to tiny dwelling,
duck heads entering low doorway;
the old man brings chairs, tells them to relax;
Baucis throws rough cloth over seats,
stirs warm embers on the hearth, revives yesterday's
fire, feeds it leaves and dry bark and old
woman's breath to produce flames; takes down
branch twigs and dry brushwood from roof,
breaks them up to put under the little pot;
husband brings vegetables from well-watered garden;
she cuts off leaves; with fork fetches
smoked bacon hanging from blackened beam, cuts
off a thin piece from the back, long-guarded,
softens it in boiling water

meanwhile, to keep from noticing
delay, they fill time with talk; a beechwood basin
hung from nail by handle is filled with warm water
for them to wash in; they shake out a couch
of soft sedge (legs and frame willow) and cover it
with cloths they use only on holidays (and even then
old and cheap—but not inappropriate for willow couch);
the gods recline; the old woman, sleeves rolled,
puts table down shakily: the third leg
uneven, she evens it with a tile; slope fixed,
she wipes level table with green mint, puts down
double-colored berries of pure Minerva, autumn
cherries preserved in wine dregs, endive and radishes,
a wedge of cheese, eggs lightly turned in ashes
not hot; all in clay dishes; then
the wine bowl (engraved of course in silver
like everything else!) and beechwood cups,
their hollows inlaid with yellow wax;

shortly, hot food is served, and wine
not very old brought back again;
then put away to make room for dessert:
nuts, a mixture of figs and wrinkled dates, plums,
small baskets of fragrant apples, grapes gathered
from purple vines; a bright honeycomb in the middle;
and above all, glad faces and good will
neither poor nor cheap

meanwhile, they notice
the wine bowl, empty, refilling itself
strangely; astonished, scared, Baucis and Philemon hold
out their hands timidly and pray, beg pardon
for the meal: no time to prepare! they prepare to sacrifice
to god-visitors their one goose, guardian
of the tiny cottage, but he's quick-winged and long
eludes slow owners; tires them out, old;
he seems to run toward gods themselves
and gods forbid his being killed: 'We're gods,
and this wicked neighborhood will get punishment deserved:
you two are given immunity from trouble:
leave your home now, follow our footsteps
up the mountain: go!'

both obey; they lean on staffs, struggle to follow
up steep hill; an arrow-shot away
from the top, they look back, see others
drowned in swamp, only their own house remaining;
while watching in amazement, weeping fate of neighbors,
that old house, small even for two,
turns temple; props become columns; straw
yellows, seems golden roof; doors engraved
and ground covered with marble; then Saturn's son
says serenely: 'Speak, honest old man,
and woman so deserving your honest husband:
what's your wish?'

Philemon talks it over a little with Baucis,
then he tells gods their joint decision:
'We want to be your priests and watch your shrines;
and since we lived our years together, that our last
moment carries us both away: I never
seeing my wife's grave, nor buried by her'

their prayer answered; made temple custodians for life;
then, broken by age and years, standing by chance
before the sacred steps, talking about events of that place:
Baucis sees Philemon turn leafy, and old
Philemon sees Baucis turn leafy too;
tree-tops grow over both faces; they speak
together while they can: 'Good-bye, spouse!'
said together; together, bushiness covers their mouths;
Bithynian locals still point out there
two trees, side by side, once bodies

old men—not foolish—told me this,
and had no reason to deceive; indeed, I saw
garlands hanging on the branches; I put fresh ones on
and said, 'You are gods if gods like you,
and those who worship shall be worshiped!'"

From "Philemon and Baucis," in *Metamorphoses*, c. 5 c.e.

PEARL S. BUCK (*American, 1892–1973*)

The jet took off at midnight. Friends came to see me off and their kindness and affection wrapped me around. But they had to return to their own lives and I had mine to face, and there was a certain comfort in being at last among strangers, to whom I need make no response. I found my seat, fastened my belt and leaned back and closed my eyes. It was the first moment that I had been totally alone since the moment that morning when the world had changed. Long ago, when I knew my child was to be permanently retarded, I learned that there are two kinds of sorrow, one which can be assuaged and one which cannot be assuaged. This one was different, yet alike in that it, too, was not to be assuaged. Nevertheless, years ago I had learned the technique of acceptance. The first step is simply to yield one's self to the situation. It is a process of the spirit but it begins with body. There, belted into my seat while the aircraft rose into the black sky of night, I consciously yielded my body, muscle by muscle, bone by bone. I ceased to resist, I ceased to struggle. Let come what would, I could do nothing to change what had already happened. The aircraft contained me, controlled me, and isolated me.

In a curious way spirit must sometimes follow body, just as at other times spirit leads. Now as the body yielded itself to the will, the spirit found it easier also to yield to the same command. Life can be inexorable but death is always inexorable. The next step is to recognize inexorability. The past becomes static. It is history and the facts of history cannot be changed. What has been done is done. One can learn from the past, one can treasure the past, but it cannot be changed. Twenty-five years had been lived in happiness, but they were lived. The End had been written. One does not go on writing a book after those two words have finished it. Another book has to be begun.

It cannot begin at once. There has to be time for total relaxation, total recognition of inexorability, total realization that the life of the past is over. Only then can new strength be summoned. I doubt even that it can be summoned. It has to grow from the very sources of the being into a new will to live. As far as the will could go that night, as the jet darted its way among cloud and stars, it was only to command the body to yield and the spirit to withdraw. At last I slept.

From *A Bridge for Passing*, 1961

YAMANOUE OKURA (*Japanese, 660–733 c.e.*)

So long as lasts the span of life,
We wish for peace and comfort
With no evil and no mourning,
But life is hard and painful.
As the common saying has it,
Bitter salt is poured into the smarting wound,
Or the burdened horse is packed with an upper load,
Illness shakes my old body with pain.
All day long I breathe in grief
And sigh throughout the night.
For long years my illness lingers,
I grieve and groan month after month,
And though I would rather die,
I cannot, and leave my children
Noisy like the flies of May.
Whenever I watch them
My heart burns within.
And tossed this way and that,
I weep aloud.

ENVOYS

I find no solace in my heart;
Like the bird flying behind the clouds
I weep aloud.

347

Helpless and in pain,
I would run out and vanish,
But the thought of my children holds me.

No children to wear them in wealthy homes,
They are thrown away as waste,
Those silks and quilted clothes!

With no sackcloth for my children to wear,
Must I thus grieve,
For ever at a loss!

Though vanishing like a bubble,
I live, praying that my life be long
Like a rope of a thousand fathoms.

Humble as I am,
Like an armband of coarse twill,
How I crave a thousand years of life!

"So long as lasts the span of life," in the *Man'yōshū*, Ancient Period, to 794 C.E.

MUHAMMAD *(Arabian/Islamic, c. 570–632 C.E.)*

Muhammad passed by some graves in Medinah, and turned his face toward them, and said, "Peace to you, O people of the graves! May God forgive us and you: You have passed on before us, and we are following you!"

*   *   *

[Muhammad said:]

Not one of you must wish for death, from any worldly affliction; but if there certainly is anyone wishing for death, he must say, "O Lord, keep me alive so long as life may be good for me, and cause me to die when it is better for me so to do."

The Faithful do not die; perhaps they become translated from this perishable world to the world of eternal existences.

Death is a blessing to a Muslim. Remember and speak well of your dead, and refrain from speaking ill of them.

*   *   *

The grave is the first stage of the journey into eternity.

Death is a bridge that uniteth friend with friend.

From *The Sayings of Muhammad*, 1941

MARTIN LUTHER *(German, 1483–1546)*

I don't like to see examples of joyful death. On the other hand, I like to see those who tremble and shake and grow pale when they face death and yet get through. It was so with the great saints; they were not glad to die. Fear is something natural because death is a punishment, and therefore something sad. According to the spirit one dies willingly, but according to the flesh the saying applies, 'Another will carry you where you do not wish to go' [John 21:18]. In the Psalms and other histories, as in Jeremiah, one sees how eager men were to escape death. 'Beware,' Jeremiah said, 'or you will bring innocent blood upon yourselves' [Jer. 26:15]. But when Christ said, 'Let this cup pass from me' [Matt. 26:39], the meaning was different, for this was the Same who said, 'I have life and death in my hand' [John 5:21, 24]. We are the ones who drew the bloody sweat from him.

"To Be Glad to Die Is Unnatural," 1532

JOHN FIRE/LAME DEER *(Native American/Sioux, 1895–1976)*

The difference between the white man and us is this: You believe in the redeeming powers of suffering, if this suffering was done by somebody else, far away, two thousand years ago. We believe that it is up to every one of us to help each other, even through the pain of our bodies. Pain to us is not "abstract," but very real. We do not lay this burden onto our god, nor do we want to miss being face to face with the spirit power. It is when we are fasting on the hilltop, or tearing our flesh at the sun dance, that we experience the sudden insight, come closest to the mind of the Great Spirit. Insight does not come cheaply, and we want no angel or saint to gain it for us and give it to us secondhand.

From *Lame Deer: Seeker of Visions*, 1972

TIBETAN PRAYER *(Tibetan/Buddhist, c. seventh–thirteenth centuries)*

When the journey of my life has reached its end,
and since no relatives go with me from this world
I wander in the bardo state alone,
may the peaceful and wrathful buddhas send out the power of
  their compassion
and clear away the dense darkness of ignorance.

When parted from beloved friends, wandering alone,
my own projections' empty forms appear,

349

may the buddhas send out the power of their compassion
so that the bardo's terrors do not come.

When the five luminous lights of wisdom shine,
fearlessly may I recognise myself;
when the forms of the peaceful and wrathful ones appear,
fearless and confident may I recognise the bardo.

When I suffer through the power of evil karma,
may the peaceful and wrathful buddhas clear away suffering;
when the sound of dharmatā roars like a thousand thunders,
may it be transformed into the sound of mahāyāna teaching.

When I follow my karma, without a refuge,
may the peaceful and wrathful buddhas be my refuge;
when I suffer the karma of unconscious tendencies,
may the samādhi of bliss and luminosity arise.

At the moment of spontaneous birth in the bardo of becoming,
may the false teachings of the tempters not arise;
when I arrive wherever I wish by supernatural power,
may the illusory terrors of evil karma not arise.

When savage beasts of prey are roaring,
may it become the sound of dharma, the six syllables;
when I am chased by snow, rain, wind and darkness,
may I receive the clear, divine eye of wisdom.

May all sentient beings of the same realm in the bardo,
free from jealousy, be born in a higher state;
when great thirst and hunger are caused by passions,
may the pain of thirst and hunger, heat and cold, not arise.

When I see my future parents in union,
may I see the peaceful and wrathful buddhas with their consorts;
with power to choose my birthplace, for the good of others,
may I receive a perfect body adorned with auspicious signs.

Obtaining for myself a perfect human body,
may all who see and hear me at once be liberated;
may I not follow all my evil karma,
but follow and increase what merit I may have.

Wherever I am born, at that very place,
may I meet the yidam of this life face to face;
knowing how to walk and talk as soon as I am born,

may I attain the power of non-forgetfulness and remembrance of
past lives.

In all the stages of learning, high, middle and low,
may I understand just by hearing, thinking and seeing;
wherever I am born, may that land be blessed,
so that all sentient beings may be happy.

O peaceful and wrathful buddhas, may I and others
become like you yourselves, just as you are,
with your forms and your auspicious marks,
your retinues, your long life and your realms.

Samantabhadra, the peaceful and wrathful ones, infinite
compassion,
the power of truth of the pure dharmatā,
and followers of tantra in one-pointed meditation:
may their blessings fulfil this inspiration-prayer.

Called "The Bardo Prayer which Protects from Fear"

PSALM 71, HEBREW SCRIPTURES

I seek refuge in You, O LORD;
    may I never be disappointed.
As You are beneficent, save me and rescue me;
    incline Your ear to me and deliver me.
Be a sheltering rock for me to which I may always repair;
    decree my deliverance,
        for You are my rock and my fortress.
My God, rescue me from the hand of the wicked,
    from the grasp of the unjust and the lawless.

For You are my hope,
    O Lord GOD,
    my trust from my youth.
While yet unborn, I depended on You;
    in the womb of my mother, You were my support;
    I sing Your praises always.
I have become an example for many,
    since You are my mighty refuge.
My mouth is full of praise to You,
    glorifying You all day long.
Do not cast me off in old age;
    when my strength fails, do not forsake me!

For my enemies talk against me;
>those who wait for me are of one mind,
>saying, "God has forsaken him;
>chase him and catch him,
>for no one will save him!"

O God, be not far from me;
>my God, hasten to my aid!

Let my accusers perish in frustration;
>let those who seek my ruin be clothed in reproach and
>>disgrace!

As for me, I will hope always,
>and add to the many praises of You.

My mouth tells of Your beneficence,
>of Your deliverance all day long,
>though I know not how to tell it.

I come with praise of Your mighty acts, O Lord GOD;
>I celebrate Your beneficence, Yours alone.

You have let me experience it, God, from my youth;
>until now I have proclaimed Your wondrous deeds,
>and even in hoary old age do not forsake me, God,
>until I proclaim Your strength to the next generation,
>Your mighty acts, to all who are to come,
>Your beneficence, high as the heavens, O God,
>You who have done great things;
>O God, who is Your peer!

You who have made me undergo many troubles and
misfortunes
>will revive me again,
>and raise me up from the depths of the earth.

You will grant me much greatness,
>You will turn and comfort me.

Then I will acclaim You to the music of the lyre
>for Your faithfulness, O my God;
>I will sing a hymn to You with a harp,
>O Holy One of Israel.

My lips shall be jubilant, as I sing a hymn to You,
>my whole being, which You have redeemed.

All day long my tongue shall recite Your beneficent acts,
>how those who sought my ruin were frustrated and
>>disgraced.

GABRIEL GARCÍA MÁRQUEZ *(Colombian, b. 1928)*

On the third day of rain they had killed so many crabs inside the house that Pelayo had to cross his drenched courtyard and throw them into the sea, because the newborn child had a temperature all night and they thought it was due to the stench. The world had been sad since Tuesday. Sea and sky were a single ash-gray thing and the sands of the beach, which on March nights glimmered like powdered light, had become a stew of mud and rotten shellfish. The light was so weak at noon that when Pelayo was coming back to the house after throwing away the crabs, it was hard for him to see what it was that was moving and groaning in the rear of the courtyard. He had to go very close to see that it was an old man, a very old man, lying face down in the mud, who, in spite of his tremendous efforts, couldn't get up, impeded by his enormous wings.

Frightened by that nightmare, Pelayo ran to get Elisenda, his wife, who was putting compresses on the sick child, and he took her to the rear of the courtyard. They both looked at the fallen body with mute stupor. He was dressed like a ragpicker. There were only a few faded hairs left on his bald skull and very few teeth in his mouth, and his pitiful condition of a drenched great-grandfather had taken away any sense of grandeur he might have had. His huge buzzard wings, dirty and half-plucked, were forever entangled in the mud. They looked at him so long and so closely that Pelayo and Elisenda very soon overcame their surprise and in the end found him familiar. Then they dared speak to him, and he answered in an incomprehensible dialect with a strong sailor's voice. That was how they skipped over the inconvenience of the wings and quite intelligently concluded that he was a lonely castaway from some foreign ship wrecked by the storm. And yet, they called in a neighbor woman who knew everything about life and death to see him, and all she needed was one look to show them their mistake.

"He's an angel," she told them. "He must have been coming for the child, but the poor fellow is so old that the rain knocked him down."

On the following day everyone knew that a flesh-and-blood angel was held captive in Pelayo's house. Against the judgment of the wise neighbor woman, for whom angels in those times were the fugitive survivors of a celestial conspiracy, they did not have the heart to club him to death. Pelayo watched over him all afternoon from the kitchen, armed with his bailiff's club, and before going to bed he dragged him out of the mud and locked him up with the hens in the wire chicken coop. In the middle of the night, when the rain stopped, Pelayo and Elisenda were still killing crabs. A short time afterward the child woke up without a fever and with a desire to eat. Then they felt magnanimous and decided to put the angel on a raft with fresh water and provisions for three days and leave him to his fate on the high seas. But when they went out into the courtyard with the first light of dawn, they found the whole neighborhood in front of the chicken coop having fun with the angel, without the slightest reverence, tossing him things to eat through the openings in the wire as if he weren't a supernatural creature but a circus animal.

Father Gonzaga arrived before seven o'clock, alarmed at the strange news. By that time onlookers less frivolous than those at dawn had already arrived and they were making all kinds of conjectures concerning the captive's future. The simplest among them thought that he should be named mayor of the world. Others of sterner mind felt that he should be promoted to the rank of five-star general in order to win all wars. Some visionaries hoped that he could be put to stud in order to implant on earth a race of winged wise men who could take charge of the universe. But Father Gonzaga, before becoming a priest, had been a robust woodcutter. Standing by the wire, he reviewed his catechism in an instant and asked them to open the door so that he could take a close look at that pitiful man who looked more like a huge decrepit hen among the fascinated chickens. He was lying in a corner drying his open wings in the sunlight among the fruit peels and breakfast leftovers that the early risers had thrown him. Alien to the impertinences of the world, he only lifted his antiquarian eyes and murmured something in his dialect when Father Gonzaga went into the chicken coop and said good morning to him in Latin. The parish priest had his first suspicion of an impostor when he saw that he did not understand the language of God or know how to greet His ministers. Then he noticed that seen close up he was much too human: he had an unbearable smell of the outdoors, the back side of his wings was strewn with parasites and his main feathers had been mistreated by terrestrial winds, and nothing about him measured up to the proud dignity of angels. Then he came out of the chicken coop and in a brief sermon warned the curious against the risks of being ingenuous. He reminded them that the devil had the bad habit of making use of carnival tricks in order to confuse the unwary. He argued that if wings were not the essential element in determining the difference between a hawk and an airplane, they were even less so in the recognition of angels. Nevertheless, he promised to write a letter to his bishop so that the latter would write to his primate so that the latter would write to the Supreme Pontiff in order to get the final verdict from the highest courts.

His prudence fell on sterile hearts. The news of the captive angel spread with such rapidity that after a few hours the courtyard had the bustle of a marketplace and they had to call in troops with fixed bayonets to disperse the mob that was about to knock the house down. Elisenda, her spine all twisted from sweeping up so much marketplace trash, then got the idea of fencing in the yard and charging five cents admission to see the angel.

The curious came from far away. A traveling carnival arrived with a flying acrobat who buzzed over the crowd several times, but no one paid any attention to him because his wings were not those of an angel but, rather, those of a sidereal bat. The most unfortunate invalids on earth came in search of health: a poor woman who since childhood had been counting her heartbeats and had run out of numbers; a Portuguese man who couldn't sleep because the noise of the stars disturbed him; a sleepwalker who got up at night to undo the things he had done while awake; and many others with less serious ailments. In the midst of that shipwreck disorder that made the earth tremble, Pelayo and Elisenda were happy with fatigue, for in less than a week they had crammed their rooms with money and the line of pilgrims waiting their turn to enter still reached beyond the horizon.

The angel was the only one who took no part in his own act. He spent his time trying to get comfortable in his borrowed nest, befuddled by the hellish heat of the oil lamps and sacramental candles that had been placed along the wire. At first they tried to make him eat some mothballs, which, according to the wisdom of the wise neighbor woman, were the food prescribed for angels. But he turned them down, just as he turned down the papal lunches that the penitents brought him, and they never found out whether it was because he was an angel or because he was an old man that in the end he ate nothing but eggplant mush. His only supernatural virtue seemed to be patience. Especially during the first days, when the hens pecked at him, searching for the stellar parasites that proliferated in his wings, and the cripples pulled out feathers to touch their defective parts with, and even the most merciful threw stones at him, trying to get him to rise so they could see him standing. The only time they succeeded in arousing him was when they burned his side with an iron for branding steers, for he had been motionless for so many hours that they thought he was dead. He awoke with a start, ranting in his hermetic language and with tears in his eyes, and he flapped his wings a couple of times, which brought on a whirlwind of chicken dung and lunar dust and a gale of panic that did not seem to be of this world. Although many thought that his reaction had been one not of rage but of pain, from then on they were careful not to annoy him, because the majority understood that his passivity was not that of a hero taking his ease but that of a cataclysm in repose.

Father Gonzaga held back the crowd's frivolity with formulas of maidservant inspiration while awaiting the arrival of a final judgment on the nature of the captive. But the mail from Rome showed no sense of urgency. They spent their time finding out if the prisoner had a navel, if his dialect had any connection with Aramaic, how many times he could fit on the head of a pin, or whether he wasn't just a Norwegian with wings. Those meager letters might have come and gone until the end of time if a providential event had not put an end to the priest's tribulations.

It so happened that during those days, among so many other carnival attractions, there arrived in town the traveling show of the woman who had been changed into a spider for having disobeyed her parents. The admission to see her was not only less than the admission to see the angel, but people were permitted to ask her all manner of questions about her absurd state and to examine her up and down so that no one would ever doubt the truth of her horror. She was a frightful tarantula the size of a ram and with the head of a sad maiden. What was most heartrending, however, was not her outlandish shape but the sincere affliction with which she recounted the details of her misfortune. While still practically a child she had sneaked out of her parents' house to go to a dance, and while she was coming back through the woods after having danced all night without permission, a fearful thunderclap rent the sky in two and through the crack came the lightning bolt of brimstone that changed her into a spider. Her only nourishment came from the meatballs that charitable souls chose to toss into her mouth. A spectacle like that, full of so much human truth and with such a fearful lesson, was bound to defeat without even trying that of a haughty angel who scarcely deigned to look at mortals. Besides, the few miracles attributed to the angel showed a certain mental disorder, like the blind man who didn't recover his sight but grew three new teeth, or the paralytic who didn't get to walk but almost won the lottery, and the leper whose sores sprouted sunflowers. Those consolation miracles, which were more like mocking fun, had already ruined the angel's reputation when the woman who had been changed into a spider finally crushed him completely. That was how Father Gonzaga was cured forever of his insomnia and Pelayo's courtyard went back to being as empty as during the time it had rained for three days and crabs walked through the bedrooms.

The owners of the house had no reason to lament. With the money they saved they built a two-story mansion with balconies and gardens and high netting so that crabs wouldn't get in during the winter, and with iron bars on the windows so that angels wouldn't get in. Pelayo also set up a rabbit warren close to town and gave up his job as bailiff for good, and Elisenda bought some satin pumps with high heels and many dresses of iridescent silk, the kind worn on Sunday by the most desirable women in those times. The chicken coop was the only thing that didn't receive any attention. If they washed it down with creolin and burned tears of myrrh inside it every so often, it was not in homage to the angel but to drive away the dungheap stench that still hung everywhere like a ghost and was turning the new house into an old one. At first, when the child learned to walk, they were careful that he not get too close to the chicken coop. But then they began to lose their fears and got used to the smell, and before the child got his second teeth he'd gone inside the chicken coop to play, where the wires were falling apart. The angel was no less standoffish with him than with other mortals, but he tolerated the most ingenious infamies with the patience of a dog who had no illusions. They both came down with chicken pox at the same time. The doctor who took care of the child couldn't resist the temptation to listen to the angel's heart, and he found so much whistling in the heart and so many sounds in his kidneys that it seemed impossible for him to be alive. What surprised him most, however, was the logic of his wings. They seemed so natural on that completely human organism that he couldn't understand why other men didn't have them too.

When the child began school it had been some time since the sun and rain had caused the collapse of the chicken coop. The angel went dragging himself about here and there like a stray dying man. They would drive him out of the bedroom with a broom and a moment later find him in the kitchen. He seemed to be in so many places at the same time that they grew to think that he'd been duplicated, that he was reproducing himself all through the house, and the exasperated and unhinged Elisenda shouted that it was awful living in that hell full of angels. He could scarcely eat and his antiquarian eyes had also become so foggy that he went about bumping into posts. All he had left were the bare cannulae of his last feathers. Pelayo threw a blanket over him and extended him the charity of letting him sleep in the shed, and only then did they notice that he had a temperature at night, and was delirious with the tongue twisters of an old Norwegian. That was one of the few times they became alarmed, for they thought he was going to die and not even the wise neighbor woman had been able to tell them what to do with dead angels.

And yet he not only survived his worst winter, but seemed improved with the first sunny days. He remained motionless for several days in the farthest corner of the courtyard, where no one would see him, and at the beginning of December some large, stiff feathers began to grow on his wings, the feathers of a scarecrow, which looked more like another misfortune of decrepitude. But he must have known the reason for those changes, for he was quite careful that no one should notice them, that no one should hear the sea chanteys that he sometimes sang under the stars. One morning Elisenda was cutting some bunches of onions for lunch when a wind that seemed to come from the high seas blew into the kitchen. Then she went to the window and caught the angel in his first attempts at flight. They were so clumsy that his fingernails opened a furrow in the vegetable patch and he was on the point of knocking the shed down with the ungainly flapping that slipped on the light and couldn't get a grip on the air. But he did manage to gain altitude. Elisenda let out a sigh of relief, for herself and for him, when she saw him pass over the last houses, holding himself up in some way with the risky flapping of a senile vulture. She kept watching him even when she was through cutting the onions and she kept on watching until it was no longer possible for her to see him, because then he was no longer an annoyance in her life but an imaginary dot on the horizon of the sea.

"A Very Old Man with Enormous Wings: A Tale for Children," 1968

SECOND LETTER OF PAUL TO THE CORINTHIANS 4:16–18, THE NEW TESTAMENT

So we do not lose heart. Though our outer nature is wasting away, our inner nature is being renewed every day. For this slight momentary affliction is preparing for us an eternal weight of glory beyond all comparison, because we look not to the things that are seen but to the things that are unseen; for the things that are seen are transient, but the things that are unseen are eternal.

CHAPTER NINE
REMEMBRANCE

"They live by memory rather than by hope," Aristotle wrote of the old in a passage quoted in our first chapter, "for what is left to them of life is but little as compared with the long past; and hope is of the future, memory of the past." Contrary to Aristotle's belief, memory—for all its susceptibility to distortion, error, and denial—is a vital source of hope for societies as well as individuals.

This chapter highlights the importance of memory as an active, creative process that makes sense of both the individual past and the collective past, thereby transmitting them to the future. In these selections memory takes various forms, including life history, memoir, scientific writing, poetry, epitaph, and short story. We hear people thinking back in time, remembering earlier selves or other people now old or dead. Some discuss unresolved social problems that compel them to continued engagement with the present. Others illustrate the importance of reminiscing, of reworking and remembering the experiences of a lifetime while searching for personal meaning. Poets muse about past lovers, memorialize the dead, or imagine their own deaths. The chapter is loosely divided into four sections: personal memory; social memory; ideas about the uses and failure of memory in old age; and memorials to the living and the dead.

The first section highlights personal memory as a vehicle of endurance, inspiration, beauty, or acceptance of the past. The contemporary African-American poet Gwendolyn Brooks introduces us to an "old yellow" couple surviving on habits, beans, and memories. At the end of her autobiography, Edith Wharton, the American novelist of upper-class Victorian manners and morals, contrasts the continuing miracle of new experiences with the "dry wood" of memories that sustain her in old age. Traveling to the site of an early love remembered is a motif common to the selections by Israeli poet Yehuda Amichai and the American Kenneth Rexroth.

In the second section, authors as diverse as Bertrand Russell and Wang Shih-Min focus on social memory as a vehicle of commitment and generational transmission. These writers remember their personal lives contextually, and pay explicit attention to historical events, cultural expectations, or social problems. In "The Pros and Cons of Reaching Ninety," the twentieth-century English philosopher Bertrand Russell confounds conventional expectations of wheelchair serenity, and instead wages a public struggle against militarism and nuclear weapons. Inspired by Russell's example, the English historian Arnold Toynbee describes his commitment to the traditional intellectual world of the humanities. "It is important to care immensely about things that are going to happen after one is dead," writes Toynbee at age seventy-five. In the excerpt from *Forty Years at Hull-House*, the American social reformer Jane Addams looks back on her Progressive-era work with Chicago's poor. Other selections reach across boundaries of chronology, race, gender, and nationality, into the lives of an African American born into slavery, a Flathead Indian from Montana, and a seventeenth-century Chinsese Confucian.

Next follows a short section—encompassing religious advice, anthropological description, and psychiatric investigation—on the uses and failure of memory in late life. "The Review of Life," excerpted from a mid-nineteenth-century American advice manual on growing old, emphasizes the religious importance of memory within the Victorian vision of old age as a resting place on the journey of life. This evangelical Protestant version of life review contrasts sharply with the secular, psychiatric theory put forward by the contemporary American geriatrician and writer Robert Butler in 1963. Failure of memory through organic disease is discussed in the original case report of Alois Alzheimer, the German psychiatrist who identified the type of dementia that bears his name.

The final section, beginning with Richard Eberhart's poem "Survivors," memorializes both the living and the dead. The selections offer portraits of remembered lives that include "ancient" New England ladies, anonymous Jewish immigrants to America, great historical figures, writers composing their own epitaphs, and by implication, our own fleeting, storied selves. In the primordial human encounter with time and death—waged variously across historical differences in culture, gender, race, class, and age—individuals use whatever tools they find or make. Remembrance, if not overwhelmed by nostalgia or resentment, may lead to gratitude for the passing gift of one's own life, as well as to hope for the future.

GWENDOLYN BROOKS (*African American, b. 1917*)

> They eat beans mostly, this old yellow pair.
> Dinner is a casual affair.
> Plain chipware on a plain and creaking wood,
> Tin flatware.

Two who are Mostly Good.
Two who have lived their day,
But keep on putting on their clothes
And putting things away.

And remembering . . .
Remembering, with twinklings and twinges,
As they lean over the beans in their rented back room that
is full of beads, and receipts and dolls and cloths,
tobacco crumbs, vases and fringes.

"The Bean Eaters," 1950

EDITH WHARTON (*American, 1862–1937*)

The world is a welter and has always been one; but though all the cranks
and the theorists cannot master the old floundering monster, or force it for
long into any of their neat plans of readjustment, here and there a saint or a
genius suddenly sends a little ray through the fog, and helps humanity to
stumble on, and perhaps up.

The welter is always there, and the present generation hears close under-
foot the growling of the volcano on which ours danced so long; but in our
individual lives, though the years are sad, the days have a way of being
jubilant. Life is the saddest thing there is, next to death; yet there are always
new countries to see, new books to read (and, I hope, to write), a thousand
little daily wonders to marvel at and rejoice in, and those magical moments
when the mere discovery that "the woodspurge has a cup of three" brings
not despair but delight. The visible world is a daily miracle for those who
have eyes and ears; and I still warm my hands thankfully at the old fire,
though every year it is fed with the dry wood of more old memories.

From *A Backward Glance*, 1934

M. F. K. FISHER (*American, 1908–1992*)

Yesterday I thought about Mr. Ardamanian and the time I let him make love
to me.

I say "make love," but it was not that, exactly. It was quite beyond
maleness and femaleness. It was a strange thing, one I seldom think of, not
because I am ashamed but because it never bothers me. When I do think
back upon it, I am filled with a kind of passive wonder that I should have let
it happen and that it never bothered me, for I am not the kind of woman

who stands still under the hands of an unloved man, nor am I in any way the kind who willy-nilly invites such treatment.

There is a novel by Somerset Maugham in which an actress lets a stranger sleep with her for one night in a train. As I recall it, she never manages to call up any native shame about this queer adventure but instead comes to recollect it with a certain smugness, pleased with her own wild daring. I do not feel smug about Mr. Ardamanian's caresses; until yesterday, I believed myself merely puzzled by their happening, or at least their happening to *me*.

Yesterday, I had to make a long drive alone in the car. It was a hundred miles or so. I was tired before I started, and filled with a bleak solitariness that gradually became self-conscious, so that before I had passed through the first big town and got out into the vineyards again I was, in spite of myself, thinking of my large bones, my greying hair, my occasional deep weariness at being forty years old and harassed as most forty-year-old women are by overwork, too many bills, outmoded clothes. I thought of ordering something extravagant for myself, like a new suit—black, or perhaps even dark red. Then I thought that I had gained some pounds lately, as always when I am a little miserable, and I began to reproach myself: I was turning slothful, I was slumping, I was neglecting my fine femaleness in a martyr-like and indulgent mood of hyperwifeliness, supermotherliness. I was a fool, I said bitterly, despondently, as I sped with caution through another town.

I began to think about myself younger, slimmer, less harried, and less warped by the world's weight. I thought with a kind of tolerant amusement that when I was in my twenties I never noticed my poundage, taking for granted that it was right. Now, I reminded myself as I shot doggedly through the vineyards and then a little town and then the peach orchards near Ontario—now I shuddered, no matter how gluttonously, from every pat of butter, and winced away from every encouraging Martini as if it held snake venom. Still I was fat, and I was tired and old, and when had it happened? Just those few years ago, I had been slender, eager, untwisted by fatigue.

I had been a good woman, too. I had never lusted for any man but the one I loved. That was why it was so strange, the time Mr. Ardamanian came to the house with my rug.

We were living near a college where my husband taught, in a beautiful shack held together by layers of paint. I was alone much of the time, and I buzzed like a happy bee through the three rooms, straightening and polishing them. I was never ill at ease or wistful for company, being young, healthy, and well-loved.

We were very poor, and my mother said, "Jane, why don't you have Mr. Ardamanian take a few of these old rugs of mine and make them into one of his nice hash-rugs for your living room? It wouldn't cost much, and anything he can do for our family he will love to do."

I thought of Mr. Ardamanian, and of the twenty years or so of seeing him come, with great dignity, to roll up this rug and that rug in our house—for my mother had a great many—and then walk down to his car lightly under the balanced load. He knew us all, first me and my little sister, then the two younger siblings, and my grandmother and the various cooks we had, and even Father. He came in and out of the house, and watched us grow, year after year, while he cleaned and mended rugs for us. Mother told us his name was that of a great family in Armenia, and, true enough, every time since then when I have seen it in books or on shopfronts, mostly for rugs, I have known it to be part of his pride.

He was small, very old and grey, it seemed, when I was a little girl. He had a high but quiet voice, deep flashing eyes, and strong, white, even teeth. He called my mother Lady. That always pleased me. He did not say Missus, or even Madam, or Lady So-and-So. He said *Lady*. He dressed in good grey suits, and although he rolled up big rugs and carried them lightly to his car, he was never dusty.

Mother went ahead with her generous plan, and Mr. Ardamanian did come to the little house near the college, bearing upon his old shoulders a fairly handsome hash-rug made of scraps. He stood at the door under the small pink roses that climbed everywhere, and he looked as he had always looked to me over those twenty years.

He bowed, said, "Your lady mother has sent me," and came in.

I felt warm and friendly toward him, this strange familiar from my earliest days, and as the two of us silently laid the good solid rug upon the painted floor, under my sparse furniture, I was pleased to be with him. We finished the moving, and the rug looked fine, very rich and thick, if not what I was used to at home—the big, worn Baluchistans, the glowing Bokharas.

Then—I do not quite remember, but I think it started by his saying, in his rather high, courteous voice, the one I knew over so many years, "You are married now. You look very happy. You look like a woman at last, and you have grown a little here . . . not yet enough here . . ." and he began very delicately, very surely, to touch me on my waist, my shoulder, my small young breasts.

It was, and I know it even now, a wonderful feeling. It was as if he were a sculptor. He had the most fastidiously intelligent hands I had ever met with, and he used them with the instinct of an artist moving over something he understood creatively, something alive, deathless, pulsating with beauty but beyond desire.

I stood, silent and entranced, for I do not know how long, while Mr.

Ardamanian seemed to mold my outlines into classical loveliness. I looked with a kind of adoration at his remote, aged face, and felt his mysteriously knowing hands move, calm as God's, over my body. I was, for those moments of complete easy-breathing silence, as beautiful as any statue ever carved in stone or wood or jade. I was beyond reproach.

I heard my husband come up the path through the mimosa trees. The old man's hands dropped away. I went to the door, unruffled, and I introduced the two men. Then Mr. Ardamanian went gracefully away, and it was not until an hour or so later that I began to remember the strange scene and to wonder what would have happened if he had led me gently to the wide couch and made love to me in the way I, because of my youngness, most easily understood. I felt a vague shame, perhaps, because of my upbringing and my limited spiritual vocabulary, and the whole thing puzzled me in a very minor and peripheral way. There had been no faintest spark of lust between us, no fast urgent breath, no need. . . .

So I found myself thinking of all this yesterday, alone in the car. I felt bitter, seeing myself, toward the end of the tiring trip, as a thickening exhausted lump without desire or desirability. I thought fleetingly of the tall, slim, ripe woman who had stood under those ancient hands.

When I got to my mother's house, I needed quiet and a glass of sherry and reassuring family talk to jolt me out of a voluptuous depression. Mind you, it was not being forty that really puzzled and hurt me; it was simply that I had got that far along without realizing that I could indeed grow thicker and careless, and let myself eat and drink too much, and wear white gloves with a hole in them, and in general become slovenly.

Almost the first thing my mother said was that she was waiting for Mr. Ardamanian. I jerked in my chair. It seemed too strange, to have thought about him that morning for the first time in many years. Suddenly I was very upset, for of all things in the world I did not want that old man who had once found me worth touching to see me tired, mopish, middle-aged. I felt cruelly cheated at this twist and I cried out, "But he can't be alive still! Mother, he must be a hundred years old."

She looked at me with some surprise at my loud protest and said, "Almost. But he is still a good rug man."

I was stunned. It seemed a proof to me of all my dour thoughts during the long ride. Oh, the hell with it, I thought; what can it matter to an old ghost that I'm no longer young and beautiful, if once I was, to his peculiar vision? "That hideous hash-rug fell apart," I said ungraciously, and paid no heed to my mother's enigmatic gaze.

When he came, he did look somewhat older—or, rather, drier—but certainly not fifteen or eighteen years so. His temples had sunk a little, and his bright, even teeth were too big for his mouth, but his dark eyes flashed politely, and he insisted on moving furniture and carrying in the clean rolls of Oriental carpet without any help. He performed neatly, a graceful old body indeed.

"Do not move, Lady," he said to my mother, and he whisked a small rug under her footstool without seeming to lift it. I stood about aimlessly, watching him and thinking about him and myself, in a kind of misery.

At the end, when he had carried the dirty rugs out to his car and had told my mother when he would come back, he looked at me, and then stepped quite close.

"Which one are you?" he asked.

"I'm the oldest," I said, wondering what he would remember of me.

And immediately I saw that it was everything, everything—not of me as a little growing child but of me his creation. His eyes blazed, and fell in an indescribable pattern from my cheeks to my shoulders to my breasts to the hidden cave of my navel, and then up over the bones of my ribs and down again to the softened hollows of my waist! We were back in the silent little house near the college, and I was filled with a sense of complete relaxation, to have this old man still recognize me, and to have him do with his eyes what once he had so strangely and purely done with his hands. I knew that it was something that would never happen again. What is more, I knew that when I was an old woman it would strengthen me, as it strengthened me that very minute when I was tired and forty and thick, that once Mr. Ardamanian had made me into a statue.

The question about seduction still remains, of course, in an academic way. Would he have done any more to me than what he did, and, indeed, would anything more have been possible—not from the standpoint of his indubitable virility, no matter what his age, but from that of our spiritual capacity to pile nectar into the brimming cup? I can never know, nor do I care.

I was filled with relief, standing passively there before my mother in the familiar room. I felt strong and fresh.

He smiled his gleaming smile, bowed to my mother, and then said directly to me, "Lady, it is good that I met you again. Goodbye."

When he had gone, as poised as a praying mantis under his last roll of rugs, my mother said, pretending to be cross, "I thought *I* was his Lady, not you!" She smiled remotely.

Mother and I talked together through the afternoon, about children and bills and such, but not about Mr. Ardamanian. There seemed no need to, then or ever.

"Answer in the Affirmative," 1983

YEHUDA AMICHAI (*Israeli, b. 1924*)

> I'm standing in a place where I once loved.
> The rain is falling. The rain is my home.
>
> I think words of longing: a landscape
> out to the very edge of what's possible.
>
> I remember you waving your hand
> as if wiping mist from the windowpane,
>
> and your face, as if enlarged
> from an old blurred photo.
>
> Once I committed a terrible wrong
> to myself and others.
>
> But the world is beautifully made for doing good
> and for resting, like a park bench.
>
> And late in life I discovered
> a quiet joy
> like a serious disease that's discovered too late:
>
> just a little time left now for quiet joy.

"A Quiet Joy," 1976

KENNETH REXROTH (*American, 1905–1982*)

> The maple leaves are brilliant
> Over the tree lined streets.
> The deep shade is filled
> With soft ruddy light.
> Soon the leaves will all have fallen.
> The pale winter sunlight
> Will gleam on snow covered lawns.
> Here we were young together
> And loved each other
> Wise beyond our years
> Two lifetimes have gone by.
> Only us two are left from those days.
> All the others have gone with the years.
> We have never seen each other since.
> This is the first time I have come back.
> I drive slowly past your home,

Around the block again and once again.
Beyond the deep pillared porch
Someone is sitting at the window.
I drive down by the river
And watch a boy fishing from the bridge
In the clear water amongst
Falling and floating leaves.
And then I drive West into the smoky sunset.

"Red Maple Leaves," 1974

BERTRAND RUSSELL (English, 1872–1970)

There are both advantages and disadvantages in being very old. The disadvantages are obvious and uninteresting, and I shall say little about them. The advantages seem to me more interesting. A long retrospect gives weight and substance to experience. I have been able to follow many lives, both of friends and of public characters, from an early stage to their conclusion. Some, who were promising in youth, have achieved little of value; others have continued to develop from strength to strength through long lives of important achievement. Undoubtedly, experience makes it easier to guess to which of these two kinds a young person is likely to belong. It is not only the lives of individuals, but the lives of movements that come, with time, to form part of personal experience and to facilitate estimates of probable success or failure. Communism, in spite of a very difficult beginning, has hitherto continued to increase in power and influence. Nazism, on the contrary, by snatching too early and too ruthlessly at dominion, came to grief. To have watched such diverse processes helps to give an insight into the past of history and should help in guessing at the probable future.

To come to more personal matters: It is natural for those who are energetic and adventurous to feel in youth a very passionate and restless desire for some important achievement, without any clear prevision of what, with luck, it may be. In old age, one becomes more aware of what has, and what has not, been achieved. What one can further do becomes a smaller proportion of what has already been done, and this makes personal life less feverish.

It is a curious sensation to read the journalistic clichés which come to be fastened on past periods that one remembers, such as the "naughty nineties" and the "riotous twenties." Those decades did not seem, at the time, at all "naughty" or "riotous." The habit of affixing easy labels is convenient to those who wish to seem clever without having to think, but it has very little relation to reality. The world is always changing, but not in the simple ways that such convenient clichés suggest. Old age, as I am experiencing it, could be a time of very complete happiness if one could forget the state of the world. Privately, I enjoy everything that could make life delightful. I used to think that when I reached old age I would retire from the world and live a life of elegant culture, reading all the great books that I ought to have read at an earlier date. Perhaps it was, in any case, an idle dream. A long habit of work with some purpose that one believes important is difficult to break, and I might have found elegant leisure boring even if the world had been in a better state. However that might have been, I find it impossible to ignore what is happening.

Ever since 1914, at almost every crucial moment, the wrong thing has been done. We are told that the West is engaged in defending the "Free World," but freedom such as existed before 1914 is now as dim a memory as crinolines. Supposedly wise men assured us in 1914 that we were fighting a war, to end war, but it turned out to be a war to end peace. We were told that Prussian militarism was all that had to be put down; and, ever since, militarism has continually increased. Murderous humbug, such as would have shocked almost everyone when I was young, is now solemnly mouthed by eminent statesmen. My own country, led by men without imagination and without capacity for adaptation to the modern world, pursues a policy which, if not changed, will lead almost inevitably to the complete extermination of all the inhabitants of Britain. Like Cassandra, I am doomed to prophesy evil and not be believed. Her prophecies came true. I desperately hope that mine will not.

Sometimes one is tempted to take refuge in cheerful fantasies and to imagine that perhaps in Mars or Venus happier and saner forms of life exist, but our frantic skill is making this a vain dream. Before long, if we do not destroy ourselves, our destructive strife will have spread to those planets. Perhaps, for their sake, one ought to hope that war on earth will put an end to our species before its folly has become cosmic. But this is not a hope in which I can find any comfort.

The way in which the world has developed during the last fifty years has brought about in me changes opposite to those which are supposed to be typical of old age. One is frequently assured by men who have no doubt of their own wisdom that old age should bring serenity and a larger vision in which seeming evils are viewed as means to ultimate good. I cannot accept any such view. Serenity, in the present world, can only be achieved through blindness or brutality. Unlike what is conventionally expected, I become gradually more and more of a rebel. I was not born rebellious. Until 1914, I fitted more or less comfortably into the world as I found it. There were evils—great evils—but there was reason to think that they would grow less. Without having the temperament of a rebel, the course of events has made me gradually less and less able to acquiesce patiently in what is happening. A minority, though a growing one, feels as I do, and, so long as I live, it is with them that I must work.

"Pros and Cons of Reaching Ninety," 1962

ARNOLD TOYNBEE *(English, 1899–1975)*

I am now seventy-five. Half my contemporaries at school and at the university were killed before they had turned twenty-seven. Ever since 1915 I have been surprised at being still alive, and rueful that my friends whose lives were then cut short have been deprived of the opportunity that I have had. In my seventy-fifth year I delivered to the Oxford University Press the manuscript of a book, *Hannibal's Legacy,* which I had been contemplating since I had lectured on the subject for the Literae Humaniores School at Oxford in 1913–14. I did not get down to working on this book till 1957. An historian needs time—more time than seems to be needed by poets and mathematicians. . . .

Every human being is a Janus. 'We look before and after.' When one is young, it is easy to look forward; one has not yet accumulated much of a past to draw one toward the backward-looking view. As one grows older, the temptation to dwell on the past and to avert one's eyes from the future grows. This tendency is well known, and it has to be resisted. If one were to fall into this backward-looking stance, one would be as good (I mean as bad) as dead before physical death had overtaken one. Lord Russell is reported to have said, when he was already far on in his eighties, that it is important to care immensely about things that are going to happen after one is dead. All ageing people ought to make this saying their own, and to act on it, as Lord Russell has done. Our minds, so long as they keep their cutting edge, are not bound by our physical limits; they can range over time and space into infinity. To be human is to be capable of transcending oneself. Compared to the range of the mind, the longest lifetime is brief. One can accomplish very little in one lifetime, even if one's life is not cut short. Anything that an individual does accomplish has meaning and value only in the larger context of society and history in which the individual plays his tiny part.

As I was born in 1889 and am still alive in 1964, I have lived to see what looks like a transition from one age of world history to another. I grew up during the later years of the forty-three years of peace in Europe that had begun in 1871. I never dreamed that this state of peace was not permanent until I was overtaken by August 1914; and on armistice day 1918 I never dreamed that I should live to see a second world war in my lifetime. I grew up in an age of stability and security for the middle class in Britain. One's family might have very little money; but, if one was moderately able, hard-working, and well-behaved, one could count on having a satisfying middle-class career. At my college in Oxford, Balliol, before 1914, any freshman who had no clear idea of what he wanted to do after he went down was put down for the Indian Civil Service by the dons as a matter of routine. An I.C.S. career was assured to any Balliol man who could not do better than that. And the contract that a successful candidate for the I.C.S. concluded with the Government of India gave the new recruit security for the rest of his life.

The mental world in which I was brought up was equally stable. It was still the mental world of the Italian Renaissance. The Greek and Latin classics become one's spiritual home; and on me, at any rate, this had the curious effect of partly detaching me from the living Western World into which I had been born. I came to look on this modern Western World with alien and unadmiring eyes. History, for me, was Greek and Roman history; mediaeval and modern history were an irrelevant and rather impertinent epilogue appended to history proper by the North European barbarians. This epilogue was not even in the main line of succession. It was a sideline. The main line had run on from the Roman Empire through the Byzantine Empire and the Ottoman Empire to the present-day Near and Middle East. This is a region of the present-day world that was alive for me. The Turkish revolution of 1908 interested me so much that it turned me into the regular reader of *The Times* that I still am today.

My spiritual home in the Graeco-Roman World has, as things have turned out, been of great practical help to me. It has been a haven of stability in the midst of a welter of change. In the living world into which I have been born, a placid phase of history has been swept away by a turbulent phase within my lifetime, but my footing in my Classical World has moderated for me the shock of this violent transition. In the barbarians' postscript to history, one paragraph has been followed by another. But history itself—that is, Greek and Roman history—still remains what it always has been.

The drawbacks of a classical education in the modern age are obvious. A traditional concentration on the Greek and Latin classics prevented me from making myself at home in the marvellous physical universe that had been opened up to view by the progress of physical science during the three centuries before the time at which I was at school. Science, and the higher mathematics that are the key to science, have remained a closed book to me. There is no adequate compensation for this loss in the faculty that I have acquired, from my drilling in Latin and Greek composition, of expressing my feelings in Greek or Latin verse when something moves me. I have never been able to write poetry in my vernacular mother-tongue; and this consequence of having taken a classical education seriously is a quaint one.

On the other side of the account, however, my classical education has given me two benefits which, to my mind, are of inestimable value. It has given me a mental standing-ground outside the time and place into which I happen to have been born; and this has saved me from over-estimating the importance of the modern Western civilization. While I do care—and care very much—about the future of the present-day world, 'my' world, in the sense of the world in which I have the greatest intellectual and emotional stake, is not this present-day Western-style one. It is the Aegean and Mediterranean World of two thousand years and more ago—of, say, Polybius's time (he lived from about 208 to about 128 B.C.). The second great benefit that I have gained from my classical education is a life-long conviction that human affairs do not become intelligible until they are seen as a whole, and a consequent life-long effort that I have made to arrive at a comprehensive view of human affairs. By the time when I was being educated, Western scholars were already shredding the seamless web of human affairs into morsels that were as minute as they were numerous, and they were examining each of these morsels under the microscope as if each of them were a self-contained universe instead of being, as it was, an inseparable part of a larger whole. I am thankful that my old-fashioned classical education saved me from being instructed in human affairs in this nineteenth-century German way. The fifteenth-century Italian way seems to me to be a much better one, because it seems to me to give a vision of human affairs that is much truer to life. The humanist student of the Classics is taught to see Graeco-Roman life as a unity. In his eyes, the languages, literature, visual arts, religion, politics, economics, and history of his Classical World are not so many separate 'subjects,' insulated from each other in thought-tight compartments; they are facets of a unitary way of life, and neither this nor they can be seen properly unless the parts are seen synoptically as contributions to the whole.

*   *   *

For my aim was to expand my horizon and my field up to the limits of my capacity. . . .

> I was running a race with the Reaper.
> I hastened; he lingered; I won.
> Now strike, Death! You sluggard, you sleeper,
> You cannot undo what I've done.

From "Janus at Seventy-Five (14 April 1964)," in *Experiences*, 1969

JANE ADDAMS *(American, 1860–1935)*

That neglected and forlorn old age is daily brought to the attention of a Settlement which undertakes to bear its share of the neighborhood burden imposed by poverty, was pathetically clear to us during our first months of residence at Hull-House. One day a boy of ten led a tottering old lady into the House, saying that she had slept for six weeks in their kitchen on a bed made up next to the stove; that she had come when her son died, although none of them had ever seen her before; but because her son had "once worked in the same shop with Pa she thought of him when she had nowhere to go." The little fellow concluded by saying that our house was so much bigger than theirs that he thought we would have more room for beds. The old woman herself said absolutely nothing, but looking on with that gripping fear of the poorhouse in her eyes, she was a living embodiment of that dread which is so heart-breaking that the occupants of the County Infirmary themselves seem scarcely less wretched than those who are making their last stand against it.

This look was almost more than I could bear for only a few days before some frightened women had bidden me come quickly to the house of an old German woman, whom two men from the county agent's office were attempting to remove to the County Infirmary. The poor old creature had thrown herself bodily upon a small and battered chest of drawers and clung there, clutching it so firmly that it would have been impossible to remove her without also taking the piece of furniture. She did not weep nor moan nor indeed make any human sound, but between her broken gasps for breath she squealed shrilly like a frightened animal caught in a trap. The little group of women and children gathered at her door stood aghast at this realization of the black dread which always clouds the lives of the very poor when work is slack, but which constantly grows more imminent and threatening as old age approaches. The neighborhood women and I hastened to make all sorts of promises as to the support of the old woman and the county officials, only too glad to be rid of their unhappy duty, left her to our ministrations. This dread of the poorhouse, the result of centuries of deterrent Poor Law administration, seemed to me not without some justification one summer when I found myself perpetually distressed by the unnecessary idleness and forlornness of the old women in the Cook County Infirmary, many of whom I had known in the years when activity was still a necessity, and when they yet felt bustlingly important. To take away from an old woman whose life has been spent in household cares all the foolish little belongings to which her affections cling and to which her very fingers have become accustomed, is to take away her last incentive to activity, almost to life itself. To give an old woman only a chair and a bed, to leave her no cupboard in which her treasures may be stowed, not only that she may take them out when she desires occupation, but that her mind may dwell upon them in moments of revery, is to reduce living almost beyond the limit of human endurance.

The poor creature who clung so desperately to her chest of drawers was really clinging to the last remnant of normal living—a symbol of all she was asked to renounce. For several years after this summer I invited five or six old women to take a two weeks' vacation from the poorhouse which they eagerly and even gayly accepted. Almost all the old men in the County Infirmary wander away each summer taking their chances for finding food or shelter and return much refreshed by the little "tramp," but the old women cannot do this unless they have some help from the outside, and yet the expenditure of a very little money secures for them the coveted vacation. I found that a few pennies paid their car fare into town, a dollar a week procured a lodging with an old acquaintance; assured of two good meals a day in the Hull-House coffeehouse they could count upon numerous cups of tea among old friends to whom they would airily state that they had "come out for a little change" and hadn't yet made up their minds about "going in again for the winter." They thus enjoyed a two weeks' vacation to the top of their bent and returned with wondrous tales of their adventures, with which they regaled the other paupers during the long winter.

The reminiscences of these old women, their shrewd comments upon life, their sense of having reached a point where they may at last speak freely with nothing to lose because of their frankness, makes them often the most delightful of companions. I recall one of my guests, the mother of many scattered children, whose one bright spot through all the dreary years had been the wedding feast of her son Mike,—a feast which had become transformed through long meditation into the nectar and ambrosia of the very gods. As a farewell fling before she went "in" again, we dined together upon chicken pie, but it did not taste like "the chicken pie at Mike's wedding" and she was disappointed after all.

Even death itself sometimes fails to bring the dignity and serenity which one would fain associate with old age. I recall the dying hour of one old Scotchwoman whose long struggle to "keep respectable" had so embittered her, that her last words were gibes and taunts for those who were trying to minister to her. "So you came in yourself this morning, did you? You only sent things yesterday. I guess you knew when the doctor was coming. Don't try to warm my feet with anything but that old jacket that I've got there; it belonged to my boy who was drowned at sea nigh thirty years ago, but it's warmer yet with human feelings than any of your damned charity hot-water bottles." Suddenly the harsh gasping voice was stilled in death and I awaited the doctor's coming shaken and horrified.

The lack of municipal regulation already referred to was, in the early days of Hull-House, paralleled by the inadequacy of the charitable efforts of the city and an unfounded optimism that there was no real poverty among us. Twenty years ago there was no Charity Organization Society in Chicago and the Visiting Nurse Association had not yet begun its beneficent work, while the relief societies, although conscientiously administered, were inadequate in extent and antiquated in method.

As social reformers gave themselves over to discussion of general principles, so the poor invariably accused poverty itself of their destruction. I recall a certain Mrs. Moran, who was returning one rainy day from the office of the county agent with her arms full of paper bags containing beans and flour which alone lay between her children and starvation. Although she had no money she boarded a street car in order to save her booty from complete destruction by the rain, and as the burst bags dropped "flour on the ladies' dresses" and "beans all over the place," she was sharply reprimanded by the conductor, who was further exasperated when he discovered she had no fare. He put her off, as she had hoped he would, almost in front of Hull-House. She related to us her state of mind as she stepped off the car and saw the last of her wares disappearing; she admitted she forgot the proprieties and "cursed a little," but, curiously enough, she pronounced her malediction, not against the rain nor the conductor, nor yet against the worthless husband who had been sent up to the city prison, but, true to the Chicago spirit of the moment, went to the root of the matter and roundly "cursed poverty."

From *Forty Years at Hull-House*, 1910

GUS ALEXANDER (*American, 1864–?*)

"I wus born in Texas one year befo' DE WAR closed. My mother wuz a slave in de cotton fiel's. My daddy wuzn't no good—wouldn't work. Dey use' to say my mother use' to pick half of his cotton rows so's he'd keep up with de other pickers. If he lagged, de driver would take a blacksnake to him. My mother die' when I wuz five months ole. It wuz always hard to keep a record on cullud chilluns' births. Dey'd say, 'Oh, you wuz born during watermelon time'—or, 'You wuz born durin' cotton pickin' time.'

"My mother's brother left where we live' when I wuz five months ole. He didn' see me no mo' 'til I wuz fifteen. I walked up to his cabin one mawnin' befo' breakfast—he wuz jes' settin' down to his breakfas', an' I walk up to his door. I wuz barefooted an' very low—I had walked miles an' miles an' wuz hungry. He hadn' seen me in nearly fifteen years, an' he said, 'Why, it's Charlotte's chile!' I felt mighty good to know he remember' me from a little baby, me bein' a orphan chile without no people much. Well, he set me down to breakfast with him and tell me lots of things about my mother.

"About de fust thing I remembers, I wuz eight-year-old. My uncle by marriage, he wuz so hard on me dat I get up one mawnin' an' take a oath to myself. I say to myself, 'De res' of de worl' can't be no harder on me den he is; so I'm gonna go 'way.'

"So there I wuz on my own 'sponsibility when I eight years ole. My daddy die in de penitentiary; so I decided to go work on de prison farm to see whut it wuz like. I wuz a hand on de prison farm to see how it wuz two different times. I decided I'd always be a law-abidin' citizen 'cause I sho didn't want to be in de pen.

"In my wanderin's I got up in Kansas. I work' on a farm for a white man fo' $3.00 a month. De good lady, dat man's wife, she save all my money for me. I bring all my money to her and she put it up for me. Den on Sat'days, I shine' shoes in town. I work' there till I have $60.00 saved up.

"My uncle fin' me an' say he gonna take me back with him. But I got away an' come back to Texas with a doctor. I wuz fifteen den, and I got to be this doctor's driver. He use' to git drunk an' git in fights. When I see him gittin' into trouble, I use' to go ketch him by de han' an' say, 'Come on. Le's go home.' He'd follow me jes' like a little chile. He use' to tell all de white folks, 'I don't care for you givin' Gus things. Give him anything you wants to; but if one of you gives him whiskey, I'll kill ye.'

"Yas'm, I have a wife. We live' together for twenty-some years. Have a boy name' Gus. Little Gus didn' have ever'thing dat wuz comin' to him. He never wuz bright, never could talk, an' he never did grow up. He live' to be twenty-two.

"My wife die' when Gus wuz jes' past twenty-one. She say to me befo' she die', 'You take care o' little Gus. Stay clost to him, but it won' be long 'cause mama or me one'll come back an' git him.' I don' pay no 'tention to her 'cause I don' b'lieve in sperrits. One night Little Gus and me went to bed jes' as usual. Nex mawnin' I look over at him, an' de little fellow wuz dead. My wife wuz right I guess.

"I learn' dat chillun an' young folks who min' de ole ones always makes good citizens. I always have been a law abidin' man, never been in jail nor in trouble. I respec' ever'body an' myself, too. Until I los' my health I never ask' help frum nobody. Now in my ole age—you know, it jes' seems like I can't git my breath—well, in my ole age, all de white folks dat I use' to work for, dey come see me. Dey tell dese cullud neighbors, 'You look after Gus—we pay you for it.'

"My wife's mother, she wuz a slave—she use' to tell us all sorts of stories about de 'paterols'. She say de cullud folks use' to slip out an' go to dances. If de 'paterols' come during de dance an' try to see if dey wuz any negroes dey knowed at de dance, de cullud folks use' to all slip out in de dark an' hide 'til de 'paterols' git tired an' leave. Ole auntie she say dat if dey come in de winter when de wuz a fire in de fireplace, she would pick up a burnin' stick an' fling coals and ashes all over ever'thing. Dat would stir up such a rookus dat de cullud folks could git out an' git hid.

"I'm ole an' can't work much no mo'—I los' all my teeth, an' my breath come so hard, too. It seem like if I could jes' git my breath, I'd be just as good as I use' to be. But I'm proud dat growin' up a orphan waif, my daddy in de pen an' my mother dead, I always git along with white folks and cullud folks too. I aint got a enemy—ever'body I know is my frien'. An' dey's white folks even dat can't say dat."

Narrative written in 1937, in *The American Slave: A Composite Autobiography*, 1979

AGNES VANDERBURG *(Native American/Flathead, 1901–1989)*

Well, when I grew up, things were different. In my time there was a lot of berries, a lot of game, fish, everything. But now everything is gone—the roots, the berries. That is what I see: they don't grow no more. The reason why is because when they are ripe, nobody prays when they grab the berries to put 'em in their mouth; they just go in there and eat off the bushes. It's the same with the roots. The oldtimers believed they had to pray for everything before they tasted it. But now, they don't believe in anything anymore. I tell my kids: I'm getting there, this February fourteenth I'll be seventy-nine; so I know a little bit about what's behind me. So I tell them: do what I was taught; then when I've gone, you'll know whatever I knew. But now you believe in the other way, you don't believe in our Indian ways.

* * *

Now, I'm trying to teach people what I know about the old ways of doing things. I teach some at St. Ignatius, beading and quill work, like that. I see kids aren't interested in school. That's the reason why what they're doing is mostly in their heads. You see on TV what's going on. That's the way a lot of them learn how to do these bad things; they even show on TV how to steal a car, how to break into a house. They show you how to open the locks, how to open windows, how to destroy cars. That's what I don't like. That's where they learn all these bad things. They don't care to learn the good way from their teacher.

* * *

Even the language is gone. Just to be funny, I start talking Indian to these kids and they look at me and say, "I don't know what you're saying." They're starting in now teaching it again in the school here. But they call and ask me what this word means. I say: You're supposed to be teachers! You got to pay me five dollars for every word. They owe me a lot of money now! [laughs]

Sometimes I show 'em how to make the sign language—you see,

Indians, they can't keep their hands still; when they talk, their hands are going. That's part of the talking. People can understand the movements. [She demonstrates] "You are talking: I hear you: what?" You see, you can pretty nearly understand just by the movements.

When I was growing up, everyone was talking Indian. So when I went to school at the Agency, it was okay to talk Indian there. But first thing I knew we had to go to St. Ignatius and there was nothing but English. Then when we'd get together and start talking Indian, we'd sure get scolded for that; they didn't want us to talk Indian. We got scared to talk. That's why a lot of Indians stopped talking their own language.

I've visited different tribes and it's the same; they just wanted to talk their own language. But all the tribes are different. The Nez Perce, for instance; you can't understand them. And the Kootenai—they talk fast. Even between here and St. Ignatius there's different words. So when the oldtimers get together we talk with sign language. We say: What kind of Indian are you? This is the way; we go like that [she shows a movement of right hand raised, then touching the back of the left hand].

Then there's what my grandparents said: When all Indians start talking one language, then you better watch it: the world's going to end. And I believe it, because they are all talking English now. But the old language is coming back slow—so they might stop it, if they try.

*   *   *

There's a place the other side of Hamilton where we've got a medicine tree. This tribe used to believe in that tree. Every fall and every spring they'd go over there. They went over there to give that tree a present. Whatever they wish for they tell that tree. You know the story? Well, they say that once a great big mountain sheep was chasing Coyote, and Coyote, he was running for his life, and he came to this tree and got behind it. The sheep charged right into the tree and rammed one of his horns in the tree and got stuck there. So Coyote said: Now this tree will be the medicine tree, and whoever comes to pray to this tree, he got to give it a payment and he can ask for anything he wants.

Just about a month ago I took some people over there. I told them: Don't just come here and laugh; you got to pay this tree. Whatever you want to be, anything you want, you tell him, but you got to pay this tree. This tree had a lot of these coins that people had stuck into it, old money, and later people came and cut into the tree so there was a bunch of holes. You could tell where there used to be a dollar, a fifty-cent piece, or a quarter—it was just like a woodpecker had been chipping on that bark. One man, oh, he was mad; he says: Why didn't I know when I was young? I said: 'Cause you didn't care! What your old grandmother knew, you didn't care to know.

Last year and this year I took some people there. But our tree is dying

377

from the top. They're saying it's on account of everybody taking things out of the tree. There's just a bunch of holes in the trunk, where people have taken the money out, because it's old money, old coins.

*　　*　　*

We still got the medicine tree, but there are no medicine men anymore. In their time, they didn't have doctors; it was the spirit that came to them that cured all different sicknesses. There was one old man that cured even for babies. That's all they depended on, was the medicine men. But now if they tried to have medicine men, they would just try to go on what they heard about the way it was. But there aren't any, anymore. The old grandmothers used to say it's because we're living in a box—that means, in a house; and in those days, they were staying in tepees, so their spirit could come to them. But not the way we live now. That's why we are not strong like the old ancestors.

From "Coming Back Slow," 1980

WANG SHIH-MIN (*Chinese, 1592–1680*)

In my youth I made a solemn resolution to uphold myself, discarding completely all the luxuries and frivolities that often corrupted young members of prominent families, thus extricating myself from the pervading worldliness and decadence. Alas, little did I expect that a prominent family would frequently incur resentment and that a brotherless man would stumble easily. I wasted months and years in timidity and vigilance, while my means were exhausted in meeting social obligations. Therefore I failed to match the glories of my forefathers by mastering one canonical classic, nor did I achieve fame and excel among my contemporaries through the practice of one art.

Now the setting sun approaches the hills, and the traveler is near the end of the road. I have not, like Hsiang P'ing [a first-century hermit], gained the freedom to roam the world, nor can I be certain that I may be granted a few more years to live—the same wish that Confucius had. I gathered all my sons and exhorted them to maintain a fraternal solidarity, lest they be vanquished one by one. It was difficult not to grieve at the death of my wife. Sorrows congest deeply in my chest, but to few of my numerous friends could I unburden myself, nor can I talk plainly with many of my relatives.

However, when I look back, I have never in all my life transgressed Confucian morality. From childhood to youth I was day and night in the company of my grandfather, so I witnessed the way he comported himself. Surrounded by his friends or family, he would sit in front of the stove, trimming the wick of the candle while discussing the classics and calligraphy, going over some historical facts, or lamenting current affairs. There was never a word about advancement, fame, or business. What I constantly saw and heard permeated my heart and mind. Consequently throughout my life I have always found serenity in being generous and loyal, have judged myself sternly in terms of purity and integrity, and have behaved as if I could never be sufficiently discreet, respectful, and yielding. Only by having done all the above did I escape the faults of superficiality and grossness. But if one places survival above honor and shamefully seeks safety at any cost, his would be merely the cautious conduct of women and children, nothing to be proud of.

I have just made a summary of my life to be kept in the family temple, whereby my descendants in future generations will be acquainted with an outline of my life history. Through the document they will trace everything back to the family instructions of my father and grandfather. They must strive to emulate former ways and do nothing to diminish the fame of the family. Perhaps someday they will restore the glory of the family by having several members simultaneously serving the government in high offices.

"Tzu-Shu (Self-Account): Conclusion," seventeenth century

ANONYMOUS (*American, nineteenth century*)

The busy day of life is over. Its pleasures, its duties, and its anxieties have passed away. The sunshine and the shade, which alternately marked its path, have alike disappeared; and the soft tints of evening are gathered over the sky.

The evening of life! Yes: life has its sunset hour, its twilight season. The dim eye, the silvered lock, and the feeble step indicate that the closing period of earthly existence has arrived. How rapid has been the flight of time! How near must be the approach of eternity!

*   *   *

. . . And life's closing hours, Christian reader, should be distinguished by serenity and repose. You must not harass and perplex yourself now with occupations which were once both appropriate and necessary, nor repine because you are unable to exert yourself as in former days. Your strength is to sit still. Old age is the resting-place in the journey of life; and the feverish heat of noontide is exchanged for the refreshing coolness of twilight.

*   *   *

The evening of life! Evening is the time for reflection. Amidst the busy and exciting occupations of the day there is seldom much opportunity for serious consideration. Well-disciplined minds, it is true, can control their thoughts, and gather them around high and holy subjects, even in those moments which are necessarily devoted to worldly business; but most persons are so harassed and engrossed by the constant claims upon their time and attention as scarcely to be able to cast a hurried glance on things which are unseen and remote; and they feel how welcome and how desirable is the evening hour for quiet meditation, for self-examination, and for the formation of wise and good purposes.

*   *   *

Retrospection! "Thou shalt remember all the way which the Lord thy God led thee these forty years in the wilderness." Old age is the most appropriate season for this consideration of the past. The judgment is not so likely to be warped by the heat of excitement, nor the feelings to be swayed by the influence of passion, as in youthful days. The veteran, as he recalls the battle-field, can mark events and form opinions far more advantageously than the soldier who is engaged in the midst of an action. Contemplate, then, your whole life from the dawn of infancy to its present decline; trace out the many windings of your pathway through the world; survey each minute feature of your changeful history.

But is it pleasant to look back? Are there not many places in our pilgrimage where memory dislikes to linger? Are there not many facts in life's early records which we feel happier in forgetting? True, the remembrance of our imperfections and our sins is painful and self-condemning; yet it is always best to open one's eyes to the truth. Enter, then, into a full and faithful examination of your past history. Scrutinize your motives by the tests with which God's word furnishes you; and try your conduct by his holy law. Let neither pride nor prejudice hide the real state of things from your view. How important is it that, on the confines of eternity, you should be kept from self-deception! Ask God himself to be your teacher. Make this your prayer: "Search me, O God, and know my heart: try me, and know my thoughts: and see if there be any wicked way in me, and lead me in the way everlasting."

What, then, is the result of your investigation? What verdict does conscience, enlightened from above, give concerning the past? It may be, nay, it must be, that you find enough in your recollections to overwhelm you with sorrow and confusion. So much selfishness and worldliness have mingled with your brightest deeds; so much unfaithfulness has been connected with your professed allegiance to Christ; so much impurity of heart and defilement of life are discovered by your rigid self-inspection, that you are ready to exclaim with the Psalmist, "Enter not into judgment with thy servant, O Lord: for in thy sight shall no man living be justified." Or perhaps your reflections on the past have convinced you that you have hitherto been living without God and without Christ in the world; that you have been so absorbed with the trifles of earth as to have forgotten the attractions of heaven; that, although a responsible being, and liable to be summoned at any moment to your final account, you have gone carelessly on in the ways of sin, and have disobeyed the commands of the Most High.

The retrospect in either case is *humbling*. Yet it leads to hope, and peace, and salvation. Both to the troubled Christian and the penitent sinner the cheering annunciation of the gospel is, "The blood of Jesus Christ cleanseth us from all sin." "Believe on the Lord Jesus Christ, and thou shalt be saved." Then, "though your sins be as scarlet, they shall be as white as snow; though they be red like crimson, they shall be as wool." "Come unto me, all ye that labour and are heavy laden, and I will give you rest." Full and free forgiveness is offered to all who seek it at his cross. Cast yourself with all your sins, however great their number or aggravated their guilt, at the Saviour's feet, saying, "Lord, save me: I perish!" and his gracious response will be, "Thy sins are forgiven;—go in peace."

*   *   *

Anticipation! Looking back should be combined with looking forward. The weary pilgrim, who recalls with mingled sorrow and gladness the events which have occurred during his journey, will also think of the rest and the welcome which wait for him in his happy home. The Christian traveller, as evening is closing in around him, and the objects of earth are fading from his gaze, loves to let his imagination dwell upon the many mansions in his Father's house, where a place is being prepared for him.

From "The Review of Life," in *Nearing Home,* 1868

ROBERT N. BUTLER *(American, b. 1927)*

. . . I conceive of the life review as a naturally occurring, universal mental process characterized by the progressive return to consciousness of past experiences, and, particularly, the resurgence of unresolved conflicts; simultaneously, and normally, these revived experiences and conflicts can be surveyed and reintegrated. Presumably, this process is prompted by the realization of approaching dissolution and death, and the inability to maintain one's sense of personal invulnerability. It is further shaped by contemporaneous experiences and its nature and outcome are affected by the life-long unfolding of character.

*   *   *

The significance of death is often inappropriately minimized by psychiatric writers, reflecting the universal tendency to deny its reality; it is also sidestepped by some writers through the use of such psychoanalytic constructs as castration anxiety, which has been held to be the basic fear. Fear of death is often conceptualized as merely manifest and not authentic.

The relation of the life-review process to thoughts of death is reflected in the fact that it occurs not only in the elderly but also in younger persons who expect death—for example, the fatally ill or the condemned. It may also be seen in the introspection of those preoccupied by death, and it is commonly held that one's life passes in review in the process of dying. One thinks of the matador's "moment of truth" during the *faena*. The life review, Janus-like, involves facing death as well as looking back. Lot's wife, in the Bible, and Orpheus, in Greek mythology, embodied an association of the ideas of looking death in the face and looking back.

But the life review is more commonly observed in the aged because of the actual nearness of life's termination, and perhaps also because during retirement not only is time available for self-reflection, but also the customary defensive operation provided by work has been removed.

In extreme cases, severe consequences of the life review seem to be quantitatively related to the extent of actual or psychological isolation. The writings of Cannon, Richter, Adland, Will, and others, suggest a relationship between isolation, or loneliness, and death. "The feeling of unrelatedness is incompatible with life in the human being," writes Will.

Reviewing one's life, then, may be a general response to crises of various types, of which imminent death seems to be one instance. It is also likely that the degree to which approaching death is seen as a crisis varies as a function of individual personality. The explicit hypothesis intended here, however, is that the biological fact of approaching death, independent of—although possibly reinforced by—personal and environmental circumstances prompts the life review.

From "The Life Review: An Interpretation of Reminiscence in the Aged," 1963

BARBARA G. MYERHOFF (*American, 1935–1985*)

Memory is a continuum ranging from vague, dim shadows to the brightest, most vivid totality. It may offer opportunity not merely to recall the past but to relive it, in all its original freshness, unaltered by intervening changes and reflections. Such magical Proustian moments are pinpoints of the greatest intensity, when a sense of the past never being truly lost is experienced. The diffuseness of life is then transcended, the sense of duration overcome, and all of one's self and one's memories are felt to be universally valid. Simultaneity replaces sequence and a sense of oneness with one's past is achieved. Often such moments involve childhood memories, and then one experiences the self as it was originally, and knows beyond doubt that one is the same person as that child who still dwells within a time-altered body. Integration through memory with earlier states of being surely provides the sense of continuity and completeness that may be counted as an essential developmental task of old age.

Freud has suggested that the completion of the mourning process requires that those left behind develop a new reality which no longer includes what has been lost. But it must also be said that full recovery from mourning may restore what has been lost, maintaining it through incorporation into the present. Full recollection and retention may be as vital to recovery and well-being as the forfeiture of memories.

Victor Turner has used the term "Re-membering," bracketing it by the hyphen to distinguish it from ordinary recollection. Re-membering, he offers, is the reaggregation of one's members, the figures who properly belong to one's life story, one's own prior selves, the significant others without which the story cannot be completed. Re-membering, then, is a purposive, significant unification, different from the passive, continuous, fragmentary flickerings of images and feelings that accompany other activities in the normal flow of consciousness. The focused unification provided by Re-membering is requisite to sense and order. Through it, a life is given shape that extends back in the past and forward into the future, a simplified, edited tale where completeness may be sacrificed for moral and aesthetic purposes. Then history approaches art, myth, and ritual. Perhaps this is why Mnemosyne, the goddess of memory, is the mother of the Muses. Without Re-membering we lose our history and ourselves.

From "Re-membered Lives," 1980

ALOIS ALZHEIMER (*German, 1864–1915*)

Alzheimer reports the case of a patient who was kept under close observation during institutionalization in Frankfurt am Main and whose central nervous system was examined by Director Sioli.

The patient showed early clinical symptoms which deviated from the common ones and could not be classified under any well-known clinical patterns. The anatomical findings were also different from those of the usual disease processes.

One of the first disease symptoms of a 51-year-old woman was a strong feeling of jealousy towards her husband. Very soon she showed rapidly increasing memory impairments; she could not find her way about her home, she dragged objects to and fro, hid herself, or sometimes thought that people were out to kill her, then she would start to scream loudly.

During institutionalization her gestures showed a complete helplessness. She was disoriented as to time and place. From time to time she would state that she did not understand anything, that she felt confused and totally lost.

Sometimes she considered the coming of the doctor as an official visit and apologized for not having finished her work, but other times she would start to yell in the fear that the doctor wanted to operate on her; or there were times that she would send him away in complete indignation, uttering phrases that indicated her fear that the doctor wanted to damage her woman's honour. From time to time she was completely delirious, dragging her blankets and sheets to and fro, calling for her husband and daughter, and seeming to have auditory hallucinations. Often she would scream for hours and hours in a horrible voice.

As she was unable to understand any particular situation, she got upset any time a doctor wanted to examine her. Only after several efforts was it possible to obtain any data.

She suffered from serious perception disorders. When the doctor showed her some objects she first gave the right name for each one, but immediately afterwards she had already forgotten everything. While reading she would omit sentences, she would spell every word or read without intonation. In a writing test she often repeated the same syllables, omitting others, and became confused and absent-minded. In her conversation she often used confused phrases, single paraphrasic expressions (milk-jug instead of cup), sometimes she would suddenly stop talking completely. She evidently did not understand many questions. She did not remember the use of particular objects. She still walked normally and had full use of her hands. There were no motoric disturbances in her gait or use of her hands. Her pupils reacted normally. She had somewhat rigid radial arteries, no cardiac hypertrophy, no albumen.

During the course of the disease symptoms appeared which could be considered focal symptoms; sometimes these were very prominent and sometimes quite faint. But they were always very mild. Mental regression advanced quite steadily. After four and a half years of illness the patient died. She was completely apathetic in the end, and was confined to bed in a fetal position (with legs drawn up), was incontinent and in spite of all the care and attention given to her she suffered from decubitus.

The autopsy showed an evenly affected atrophic brain without macroscopic foci. The larger cerebral vessels showed arteriosclerotic changes.

The Bielschowsky silver preparation showed very characteristic changes in the neurofibrils. However, inside an apparently normal-looking cell, one or more single fibres could be observed that became prominent through their striking thickness and specific impregnability. At a more advanced stage, many fibrils arranged parallel showed the same changes. Then they accumulated forming dense bundles and gradually advanced to the surface of the cell. Eventually the nucleus and cytoplasm disappeared, and only a tangled bundle of fibrils indicated the site where once the neuron had been located. . . .

On the whole, it is evident that we are dealing with a peculiar, little-known disease process. In recent years these particular disease-processes have been detected in great numbers. This fact should stimulate us to further study and analysis of this particular disease. We must not be satisfied to force it into the existing group of well-known disease patterns. It is clear that there exist many more mental diseases than our text books indicate. In many such cases, a further histological examination must be effected to determine the characteristics of each single case. We must reach the stage in which the vast well-known disease groups must be subdivided into many smaller groups, each one with its own clinical and anatomical characteristics.

> From "A Characteristic Disease of the Cerebral Cortex,"
> in *The Early Story of Alzheimer's Disease*, 1906

RICHARD EBERHART *(American, b. 1904)*

Superior elan
Sometimes offends.
One cannot stand it.
To be clear

In mind and body,
Dominating
A scene at eighty-eight

Makes one think
Too much
On height elan,
Abateless ability,

Breaks reality
Into a special claim
On the nature of man,
Especially of women

Who live longest,
Sometimes an eagle-gilt eye
Surveying the scene
From elan,

Elan's proud claim,
Gives dismay
If humility
Exists,

And if it does not,
Gives dismay

Anyway,
Because

The people suffer,
Have credible
Troubles,
Real heartbreak,

And death comes too soon
To any of them,
These sufferers,
Lauded commoners,

Yet ancient ladies,
Graceful, elegant-pictorial,
Eke on,
Drive from Boston to Maine

At ninety,
Play golf at ninety
At Castine,
A way from sorrow,

It is no ambage
To see these etched beings,
Who have evaded ill
By some mysterious principle

We do not know,
High-spirited,

They spring me
Into empathy

With those who have suffered and lost,
With imperfection,
The common lot,
Nature ruthless,

But the theme of this poem
Is that nature is
Not ruthless to them,
Seemingly,

To have joy at ninety,
Ability to drive a car

Three hundred miles without fatigue
Ought to be celebrated.

I am bemused,
I have seen too much love
Gone wrong,
Lives wasted by time,

Am challenged
By too much
Goddess control,
I cannot accept

That to live long means truth
When I think
Of Keats, of Hopkins,
Of Dylan Thomas.

"I hope to see you next year"
Comes across the bay,
A common report
Carried across the water

On an evening still and full
Of falling sunlight by the ocean.
Of course we do
We all do,

We want five chick swallows
In a nest
Under the areaway
To prosper,

And as the mother and father
Gather bugs
And stuff them
In yellow mouths

We watch the process
Until one day
Five swallows
Take their maiden flight.

They make it
Up to the rooftree,
Sit there expectant,
While father and mother

Fly in to feed them
Still; the next night
They retreat
Near the nest,

Bunched five in a row,
Fed still,
A revelation,
How splendid.

Even after mid-July,
The full moon,

The parents feed the young,
Teaching them to fly.

The laws of nature
Are from ancient time,
Why then
Not salute

Old ladies full of grace
Who have
Outwitted time,
Or so it seems,

Continue sportively
Guessing, truthward, at
Genes, environment,
Will, and chance.

"Survivors," 1980

MARC KAMINSKY (*American, b. 1943*)

Memories not in me only, but in me through my mother's mother,
reaching back beyond her sepia photographs, seamstress
girls on a solidarity lunch break, her factory days
of 1911, to her barrel-chested wine merchant father in
Besarabia, now vanished, and her grandmother's memories
of migration, now vanished, and memories of generations
of fugitives, all landing at once in America, there to
find nothing they dreamed of, the repeating history of
men running away from women, of women being abandoned
or leaving their men.

And memories of the *agunahs*, the abandoned ones with varicose
    veins, and three hungry mouths, and the slow wasting
    of the children's bodies by hunger, half-seen by candle-
    light, blessing the candles for Sabbath, helpless

And the men running after a living, breathless, peddlers,
    piece-workers, jabbering Yiddish, thousands of men
    on Hester Street, called the Pig Market, and the boss
    shouting You, you, and you, three out of ten got work,
    eighty-five cents a day, sixteen hours a day, a year
    gone, and no money saved, helpless, no candles to bless,
    Gold Street not the name of a place but another false
    messiah in a long succession of false messiahs, another
    letter sent back home without rubles, without the
    steamship ticket promised a year ago, seven years ago,
    in the stupid hope of the setting out

They carried their sewing machines on their shoulders,
    walking the streets, nowhere to go, the women at home
    growing beards, getting stranger, feeding their children
    on "tongue sandwiches," a slice of Yiddish endearments
    between two slices of thin air, the men desperate,
    casting humpbacked shadows on tenement walls, looking up
    cousins they would never have spoken to back home, who
    spanked them in the toilets for a mispronounced phrase
    of Gamara, meals of humiliation, bread of affliction,
    another Passover in America, ready to spit, close to
    tears

How many men left how many women, running away to Milwaukee,
    running to California, Jewish cowboys, Jewish gold
    rushers, how many women suffocating with fifteen people
    sleeping on the bedroom floor, traveling steerage class
    from birth to the end of hope, how many women, the
    agunahs, putting their heads in the oven when there were
    no words left for a tongue sandwich

Or putting ads in the *Daily Forward*, whole *agunah* sections,
    how many women, the repeating history of emigration,
    and mug shots of how many men, cursed to work without
    hope, If Moishe Leib reads this, if Zev Aaron reads
    this in Chicago, let him think of his faithful wife
    Rivkah Leah, let him remember his devoted wife

Dvorah Esther, with whom he stood under the marriage
canopy in the eyes of God, with whom he conceived
Mani, the light of his father's eyes, who goes without
shoes, with whom he conceived three precious daughters,
let him remember Benjamin, his Kaddish, who mixes with
bad company, with whom he begot Fanya, who left the
ways of her fathers and is living in sin, with whom
he begot his seventh child Reuven, who still remembers
his father and continually cries out for him, let
him remember, if he reads this, in California, in
Chicago, anywhere in the West, may it find its way
to him, and let him return, if he reads this, let him
think of his wife and children without rancor and let
him turn to us and let him return

Strange women stepping off the boat with thin bundles, his
children, and is this what he worked for, one year,
seven years, this family that he no longer knows,
who no longer knows him, the repeating history in me
of the separation of how many women and how many men

Or the women in Besarabia, or the Ukraine or the outskirts
of Warsaw, feeding themselves on infrequent letters,
eighty-five cents a day, and no steamship ticket at
last, no safe passage into America, and the radiant
Yiddish, the Yiddish of blessings, Yiddish of the
mystical spheres of splendor and the song of the bride
of Sabbath, Yiddish of hope, losing all touch with
the sky in the Pig Market, the boss shouting You,
you, and you, and then later it was full of disguises,
the girls in the tenements hitching up their skirts
and pouring pitchers of water into the hot tubs,
or bending over ironing boards with half-open blouses,
boys of nine sorting and marking the laundry, the
Yiddish of holy sparks giving way to a bookkeeper's
tongue of how much earned, how little saved, and
apologies, mixed with prayers for forgiveness, until
the men couldn't bring themselves to write any more

How many men in the repeating history of failure and running
away, and taking up other names and other families,
and repeating women how many lives in memory living

how many repeated lives in me, fugitive, working,
conflicted, saying in a language losing all touch
with the sky, You, you, and you!

"Pig Market," 1982

W. H. AUDEN (American, 1907–1973)

When there are so many we shall have to mourn,
When grief has been made so public, and exposed
    To the critique of a whole epoch
      The frailty of our conscience and anguish,

Of whom shall we speak? For every day they die
Among us, those who were doing us some good,
    And knew it was never enough but
      Hoped to improve a little by living.

Such was this doctor: still at eighty he wished
To think of our life, from whose unruliness
    So many plausible young futures
      With threats or flattery ask obedience.

But his wish was denied him; he closed his eyes
Upon that last picture common to us all,
    Of problems like relatives standing
      Puzzled and jealous about our dying.

For about him at the very end were still
Those he had studied, the nervous and the nights,
    And shades that still waited to enter
      The bright circle of his recognition

Turned elsewhere with their disappointment as he
Was taken away from his old interest
    To go back to the earth in London,
      An important Jew who died in exile.

Only Hate was happy, hoping to augment
His practice now, and his shabby clientèle
    Who think they can be cured by killing
      And covering the gardens with ashes.

They are still alive but in a world he changed
Simply by looking back with no false regrets;

All that he did was to remember
Like the old and be honest like children.

He wasn't clever at all: he merely told
The unhappy Present to recite the Past
    Like a poetry lesson till sooner
    Or later it faltered at the line where

Long ago the accusations had begun,
And suddenly knew by whom it had been judged,
    How rich life had been and how silly,
    And was life-forgiven and most humble.

Able to approach the Future as a friend
Without a wardrobe of excuses, without
    A set mask of rectitude or an
    Embarrassing over-familiar gesture.

No wonder the ancient cultures of conceit
In his technique of unsettlement foresaw
    The fall of princes, the collapse of
    Their lucrative patterns of frustration.

If he succeeded, why, the Generalised Life
Would become impossible, the monolith
    Of State be broken and prevented
    The co-operation of avengers.

Of course they called on God: but he went his way,
Down among the Lost People like Dante, down
    To the stinking fosse where the injured
    Lead the ugly life of the rejected.

And showed us what evil is; not as we thought
Deeds that must be punished, but our lack of faith,
    Our dishonest mood of denial,
    The concupiscence of the oppressor.

And if something of the autocratic pose,
The paternal strictness he distrusted, still
    Clung to his utterance and features,
    It was a protective imitation

For one who lived among enemies so long;
If often he was wrong and at times absurd,
    To us he is no more a person
    Now but a whole climate of opinion,

Under whom we conduct our differing lives:
Like weather he can only hinder or help,
     The proud can still be proud but find it
     A little harder, and the tyrant tries

To make him do but doesn't care for him much.
He quietly surrounds all our habits of growth;
     He extends, till the tired in even
     The remotest most miserable duchy

Have felt the change in their bones and are cheered,
And the child unlucky in his little State,
     Some hearth where freedom is excluded,
     A hive whose honey is fear and worry,

Feels calmer now and somehow assured of escape;
While as they lie in the grass of our neglect,
     So many long-forgotten objects
     Revealed by his undiscouraged shining

Are returned to us and made precious again;
Games we had thought we must drop as we grew up,
     Little noises we dared not laugh at,
     Faces we made when no one was looking.

But he wishes us more than this: to be free
Is often to be lonely; he would unite
     The unequal moieties fractured
     By our own well-meaning sense of justice.

Would restore to the larger the wit and will
The smaller possesses but can only use
     For arid disputes, would give back to
     The son the mother's richness of feeling.

But he would have us remember most of all
To be enthusiastic over the night
     Not only for the sense of wonder
     It alone has to offer, but also

Because it needs our love: for with sad eyes
Its delectable creatures look up and beg
     Us dumbly to ask them to follow;
     They are exiles who long for the future

That lies in our power. They too would rejoice
If allowed to serve enlightenment like him,

Even to bear our cry of "Judas,"
As he did and all must bear who serve it.

One rational voice is dumb: over a grave
The household of Impulse mourns one dearly loved.
Sad is Eros, builder of cities,
And weeping anarchic Aphrodite.

"In Memory of Sigmund Freud (d. Sept. 1939)," 1940

ROBERT FROST (*American, 1874–1963*)

Mary sat musing on the lamp-flame at the table,
Waiting for Warren. When she heard his step,
She ran on tiptoe down the darkened passage
To meet him in the doorway with the news
And put him on his guard. "Silas is back."
She pushed him outward with her through the door
And shut it after her. "Be kind," she said.
She took the market things from Warren's arms
And set them on the porch, then drew him down
To sit beside her on the wooden steps.

"When was I ever anything but kind to him?

But I'll not have the fellow back," he said.
"I told him so last haying, didn't I?
If he left then, I said, that ended it.
What good is he? Who else will harbor him
At his age for the little he can do?
What help he is there's no depending on.
Off he goes always when I need him most.
He thinks he ought to earn a little pay,
Enough at least to buy tobacco with,
So he won't have to beg and be beholden.
'All right,' I say, 'I can't afford to pay
Any fixed wages, though I wish I could.'
'Someone else can.' 'Then someone else will have to.'
I shouldn't mind his bettering himself
If that was what it was. You can be certain,
When he begins like that, there's someone at him
Trying to coax him off with pocket money—
In haying time, when any help is scarce.
In winter he comes back to us. I'm done."

"Sh! not so loud: he'll hear you," Mary said.

"I want him to: he'll have to soon or late."

"He's worn out. He's asleep beside the stove.
When I came up from Rowe's I found him here,
Huddled against the barn door fast asleep,
A miserable sight, and frightening, too—
You needn't smile—I didn't recognize him—
I wasn't looking for him—and he's changed.
Wait till you see."

        "Where did you say he'd been?"

"He didn't say. I dragged him to the house,
And gave him tea and tried to make him smoke.
I tried to make him talk about his travels.
Nothing would do: he just kept nodding off."

"What did he say? Did he say anything?"

"But little."

      "Anything? Mary, confess
He said he'd come to ditch the meadow for me."

"Warren!"

      "But did he? I just want to know."

"Of course he did. What would you have him say?
Surely you wouldn't grudge the poor old man
Some humble way to save his self-respect.
He added, if you really care to know,
He meant to clear the upper pasture, too.
That sounds like something you have heard before?
Warren, I wish you could have heard the way
He jumbled everything. I stopped to look
Two or three times—he made me feel so queer—
To see if he was talking in his sleep.
He ran on Harold Wilson—you remember—
The boy you had in haying four years since.
He's finished school, and teaching in his college.
Silas declares you'll have to get him back.
He says they two will make a team for work:
Between them they will lay this farm as smooth!
The way he mixed that in with other things.

He thinks young Wilson a likely lad, though daft
On education—you know how they fought
All through July under the blazing sun,
Silas up on the cart to build the load,
Harold along beside to pitch it on.''

"Yes, I took care to keep well out of earshot.''

"Well, those days trouble Silas like a dream.
You wouldn't think they would. How some things linger!
Harold's young college-boy's assurance piqued him.
After so many years he still keeps finding
Good arguments he sees he might have used.
I sympathize. I know just how it feels
To think of the right thing to say too late.
Harold's associated in his mind with Latin.
He asked me what I thought of Harold's saying
He studied Latin, like the violin,
Because he liked it—that an argument!
He said he couldn't make the boy believe
He could find water with a hazel prong—
Which showed how much good school had ever done him.
He wanted to go over that. But most of all
He thinks if he could have another chance
To teach him how to build a load of hay—''

"I know, that's Silas' one accomplishment.
He bundles every forkful in its place,
And tags and numbers it for future reference,
So he can find and easily dislodge it
In the unloading. Silas does that well.
He takes it out in bunches like big birds' nests.
You never see him standing on the hay
He's trying to lift, straining to lift himself.''

"He thinks if he could teach him that, he'd be
Some good perhaps to someone in the world.
He hates to see a boy the fool of books.
Poor Silas, so concerned for other folk,
And nothing to look backward to with pride,
And nothing to look forward to with hope,
So now and never any different.''

Part of a moon was falling down the west,
Dragging the whole sky with it to the hills.

Its light poured softly in her lap. She saw it
And spread her apron to it. She put out her hand
Among the harplike morning-glory strings,
Taut with the dew from garden bed to eaves
As if she played unheard some tenderness
That wrought on him beside her in the night.
"Warren," she said, "he has come home to die:
You needn't be afraid he'll leave you this time."

"Home," he mocked gently.

                  "Yes, what else but home?
It all depends on what you mean by home.
Of course he's nothing to us, any more
Than was the hound that came a stranger to us
Out of the woods, worn out upon the trail."

"Home is the place where, when you have to go there,
They have to take you in."

                 "I should have called it
Something you somehow haven't to deserve."

Warren leaned out and took a step or two,
Picked up a little stick, and brought it back
And broke it in his hand and tossed it by.
"Silas has better claim on us you think
Than on his brother? Thirteen little miles
As the road winds would bring him to his door.
Silas has walked that far no doubt today.
Why doesn't he go there? His brother's rich,
A somebody—director in the bank."

"He never told us that."

                 "We know it, though."

"I think his brother ought to help, of course.
I'll see to that if there is need. He ought of right
To take him in, and might be willing to—
He may be better than appearances.
But have some pity on Silas. Do you think
If he had any pride in claiming kin
Or anything he looked for from his brother,
He'd keep so still about him all the time?"

"I wonder what's between them."

"I can tell you.
Silas is what he is—we wouldn't mind him—
But just the kind that kinsfolk can't abide.
He never did a thing so very bad.
He don't know why he isn't quite as good
As anybody. Worthless though he is,
He won't be made ashamed to please his brother."

"I can't think Si ever hurt anyone."

"No, but he hurt my heart the way he lay
And rolled his old head on that sharp-edged chair-back.
He wouldn't let me put him on the lounge.
You must go in and see what you can do.
I made the bed up for him there tonight.
You'll be surprised at him—how much he's broken.
His working days are done; I'm sure of it."

"I'd not be in a hurry to say that."

"I haven't been. Go, look, see for yourself.
But, Warren, please remember how it is:
He's come to help you ditch the meadow.
He has a plan. You mustn't laugh at him.
He may not speak of it, and then he may.
I'll sit and see if that small sailing cloud
Will hit or miss the moon."

                        It hit the moon.
Then there were three there, making a dim row,
The moon, the little silver cloud, and she.

Warren returned—too soon, it seemed to her—
Slipped to her side, caught up her hand and waited.

"Warren?" she questioned.

                    "Dead," was all he answered.

                      "The Death of a Hired Man," 1914

WILLIAM CARLOS WILLIAMS (*American, 1883–1963*)

There were some dirty plates
and a glass of milk
beside her on a small table
near the rank, disheveled bed—

Wrinkled and nearly blind
she lay and snored
rousing with anger in her tones
to cry for food,

Gimme something to eat—
They're starving me—
I'm all right I won't go
to the hospital. No, no, no

Give me something to eat
Let me take you
to the hospital, I said
and after you are well

you can do as you please.
She smiled, Yes
you do what you please first
then I can do what I please—

Oh, oh, oh! she cried
as the ambulance men lifted
her to the stretcher—
Is this what you call

making me comfortable?
By now her mind was clear—
Oh you think you're smart
you young people,

she said, but I'll tell you
you don't know anything.
Then we started.
On the way

we passed a long row
of elms. She looked at them
awhile out of
the ambulance window and said,

What are all those
fuzzy-looking things out there?
Trees? Well, I'm tired
of them and rolled her head away.

"The Last Words of My English Grandmother," 1939

399

MURIEL RUKEYSER (*American, 1913–1980*)

From you I learned the dark potential
theatres of the acts of man holding
on a rehearsal stage   people and lights.
You in your red hair ran down the darkened
aisle, making documents and poems
in their people form the play.

Hallie it was from you I learned this:
you told the company in dress-rehearsal
in that ultimate equipped building   what they lacked:
among the lighting, the sight-lines, the acoustics,
the perfect revolving stage, they lacked only one thing
the most important thing.   It would come tonight:
The audience   the response

Hallie I learned from you this summer, this
Hallie I saw you lying all gone to bone
the tremor of bone   I stroked the head all sculpture
I held the hands of birds   I spoke to the sealed eyes
the soft live red mouth of a red-headed woman.
I knew Hallie then I could move without answer,
like the veterans for peace, hurling back their medals
and not expecting an answer from the grass.
You taught me this in your dying, for poems and theatre
and love and peace-making that living and my love
are where response and no-response
meet at last, Hallie, in infinity.

"H.F.D.," 1944

CHRISTY BROWN (*Irish, 1932–1981*)

Only in your dying, Lady, could I offer you a poem.

So uncommonly quiet you lay in our grieving midst
     your flock of bereaved wild geese
pinioned by the pomp and paraphernalia of death
     for once upon a rare time wordless
beyond the raw useless grief of your nine fine sons
     the quiet weeping of your four mantillaed daughters
gathered in desperate amity around your calm requiem hour
     and almost I saw you smile in happy disbelief
from the better side of the grave.

Only in your dying, Lady, could I offer you a poem.

Never in life could I capture that free live spirit of girl
       in the torn and tattered net of my words.
Your life was a bruised flower
       burning on an ash-heap
strong and sure on the debris of your broken decades
       unwilting under a hail of mind-twisted fate
under the blind-fisted blows of enraged love
       turning ever toward the sun of a tomorrow
you alone perceived beyond present pain.

Only in your dying, Lady, could I offer you a poem.

You were a song inside my skin
       a sudden sunburst of defiant laughter
spilling over the night-gloom of my half awakenings
       a firefly of far splendid light
dancing in the dim catacombs of my brain.
       Light of foot and quick of eye for pain
you printed patterns of much joy upon the bare walls of my life
       with broad bold strokes of your Irish wit
flaming from the ruins of your towers.

Only in your dying, Lady, could I offer you a poem.

With gay uplifted finger you beckoned
       and faltering I followed you down paths
I would not otherwise have known or dared
       limping after you up that secret mountain
where you sang without need of voice or words.
       I touched briefly the torch you held out
and bled pricked by a thorn from the black deep rose of your
  courage.
       From the gutter of my defeated dreams
you pulled me to heights almost your own.

Only in your dying, Lady, could I offer you a poem.

I do not grieve for you
       in your little square plot of indiscriminate clay
for now shall you truly dance.

O great heart
    O best of all my songs
       the dust be merciful upon your holy bones

                                 "For My Mother," 1971

MBELLA SONNE DIPOKO *(Cameroonian, b. 1936)*

I am tempted to think of you
Now that I have grown old
And date my sadness
To the madness of your love.

All those flowers you hung
On my gate
All those flowers the wind blew
On the snow!
Why must I remember them now
And recall you calling me
Like a screech-owl
While I watched you
Through the window-pane
And the moon was over the Seine
And Africa was far away
And you were calling
And then crying
In the snow of exile
And the neighbour's dog barking as if bored
By the excesses of your tenderness?

When I came down for you
And opened the gate
Cursing the cold of your land
You always went and stood
Under the poplars of the river Yerres
At the bottom of the garden
Silently watching its Seine-bound waters;
And the moon might take to the clouds
Casting a vast shadow
That sometimes seemed to reach our hearts.

And then following me upstairs
You stopped a while on the balcony
As high as which the vines of the garden grew
With those grapes which had survived
The end of the summer
You picked a few grapes
Which we ate.
I remember their taste
Which was that of our kisses.

And then in the room
You in such a hurry to undress
And you always brought
A white and a black candle which you lit.
Their flames were the same colour
Of the fire glowing in the grate
And you were no longer white
You were brown
By the light of the fires of love
At midnight
Years ago.

"A Poem of Villeneuve St. Georges (for M–C)," 1972

LANGSTON HUGHES (*African American, 1902–1967*)

I don't mind dying—
But I'd hate to die all alone!
I want a dozen pretty women
To holler, cry, and moan.

I don't mind dying
But I want my funeral to be fine:
A row of long tall mamas
Fainting, fanning, and crying.

I want a fish-tail hearse
And sixteen fish-tail cars,
A big brass band
And a whole truck load of flowers.

When they let me down,
Down into the clay,
I want the women to holler:
Please don't take him away!
    Ow-ooo-oo-o!
Don't take daddy away!

"As Befits a Man," 1935

SIR WALTER RALEIGH (*English, c. 1554–1618*)

Even such is time, which takes in trust
Our youth, our joys, and all we have,
And pays us but with age and dust,

Who in the dark and silent grave
When we have wandered all our ways
Shuts up the story of our days,
And from which earth, and grave, and dust
The Lord shall raise me up, I trust.

"The Author's Epitaph, Made by Himself," c. 1618

FLORIDA SCOTT-MAXWELL (*American, 1883–1979*)

You need only claim the events of your life to make yourself yours. When you truly possess all you have been and done, which may take some time, you are fierce with reality. When at last age has assembled you together, will it not be easy to let it all go, lived, balanced, over?

From *The Measure of My Days*, 1968

CREDITS

The editor and publisher gratefully acknowledge permission to reprint the following material:

Addams, Jane: From *Forty Years at Hull-House* by Jane Addams. Copyright 1910, 1930, 1935 by The Macmillan Company, renewed 1938, 1958 by John A. Brittain. Renewed 1962 by Macmillan Publishing Company. Reprinted by permission of Macmillan Publishing Company.

Agosin, Marjorie: "Mi Estómago" by Marjorie Agosin is reprinted from *Women and Aging*, edited by Jo Alexander, translated by Cola Franzen, by permission of Calyx Books. Copyright © 1986 by Calyx Books.

Alexander, Gus: From *The American Slave*, Supplement, Series 2, Vol. 2, Texas Narratives Part I, pp. 34–36, edited by George Rawick. Published by Greenwood Press, an imprint of Greenwood Publishing Group, Inc., Westport, CT. Reprinted with permission.

Alzheimer, Alois: "A Characteristic Disease of the Cerebral Cortex" by Alois Alzheimer, translated by Katherine L. Bick. From *The Early Story of Alzheimer's Disease*, edited by Katherine L. Bick, Luigi Amaducci, and Giancarlo Pepeu, published by Liviana Editrice spa in 1987.

Amichai, Yehuda: "A Quiet Joy" from *The Selected Poetry of Yehuda Amichai* by Yehuda Amichai, edited and translated by Chana Bloch and Stephen Mitchell. English translation copyright © 1986 by Chana Bloch and Stephen Mitchell. Reprinted by permission of HarperCollins Publishers, Inc. and the author.

Aristotle: From *Rhetoric* translated by W. Rhys Roberts, from *The Oxford Translation of Aristotle* edited by W. D. Ross, vol. 11 (1925). Reprinted by permission of Oxford University Press (Oxford).

Arnheim, Rudolf: From "On the Late Style of Life and Art" by Rudolf Arnheim. From *New Essays on the Psychology of Art* published by the University of California Press in 1986. Copyright © 1986 The Regents of the University of California. Reprinted by the permission of the Regents of the University of California and the University of California Press.

Arnott, Kathleen: "The Calabash Children" from *African Myths and Legends* retold by Kathleen Arnott. Copyright © 1962 by Kathleen Arnott. Reprinted by permission of Oxford University Press (Oxford).

Athanasius: From *Athanasius: The Life of Antony and the Letter to Marcellinus*, translation by Robert C. Gregg. Copyright © 1980 by The Missionary Society of St. Paul the Apostle in the State of New York. Used by permission of Paullist Press.

Auden, W. H.: From "In Memory of Sigmund Freud," copyright 1940 and renewed 1968 by W. H. Auden. "Old People's Home," copyright © 1970 by W. H. Auden. Reprinted from *Collected Poems* by W. H. Auden, edited by Edward Mendelson, by permission of the publishers, Random House, Inc. and Faber and Faber Ltd.

benShea, Noah: From *Jacob Baker* by Noah benShea. Copyright © 1989 by Noah benShea. Reprinted by permission of Villard Books, a division of Random House, Inc.

Benét, Stephen Vincent: "Old Man Hoppergrass" from *Selected Works of Stephen Vincent Benét*. Copyright 1936 by Stephen Vincent Benét. Copyright renewed 1964 by Thomas Benét, Stephanie Mahin and Rachel Lewis Benét. Used by permission of Brandt & Brandt Literary Agents, Inc.

Berenson, Bernard: From *Sunset and Twilight: From the Diaries of 1947–1958* by Bernard Berenson, edited by Nicky Mariano. Copyright © 1963. Reprinted by permission of the Estate of Bernard Berenson represented by Sabina Anrep c/o the Antonella Antonelli Literary Agency.

Bhagavad-Gita, The: From the *Bhagavad-Gita*, translated by Barbara Stoler Miller. Translation copyright © 1986 by Barbara Stoler Miller. Used by permission of Bantam Books, a division of Bantam Doubleday Dell Publishing Group, Inc.

Black Elk: From *Black Elk Speaks* by John G. Neihardt. Copyright 1932, © 1959, 1972 by John G. Neihardt. Copyright © 1961 by the John G. Neihardt Trust. Used by permission of the University of Nebraska Press.

Bontemps, Arna: "A Summer Tragedy" by Arna Bontemps. Copyright 1933 by Arna Bontemps: renewed. Reprinted by permission of Harold Ober Associates, Incorporated.

Bourke-White, Margaret: "My Mysterious Malady" from *Portrait of Myself* by Margaret Bourke-White.

405

REFERENCES

Aesop: "The Man, the Horse, the Ox and the Dog" from *Aesop's Fables*, translated by James and Townsend. Published by J. B. Lippincott in 1949.

Anonymous: From "The Review of Life" by an anonymous author from *Nearing Home* by William E. Schenk. Published by Presbyterian Board of Publications, 1868.

Avicenna: "On the Causes of Health and Disease: the Necessity of Death" and "The Regimen for the Physically Matured" from *The Canon of Medicine of Avicenna*, translated by O. Cameron Gruner. Published by The Classics of Medicine Library, Gryphon Editions, 1984.

Bacon, Sir Francis: "The Differences of Youth and Age" from *The Histories of Life and Death*, 1638.

Bandaline, J., M.D.: "The Struggle with Old Age" from *Medical Record, A Weekly Journal of Medicine and Surgery*, New York, July 18, 1903, Vol. 64, No. 3.

ben Azariah, Rabbi Eleazar: "Ethics of the Fathers" from *Voices of Wisdom: Jewish Ideals and Ethics for Everyday Living* by Francine Klagsbrun. Published by Pantheon Books, a division of Random House, Inc., 1980.

Bronte, Charlotte: "Letter 306 to W. S. Williams, Oct. 2nd, 1848" from *The Brontes: Life and Letters*, Vol. I by Clement Shorter. Published by Hodder and Stoughton, 1908.

Browne, Sir Thomas: From *Christian Morals*, from *Religio medici*, 1643.

Browning, Robert: "Rabbi Ben Ezra" from *Dramatis Personae*. 1864.

Carlisle, Sir Anthony: From *An Essay on the Disorders of Old Age and on the Means for Prolonging Human Life*, 1819.

Carroll, Lewis. "You Are Old Father William," from *Alice's Adventures in Wonderland* by Lewis Carroll. Published by Macmillan and Co., 1866.

Dipoko, Mbella Sonne: "A Poem of Villeneuve St. Georges (for M-C)" from *Black and White in Love*. Published by Heinemann, London, 1972. George Bell and Sons, London, 1875.

Donne, John: "Death, Be Not Proud" from *Holy Sonnets*.

Emerson, Ralph Waldo: "Terminus" from *Poems of Ralph Waldo Emerson*, edited by Donald J. Adams. Thomas Y. Crowell Company, 1965.

Farnham, Eliza Wood: From *Women and Her Era*, Vol. 1, 1864.

Gaskell, E. C.: From *The Life of Charlotte Bronte* by Mrs. Gaskell, 1857.

Goethe, Johann Wolfgang von: from *Conversations of Goethe with Eckermann and Soret*, translated by John Oxenford. Published by George Bell and Sons, London, 1875.

Hasidic Tale: From *Voices of Wisdom: Jewish Ideal and Ethics for Everyday Living* by Francine Klagsbrun. Published by Pantheon Books, a division of Random House, Inc. 1980.

Hippocrates: From *The Genuine Works of Hippocrates*, translated by Francis Adams. The Williams and Wilkins Company, 1939.

Holmes, Oliver Wendell: "The Professor's Paper" from *The Autocrat of the Breakfast-Table*. Macmillan and Co., Ltd., 1903.

House, Abigail: From *Memoirs of Abigail House*, 1861.

Isidore of Seville: From *Etymolgiae*, translated by J. A. Burrow, 1911.

James, Henry: From *A Passionate Pilgrim*, 1871.

Judah, ben Tema, Rabbi: From "Ethics of the Fathers" from *Voices of Wisdom: Jewish Ideals and Ethics for Everyday Living* by Francine Klagsbrun. Published by Pantheon Books, a division of Random House, Inc., 1980.

King James Version of The Bible: John 12:3; Matthew 2:17–18; Matthew 25:14–30.

Kohut, Heinz: From *The Search for the Self, Selected Writings of Heinz Kohut: 1950–1978*, Vol. 2, edited by Paul H. Ornstein. Published by International Universities Press, Inc., 1978.

Li Mi: "A Pleading Memorial" from *A Treasury of Chinese Literature: A New Prose Anthology*, translated and edited by Chu'u Chai and Winberg Chai. Published by Appleton-Century, 1965.

Lowell, Amy: "Music" from *Sword Blades and Poppy Seeds*, 1914.

Manu: From *The Sacred Books of the East*, Vol. XXV, *The Laws of Manu*, edited by Max Muller and translated by G. Buhler. Published by Clarendon Press, 1886.

Mather, Cotton: "Liberatus" from *The Angel of Bethesda*, edited by Gordon W. Jones. American Antiquarian Society and Barre Publishers, 1972.

Metchnikoff, Élie: From "Natural Death" and "Should We Try to Prolong Human Life?" from *The Prolongation of Life*, edited and translated by P. Chalmers Mitchell. Putnam, 1908.

Nicholls, A. B.: Letter to Ellen Nussey from *The Brontes: Life and Letters*, Vol. II by Clement Shorter. Published by Hodder & Stoughton, 1908.

Niebuhr, Richard R.: "Pilgrims and Pioneers" from *Parabola* Magazine, Vol. 9, No. 3, August 1984.

Raleigh, Sir Walter: "The Author's Epitaph, Made by Himself."

Rūdakī: "Lament in Old Age" from *Early Persian Poetry* by A. V. Williams Jackson, translated by A. V. Williams Jackson. Published by Macmillan Publishing Co., 1920.

Sappho: "To Her Pupils" from *The Poems of Sappho*, translated by P. Maurice Hill. Published by Staples Press.

Schopenhauer, Arthur: "The Ages of Life" from *Arthur Schopenhauer, Counsel and Maxims*, translated by T. Bailey Saunders, 1890.

Shakespeare, William: From *As You Like It* from *The Complete Works*, edited by W. G. Clarke and W. Aldis Wright, 1853.

Shakespeare, William: Sonnet 73: "That Time of Year . . ." from *The Sonnets by William Shakespeare*. A Signet Classic. Published by The New American Library, 1965.

Shakespeare, William: "The Passionate Pilgrim" from *The Complete Works*, edited by W. G. Clarke and W. Aldis Wright, 1853.

Smith, John Stores: From "Personal Reminiscences of Charlotte Bronte," from *The Brontes: Life and Letters*, Vol. II by Clement Shorter. Published by Hodder & Stoughton, 1868.

Southey, Robert: "The Old Man's Comforts and How He Gained Them."

Stowe, Harriet Beecher: From *Uncle Tom's Cabin or Life Among the Lowly*, 1852.

Tennyson, Alfred Lord: "Ulysses" from *Alfred Tennyson, Poetical Works*. Oxford University Press, 1959.

Thoreau, Henry David: From *Walden*.

Tu Fu: "The Roof Whirled Away by Winds" from *White Pony: An Anthology of Chinese Poetry*, edited by Robert Payne. Translated by Pu Chaing-Hsing. Published by John Day-Mentor Books, 1947.

Twain, Mark: Speech on his seventieth birthday from *Complete Essays of Mark Twain*, edited by Charles Neider. Doubleday, 1963.

Vogelweide, Walther von der: from "Elegy" from *The Poems of Walther von der Vogelweide*, translated by Edwin H. Zeydel and Bayard Q. Morgan. Published by the Thrift Press, 1952.

Whitman, Walt: "Thanks in Old Age" from *Leaves of Grass*.

Wilde, Oscar: From *The Picture of Dorian Gray*, 1891.

Williams, Margery: From *The Velveteen Rabbit or How Toys Become Real*.

Yeats, W. B.: "When You Are Old" from *The Rose*, 1893. "The Wild Swans at Coole" from *The Wild Swans at Coole*, 1919. Published in *The Poems of W. B. Yeats: A New Edition* edited by Richard J. Finneran, Macmillan Publishing Co.

AUTHOR INDEX